THE
DISAPPEARING

ALSO BY LORI ROY

Bent Road

Until She Comes Home

Let Me Die in His Footsteps

THE
DISAPPEARING

A NOVEL

LORI ROY

DUTTON

DUTTON

An imprint of Penguin Random House LLC
375 Hudson Street
New York, New York 10014

Copyright © 2018 by Lori Roy

Penguin supports copyright. Copyright fuels creativity, encourages diverse voices, promotes free speech, and creates a vibrant culture. Thank you for buying an authorized edition of this book and for complying with copyright laws by not reproducing, scanning, or distributing any part of it in any form without permission. You are supporting writers and allowing Penguin to continue to publish books for every reader.

DUTTON and the D colophon are registered trademarks of Penguin Random House LLC.

LIBRARY OF CONGRESS CATALOGING-IN-PUBLICATION DATA

Names: Roy, Lori, author.
Title: The disappearing : a novel / Lori Roy.
Description: New York, New York : Dutton, [2018]
Identifiers: LCCN 2017036790 (print) | LCCN 2017049774 (ebook) |
ISBN 9781524741952 (ebook) | ISBN 9781524741938 (hardcover) |
ISBN 9781524741945 (trade pbk.)
Classification: LCC PS3618.O89265 (ebook) | LCC PS3618.O89265 D57 2018
(print) | DDC 813/.6—dc23
LC record available at https://lccn.loc.gov/2017036790

Printed in the United States of America
10 9 8 7 6 5 4 3 2 1

Set in ITC Galliard Std
Designed by George Towne

This book is a work of fiction. Names, characters, places, and incidents either are the product of the author's imagination or are used fictitiously, and any resemblance to actual persons, living or dead, business establishments, events, or locales is entirely coincidental.

RO452552007

FOR ALL THE BOYS WHO RAN,

AND THOSE WHO WANTED TO

THE
DISAPPEARING

LANE

LANE WALLACE IS alone inside Rowland's Tavern when the front door flies open. A man stumbles inside, bringing with him a spray of rain that throws a shine on the hickory-brown floors. He scans the dark room, stomps his feet, and draws both hands over his round, wet face. If the man says anything, Lane doesn't hear him for the rain pounding the tin roof and the palm fronds slapping the front windows. It's supposed to rain through the night, and all around Waddell, people will be keeping a close eye on the river.

Lane smiles because maybe the man is a friend of a friend and not a stranger. She's expecting a big crowd tonight, and one of her regulars might have invited him. But he doesn't smile back. Slipping her phone from her back pocket, she lays it on the bar top where the man will be sure to see it. It's a subtle warning, but if the man is looking for trouble, it'll make him reconsider.

He's a little on the heavy side; doughy, a person might say. From behind the bar, Lane asks the man if a beer'll do him, and as he slides into a booth near the front door, he nods. Her regulars, men who've known her all her life, or rather who have known her father, won't show up for another hour or so, but Rowland Jansen will be back any time now. He ran out to move his car and Lane's to the higher and drier ground of the parking lot out front, so she won't be alone with the man for long.

Even though it's raining, her regulars will come, because after twenty years, this is the night Lane Wallace becomes Lane Fielding again. They'll come to toast the occasion of her divorce and tell her they never liked that no-good, cheating Kyle or the twelve novels he's written. These regulars are Lane's only friends here in town. Since moving back to Waddell six months ago, a move her divorce demanded after living up north for the last twenty years, she's managed to avoid the friends she had when she was growing up here. To her, they're painful reminders of a past she'd rather forget.

Her regulars, men twice her age, have been enough for Lane since moving home. They've even managed to forgive her one indiscretion three months ago with Rowland, her married boss, or to at least ignore it. She's one of them again now that she's back in town, and they're always telling her it's high time she be proud of Waddell and of the family she was born into. Not one of them believes what they call the hogwash that's been spread about Lane's father by the newspapers and television for the last five years. We're glad to have you back, they say instead. Yours is a fine Southern name passed down by fine Southern gentlemen. No need for any more shame. Damn the newspapers. Damn the state too.

Maybe if the man, this stranger, had sat at the bar like most singles do, Lane wouldn't bother calling Sheriff Mark Ellenton. But he didn't, so she grabs her phone and dials, because she did, after all, make the sheriff a promise.

About ten days ago, a student from Florida State disappeared. Even before the Tallahassee police made their way to Waddell in search of Susannah Bauer, Mark stopped by the bar and made Lane promise to call him if ever she found herself alone with a customer she didn't know. Having two daughters to think of, Lane couldn't afford to be careless, and Mark couldn't bear the thought of anything happening to her. That's what he said, but what he meant, and what hung in the air as it has for more than twenty years, was that he couldn't bear anything happening to her *again*.

This latest girl's disappearance has brought back bad memories for those old enough to remember the late seventies and a man named Ted. Lane was too young to remember when he passed through Waddell, taking with him a twelve-year-old girl who was never seen again, but plenty of her customers remember. He ate lunch at Olson's Café that day and had a tire patched just down the road from Rowland's. Such an ordinary-looking fellow, folks remember. Just as they surely did in 1974 following the disappearance of that young girl, when news of Susannah Bauer's disappearance hit ten days ago, folks started locking doors and taking note of out-of-state license plates.

With her phone pressed to one ear, Lane leans against the bar and studies the back of the strange man's head. The call to Mark's phone rings a few times, but before it rolls to voicemail, the front door opens again. Much like the first man who stumbled inside, the three men who cross over the threshold bring with them another spray of rain.

"Towels are there by the bar," Lane says to the men, and ends the call because four strangers are safer than one.

If she's being honest with herself, the strange man had only been an excuse for her to reach out to Mark. He's the only one she's been happy to see again in the months she's been back, and given that he never married and that he finds reason to stop by the bar more often than necessary, he's seemed happy to have Lane back as well. But since the night she slept with Rowland, Mark hasn't been coming around as much.

She takes the three men for Southerners and whiskey drinkers, and she's right. She hollers to the man sitting at the booth that she'll be right with him, and as she tips a bottle of Woodford over the first tumbler, the ice inside popping and cracking, the men talk among themselves, poke at their cell phones, jot things on small spiral notepads. These three aren't tourists, and they aren't locals here for Lane's party. They've been here before, though not these three exactly, but ones just like them, and they'll certainly come again. Many years ago, Lane was one of them. But then Kyle's fifth book became a bestseller, and he said to Lane, why bother with your career when you have the girls to look after now, and so she quit. These three men are reporters.

"Think you fellows should stick to one round," Lane says.

"Just getting started," the dark-haired one says.

Lane grabs a dry towel from the stack and pulls a longneck from the cooler. "You're journalists?"

"That we are, ma'am." It's the one with silver hair.

"How do you know we're reporters?" the smallest one says.

"If ever there was a news-weary town, gentlemen," Lane says, walking toward the end of the bar, "this is it. Trust me. You're best off sticking to one round."

It hadn't taken the Tallahassee police long to make their way to Waddell after Susannah disappeared. The newspapers and television stations were bound to follow, so it's possible these re-porters are here to cover Susannah, but not likely. It'll be Lane's father who has brought them to town. Reporters have been com-ing to cover Neil Fielding's story for at least five years, long before Lane returned home.

Stories like the one about Lane's father win awards and launch careers. In the beginning, the reporters came only from Florida, but as the story grew, they began driving in from all over the South. From her Brooklyn apartment where she lived with Kyle and the girls for the last twenty years, Lane tracked the reporters' bylines across the country. And within the last six months that Lane's been back, they've begun flying in from New York, Illinois, and from as far away as California. With every new development, the details become more shocking and more reporters come, and the wound here in Waddell so many had hoped would heal has instead festered.

IT'S THE RAIN and thunder that make Lane creep instead of walk toward the man sitting alone at the booth. It's divorce and being on her own for the first time in twenty years. It's her body being softer than when she last lived here and her blond hair having faded to a blurry brown. It's living in her parents' house and hating that she knows which floorboards creak and which kitchen drawer comes off its track. And it's the music, the soulful slow notes plucked on an acoustic guitar that float through the speakers over-head and remind her how many years are lost and that she's right back where she started.

"Here you go," Lane says, setting the beer on the table.

The man, new to the bar and having come here on the same day as the reporters, is probably a relative of one of the men her father harmed. As the man reaches for the beer, he turns toward

Lane, but not in the sudden way she feared. He turns slowly, his eyes not looking quite at her but instead at an empty spot over her shoulder. He's not much older than her oldest daughter, Annalee. Twenty-one at most. Like the rest of him, his face is doughy. His eyes, an icy blue, jump from the beer to that empty spot over Lane's shoulder and back again. As if the man wants to say something but has to think it over, he works his lips together.

"Annalee's not at work," he says. He stares at the tabletop, and his voice barely rises above the rain.

"Pardon?"

"Annalee," he says. "She's your daughter."

The man isn't about Annalee's age. Lane was wrong to think so. He's mid-twenties at least. He could be nearly thirty.

"It's Monday," the man says, now holding one hand with the other as if trying to trap it. "And she works at the restaurant on Mondays."

"Do you have a job there too?" Lane asks, letting out the breath she'd been holding. He must be asking about Annalee because they work together.

"Butchers and whores," the man says, working his lips in that same way.

Lane glances at the three reporters sitting at the bar. They heard what the man said because they've all turned to face Lane, and the dark-haired reporter is preparing to stand, one foot resting on the ground. She waves them off.

This isn't the first time someone has called the Fieldings butchers and whores. While Lane's regulars won't let themselves believe what the papers report about Lane's father, plenty of others in town do, and they branded the Fieldings butchers. Plenty of those same people, especially parishioners over at the New Covenant, branded Lane a whore after her one night with Rowland. Or rather, Hettie Jansen, Rowland's wife, branded her a whore, and like a snappy headline, it caught on. Butchers and whores.

But Hettie wasn't the first to call Lane such a thing. She had been a girl when first someone called her a whore, and back then, her own father had been the one to do it. You're a whore, he had said to the thirteen-year-old Lane, his warm breath making her eyelids flutter. That's the day she began hatching a plan to leave Waddell. Her marriage to Kyle had been her way out, and her divorce from him twenty years later had forced her return.

"I understand you're angry with my father," Lane says, backing away. It's her standard response, the thing Mark—Sheriff Ellenton—advised her to say. Defuse and evade. "And you have every right to be, but please leave my daughter out of it."

She was right after all. The missing girl hasn't brought the reporters to town. Something is getting ready to break in her father's story, and that's why this man and these reporters have come. Like the others before him, the man is angry because Lane's father has never been punished. Still, she can't allow such hatred, no matter how justified, to settle on her children. This is the reason she'll have to leave Waddell as soon as she can save some money.

"Trouble?" the dark-haired reporter asks as Lane walks back to the bar.

Ignoring the man's question, Lane grabs her cell phone and punches in a message to Annalee. WHAT'S UP, she types. Lane already knew Annalee wasn't at work. The restaurant called her early in the day and told her not to come in because of the rain. A message pops up. PUTTING ON SUPPER, it reads. ANYONE CAUSING TROUBLE AT THE HOUSE TODAY, Lane types. Annalee answers, NOPE. ALL QUIET.

For the third time, the bar's door opens, and Rowland Jansen walks inside. As he pulls off his hat, Lane tucks her phone back in her pocket. People used to notice Rowland for his blond hair, but it's long since darkened, and now they most notice his height—a good six and a half feet.

"Reporters," Lane says, and nods toward the three men.

"Not looking to cause any trouble." It's the small one.

"Well, here's the thing about reporters," Rowland says, brushing a hand over Lane's hip and stomach as he passes her by. "I have a bar full of regulars coming here tonight, and I don't care to deal with them dealing with the three of you."

Lane slips around to the other side of the bar to put herself beyond Rowland's reach. Though he hasn't said out loud that he hopes their one night together will lead to more, he's become ever more familiar in the weeks since—too familiar.

Draining his glass in one swallow, the silver-haired reporter slaps a twenty on the bar. "The Fielding Mansion," he says. "You know it? Place where Neil Fielding lives? GPS can't find it."

"Never heard of it," Rowland says, a lie he has often told.

Leaning against the bar where Rowland won't happen to brush against her again, Lane glances at the odd man still sitting alone. He has swung his legs around the end of the booth as if preparing to stand and is slapping himself in the forehead, again and again, with one hand.

"We were told to look for the giant elm," the silver-haired one says. "What about you, ma'am? You know where we'll find the Fielding Mansion?"

"Nope," Lane says. "Never heard of it." She's told the lie a good many times too.

Pulling a business card from his wallet, the reporter slides it under the tip jar. "If you happen to remember."

Lane nods but says nothing. It's an oak tree, she could tell them but won't. She could also tell them she's a Fielding and she grew up in that house and lives there now. But she won't do that either. First thing tomorrow morning, she'll have to prepare Erma and the girls. They all need to brace themselves for whatever has brought the reporters to town.

For a moment, the rain and wind are louder. A fine mist blows across Lane's face as the front door opens and falls closed. The booth where the man was sitting is empty.

2

TALLEY

TALLEY STANDS IN front of the attic door, both hands wrapped loosely around its glass knob. All night, Annalee's been in her room. She slammed her door when she went in there because she was angry at Talley. Talley thought to knock and apologize, but she didn't because sometimes, most of the time, Annalee scares her. An hour ago, Mama came home from the bar where she works, and now everyone is asleep. Squeezing the glass knob, Talley turns it and pushes open the door.

The door to the attic is like every other door in the house—made of wood, six panels, painted white—but it's only half as tall as a door should be. The day they moved in with Grandma Erma and Grandpa Neil, Mama showed Talley and Annalee the attic door with its old-timey glass knob. It's dusty and dirty up there, she said, and you'll catch a rusty nail. I want you to promise me. Never go in the attic.

Old as they are, the stairs to the attic are solid. It's a damn good house, Grandpa Neil is always saying. Built to stand up to Union soldiers. Grandma Erma says this place—the oaks outside, the tabby ruins where the slaves once lived, the heavy drapes, most especially the attic—is filled with the ghosts of days gone by.

At the top of the narrow stairwell, Talley drops to her knees and leans into the attic. No glass covers the windows up here, only metal vents, and because the rain has stopped, she can hear the river running alongside the house. Grandma says the attic's open windows are how the roof rats sometimes get inside. Holding the flashlight in both hands, Talley flips it on and sweeps the white stream of light across the long, narrow room. From a far corner, something rustles; it scurries, and then there is silence.

Ever since arriving in Florida, Talley has been leaving food for the boys who run. Even though the school where the boys once lived and where Grandpa Neil once worked closed three years ago, Talley still leaves the food, just like Mama did when she was a girl. Leaving the food makes living in Florida a little less lonely. Sometimes, when she's alone in her room, Talley talks to the boys. They always have light brown hair in her imagination and bright blue eyes, and they think Talley is special and smart. They say thank you for the food because they sure did need it and Talley sure was brave to leave it. And then a few weeks ago, it happened. Then again and again. The food Talley was leaving on the fence post near the river had begun to disappear. Now, every night she waits for the house to grow quiet, climbs the stairs, and watches out the attic window in hopes of seeing who is taking her food.

When they still lived in Brooklyn, Mama would tell stories

about the boys who ran. Every night of her childhood, at least up until she was thirteen, Mama would sneak leftovers and leave them on the fence post near the river. Something bad happened to Mama when she was thirteen, and that must be why she stopped. Sometimes Grandpa talks about it, but he mostly mumbles and makes no sense, what Grandma calls talking gibberish, so Talley never has figured out what happened.

Before they moved to Florida, Mama told lots of stories about her home and said that maybe one day they'd visit. Florida was far from Brooklyn, at least a two-day drive. The sun always shone in north Florida, Mama said, and the flowers bloomed all year. There were alligators and tupelo honey and sweet magnolias. But when the day came that Mama said they were moving to Florida, Talley didn't dream of any of those things. Instead she dreamed of leaving food for the boys who ran.

The school where the boys lived before it was closed is directly behind Grandma Erma and Grandpa Neil's property. Boys from all over Florida were sent there for doing things like skipping school and stealing cars. Sometimes one of those boys would try to run away. In the days before a fence was built around the school, the sound of sirens carried across the whole of Milton County. Didn't need no fence, Grandpa would sometimes say. Back in those days when he was in charge of the school, didn't need no fence to keep them boys where they belonged.

If one of those runaway boys was new to the school, he might mistakenly run straight for Grandpa's land. This is why Mama would leave the food and a note too. Don't come this way, she would warn them in her notes. That's how brave Mama was when she was a girl, and how brave Talley hopes to be too. Talley once asked Mama straight out why at thirteen years old she stopped leaving the food. Did the boys not need it anymore? Did they stop running? Mama shook her head. They still ran, she said, but my food, my notes, couldn't save them.

IT'S A PERSON. At first, that's all Talley knows for sure. At the attic window that looks down on the drive, she presses her face against the metal vent and stretches her eyes wide. He or she comes from the house. A boy, if it were one of the boys who run, would come from the trees that separate Grandpa's property from the school. But this person looks to have walked out the back door off the kitchen, and as the shadow crosses the drive, it turns into a girl, and because it has long hair and small shoulders and tips onto its toes as it walks, it turns into Annalee.

Talley stares hard at Annalee and the drive below and holds up one hand to the side of her face so she can't see the giant oak growing nearby. That old tree frightens Talley on nights like this, when the moss quivers and shadows slip in and out of its branches. Soon after they moved in, Grandpa told Talley about the terrible things that happened at the tree a long time ago. She asked Mama if Grandpa's stories were true, and Mama got angry at Grandpa and told him to mind his business.

Pinching the blades on the window's metal vent, Talley adjusts them until she gets the best view out the window. Annalee walks up to her truck, opens the door, reaches inside, and begins to push. Like she always does, she has backed her truck in so now it's pointing the right way. Many other times in the past few weeks, while watching out the attic window, Talley has seen Annalee do this same thing. Each time, she should have told Mama what Annalee was up to because Talley knew it was wrong. But the part of Talley that made her afraid to do things like climb the old oak outside Grandma's kitchen window stopped her from telling on Annalee.

Probably because the ground is soft and wet, Annalee has a hard time getting the truck to move, but once it starts rolling, she jumps in and pulls the door closed. Without switching on the headlights, she starts it up and the truck rolls on down the drive until Talley can't see it anymore. Grabbing the flashlight, Talley runs on her toes toward the other end of the attic.

Mama would be angry to know Talley is here in the attic. Daddy would be angry too, but he lives in Europe now and never calls because it's always too early or too late. Thinking about Daddy living so far away makes Talley sad, but every day that he doesn't call, she misses him a little less. Sometimes she wonders if Daddy will skip so many phone calls, she'll stop missing him altogether.

Mama would be angry too if she knew Talley has been walking down to the New Covenant Church to watch the girls who go there for the Little Sisters of the South meetings and that they won't let Talley join because they're afraid of Grandpa Neil. Mama was a Little Sister, but she quit when she was a teenager. Even if Mama stopped wanting to be a Little Sister, Talley wants it more than anything else here in Florida. If she's a Little Sister, she'll learn to be like every other girl because every other girl she knows is a member. Being like everyone else has to be easier than being different.

But Mama will be angriest to know Talley is friends with Daryl, who works at the New Covenant Church, and that he is helping her grow a garden so the Little Sisters will change their minds and let her join. Daryl is much older than Talley, and Mama won't like that at all.

Talley's only other friend was Susannah Bauer before she disappeared. More than anyone she's ever known, even Daddy, Talley misses Susannah. All around town and probably all around the whole state, people are looking for her. Some in town say everyone should keep a close eye on the blond girls. They must think Susannah being blond means something, and they're afraid another girl will be next, though they never say which girl it will be. Mama and Annalee both have blond hair, but Mama's isn't as blond as Annalee's. Talley has the lightest hair of all three, and she sometimes worries that means she will be the next to disappear.

At the other end of the attic, Talley drops to her knees and presses her face to the vent that looks out the front of the house. Annalee's two red taillights have reached the end of the road. She takes a right turn, and soon her truck is out of sight, but before Talley pushes away from the window, another set of headlights pops on. They come from a car parked at the intersection where Annalee turned. The car sits there, its headlights throwing a smoky yellow glow. From somewhere far away, thunder rumbles. After a few moments, the car's lights begin to move, rolling slowly forward, and they follow in Annalee's path.

3

DARYL

21 days before Susannah disappeared

AS I PUSH my shopping cart from aisle to aisle, one of the front wheels wobbles and pulls hard to the left. I'm here to wait for the girl who comes to town twice a month. Susannah Bauer is her name. Usually, she comes here to this grocery store on the first and the third Saturday. Usually, but not always.

My forearms ache from trying to right this cart for the past thirty minutes. It rattles, this cart with the bum wheel, and people who pass me say I should leave it and try another. Don't you hate it when you get a bum one? they say to me. And I nod and smile because that's what they do. I hate it when I get a cart with a bum wheel.

As I watch for Susannah Bauer, I look for my brother too among all the faces here in this grocery store and at the church where I work and on the sidewalks around town. I haven't seen him, Wayne is his name, since I was seven or eight years old, but I think I'll know him when I do. Twenty years ago, maybe more, a judge sent my brother to the school for boys here in this town for stealing a lawn mower. Wayne is the reason I came to Waddell, and I hope to stay until I find him.

Wayne was seventeen the last time I saw him. As he disappeared in the back of a brown car, Mother pushed her wiry dark hair from her face, said good riddance, and moved us north. Far north. When I asked Mother how Wayne would know where to find me, she pointed a finger in my face and said she hoped he never would and that I had better hope the same.

It's almost five thirty, and the girl, Susannah Bauer, should be here in the store by now. Sometimes she comes to my work to borrow tools. All day, every other Saturday, I wait in my shed for her, but she didn't come today, so I hope to see her in the store.

Susannah Bauer is one of the students from Florida State who volunteers at the Fielding Mansion on the Fielding Plantation. I know where it is because it shares a fence with the school for boys. When I first moved to town a year ago, I went to the school to look for my brother, but it was empty. Mother, when I was still a boy, told me the school wouldn't be so bad for Wayne. They play games there, she said. Basketball and soccer and football too. You know how Wayne loves football, she said. But there were no boys playing the day I drove to the school. There were only two guards who, through a silver fence, told me the school was closed and ordered me to go away. Sometimes I still drive by because maybe Wayne's looking for me just like I'm looking for him.

The grounds at the school are always freshly mowed. I don't know who tends them, but I know Susannah and the other volunteers don't. They only see to taking care of the Fielding Mansion because it's old and part of Florida history. Every Saturday that the volunteers come to the house, Susannah comes too, and now that the sun is setting later in the day, she comes here to shop for sandwiches and bottled water so the others will stay and work longer. Sometimes she buys ice-cream bars too, and at her car, she unloads them into a foam cooler and packs them with ice.

Seven times, Susannah has come to me and asked to borrow a tool. Reverend says the students are allowed to borrow them because they are working to preserve some part of Florida history, so I told Susannah of course I'd loan her the edger or the wheelbarrow like they were mine to give. I wanted her to believe I was the important one. I like that she smiles at me on those days, and I smile back as I wonder what her skin must feel like. I think it would be warm and soft like her voice.

I asked Susannah once if she ever saw anyone over at the school for boys. She shook her head and crossed her arms. Just because we care about the history of the home, she said, doesn't mean we condone what that man did. I didn't know who that man was, but I didn't like making Susannah angry. I never asked her about the school again.

WAITING AND WATCHING for Susannah, I've walked the aisles three times. I'm squeezing the cart's handle, pushing with my left hand and pulling with my right. The wheel is still drifting. I turn because I think that's her laugh coming from over near the frozen food, and my cart bumps against something. It stops short, and the handle rams into my gut. I double over because it's caught me just so, and I can't draw in a breath.

Her squeals are muted, this new girl who has run her cart into me. It sounds as if she's cupped a hand over her mouth. I pinch my eyes closed. A buzz comes from overhead. It's the lights. Even through my closed eyelids, I can see they don't throw a steady glow. One aisle over, the freezers make a humming sound. The scent of bleach tints the air. And there is the laugh again, a giggle, really. It's Susannah Bauer's voice. I'm sure of it, coming to me from one aisle over. Still tasting the bleach, I gasp, finally am able to inhale, and open my eyes. And then comes a string of apologies.

I like it, the sound of this new girl's voice. Even before I see her face, I like the sound of her. Her voice is clear and soft, nearly like a whisper. A small hand wraps around my forearm. It's pale, and I'd like to trail a finger over the fine blue veins that run along the back of her hand, but I don't because her face is here alongside mine. She's bent down next to me, nearly crouched beneath me so she can look up into my eyes.

This is how it begins. Not often or sometimes, but always it begins with a hitch in my breathing. Something like the way you suck in air when startled. Not startled in a bad way. It's the hitch in your breath you must feel when a woman first removes her blouse for you and she's wearing no underclothes beneath. The shock of it must make you draw in a breath and then you let it out long and slow, always through your mouth because to do so will make the vision last a moment longer. This is how it always begins.

I don't like them, the girls, to remember me. Or rather, I'd like them to remember me, but I can't let that happen. I don't want them to ever look back and remember a strange man from the gas station or the ticket booth at the theater. I don't speak to them, never get so close as to do that. I don't open a door for them or pick up a set of keys they might drop. I'm safer if they don't notice me and if I stay far away. I'm safer because I wonder sometimes what my needing so badly to be near them, needing so badly for them to soothe what's inside me, will one day force me to do. Susannah is the only girl I've ever talked to and only because she came and found me at the church. She asks me for help on those days, and sometimes she brushes past so that our arms touch and I can smell her and so she will remember me. That makes her special, I think.

This girl too, this one here beside me who has run her cart into mine, will remember me. She will remember, and so I shouldn't look at her. I should close my eyes again, brush her away as if I'm just that angry. But she's apologizing over and over and asking what can I do, what can I do? Her tiny hand strokes my arm, lightly. What can I do?

I shake my head as I look into her small face. It's delicate, and her chin would easily rest in the palm of one hand. In the palm of my one hand. Her eyes are a watery blue. They're round and too large for her small face. They're right there beneath me, looking up at me. Her mouth is slightly parted. The tip of her tongue pokes out, wets her lips. I'm so sorry, she says again. What can I do? I shake my head and force myself to stand straight.

"No worries," I say, and back away until her small, pale hand slides from my arm. "I'm fine now."

"Your bread," she says, bending to pick up the loaf I dropped. "But not this one." She slides the dented loaf back on the shelf and grabs another. "Whole wheat. It's all I ever buy. That other stuff is garbage."

I toss the bread in my cart but say nothing. I don't want to take notice of the blond hair pulled back and tied off with a single band. Yellowish blond, not an ashy blond. Always light and blond and smooth. The girls, these blond girls, shimmer and catch the light. To look at them quiets what's inside me. Their hair is never wiry like Mother's. Never dark and streaked with gray. I don't want to notice that this girl's hair must surely fall well past the shoulders when let down. Or her age. Seventeen, most likely. Maybe eighteen. She's taller than I would have thought when looking only at her face, but still she's frail in a way, slender, slight. She'll be tender, and she'll be the oldest in the family because she's doing the shopping, and she's here in this store, same as me, because it sells cheap food and so she'll come from a modest, maybe poor home.

She'll live here on the east side of town because there is another Food Lion on the west side. And she's local. No doubt. Her skin is not sunburned, and her clothes aren't wilted from a day tubing down the river. It's summertime and she's the oldest and she comes from no money so she'll have a job, a part-time job for the summer. There's something written on the left side of her shirt where a breast pocket might normally be. I don't let my eyes settle there because I really don't want to know what it says, but I already do. Even from this distance and even though the letters are mostly a blur. She works at the Wharf, likely bussing tables because she wears a crew neck and not a collared shirt. A red name tag is pinned beneath the emblem. I lean forward just enough to read it. ANNALEE, it reads.

School just let out for the summer, so it might be her first day on a new job or maybe she's worked there a few months. She'll be hoping to get promoted to waitress soon. That's where the real money is, and she'll need it because no one at home is giving it to her. Her shirt is clean, so she's on her way to work. Saturday-evening shift. Perhaps every Saturday. I try not to notice any of this because I don't want to ever think of her after today.

There is Susannah's laugh again, and I remember why I'm here. It's high-pitched and louder, clearer, so it's closer. And there's another voice too. The second voice is deep, a man's voice. He's begging for beer. Buy those poor kids a few cold ones for their hard work. It's the least you could do. Buy me a few while you're at it. I recognize the voice. He's the son of Hettie Jansen. Miss Hettie is the secretary at the church where I work. She has long dark hair that is streaked with gray. It makes her look older

21

than I think she really is. Jimmy is her boy's name. Jimmy Jansen. He's taller than me, though not much taller. And thinner too, and he has blond hair. His mother, Miss Hettie, calls him a boy, so I do too, but he isn't a boy. He's big as any man.

I try not to look toward the voices, toward his voice or Susannah's, but I do. It's a quick glance to see if they are standing together at the end of the aisle and walking this way. The thought of the boy being so tall and blond standing next to Susannah, so small and tender, makes my hands knot up into fists, and I slap them against my thighs. I slap harder and harder. The pain I feel is the pain I want the boy to feel. But Susannah is not there, and neither is he. When I turn back to the girl, she is looking too. She has stopped apologizing to me and is staring at the same empty spot at the end of the aisle.

This new girl's worry for me had made her lips pucker and her brows droop, but the sound of a man's voice and the giggle of another girl changes her face. Her brows pinch instead of droop and her lips form a hard line instead of a round pucker. She takes a few quick steps up the aisle to follow the giggles and the man's deep voice.

The girl says nothing more as she walks away. She has a spring to the way she walks, lifts ever so slightly onto her toes with each step. She's finished with me and has left behind her cart. It's empty. She's not here doing the shopping on her way to work. That would make no sense. Like me, she's here at this store for another reason. She's here because of the man, the boy, who is talking and laughing with Susannah Bauer.

Already, I feel it. The thing that grabs hold. The hitch in my breathing. The thing that finally catches. And I know I'll have to see her—this new girl named Annalee—again.

ERMA

AT FIRST, ERMA figures she's hearing her granddaughters, up and about for the day. But no, that's not it. And then she thinks it's the rustling of leaves on the old oak growing outside her kitchen window. She'd have a nice sunny kitchen on a morning like today if not for the old tree, but there's not breeze enough outside to stir a lit candle, so it won't be those leaves. Maybe it isn't that she hears something out there; it's that she feels it. Like the ache in her hip that flares up with the rain. It's a set of tires, and it's headed this way.

Leaning over the kitchen sink as best she can, Erma pushes aside the curtains, vintage lace she washes only by hand. Sure enough, a white van is turning into her driveway. She steps back and drops the curtain before anyone gets a look inside. That old tree is how the white vans find the house. Even though Erma pried the address off the mailbox down by the road, those reporters know to take a left at the giant live oak, the grandest in all of Milton County, Florida, and that'll be the Fielding Mansion.

More than fifteen years ago, a couple of fellows from the county said the tree had seen the last of its better days. Yes, it's a beauty of a tree, those fellows said, and shook their heads as they glanced at each other. They knew, like most folks knew, such a tree came with a sad and painful past. But you see all this moss, the way it trails from nearly every branch, they went on to say. Such a lot of moss is a sign the tree is dead or dying. Moss does so love a dying oak. One good storm'll bring it down. Best you tend it now.

Back when the tree was first diagnosed, Neil, newly retired from the school and still touching up his hair with cheap black dye, was too busy to be bothered with it. He was too busy visiting the fellows down at the meal center, claiming he was tending the elderly, when in truth he was tending his poker habit. And he was too busy tugging his blue pleated slacks up over his bulging stomach while flirting with the church ladies on potluck Wednesdays. Even though Neil wasn't such a handsome man, those ladies giggled and touched him on the forearm as he told them unseemly jokes, sometimes going so far as to whisper the nastiness in their ears. It has surely been a long time since Neil whispered in Erma's ear, but she remembers well how his warm breath, so often smelling of tobacco and stale coffee, tickled and caused her a shiver. She figured those ladies were feeling that same tickle, though what tickled Erma was fear.

SOMETHING OUTSIDE IS causing an awful ruckus. Erma starts to take a peek out her kitchen window but remembers she already did. When this confusion happens, as it so often does, she rubs her eyes. It helps to clear the cloudy haze that swells inside her head. It's a van. That's what it is. Those vans coming are mostly what cause her thoughts to turn thin and wispy, trail away like puffs of smoke. Sometimes her heart pounds hard inside her chest and she struggles to get her air. It's the vans. And if the white vans are coming, that Bonnie Wiley from across the road will be coming too, bringing with her all her witchy nonsense.

Once outside the kitchen door, Erma leans heavy on the metal railing as she climbs down the three steps and winces when she reaches the ground. She's barefooted, for pity's sake. Hiking the hem of her housedress, she shuffles toward the main drive. Just underfoot, a few strands of straw are scattered. Bonnie Wiley spreads them almost nightly—thirteen strands in all, always thirteen, that she's broken off a broom. That broom must be nearly bare by now for all the straw she's snapped off and dropped outside the Fieldings' door. Erma plants a heel in the middle of one brittle strand and snaps it in two.

Erma is wearing her lavender housedress today. Not one of her nicer ones, but one of a few that still fit. Back when the vans first started pulling into her drive, she would have seen to her hair and touched up her velvety pink lipstick before going outside to meet them. Back then, the salon would still take her appointments— every Friday morning, ten o'clock sharp—and she was still welcome over at the New Covenant. But she's altogether gray now and will likely stay that way, and it's been three years since the elders over at the New Covenant sent a letter offering that, due to increasing pressures from concerned members, the reverend would see to worshiping with the Fieldings in their home.

Please understand, the reverend said. More reporters are coming to town in the wake of the school closing its doors. No one down at the church wants that type of attention. Erma told them no, thank you very much, she wouldn't be taking services at home, and she hasn't been to the church since.

Straight ahead, the first van rolls to a stop, the passenger-side door opens, and a man wearing a blue suit steps out. Another two pull in behind the first. Lifting her chin, Erma settles her hands on her hips and plants her feet wide. Lane and the girls are finally back home. Praise be, after all these years, and Erma darn well won't be letting these troublemakers anywhere near this house. Shoring herself up, she presses one flat palm out in front of her and hollers for the vans to stop.

THOSE FELLOWS FROM the county had been wrong. The tree never came crashing down on the house, but it has caused a load of trouble. Every reporter, photographer, lawyer, and lookie-loo from as far away as New York and California eventually finds his way to the Fieldings' house. With every new development over at the school, every new lawsuit filed, every new judgment made by a court, every grave unearthed, the story grows and more reporters from more newspapers come searching. Shoot out down Route 121—some maps call it Blue Spring Road, some call it South Highway—and look for the big oak. When you see that giant of a tree, you'll know you're at the right place. The Fieldings' place.

"Good morning, Mrs. Fielding," the man wearing the blue suit and red tie says. He has silver hair and is older than most of the fellows who have come before him. The bigger the story has grown, the better dressed these fellows have become.

"You all go on now," Erma hollers.

From over by the river comes a hollow grunt—Neil rubbing a metal file over a post driven down into the dirt. He and Talley will be back there among the cypress trees where Neil coaxes worms with his songs. Talley will be dashing about, plucking up those worms and dropping them in her pail. Erma needs to send away these reporters before Talley finishes and comes back to the house, but before she can holler out at the reporters again, a black-and-white car, the sheriff's car, appears from behind those vans. It rolls slow, real slow, past the man in his fine clothes, and stops in front of Erma. Sheriff Ellenton, Mark Ellenton, throws open his door and steps out of the car.

"You all get on," the sheriff says to everyone climbing out of the vans. "You know you're not meant to use this drive."

Erma has known Mark all his life, he and Lane running around together since they were near babies, and he's grown into a fine man.

"Just one question," the silver-haired one says. "Will you be going to the press conference, Mrs. Fielding? Will your husband attend?"

"Mrs. Fielding won't be talking with you fellows today," Sheriff Ellenton says. "You all get on now."

The silver-haired man tries once more, and then he and the others climb back into their vans.

As soon as they're gone, Mark turns to Erma. "Sorry to trouble you so early, Mrs. Fielding."

"No trouble at all," Erma says. She's happy Mark has run off those reporters, and maybe he's brought news of Susannah Bauer too. Folks in town are saying it's just like when that fellow, Ted, came through. They talk like they can smell it in the air and like Susannah is only the first. But Erma doesn't believe it. Sometimes young girls run off and come back on their own. That's what she's hoping Mark will tell her, if not today, then one day soon. Lock your doors, folks have been saying since the day the police came to town looking for Susannah, but Erma's been locking her doors for years.

"Come on in for coffee," she says to Mark. "Just brewed a fresh pot."

"Afraid I can't, ma'am," Mark says. "I'll be needing to talk to Lane if you wouldn't mind rounding her up."

LANE

THOUGH HER BEDROOM windows are locked up tight and the drapes are drawn, Lane can still hear gravel kicking up from under a set of tires. It'll be a reporter, probably one who was in the bar last night, and she remembers. She's divorced now. It's official. She pushes off the bed slowly, giving her legs time to adjust because the alcohol hasn't burned off yet. She had been right about the rain not keeping her regulars away. They'd shared shots and stories of their own divorces until well past midnight. Steadying herself with one hand on the footboard, she flips on the television, already knowing what she'll see.

The Fielding house, though the reporters always call it the Fielding Mansion or the Fielding Plantation, fills the screen. The local stations usually use the same photo when they have something new to report about Neil and the school. It was taken long before the family, mostly Neil, sold off the bulk of the property. The picture has a sepia tone to it, an orange cast meant to remind people Neil Fielding lives in a house where slavers once lived, and isn't that somehow telling?

She starts to pull on the jeans she wore to work last night, but they smell of smoke, so she digs her car keys and a stack of rolled-up bills from the front pockets, drops them on her bed, and slips on shorts and a T-shirt instead. Grabbing her sunglasses from the nightstand, she switches off the television, runs up the stairs, and taps on Annalee's bedroom door.

"Annalee," Lane says. "You up?"

She knocks again, louder this time. "You awake?"

Still no answer. Turning the knob slowly, Lane pushes open the door. The sheets are twisted, the bedspread hangs off the end of the mattress, and dirty clothes are scattered across the floor. It's all too familiar, walking into an empty bedroom that shouldn't be empty. Teenagers being teenagers, Kyle had been inclined to say when the same happened in Brooklyn. But this is the first time it's happened in Florida. Annalee has been happier here, seems to have left behind some of the aches of the teenage years. She has friends, something Talley has struggled with, and a job.

Lane will stick to the back office at the bar today and tonight and be able to avoid any more reporters. Rowland will fill in, and it'll give her a chance to get caught up on the bookkeeping. Rowland hired her mostly for her ability to enter receipts, pay bills, and balance a bank account, skills she developed after she and Kyle suffered underpayment penalties on their tax returns two years in a row. But Annalee doesn't have a back office to hide in. When last a day started like this, two of those reporters pieced together the family tree and made their way to Annalee's station at the restaurant. When she tried to clear their table, they asked how it felt to live with a man like Neil Fielding and had she ever seen the scars on the back of his right hand? She offered to tell them for a hundred bucks. After that, Lane decided no more working for Annalee on the days the reporters come to town.

Back downstairs, a stream of warm air blowing across the foyer means Erma has left the kitchen door open. Someone out there is hollering for the reporters to get going. It's Mark Ellenton's voice. Lane's sure of it. And she is sure the reporters are here in search of her father.

Starting about five years ago, a group of men—they had been children in the fifties and sixties—found one another on the Internet, and their silence was broken. Through blogs, e-mail blasts, and websites, they discovered stories similar to their own. As their numbers grew, their voice grew, and they were finally heard. They spoke for themselves and for those who had already passed on. They had lived their entire lives, many of the victims, believing they were alone. Believing they were the only ones to remember a small white house and the man with a leather strap. Together, they demanded that people listen and that someone be held responsible.

They are the men who all say they were beaten in a Florida reform school when they were boys as young as eight. Some beaten nearly to death. They were so often boys from poor homes whose families were kept separate from them by distance and poverty. The school that Lane grew up looking at from her bedroom window was open only two years when the first incidents of abuse were recorded. That was one hundred years ago, long before Neil Fielding took charge of the school's discipline. There were countless reports of the violence, some even that made it all the way to Washington and the Senate floor, but no one ever took notice. Nothing was ever done. Not until the men found one another on the Internet. They all say Lane's father is the man mostly responsible for the things they'll never forget.

Before walking outside to face the reporters who have come today, Lane grabs her cell phone and types in a message to Annalee.

CALL HOME BEFORE YOU GO TO WORK.

WHEN MARK FINALLY stopped in at the bar last night, the odd man was long gone, the music had been turned up, and the bar's crowd was a mix of regulars celebrating with Lane and reporters killing time until the next day. After first confirming with Rowland that there had been no trouble between the reporters and the locals, Mark wrapped Lane in a loose-fitting hug and congratulated her on being newly single. He was damp and smelled like soap, and he talked to Lane in that voice of his. It had always had a way with her. It was deep, and his words, as he spoke them, glided from his mouth, one after another, each slower than the last. He was a man who knew about things like silky black river water and roosting bats and shoal bass big as a man's forearm.

Lane had finished off a few drinks by the time Mark arrived and at least three shots of whiskey, and she held on to him too long. After that night with Rowland, she started limiting herself to one beer a night, but that promise hadn't held during the party. Mark pulled away first, and once he untangled himself, he told Lane a press conference at the school had brought the reporters to town and said to give a call if she had any trouble. And then he shook Rowland's hand as if Lane's divorce was reason for him to celebrate too. Rowland slipped an arm around Lane's shoulder and said he'd see to taking care of her. Lane pushed him away, but the damage was already done.

Plenty more reporters made their way to the bar after Mark left. No more of her father's accusers or their relatives came, at least none that Lane picked out of the crowd. After the first three reporters left, a dozen more arrived. Lane recognized a few, but the rest were new to her, which meant interest in the story had spread yet again. None asked about the missing girl, but they all wanted to know how to get to the Fielding Mansion. As the night went on, the alcohol fooled her into thinking she was one of them again. She talked bylines and relived past stories, even flirted with a few. The more she drank, the harder it was to claim she'd never heard of the Fielding Mansion. And then one asked . . . isn't Fielding your new name?

The smartest among them pieced it together. Fielding wasn't Lane's new name. It was her original name. You were married to Kyle Wallace. That's right, isn't it? Man, I love his books. And then there was that one reporter, there was always that one who pointed at her and said, I know who you are. You're Neil Fielding's daughter. You're the one who was abducted. You're the one that boy from the school took. You were thirteen, right? I understand your father found the boy. Is that true? What happened to him? And what about all the other boys who were sent to that school? What do you think about the things your father did to them? Is that why you stayed away all these years? Come on, tell us, what do you remember?

In all her years living up north with Kyle and the girls, Lane was never asked about that day. Now she is asked almost every time the reporters come to town. Whenever one of them questions her about having been abducted, she tells them only that it was a family matter. Neil kept the whole thing out of the papers. So even though Lane never asks the reporters to disclose their sources, she always knows it had to have been someone born and raised in Waddell, a local, who told them.

Year after year, when she was still working as a reporter and in the years since when she was home with both girls, Lane searched for something, anything, that would tell her what happened to the boy Neil said took her when she was thirteen. She researched crimes, abductions, kidnappings, and assaults reported in the town of Waddell in 1990, or, more specifically, Saturday, April 7, 1990. She hunted for any sign of the boy. Was there a boy who was injured at the school that April seventh? Was there a boy who died that day? Every year, every month, nearly every day, she's looked for the boy Neil blamed and found nothing.

"GOOD TO SEE you, Lane," Mark calls out as she walks across the drive toward him. He's not yet shaved this morning, and his dark stubble is visible even from a distance. "Sorry about the hour."

"Expecting trouble?" Lane says as the last van pulls away.

"Just a press conference," Mark says. "But not here about that."

All her years away from Waddell, Lane thought often of Mark, imagined the kind of father he would have been, the kind of husband, the kind of life she might have had if she'd have chosen him instead of Kyle. And up until the rumors about Lane and Rowland Jansen began, she believed Mark had thought of her all those years too. But if he had, he wouldn't have let go so easily, or perhaps he never grabbed on. Perhaps the thing Lane thought had begun growing between them after she moved back had only been growing in her imagination.

"He's here looking for Annalee," Erma says, blotting her cheeks with a cotton dish towel.

"That right?"

"Wondering if she's around?" Mark asks.

"Was going to have her call in sick to the restaurant," Lane says, working through the possibilities of what kind of trouble Annalee has gotten into. "When I heard the vans outside, I went to wake her, but she was already up and out. She in some kind of trouble?"

Lane had been prepared for reporters when she first walked outside. Soon after moving back to town, she wrote lists of questions she might be asked concerning Neil, because preparation was the best way to avoid being shocked into saying something she might otherwise regret. She'd learned while working as a reporter the effectiveness of an unexpected question. She shared the questions with Erma too, but she refused to study them. Instead, she would say, You were never like them, were you, Laney? You never shouted at people or blocked their driveways?

During Lane's years as a reporter, she did shout questions and block drives. She'd believed anything that led to the truth was justified. She still believes in the truth, wishes desperately more people cared about it, most especially as it relates to her father, but now she understands what all her reluctant sources had understood. The instinct to protect can be far stronger than the desire for truth.

"That mean you haven't seen her this morning?" Mark asks.

Lane shakes her head. "Erma?"

"Not hide nor hair."

"Bed been slept in?" Mark asks.

"No telling," Lane says. She's being evasive, protecting Annalee, though she doesn't know from what. "Never gets made. What is this all about?"

"And last night?" Mark asks, glancing between Lane and Erma. "Either of you see her last night?"

"She was supposed to work," Lane says. "But they told her not to come in. The rain and all. She was here when I got home."

"And, Erma, what about you? You see Annalee last night?"

"We had supper," Erma says, worry already turning her cheeks and neck red. "All of us. Seen her off to bed."

To put a little distance between herself and Erma and because she's feeling a chill, Lane walks from the shade of the oak into the sunlight. As she motions for Mark to follow, she pulls out her cell phone. The screen is dark and empty. Still nothing from Annalee, and she's sure of it now. Something is wrong.

"What is it, Mark?"

From the earliest days in her journalism career, while speaking to someone in the wake of a car crash or a downtown shooting, she learned to recognize this—the beginnings of fear settling in. Even at the height of a summer day, a person, a victim, a witness, would sometimes shiver and look at Lane as if surprised to see her though she'd been talking with him, interviewing her, for twenty minutes. Could we step out into the sun? he or she would say. I'm so darn cold.

"Kids from Tallahassee still coming around?" Mark asks.

"Couple times a month," Lane says. Her shoulders drop, and her chest shudders as she exhales. She immediately regrets the feeling, but she can't stop it from settling in. It's relief. "So, that's what's brought you? More questions about Susannah?"

Since Lane was a child, twice a month, students from Florida State who are studying things like architecture, history, and preservation have helped with the upkeep of the house and grounds. The students get experience and college credit, and it's the only way the Fielding family has been able to stay on the property, the costs of maintenance being so high. Twice, in the nearly two weeks since Susannah Bauer disappeared, police officers from Tallahassee have been to the house because Susannah was one of the regular volunteers. She was seen at the nearby Food Lion deli counter the day she disappeared, driving the car of another volunteer, but the grocery store wasn't her last stop. She came back to the house to drop off sandwiches for the other volunteers, and at around six o'clock, she caught a ride with a few of the other students. They dropped her at home, or so they said, and she hasn't been seen since.

This is what Lane told the police both times they questioned her. She hadn't seen anything or anyone unusual and didn't know if Susannah had a boyfriend. It was probably all in Lane's imagination, the fear that those police officers doubted her story. In the years since Lane left Waddell, the town split into two sides—those for Neil Fielding and those against. To some, the school where Neil had worked had meant jobs and a livelihood. They claim it helped young children find a better path, and they use the shocking nature of Neil's crimes to discredit his accusers. Who would believe anything so horrific? Most of all they resent the journalists who roll into town with cameras, tape recorders, and bylines. To others, the school brought shame. They are the ones who understand what is unbelievable is nonetheless possible. One town. Two sides. And the Tallahassee police are probably no different.

Each time she spoke to the officers, Lane assured them Neil never saw Susannah. Besides, he's an old man, though Lane sometimes forgets. Her throat might tighten; her breath might turn shallow. An upset chair is all it takes, even after twenty years. Or a door slammed by the wind. It's enough to make her forget, if only for an instant, that Neil is an old man now. For that moment, she's a teenager again and is afraid of him. She's afraid of the slamming doors, the toppled furniture, Erma's cries from behind a closed door. But no one else except Erma would feel that way. When other people see Neil, they see a tired, crippled old man. We have no reason to suspect your father, the police said each time.

"Come on in the kitchen," Lane says to Mark. "But not sure what new I can tell you."

"Not here about Susannah Bauer," Mark says.

No one else would notice the small change in Mark's voice, the way it softens, slows ever so slightly, but Lane hears it. It's something that only happens between people who've known each other their whole lives. She stops and turns. It's a slow turn, and yet it leaves her dizzy.

"Then what is it?"

"Likely nothing." Mark takes a few steps toward Lane.

Forgetting about her red eyes and the dark smudges under them, Lane pulls off her sunglasses. "Just tell me."

After the initial chill, the world starts to shrink in on a person. That's another thing she learned early in her professional career. It's happening to her now. Her ears feel as if they're stuffed full of cotton. A woman once described it that way as she tried to make Lane understand what it was like when a police officer knocked on her door at two A.M. Did you have a daughter? the officer had said. Not do you have a daughter, but *did* you have. I saw that officer's lips making those words but couldn't hear a sound. All of it, like cotton in my ears.

"Couple fellows fishing out on the river this morning seen a truck parked there where the tracks cross over. You know the spot?"

"Yes, I know it," Lane says. She and Mark together knew the spot as kids.

At first, it was just a tickle, an itch at the base of her neck that told her something was wrong. But now that feeling has crept around her shoulders and settled in her chest and throat.

"Seen it parked back in there," Mark says. "River rose up around it. Figured it was left for stuck."

"And it's Annalee's."

Mark nods. "Had to been driven down there last night before the rain started up heavy again."

"And Annalee? Did they see her too?"

"No," he says. "Was hoping I'd find her here. Figured maybe she had to leave it and find another way home."

Lane nods, glances at the empty spot where Annalee's truck should be parked. The sound of Neil singing for worms drifts over from the river. There's that dizziness again, as if she's slipping in and out of childhood.

"Strange thing, though," Mark says. "Driver's-side door was left open."

Hearing something so typical of Annalee steadies Lane. Talley would never do anything so careless, but Annalee would. She'd leave a door hanging open and not for a moment think about the terrible time they'd have drying out the seats and floor mats. If leaving the door hanging open is understandable, then the rest must be too. But before she can say any of this, Mark raises a finger to silence her, slips his phone from his front pocket, and excuses himself.

Walking a few feet away, Mark takes the call, and as he begins to talk, he turns his back on Lane. Her chest pumps faster, straining against the weight that has settled there. Sweat gathers on her upper lip. She hits the number 2 on her phone, speed dial for Annalee. It goes straight to voicemail. She ends the call and tries again.

When the subjects of Lane's many interviews over the years would stumble from the shade to the sunlight, asking Lane if she felt the chill too, or stare at her mouth as if struggling to decipher whatever question she was asking, she'd tell them to inhale through their noses and exhale through their mouths. She does that now for herself. After a few moments, Mark tucks the phone in his pocket and continues to stand with his back to Lane. He stands like that for too long, longer than he needs to. When he finally turns, Lane begins to talk.

"I think you're right," she says, talking fast so Mark can't tell her any more bad news. "She probably got a ride with a friend. Probably spent the night somewhere and hasn't woken up yet."

"I'd say get to calling everyone you can think of."

"That's what it is," Lane continues, trying to smile. "She's sleeping it off somewhere."

When packing up to move back to Florida, Lane worried it wasn't the best choice to move halfway through the school year, but it had been the only choice. Kyle didn't renew the lease on their apartment, something he failed to tell Lane until after she heard another woman's voice on his phone. Lane hadn't worked in years and didn't get enough money from the divorce to touch a Brooklyn apartment. Moving back to Florida, even if just for a short while, had been the only choice. But it's worked out well enough, especially for Annalee. She complained at first, thought people talked too slow in north Florida and that the size of the roaches was horrid and the humidity was draining every intelligent thought she'd ever had. But then she made friends, at least a handful, and the complaining stopped. She could be with any one of them.

"They've found a few things, Lane," Mark says, holding up a hand to stop her before she starts talking again. "A purse, mostly empty, caught up in some trees and whatnot. And a sandal."

"Could belong to anyone." She's arguing with him now, something she's seen plenty of people do when facing yet more bad news.

"Yes, that's true enough," Mark says, taking one of Lane's hands.

They stand like this, Lane letting him hold her hand in both of his, her arm stretched across the distance between them. She's known him all her life, loved him a good part of it, and he's loved her too, so she knows the silence means something.

"And?" Lane says.

"They've confirmed blood in the cab of her truck. Not much. But they're certain."

Lane doesn't speak. She looks at Erma standing nearby, her hands folded, her head lowered as if she has heard what Mark said. For days, almost since the day Susannah disappeared, Lane's customers have been saying, keep a close eye on the blond girls. Back in the seventies, Ted had favored the dark-haired girls, but Susannah was a silky blonde. Lane didn't like them saying those things because her girls were blondes too, silky blondes. Every time one of her customers summoned that notorious name, she realized they must have also summoned it back in April of 1990 when she was thirteen and they feared the worst for her. Hush up, the all of you, she said every time that name was mentioned. She was trying not to let fear work its way in, but even then, she felt it. They were tempting fate.

"I'd like you to come on with me," Mark says. "Have a look at what they brought in. Tell me they don't belong to Annalee. And I'm thinking she'll beat the two of us home."

Lane can't hear the words, can only see Mark's mouth moving as he motions for her to get in his car instead of driving her own, and she's thinking of the river. She's thinking of the poison ivy Mark always got into whenever they went there as kids. She's thinking how the river swells with a heavy rain, how the rapids flare up where usually there are none. She's thinking of the spots where the banks are steep and how the water tumbles over limestone shelves buried just beneath the surface. And she's thinking of Susannah Bauer and Annalee, both with their silky blond hair.

6

TALLEY

HURRYING GRANDPA NEIL along this morning, although there isn't much hurry in Grandpa, Talley carries his stob and rooping iron. A small pail hangs from one of her wrists, and the sun is already burning the tops of her shoulders. Mama says the same sun shines over Florida and New York, but it doesn't feel the same. The air is different too. Grandma says it's so heavy with humidity some days that she'd like to wring it out in her kitchen sink and hang it to dry on the line.

Making a show of studying the ground by kicking at it with his sneakers, Grandpa Neil picks the same spot he always does. Talley jams the stob in the ground and hammers on the three-foot-long stake with a flat rock until it's good and stable. Then she hands Grandpa the rooping iron, a metal file about eighteen inches long and a few inches wide. Grandpa lowers himself onto the trunk of a fallen tree and begins rubbing his rooping iron across the wooden stake, the two of them hatching a hollowed-out grunt Mama says sounds more like a pig snorting than any kind of song she ever heard. Grabbing her pail, Talley tells Grandpa she'll be back before the first worm pops and takes off running for the fence post. This is her favorite part of every day—the moment she sees if the boys who run have taken her food again.

Usually, after Talley gathers all the worms Grandpa sings from the ground, always being careful to cover them over in her pail with cool, damp dirt, she dumps them in Grandma Erma's garden. She says those worms are the key to her sweet tomatoes and creamy smooth butter beans, but today Talley will take the worms to the church and dump them on her own garden.

Talley has been going to the church to watch the Little Sisters for a long time, but she met Daryl only about three weeks ago. Susannah Bauer wasn't missing yet when Talley and Daryl first became friends and started her garden, but then the police came and said Susannah was gone and asked Mama questions. Talley was especially glad to have Daryl as a friend after that day because she didn't think about Susannah as much when she was thinking about her garden and Daryl and the Little Sisters of the South.

Planting a garden had been Daryl's idea. He said the Little Sisters love to garden and they'd let Talley join if she had one of her own. Most days, he's nice to Talley and she's glad because without Susannah Bauer, he's Talley's only friend. But sometimes he gets angry, slaps himself on the forehead, and stomps back and forth inside his small shed, sweat bubbling up across his top lip and forehead. Talley goes home on those days wishing she had a different grandpa so the girls at school would like her better and she wouldn't need Daryl as a friend.

———

ONCE SHE'S RUN beyond the shade of the hardwoods that line the river, Talley slows to a walk. She lifts her knees high to step through the bristly grass growing near the clothesline, pulls a red kerchief from her back pocket, and ties it on her head. Glancing back to make sure Grandpa isn't watching, she ducks under the line where Grandma has already hung out the sheets and pillowcases, all of them still damp and leaking a hint of bleach. As she stoops under the last one, she sees it. Straight ahead stands the fence post, and her tub is gone. For a fourth time, one of the boys who runs has taken her food.

"Look there," Grandpa Neil shouts.

Talley swings around. Grandpa has stopped his worm singing. If he's pointing at something, she can't see because of the laundry. But she can see Grandma and Mama standing in the shade of the giant oak, and a man with a hat on his head is standing with them. It's Sheriff Ellenton. He usually comes when there's news about the school and the boys who once went there but are now grown-up old men.

A thick row of trees and a chain link fence topped with coils of barbed wire separate the school for boys from Grandma and Grandpa's house, but the fencing wasn't always there. When Mama was a little girl, only the trees separated the house from the school. Talley once asked Mama if she had been afraid of what would happen if one of those boys snuck through the trees. Mama said she worried about it plenty, but she hadn't been worried about herself. She had been worried about what would become of the boys.

Keeping an eye on the sheriff's car, Talley leans on the fence post and uses her foot to push aside the bristly grass that's still damp from last night's rain. She squats to get a better look, and as soon as she does, she wishes she hadn't. The white tub with a lid that leaks is lying right there on the ground.

"They're here looking for Lane," Grandpa shouts out again. "Get me up there to the house so I can talk to them police."

Before running back to Grandpa and the worms, Talley picks up the tub. It's heavy, still filled with the pork chop and biscuit she took from last night's leftovers. Brushing a few leaves from it, she sets it back on top of the post. She'll pick it up and take it inside later so Grandma, Mama, and Sheriff Ellenton won't see her with it. Maybe that's why the sheriff has come. He found out Talley's been leaving food and someone has been taking it.

"Don't worry about that now, girl," Grandpa says when Talley ducks under the last sheet and reaches for her first worm. "One of them boys has took Lane. Damn it all, I know it."

Grandpa grunts and leans forward to grab on to his wooden stake. Mama says he forgets things sometimes. He forgets Talley is his granddaughter and Mama is a grown woman. He thinks he still works at the school and the boys still live there. He forgets how many years have passed. And when Grandpa forgets his years, Talley doesn't like to be around him.

"No one took Mama," Talley says. "I see her right over there."

Talley turns to point at Mama, but she and the sheriff are gone, and Grandma is waving like she's calling Talley to the house.

"She's just a girl," Grandpa says. "Hate to think what one of them boys will do to her."

"Mama's not a girl, Grandpa," Talley says. Grandma is waving both arms now, waving them high over her head like Talley needs to come quick. Real quick.

Grandpa Neil says nothing more and is staring at Talley like he does when he forgets where he is. It's the look that most scares Talley and the reason she doesn't much like worm hunting.

"Let's go find Mama, Grandpa," Talley says, because sometimes

Mama says to tell Grandpa whatever he wants to hear. "I think Grandma wants us to come inside."

Talley's pail is empty. She'll have no worms to dump on her garden, but she'll still go to the church. Today is the last time the Little Sisters will meet this summer, and when the meetings start up again in the fall, Talley's garden will be dead. This one last time, she'll go to the church in hopes that the Little Sisters will like her garden and let her join. Being one of them is the only way she'll learn where to place her silverware when she's done eating and how to fold a napkin and properly address an envelope. At lunch in the school cafeteria, the boys always stand when the Little Sisters walk up to the table and the girls say thank you and wait until the boys invite them to sit. Talley wants to learn all those things even though Susannah once said Talley shouldn't worry about napkins and envelopes and boys who stand.

One more time, Talley will go to the church, but only once more. Yesterday when she went, Daryl grabbed her and scared her, so after today, she thinks she'll never go again.

DARYL

14 days before Susannah disappeared

FOR SEVEN DAYS, I've tried to forget the new girl from the grocery store, and I've thought of Susannah Bauer instead. I've sorted through my tools and prepared for what Susannah will borrow when next she stops at the church to see me. She'll come to town one more time, that's what she promised me, and then she'll be gone. This is why I've met the new girl. Because Susannah is going away to grad school. I've tried not to think of the new girl, Annalee is her name, because she'll remember me and I don't like the girls to remember me. But still I can't stop myself.

It's a Saturday when I go to the restaurant where the new girl works. I sit on a stool at the bar and the man pouring drinks knows me straightaway. He has a thick silver mustache and a round, fleshy nose. Sliding a beer across the bar, he says it's on the house for the kid who mows the church grounds. I rest my arms on the smooth wooden bar because it's what the others are doing, and I want them to think I've been in a place like this before. I wrap my hands around the glass. White foam spills over the rim and seeps through my fingers.

It's June, so even though it's suppertime, the sun is long from setting, and it's hot. Hotter than grease on a griddle, they say— the old men and old women too who come to the church—before hurrying inside where I have the air conditioner working better than ever. Sometimes, I ask them if they've ever met a fellow named Wayne who knows how to hold a football and that long-beard turkeys roost near water, but the only Waynes they know are old men. None of them are my brother.

A few men pat me on the back and say how good it is to see me enjoying a Saturday night on the town. Young fellow like you needs to see to a good time. Another beer slides across the bar. I think this means I'm meant to hurry along, so I finish the first by taking one long drink. It swells as I swallow, and I choke on the foam. Slow down there, champ. The new beer is colder and wet-ter than the first, so I take a smaller drink. It chills my insides. I smile at the men without looking in their eyes and nod along and think maybe I won't have to look for the girl from the grocery store because these people like me and now I have somewhere to go on Saturday nights.

I spend most Saturdays, and every other night too, alone in my apartment. The walls are gray, and sheets hang over every window because I don't like to imagine people looking inside. Every Saturday, I hear the neighbors open and close their doors as they go out for the night. Their keys jingle when they walk toward the stairwell, and later, much later, when they return, their headlights flash across my windows. I always wait up to hear them come home so it'll be like I just came home too. I'll have the feeling, if only for those moments, that I've been with these people and talked with them and laughed with them.

I try to listen to their conversations once their doors close so I'll know where they've gone. Was it to a movie? To supper? Did they meet friends, and did they have one too many and boy they are going to feel it tomorrow. I listen so if Reverend asks what I did with myself over the weekend, I'll have something to tell him.

But now I'm the one out for a Saturday night. When I go home, I might even stumble because I've had one too many. Boy, will I feel it tomorrow, and I'll come here again next Saturday night, and I won't even be looking for the girl from the grocery store but I will continue to look for my brother. And this is when I see her. Yes, I'm certain, she's the girl from the grocery store. She carries a tub filled with dirty dishes, half-empty glasses of soda, and wadded-up paper napkins. I'm certain it's her. Annalee.

IT EXHAUSTS ME in the end, what happens after I feel the hitch in my breathing. I know the ache that will follow, and this is what exhausts me most. The ache to see them again, to know when they'll come and where they'll go and when they'll come again. When they're near, even across a parking lot or standing at the front of a line while I'm at the back, my insides quiet and soften. I can hear all of what's around me, and the air is clear and light. My heart beats steady and easy. But then they're gone so quickly, and without them, the air becomes heavy again and cloudy and slowly what's inside begins to tighten and draw up into knots. When I can't be near them, I ease this ache by drawing maps and circling their houses and schools and the places they work. But the ache will eventually break through, and I'll need to see them again. What will happen, I sometimes worry, when seeing them—even if from a distance—is no longer enough? This is what will become of me and the ache that will follow the new girl named Annalee. Already it exhausts me.

Like she was when I saw her in the grocery store, Annalee is wearing a bright blue shirt. She'll still be hoping to make waitress soon. It's nearly eight o'clock, which means she likely has a few more hours to work. I remember a tiny chin, and though I can't see them from my stool, I remember watery blue eyes too. Her blond hair hangs loose around her shoulders today. Only the very front has been pulled back from her face. She has a certain way of turning her head so her hair fans out as it swings around. It's something she does, I think, so people will notice her.

I was right about her hair being the perfect length and the perfect color, and I know it'll have the perfect feel too, would have the perfect feel if I were ever to touch it. But the color is enough. It glows in the late-day sun shining through the windows, and the tangles inside me loosen, the noises quiet, and I exhale.

As Annalee walks across the crowded restaurant, her shoulders roll forward from the weight she carries. At the next table, she sets down the tub and begins to fill it with dirty dishes. Other waiters and waitresses pass her by as they carry hot dishes and cold drinks to waiting tables, but she doesn't smile or say hello or push aside a chair that might stand in their way. When she looks toward me, I sit tall, my back stretching and straightening, but she's really looking toward the front door. From behind me, someone calls out her name.

"Annalee. Annalee."

It's a girl's voice. Right away, I know I've heard it before, and the sound of it makes me close my eyes and inhale deeply through my nose. The voice is sweet, light, not raspy and worn by cigarette smoke and brown liquor. The girl's voice makes me want to smile because things will be better now. Maybe like a mother's voice should make me feel. Maybe like that.

"Annalee, where should we sit?"

Like the blue eyes and blond hair, I remembered Annalee's name correctly too from the day in the grocery store. She waves and drops down on the wooden bench at the table she is cleaning, leans back in the seat, gathers her hair in both hands and lifts it off her neck. She stretches. Her spine arches. Her chest lifts up and out. It's another thing she does so people will take notice.

Shifting in my seat, I look for the girl who called to Annalee. Close enough I could reach out and touch her shoulder, she walks past me, and she's followed by an older woman. From her seat at the table, Annalee opens her eyes but doesn't bother to lean forward. I think she might smile, but she doesn't, and she waves the girl and older woman to her.

The woman is certainly Annalee's mother. They look alike, the two of them. Same blond hair, though the mother's is closer to a pale brown. Same smooth skin. The mother slides onto the empty bench, and Annalee stands so the young girl can take her place. I know the younger girl from someplace. I'm certain of it. I close my eyes and listen for the sound of her voice beneath all the other voices.

The girl is nine, maybe ten years old, and I've seen her sitting cross-legged on a curb. She and Annalee are about the same age difference as Wayne and I. The younger sister's hair is pulled back from her face and tied off with a bow I'm certain she doesn't much like. She's the girl who comes to the church on Tuesdays. She waves to me most days as she watches the girls who come to the meetings of the Little Sisters of the South. I know why she does it, because I watch Susannah and all the others for the same reason. The young girl is lonely and comes to the church so she can watch and listen and almost be one of them. If she can see them, at least be near them, she won't ever be truly alone.

My second beer has gone warm. I drink from it, but it's bitter now. I worry I'll spit it out if I try to finish it. The baseball game is in the bag, not for our team but for the other. That's what the men say. I'll go back to my apartment and fumble with my keys and maybe fall into my neighbor's door. But before I go, I'll take one last look.

The young girl at the table, the one who comes to the church on Tuesdays, is Annalee's younger sister. She must feel me looking at her, because her eyes scan the room until they land on me sitting on my stool. It takes her no time to recognize me. She has the same tiny, heart-shaped face as her sister. So much the same as Susannah Bauer too. So much the same. It's something they have, all of them. The sweetness and kindness. It's a freshness too that they all share. Straightaway, the young girl smiles and raises a hand to say hello. Now I know how to find her and where to find her and that means I can find Annalee too.

8

LANE

AS MARK AND Lane drive from her house to the sheriff's office, she makes several phone calls. Already she regrets her feelings of relief when she thought Mark had come about Susannah Bauer. Just like her customers who said to keep an eye on the blond ones, she was tempting fate.

With each phone call, Lane has to tell people twice who she is. Lane Wallace, Fielding, I mean. I used to know your mother, or I grew up with your father. Yes, I'm Annalee's mother. Annalee who works with you. Annalee who graduated with you. Yes, Annalee who lives at the Fielding Mansion. Lane has worked hard to keep her past from Annalee and Talley. She's avoided old friends who might say something about what a shame it was, the thing that happened to Lane all those years ago, or you're doing so well now, or so glad you were able to have children despite what happened. But now, when Lane needs her old ties so their children will help her find Annalee, they're not there.

By the third call, Lane snaps at the girl on the other end. Annalee mentioned her over breakfast just the other morning. Nancy Perry. They had three classes with each other during Annalee's one semester at the high school, and just two nights ago, they met to see a movie. At least that's what Annalee told Lane. You have to remember her, Lane said. But Nancy doesn't really know Annalee. I'm sorry, she says. I think Annalee sat behind me in Calculus. She was new this year, right? Only came for second semester?

Every call is the same. Even the girl who works with Annalee doesn't really know her. She keeps to herself, the girl says. No, I don't know anyone who might have heard from her. Yes, I'll call if I see her.

As Lane continues to search for more numbers to call, Mark drives fast through town and Lane must cling to the handle in the car's door panel every time he takes a turn. She's read about it, written about it, listened to police officers talk about it. Just the thought makes her lungs stiff and her throat swell. Mark is driving fast because time is a thing that can't be squandered in the case of a missing person.

At the entrance to the sheriff's office, a redbrick building Lane remembers only from the Easter egg hunts hosted there every spring of her childhood, Mark reaches across her and pulls open the glass door. He cups her elbow and guides her so she won't bump against a wall or trip over the threshold as she continues to page through the contacts on her phone, looking for someone, anyone else she can call.

She doesn't have enough numbers. Annalee must have more friends, and probably she does, but Lane doesn't know their names and certainly doesn't have phone numbers for them. Annalee's eighteen now. She needs her space and for Lane to show trust in her. It's something Lane never had growing up because she was, from the time she was thirteen, *that* girl, and when everyone thinks they know your worst secret, you become something less than everyone else. Nothing about your life is private or even decent. No one trusts you either, because when tragic things happen to a person, the tragedy sticks.

As Lane and Mark walk into the building, a rush of cold air sweeps past them. It ruffles Lane's hair and stirs up the smell of smoke, a leftover from last night. She tries to draw in the dry, icy air so it will snap her to attention. She's been like this, not quite at attention, since leaving her home and husband of twenty years. It's why she never noticed that all those stories Annalee told about school and work and the people she was spending time with were just that—stories.

Lane has been absent somehow, has missed what should have been apparent. She wasn't letting Annalee grow up or giving her space. That's not why she doesn't know Annalee's friends or their phone numbers or that Annalee isn't well liked at work. That's what Lane was telling herself to make it all easier, so she could stay out late at the bar, drink too much whiskey, and sleep with a married man. Annalee must have been lonely to make up friends, but Lane hadn't noticed.

With a sweeping gesture, Mark guides Lane through the first door on the right. It leads to a conference room of sorts. A dark laminate table with metal legs fills the long, narrow room and a half-dozen chairs surround it. Someone has placed two plastic bags in the center of the table. Both have been left open to allow what is inside to dry, and the yellow evidence tags have been turned upside down, likely so Lane won't see what is written there. She pushes aside a chair, leans forward, and reaches for the closest bag, but Mark's hand on her shoulder stops her.

"I need you not to touch anything," he says.

Like the blood and the door left open on Annalee's truck, this is another sign of trouble. They'll have gathered the same types of evidence in their search for Susannah Bauer. Lane wonders now, as she stares down on the two bags, if they've found anything of Susannah's and what did they find and where. Those are among the first questions she would have asked if she were covering this story. Might the two cases be related? she'd have been thinking. As much as she didn't like her customers talking about it at the bar, they'd been right. Two girls, similar ages, similar in looks and hair color, missing from the same area. But she doesn't ask Mark any of these questions because she's too afraid of the answers.

"They're wet from the river?" Lane asks. The desire to grab hold of those bags and the things inside is strong, as if grabbing them would be the same as grabbing hold of Annalee. She folds her arms to stop herself from reaching out again.

Mark nods. "You recognize them? Either one?"

A brown clutch, not much bigger than an envelope, is inside the closest plastic bag. It's a darker brown than Lane remembers, but that's because it's wet. It has a faux gold buckle and closes with a magnetic snap. She wonders for a moment if the magnet still works.

"Can I sit?" Lane asks.

Mark nods and pulls out a chair. Bracing her hands against the laminate tabletop, Lane lowers herself slowly. The ground is uneven underfoot, except that it isn't.

"Why is there just one sandal?" she asks, looking over her shoulder at Mark.

"Is it Annalee's?"

The single brown leather sandal is harder to look at than the purse. It sits flat on the table as if ready for Annalee to slip her foot into it. A single green leaf, maybe from an azalea bush, is stuck to the sole where her heel would rest.

"They could have fallen out of her car, right?" Lane says, clinging to the table's edge. "Since she left the door open."

"So they belong to Annalee?"

Lane nods.

"You're certain? Good many shoes look alike."

"She poked an extra hole in the strap," Lane says. She knows she's the one talking, but her voice comes to her as if from across the room. "I told her they were too big when she bought them." She points without standing because the ground is still tilted. "Look there near the buckle. You'll see she nearly ruined the strap. Did the same to both."

"The purse too?"

"Yes," she says, though she doesn't want to. She doesn't want to be here in this room or looking at the purse and sandal because all of these things might mean Annalee really is gone. "They both belong to Annalee."

MARK ELLENTON WAS the first boy Lane ever had sex with. They had lain together in the back of his El Camino, huddled under a blanket because it was February. His hands shook when he fumbled with the white buttons on her blouse and then when he touched her. She had hoped it was the cold or maybe the thrill, as if she were somehow that thrilling, but mostly she'd worried his hands shook because he was afraid. Afraid he would hurt her. Afraid he would shake loose painful memories. Afraid she was still broken even four years after she was abducted and suffered God knows what. They'd stayed until nearly sunrise, the air turning heavy and damp. It had happened down at the river, the spot where the tracks cross over. The same spot where Annalee's truck is now parked.

"Well," Mark says, drawing one hand over his mouth and sitting on the table's edge. "You'll keep calling her friends, because that's how we'll likely find her."

Lane nods though she's already made six calls. Not one of those people knew Annalee as a friend, and Mark knows this. He's being optimistic, trying to keep Lane calm by giving her a task, something to make her feel useful so she'll hold on. That's what she's doing now—barely holding on.

"Neil having any more trouble of late?" Mark asks. "Any more calls in recent weeks, letters? People showing up at the house?"

"You mean besides reporters?"

"Yes, besides reporters."

"Bonnie Wiley," Lane says, forcing herself to exhale so she'll begin to breathe normally again.

"Doing anyone harm? Causing any trouble?"

"Tortures Erma to have her hollering up at the house all the time," Lane says. "But she's never hurt anyone."

"Anything else?"

"We get a picketer or two occasionally, down at the bar. You've seen it. People get wind I'm his daughter. Mostly out-of-towners. I've offered to quit, even."

The night Lane offered to quit was also the one night she slept with Rowland, and Mark will know this. Though maybe he thinks it's happened many nights. Maybe he thinks it's still happening.

The police had to be called the night the picketers targeted Lane and the bar, and Mark came too. When it was over and everyone had gone, Lane sprayed down the bar mats, draped them over the stools to dry, and accepted the shot Rowland offered.

She'd been in town only a couple of months at that time and hadn't shaken off the shock of Kyle letting her go. She'd told no one that she'd offered to stay with him despite all the women he'd admitted to and that he said no thank you. She'd grown accustomed to life without Kyle quickly enough, even slipped easily back into the patterns of childhood in this town though it pained her to feel it happen so quickly, but the humiliation was harder to shake off. It trailed her for months, constantly reminding her that those twenty years of marriage had been a lie and she'd been the fool.

By the third shot, she couldn't stop herself from crying. She covered her face over with both hands and turned her back on Rowland. He surely thought her family name was the cause of her tears and wrapped one arm around her shoulders. That's the moment she should have stepped away from him, but instead she leaned in.

"I won't never let anything else bad happen to you," he said, pressing his mouth to her ear. His breath was warm on her neck. He was familiar, like they could have been kids again, their entire lives ahead of them. She had yet to waste twenty years of her life. She had yet to be made a fool.

"You have a home here," Rowland said. He paused, waiting for her to pull back or lower her eyes, but she didn't, so he held her face with both hands and kissed her.

"Take me home," Lane said, and when she invited him into her bedroom, it was because she needed to show him, if only him, she wasn't damaged.

But it happened only once. Even as Rowland lay next to her in her bed, she knew it was wrong, that it would hurt Rowland's wife and Mark too and that she'd feel shame in the morning. But mostly she knew sleeping with Rowland would prove nothing, solve nothing. It would definitely change nothing.

"Annalee seeing anyone?" Mark asks. "Someone who might be keeping her out all night?"

Lane shakes her head.

"But she was?"

"Yes," Lane says. "She was."

The night she handed Rowland her keys and invited him into her bedroom, she never considered what it might mean for Annalee. She'd been dating Rowland's son up until that night. By the next day, Rowland's wife had moved out of their home, and Annalee and Jimmy were forbidden—that was the word Hettie used when she called Lane—from seeing each other ever again.

Within hours, it seemed, everyone in town, including Mark, knew what had happened, though Lane never knew how the news spread so quickly. She offered to quit, but Rowland said no and cupped her chin with one hand. That was her first hint he wanted more. You're going nowhere, Rowland said. He decided who worked in his bar, no one else, not even Hettie. In truth, everything Rowland owned, including the bar, was because of his wife's family money. She'd been Hettie Martin before marrying Rowland, and Martin meant sugarcane money in Waddell, Florida, where Martin Avenue cut through the center of town. "Leave her to me," Rowland said, like a man who had been through this before, a fact Lane clung to in the months that followed. There was comfort, no matter how misguided, in being one of many.

"So Annalee's not dating Rowland and Hettie's boy anymore?" Mark says, pushing off the table and reaching to pull open the door leading to the hallway. "You sure about that?"

Lane swivels around in her chair, looks up at him, but doesn't stand. "You think Jimmy has something to do with this?"

"I just need to know who she might have been seeing."

Lane shakes her head. "Ended at least three months ago."

"She end it?"

Again, Lane shakes her head. An overhead vent blows icy air down on her. The tips of her fingers have grown cold, numb. She presses them to her forehead and cheeks.

"He did," Lane says. "Well, really, Hettie did. And I told Annalee."

She won't have to say any more. Mark already knows the answer to every one of his questions, but he must ask because he's investigating and not gossiping.

"Annalee take it hard? Being told she couldn't see Jimmy anymore?"

"At first," Lane says. "Mostly mad at me. She'd heard, maybe from Jimmy, about Rowland and me and must have figured that's what set Hettie off. But she didn't stay mad for long. It seemed to pass." She stands but makes no move to walk out the door Mark still holds open. "I'm right, aren't I? You think Jimmy has something to do with this."

"We're rounding him up," Mark says, gesturing for her to walk out ahead of him. "We'll see to where he was last night. Let's just get you home for now."

Lane shakes her head, not moving from her seat. It's settling in now, the gravity of what she did by sleeping with Rowland. She had wanted to forget it ever happened, to shower it away. People would forget. Hettie would forgive because apparently she had forgiven others. But Lane had been wrong, and maybe this is what she gets.

"I want you to take me to the river," she says.

On the drive over to Mark's office, Lane had remembered rapids rushing over the limestone riverbed and the slippery clay banks there under the tracks. She had imagined the swim lessons the girls would have had if they grew up in Florida but didn't because they grew up in a Brooklyn apartment. She had thought about two girls with the same silky blond hair. Now she's thinking of

Jimmy Jansen, big enough to play basketball but choosing baseball like his father. Jimmy, who Lane thought was a good influence on Annalee. He had plans for college and held down a part-time job. She had missed so much about her own daughter. What might she have missed about Jimmy Jansen?

ERMA

INSTEAD OF USING the side door off the kitchen, Erma follows Neil and Talley toward the proper back entrance. Before Mark and Lane left, Erma overheard them talking about Annalee's whereabouts and Susannah Bauer's too. Hearing the two girls' names together was like hearing Neil's tires grind too quickly to a stop back in the days when he was still driving. Not altogether unusual, but frightening just the same and enough to make Erma brace herself.

It used to mean something to Erma, using the front and back entrances instead of the side. It was a responsibility of sorts, thrust upon her when she married into the Fielding family, a union Erma's mother had insisted upon. Erma had tried to be happy about it. Grateful, at least. Erma's family had a lineage worthy of the Fieldings, and once married to Neil, Erma would be charged with maintaining something, history perhaps, some finer part of life. Only a woman of a certain pedigree could do that. But Neil didn't choose Erma for her pedigree, not like her mother said. He chose her because of the beauty she had in those early years. He liked her thick blond hair and the way her tiny waist made the other parts of her seem rounder and all the more pleasing. He would draw his fingers through her hair, trail his hands over her curves, and say he didn't even care that she came from nowhere.

When Lane was a teenager, she stopped wanting any part of the history Erma tried to preserve. Beginning with that April when Lane was only thirteen, Erma worked every day to make things just so for Neil to ward off his outbursts. When she failed and he and Lane argued, Neil would finish the argument, no matter what it was about, by screaming at Lane. Everything I had to do was to stop shame being brought on this family, Neil would say. This was when Lane began refusing to walk through the front doors or back. She'd use only the side door off the kitchen, just as the people who once worked here had to do. Slaves, Lane would say, correcting Erma. They were slaves. And when she grew older still, she would say, don't try to sugarcoat it, Erma, and when did she begin to call her own mother Erma?

Before passing between the fluted columns that stretch two stories high, Erma pauses. Leaning against one of the columns, she tries to grab hold of the thoughts swirling around her head because when one drifts off, the others tend to follow. The perfect symmetry of the house—four columns, six windows to the left, six to the right, the bold and simple moldings—usually gives her comfort. She likes to imagine the goings-on inside her head are the same as the house—orderly and solidly built.

Susannah, before she disappeared, loved the Fielding house

and its thick moldings and precise symmetry, and she made Erma love it again too. Susannah would fret about what grade of sandpaper to use and how best to repair the chipped enamel sink when others simply wanted to replace it. On one of her first visits, she used the Internet to track down the heart yellow pine that was the only good choice for repairing the floors in the foyer. We can't get it new, Susannah had told Erma. First-generation pines, once gone, they're gone for good.

Susannah was a girl who knew about all kinds of things, but she was also a girl who talked to Erma and listened to her, and those two simple things made Erma whole again. Susannah's friendship made Erma eager to rise in the morning and to brew fresh coffee and to even put a brush and some hairspray to her hair. Every day since Susannah disappeared, Erma's read the newspaper and watched the news and prayed for her safe return. Before Lane and the girls moved home, Susannah was Erma's only reminder that she could still find joy in her life. And six months ago, because Erma asked and because Susannah was a girl who knew about things, Susannah taught Erma how to fire a gun.

ONCE INSIDE THE doors, Erma frowns to see someone has tracked mud into her house. Before she can holler out for someone to come help with this mess, Talley walks from the kitchen with a spray bottle and a roll of paper towels in hand.

"You're a dear," Erma says, glancing down to see she's tracked in her own set of prints.

Talley stares at Erma as if wanting to say something.

"You worried about Annalee, child?" Erma says. "I'm sure she'll be home before you know it."

"Is Annalee gone like Susannah?" Talley asks.

65

"Oh, heavens no," Erma says, wrapping her arms around Talley and pulling her close. "Neither of them is gone."

Erma takes a quick look at all four corners of the foyer. Just by cracking the silence with that question, the child may have conjured who knows what. Erma's overheard folks in the grocery saying one missing girl might mean another is close behind. Just like what happened back in the seventies, they worry aloud to one another.

"Don't you concern yourself about Annalee or Susannah. Mind, Annalee'll be in a good bit of trouble when she brings herself home, but it won't be your hide suffering it."

Annalee hasn't taken to Erma in nearly the same way as Talley. Annalee is frightened of Erma's old age, is the best Erma can figure. It scares some people to see up close what will eventually become of them.

"She'll be home before dinner is ready." Erma kisses the top of Talley's head one, two, three times. A lucky three times. "And Susannah will be back just any day now too," she says, hoping that by saying these things, she'll make them so.

"Yes, ma'am," Talley says, giving the floors a squirt of the cleaner. "Grandpa's got the news on. There's pictures of our house on the television, and I just saw Miss Bonnie."

"You seen Bonnie Wiley on the television?"

"No, ma'am. Just now," Talley says, wiping big circles on the pine floors. "Outside the kitchen."

"She's right outside?" Erma says, and quick as Talley says Bonnie Wiley is here, the air turns sweet and spicy. It's the smell that follows Bonnie Wiley everywhere she goes. Some witchy concoction she burns all day, every day. "She's here at the house?"

Bonnie's probably setting more of those black candles on Erma's porch. The last time Bonnie did that, the deputies had to come, and when they blew out the candles, they sprayed black wax across Erma's porch that she's still, to this day, scraping clean.

"You get on upstairs, won't you?" Erma says to Talley, giving the girl another three kisses on her warm head. Sweet Talley, who's so easy to love and is so like Lane at this same age. So like Lane before that April when she was thirteen. "And don't come down until I've called you to."

It started just over five years ago. After the school had been locking up boys for better than a century, a group of grown men found one another on the Internet. They planted a tree on the school grounds and said they had been beaten there, most of them during the 1950s and '60s. Pointing to a small white building, they said they were beaten right there when they were boys as young as eight years old, some claiming until nearly dead. Bonnie Wiley, who lives right across the road, says her brother was one of those boys, and he never came home.

The men, who had each lived most of his life thinking he was alone, found a voice in their numbers, and the state could no longer ignore them. The governor said, "Justice cries out for a conclusion," and so folks started to investigate. There were accusations of boys being beaten, of boys being killed, and of boys disappearing and never being found. After a hundred years, the citizens of Florida were due answers, and someone needed to be held accountable.

Even as the school was still in operation, folks began to dig through boxes of paperwork and death certificates. Researchers found handwritten notes in tattered record books and letters sent to mothers. We're sorry we can't find your boy. We're sorry your boy took ill. We're sorry your boy is gone. They searched for evidence of beatings, and they tried to—but couldn't—match that paperwork to the thirty-one white crosses that stood in the school's overgrown cemetery not so far from that small white building and the tree those old men planted. Folks began to wonder who was buried there on the school grounds and how had they died.

Neil worked at the school during the years when most of the old men were sent there, and most every man who said he was beaten remembered Neil's name. Not long after the men planted their tree, Neil had to go to a room at the county courthouse and answer questions in front of men in suits. He wore his favorite sweater despite it being summer because rooms like the one where they took him are kept bitter cold by the air-conditioning.

They asked Neil did he ever beat those boys, any of those boys, during the 1950s and '60s? What about the years after? What about a boy in 1990? What about the boy folks say took your daughter? Did Neil swing a leather strap through the air and whip those boys, any of those boys, a dozen times, two dozen, three or four dozen times? Did he lift his hand so high in the air as to brush his knuckles against the low-hanging ceiling, doing it so many times he drew blood, not only from those boys but from the back of the hand he brushed across the rough ceiling over and over again? Did he chain them, hog-tie them, throw them in a cell? No, he told them. Two straight days, he told them no. And Erma believed him. She had no other choice.

BACK IN THE kitchen, Erma leans over the sink to get a look out the window. She hasn't thought much about curses and things that loom and crack the silence since she was a little girl living in south Florida, but then, a few years ago, Bonnie Wiley moved in across the road, and now Erma's thinking about hanging a mirror outside the front door to trap Bonnie Wiley's witchy ways before they seep inside.

Maybe that was the hem of a housedress disappearing around

the corner of the house or maybe not. Listening and hearing nothing, she kneads at that sore hip with the heel of one hand, turns, and in the foyer, she takes her address book from the credenza's top drawer.

She can't help that her hands are shaking. They do that sometimes for no reason whatsoever, but now they're doing it because Bonnie Wiley is near. She'll call Mark and tell him Bonnie Wiley is here snooping around, and if some terrible luck has befallen poor Annalee, Bonnie Wiley might be the cause of it. They also ought to consider that Bonnie Wiley might have had cause to bring harm to Susannah Bauer too. She was like family to Erma, and a woman like Bonnie would know that.

When Erma lands on the page that lists Mark's cell number, she reaches for the phone just as it starts to ring. Reporters. First they come in vans, and then they begin to call. They'll call all day and as late as nine at night. Staring at the ringing phone, Erma backs away and crosses into Neil's room.

Long before it became known as Neil's room, it was called the drawing room, where ladies would retire after a lovely supper. In its grand days, the room was filled with fine furniture, delicate fabrics, and a crystal chandelier hung in its center. But then Neil's troubles began, his health turned, and he was no longer able to climb the stairs to their bedroom. He took to sleeping, eating, and spending every other waking moment here in this room. It smells of him now, and all the fine furnishings and fabrics have been boxed up and stored in the attic or crowded into other rooms.

"Turn off that contraption," Erma says of Neil's television. There was a time, though her better judgment knows that time has passed, when Erma would have suffered for a comment like that.

At the closest of the two windows, she pinches the seam where the drapes meet, gingerly so as not to damage the deep-red damask, squeezes the clothespin, and pulls it off. The television goes quiet, but when she turns, she sees Neil has only muted it. Pulling the drapes apart just enough, she peeks outside.

On the porch, a shadow passes by. Maybe a shadow. The ceiling out there is painted blue because evil won't pass beneath a blue ceiling. That's what Erma's mother always said, and her mother before her. But Bonnie has walked this porch a dozen times, maybe more. The blue ceiling did nothing to keep her away then, and it will do nothing now. Erma steps up to the window, and through the sheers that still hang closed, she sees her.

That's Bonnie Wiley all right, walking along the porch. She has neared the front of the house and is stopping to press her face to each window she passes. She shuffles like an old woman might shuffle, or rather she shuffles like an old woman because she is an old woman. Bonnie Wiley might be twenty years Erma's junior, but she has the most atrocious posture and looks to have not eaten a decent meal her entire life.

"You go on home, Bonnie Wiley," Erma hollers at the closed window. Behind her, the phone starts ringing again. On and on, it rings. "We got trouble here today and I'm wondering if it's your doing."

THE SCHOOL, THAT'S what they called it, the school, closed three years ago. The state blamed budget cuts, but Erma never believed that was the real reason. By the time the school closed, the entire country was coming to know about the town of Waddell and the school's shameful past. Closing the school had been an escape attempt. If there was no more target, the state must have strategized, people would stop taking aim and forget. But the three years since have proven the state wrong.

By the time the school shuttered its doors, Neil had stopped going to potluck Wednesday or playing poker with the other old men, and he and Erma had stopped attending services. It was odd to think the school had still been open when they were digging through records and trying to match death certificates to the white crosses someone had pounded into the ground. That'll be the end of it, the whole town thought when the school closed.

And then the state tried to sell the school and the property it stood on, including the little building where the boys were whipped and the unmarked graves of the ones who died. The state, after concluding its investigation, said there were thirty-one crosses in the cemetery, and they had found thirty-one names in the school's record books to go with them. They said the boys who were buried in those unmarked graves had died of things such as fire or influenza. They didn't know which body went with which name, but they were satisfied they knew enough.

Then folks from a university down in Tampa came. They ran radar machines over the ground and said those thirty-one white crosses weren't marking nearly enough graves. At least another twenty people, most likely boys, were buried there, maybe some who died when Neil was working at the school, maybe some who died long before. No matter, a judge said. The state couldn't sell the land until someone accounted for those twenty unnamed dead boys.

The ringing phone has stopped, and not hearing anything more of Bonnie Wiley, Erma takes another peek outside. Bonnie is still out there. At the window nearest the front of the house, she stops and turns. She wears a floor-length white quilted housedress and black sneakers that poke out from under the hemline with each step she takes.

"I know you got troubles," Bonnie hollers. "But it ain't because of me. I know why them reporters was here at your house. All your money can't protect you now, Erma Fielding." Even though Bonnie hollers, her voice barely carries through the closed windows. "I'll tell you why they come and you won't think you're so high-and-mighty then."

"It's mighty strange, Bonnie Wiley, you being here just now," Erma hollers back. "Maybe you know where my granddaughter is."

Bonnie looks from window to window, not seeing Erma. It'll be the glare of the sun bouncing off the glass that keeps Bonnie from seeing inside.

"Don't know nothing about your granddaughter," Bonnie shouts. "Ain't here about her. They have a picture now. A rendering, they're calling it. Dug up the head of one of those boys over there at the school and sketched what he'd have looked like."

"You get on," Erma says. That phone starts ringing again. "Get on before I call the sheriff and tell him you're up to no good."

"Go have a look at that television of yours," Bonnie calls, and this time her eyes settle on Erma. She shuffles straight to the window where Erma stands. "They're going to show us his picture just anytime now. Going to be my own brother they find there one day. None of your money will help you then."

"You get on, Bonnie Wiley," Erma hollers one last time. "And heaven help you if you've tangled with my family."

Mark and Lane will be back soon and if, God forbid, they haven't found Annalee yet, Erma will tell Mark that Bonnie Wiley is up to no good. Mark isn't afraid of Bonnie because he doesn't believe in her conjuring. More than once, he's been here to gather up bundles of smoldering sage Bonnie placed at each corner of the house or dozens of slender sticks sharpened at both ends that she scattered at the foot of every door leading inside.

Mark is like Annalee in this way, neither one of them fearing Bonnie or her witchy ways, but Mark has never taunted Bonnie or made fun of her like Annalee does. Erma has heard Annalee laugh at Bonnie, something that makes Erma fear for Annalee now all the more. Don't go poking the bear, Erma's own mother used to say. You'll be sorry when the bear pokes you back.

There's that phone again. It'll keep on ringing the whole day long, all those reporters thinking like Bonnie Wiley. They don't realize there's no great money to go along with this house or the name that's one of the oldest in the state. Erma can't hardly buy herself a new housedress. A person surely can't think she's high-and-mighty when she can't buy a single dress. Stepping away from the window, she walks into the foyer, grabs the phone by its base, and yanks it from the wall. The ringing stops.

The worst day, the day Erma knew Neil would never leave this house again, came a year ago when that group of folks from the university in Tampa got the right to dig up the bones in the school's cemetery. They hoped to test those bones and give them names and return them to their families. No matter the cries from so many who couldn't bear the thought of strangers disturbing graves, digging them up with machines and shovels, the state of Florida said they could go ahead. Folks have a right to know how many people died here and who's buried here. They have a right to bring their little boys home.

The people from the university waited until this past winter to do their digging on those graves. They were waiting for lower water levels, they said into the news cameras, and weather that was a bit more forgiving. They dug up coffin nails, zippers, buttons, and buckles. They even dug up a marble. And they found bones they shipped off to a laboratory in Texas that will one day say who the remains belong to.

Soon enough, they'll have a name for one of the boys they're digging up, and maybe they'll know when he died and how he died or maybe they won't. Any day, those reporters will come and say they've identified some of those old remains. Dozens of boys will be dug up, and each time they match one to his family, they'll take a look to see what year the boy died and then they'll question Neil. Did you have a beef with this boy? What about that one? Did you beat him? Did you kill him? And if the bones happen to date back to April 1990, they'll ask . . . Is this the boy who took your little girl?

10

TALLEY

GRANDMA TOLD TALLEY to march herself upstairs, but Miss Bonnie is still outside shouting about the boys from the school, so Talley tiptoes instead. Mama is always telling Talley there's no reason to fear Miss Bonnie, but Grandma makes Talley promise to keep her distance. Miss Bonnie's brother is buried in a cemetery over at the school for boys with lots of other boys. Grandpa says it's a wonder Miss Bonnie doesn't fuss about her brother being buried with the colored boys, being as where she's from.

Twice Miss Bonnie has scattered dirt from the school's cemetery outside Grandma and Grandpa's front door. She says the dirt is cursed and it'll make Grandpa sorry for what he's done. But in all her shouting, Miss Bonnie never said anything about her brother being buried with black boys. Bones are bones, is what Talley thinks.

Once upstairs, Talley stops outside Annalee's room, presses her ear to the door, rests a hand on the glass knob, and listens. Talley's never seen one of those dug-up graves at the school, but if she ever does, it will surely remind her of Annalee's room—a place where she doesn't want to step too close to the edge. Turning the knob, Talley slips inside the room and pulls the door closed.

A few days ago, maybe it was a week ago, from the window in the attic where she goes to watch for the boys who run, Talley saw Annalee sneak out of the house. Just like every other time Annalee snuck out, she was back the next morning. But one thing was different. Annalee was happy that morning, smiling, even, and she told Talley she was going to run away one day soon and get married and never come back to Waddell. She loved Jimmy Jansen, and he loved her too. But you can't tell a soul, Annalee said. Not even Mama. Before they left Brooklyn, Talley would have been happy to share a secret with Annalee. That would have put them on the same side, and being on the same side as Annalee was a safer place to be. But Susannah had been missing for a few days by then, and not even sharing a secret with Annalee made Talley feel better.

Talley thought to tell Mama about Annalee's secret, but just to hear Annalee wanted to run away from home would have hurt Mama just like it hurt her when Daddy left. After all these months of living in Florida, Mama was finally getting out of bed in the mornings and looking as if she'd slept. It would all go away if Mama knew Annalee wanted to leave.

So Talley kept Annalee's secret, and every time she saw Annalee sneak out, last night included, she worried she would never come back. Talley was afraid to tell Mama and afraid not to. When she couldn't keep the secret inside any longer, she told Daryl. He always talked to Talley like she was a grown person, but instead of helping, he slapped his forehead and said over and over that it wouldn't be fair if Annalee got to run away forever. He frightened Talley. She backed away from him and crossed her arms over her chest. That was the first day Talley thought about never going back to see Daryl or her garden ever again.

And then came yesterday, when Talley went to the church to water her plants. Daryl told her that Jimmy didn't truly love Annalee. It was all a lie, a trick to hurt Annalee. Jimmy was never going to marry her or run away with her. He was going away to college without Annalee. Daryl made Talley promise to tell Annalee everything he said. Little Sisters always keep their promises, he said, so last night, Talley kept her promise, told Annalee everything, and now she's gone.

Once inside Annalee's room, Talley quickly looks around. As usual, Annalee's bed is unmade, and dirty clothes are scattered around the floor. Talley walks slowly through the room, and at the closet, she pushes aside Annalee's clothes, uncertain what she's looking for. From there, she crawls a few feet to the bed, lifts the bedspread, and looks underneath.

When they were preparing to leave Brooklyn six months ago, Mama bought all three of them a blue bag and told Talley and Annalee to pack everything they'd want when they stayed overnight in a hotel. Annalee was angry about the move and yelled at Mama. She said if Mama were a better wife, Daddy wouldn't be leaving her. Annalee didn't care what she took to Florida because it was a horrid, hot place filled with hicks, so she grabbed handfuls of clothes from her drawers and stuffed her bag full.

Talley did the opposite. She counted out underwear and socks and planned for warm weather and cold. Maybe this bag was all she'd have for now and forever. Finally, Mama started shoving things in Talley's bag like Annalee had shoved things in hers. Talley stood in the corner and cried. She didn't care if Florida was horrid and hot. She cared only about Daddy not going with them and that they wouldn't be a family anymore. Seeing Talley cry that day made Mama cry too. She stepped aside and told Talley to take all the time she needed.

Downstairs, the phone has stopped ringing, which probably means Grandma unplugged it. Reaching under the bed, Talley grabs hold of a thick strap and hauls out one of those blue bags Mama bought for her and Annalee. She yanks on the zipper, and once it's open, she jerks her hands away.

Neatly folded clothes fill the bag. Only Grandma can fold clothes so every shirt is the exact same size as the next. Grandma washes clothes on Mondays and linens on Tuesdays. She scrubs floors on Wednesdays and washes windows on Thursdays. These clothes went from Annalee's hamper, because Grandma will wash only what's in the hamper, to the pile of folded laundry Grandma always leaves outside Annalee's door on Monday afternoons, and lastly into this bag.

Annalee had to have packed this bag yesterday because yesterday was Monday and Monday was laundry day for clothes. Probably she was planning to run away last night with this bag of neatly folded shirts and shorts, but something changed, and maybe Talley is the reason. At first, Annalee laughed when Talley told her Jimmy didn't really love her and wasn't going to run away with her. She stopped laughing when Talley said Daryl was the one who told her everything.

Hearing Daryl's name surprised Annalee. Her eyes, already too big for her face, stretched even wider, and her chest started pumping harder and faster. Something about Daryl's name frightened Annalee or made her angry or both. She grabbed Talley by the arm, told her to say it exactly as Daryl had said it. Talley told Annalee that Jimmy's mother, Miss Hettie, would never let them get married and that Jimmy didn't love her. It was all a trick and Jimmy was going to sneak off without even telling Annalee good-bye. Annalee called Talley a liar, stomped out of the kitchen and up to her room, and that was the last time Talley talked to her.

Talley should be relieved to think, hope, Annalee didn't run away since her bag is still here, relieved like she was this morning when she first thought the boys had taken her food. That good feeling is the reason she leaves the food. Thinking she is helping those boys and that maybe they need her, even if deep down inside she knows they aren't real, makes Talley happy. And every time she finds the food on the ground, she feels certain something bad has happened to one of those boys. Finding this packed bag under Annalee's bed is making her feel the same way. She's feeling certain something bad has happened to Annalee. She's feeling certain Annalee is gone and that she isn't coming back.

PUSHING THE BLUE bag under Annalee's bed, Talley grabs her sneakers and walks down the back staircase into the kitchen. The house is quiet, which means Grandma Erma is sleeping as usual in the parlor. But Grandpa is awake. He won't have heard Talley, because his hearing isn't so good, but something makes him holler out to her.

"Come here to me, girl," he says. "Come and see what's on the television."

Every day, Grandpa Neil wears the same thing—brown socks that hang too long off the ends of his toes, tan pants, a brown belt split from too much wear, and a white undershirt. Sometimes, he doesn't change his shirt for days. He'll get a stain on a Monday, pickle juice or tomato soup, and it'll still be there come Thursday. Grandma will get after him to take the wretched thing off, and sometimes Mama will have to join in, it taking the both of them to yank it over his head.

Talley has watched Mama and Grandma do this before, and she tried not to stare at Grandpa as he sat bare-chested. His chest had drooped and was covered by wiry gray hair, and his arms and belly sagged. Grandpa stood tall when he was a younger man. Talley's seen the pictures to prove it. He wore a brown cowboy hat and boots back then, and he smoked a pipe. Every so often, he still smokes one. Sometimes Talley will wake during the night and smell the sweet, spicy pipe and wonder if Grandpa is awake and smoking, or if the smell is left over from days gone by.

"Come and see," Grandpa says again as Talley walks into his room. "Look at what they drew up."

When Talley is within arm's reach, Grandpa grabs her by the wrist and points at the television. A picture, a drawing of a young boy, fills the screen. If Talley were to see him at school, she'd think he was probably a new kid who would be in her class. Looking at his face—the rounded cheeks, the soft lips, eyes almost too large for his head—makes Talley feel bad for the boy.

"I told them there was only one place we buried them boys," Grandpa says. "Black or white. Didn't matter one bit to us. Damn well told them. One cemetery for all them boys."

"They made a drawing of a boy they dug up from the ground?" Talley says, staring at the television.

"You bet." Grandpa drops Talley's wrist and picks up the remote control with the hand that doesn't work so good. "Buried them all together. Thought they'd only find white boys. But Garrett was a black boy. Garrett Wilson. That's him all right."

Grandpa pokes at his remote, and when his talking turns to mumbling, Talley begins to back away, the face of Garrett Wilson watching her from the TV as she goes. The sun will be getting higher, and if she's late to the church, Daryl might not let her show the Little Sisters her garden. Where the drawing room turns into the foyer, she swings around, hurries through the kitchen, grabs her shoes, and runs out the side door.

Across the street, Miss Bonnie has probably seen the same thing Talley and Grandpa saw. Miss Bonnie is white, plain old white, so the boy they dug up and drew is not her brother. She thinks Grandpa beat her brother with a leather strap until he was dead. Talley wants to ask Grandpa if he remembers all the boys who went to his school, or does he only remember Garrett Wilson? But she won't because she's afraid of what he might say.

DARYL

11 days before Susannah disappeared

SUSANNAH BAUER COMES to town only on the first and third Saturdays of the month. Because I can't catch sight of her on the days she is away, or even the scent of her, I study my maps and trace the way from me to her. I imagine where she is so I can imagine myself with her, and if I'm with her, I'm not alone and a stillness will settle in. But now I have Annalee. She lives here in this town every day, and I know how to find her because I know her younger sister.

Every Tuesday morning, the younger sister comes to the church, and today is Tuesday, so I wait, reminding myself again and again that the younger sister isn't Annalee, only looks like Annalee. I pull dollar weeds under the oaks where the ground is shaded and damp.

The long white roots, like slippery strands of twine, easily give way in the softer dirt. I toss them to the left and right until I have a good mess in need of a good raking.

The girl comes every Tuesday because the Little Sisters meet in the church on Tuesdays and she hopes they'll be her friends. The Little Sisters come here to learn what it means to be a young lady, that's what Reverend says. Every good woman in town who's a proper lady was once a Little Sister. When I first started here, Reverend said I should keep to the back of the church until the parents became accustomed to me, but I think they know me now, at least well enough that I can kneel here in the cool shade and pull weeds. As cars begin to roll up to the curb, I count the footsteps going into the church. When I have counted twelve, I sit back on my heels and brush my hands together. The girl sits on the curb across the street, exactly where I knew I would see her.

"Do you mind?" I call out loud enough that the girl will hear.

At the sound of my voice, she lifts her head, unwraps her arms from around her legs, and sits tall. Her loose hair hangs well past her shoulders. It shimmers, almost glows, where the sun hits it.

"The rake," I call out, louder still. "There, behind you. Do you mind?"

The girl turns to look where I've pointed. Right behind her, my rake leans against a tree where a person would think I left it, accidentally, mistakenly. I mowed the grass yesterday and gathered up all the stray leaves and clippings. And then I left the rake.

Rocking forward, the girl stands. She wears a tan skirt much like the tan skirts the Little Sisters of the South wear. Her hair hangs to the middle of her back, and while I can't see from this distance, it is likely cut in the same fashion as Annalee's. I turn away, close my eyes, and remind myself this girl is only the sister.

My breath is coming too fast. I try to slow it by blowing out through my mouth. Seeing one is not the same as seeing the other.

I've never had to think this before, but she is too young to be what I need. Still, she'll be kind like Annalee and like all the other girls, caring and considerate. This younger sister will help me, and just as I think it, she grabs the rake, checks both ways before crossing the street, and then jogs toward me. That's the thing about girls like Annalee and her sister. And Susannah Bauer too. They'll jog instead of walk to bring you things because they're kind like that.

While she's still beyond the shade of the oaks, the girl stops and holds the rake out to me. This is the closest I've come to her and nearly as close as I was to Annalee in the grocery store. The girl's cheeks and the tip of her nose are red, and she smells of sunscreen.

She is ten years old or nearly so if she wants to join the Little Sisters. And she walks here. I have never seen her climb from one of the cars, so she lives close. She's breathing heavily from her jog across the street and from the excitement of being this much closer to where the girls meet every Tuesday.

"Do you want to see?" I ask her as I take the rake from her hand.

Our fingers nearly touch but not quite. I don't let them. I'm shaking, and I don't want her to see. People are frightened by a man who shakes to be so near them or who stares at them or who follows them from one place to the next. The shaking frightens me too because it's a reminder that being near the girls may not always be enough.

"The Little Sisters," I say. "We can see them through there." And I point at a window at the back of the church.

Holding up one hand to shield her eyes, the girl squints across the church lawn. The glow of the sun coats one side of her face and hair. She rolls her lips in on themselves as if she's thinking hard on what is the best thing to do.

"You go on," I say, pulling the rake through a patch of discarded weeds as if I'm not so interested in her. "Go on and have a look." And I give a nod in the direction of the window and remind myself to smile. "No harm. Run there and back. No one'll ever know. But first, tell me your name."

"Talley, sir," she says. "My name is Talley."

I tell her she doesn't have to call me sir and that my name is Daryl.

She smiles at me, turns, and runs toward the window. When she returns, she is breathless again and smiling. Already she's forgotten I'm a stranger to her.

"I saw them," she says. "They sit in a circle, crisscross on the floor, just like I knew they would. Miss Hettie leads them."

The bridge of her nose and the round knobs at each shoulder sparkle with tan freckles. Her white teeth are straight and clean. I smell her peppermint gum, can almost feel puffs of her fresh, warm breath on my skin.

"Do you know Miss Hettie?" I say.

The girl wipes a hand across her mouth. "She's married to Mr. Jansen. My mom works for Mr. Jansen."

It's one more thing I know. The mother works for Rowland Jansen, and he owns a bar on the other side of town.

"Does she tell you about the Little Sisters of the South?" the girl asks.

I nod. "I'm making a garden for them. You should come see it next time."

"Today," the girl says. Talley. I have to remember Talley is her name. "I want to see it today."

"Next time," I say. "And you'll help me with the weeding and watering."

"Gardening is a badge," the girl says. Her eyelashes flutter because her face is tipped toward the sun.

"Yes," I say. "I know. So you'll help me. And we'll put in some plants special for you. Maybe then you'll get your own badge and you can join."

Because she's forgotten I'm a stranger, she tells me she hasn't lived in Waddell too long and that once she joins the Little Sisters of the South, she'll have many friends. Everyone in her class belongs, and when she belongs too, she'll learn all their secrets. She'll know what to do and what to say once she is a Little Sister and then she'll be just like everyone else. I nod because she's right, and I ask how far is her walk. Is it safe for you to walk home alone? I ask. I live in the plantation house, she says, because everyone knows the plantation house. The Fielding Mansion.

"I live there with my grandma and grandpa," she says. "My mama too and my sister."

I think her grandfather is the one Susannah Bauer called "that man." He's the one she doesn't condone. The folks at church sometimes whisper about all that nonsense going on over at the school and what of poor Neil Fielding. It's a shame he and Erma don't come around to services anymore, some say, but we reap what we sow. Others say, a terrible ending for a damn fine man. I know now that Neil Fielding is Annalee's grandfather and Talley's too.

She goes on to tell me about the house and the great oaks and the gun her grandfather keeps and the school on the other side of the fence. As if she's happy to have someone listen to her, she talks and talks, and listening to so many things about Annalee's life eases the tightness inside me. I hear Talley clearly, have no trouble latching on to her words, when she says ghosts live at her house and tells me about the food she leaves for the boys who run. Every day she checks the fence post by the river to see if anyone has taken it. So far, no one has. And I begin to wonder if maybe my brother was one of the boys who ran.

LANE

LANE MUST LEAVE behind the things bagged and sealed—
Annalee's purse and her one sandal. Looking back at the long
table, she lingers at the conference room door Mark still holds
open for her.

"Annalee will need her purse," she says.

During her days as a reporter, she saw others do the same,
want to protect some part of what their loved ones left behind.

"I'll see they get back to her," Mark says.

Riding in the car now on their way to the river, Lane continues to call Annalee's phone and the home phone. Annalee's goes
straight to voicemail, and in between calling Annalee, Lane calls
Erma. The phone at home rings four, five, six times. Erma probably isn't answering because the reporters will have been calling.

"We weren't so different, were we?" Lane says without looking at Mark. "Stayed out all night a few times. Remember?"

The blood in Annalee's truck doesn't have to mean anything. It doesn't have to mean Annalee is another blonde like Susannah. It could have come from a busted-up knuckle Annalee got while trying to push the truck to higher, drier ground. And maybe Annalee and Jimmy didn't really break up and are now, at this moment, waking together and scrambling to get home. That would explain why Annalee got over the loss of Jimmy so quickly. There had been no loss. Plenty of folks around town said the same when Susannah Bauer first disappeared. Probably she ran off with some fellow, they said down at the bar, though they stopped saying that when day two came and went with no word of her whereabouts.

Annalee being in love is the most likely explanation for why she stayed out all night. Even if she woke and realized her mistake, she wouldn't bother giving Lane a call, might even enjoy the worry she caused. Lane feels it sometimes, has even wondered if it's normal . . . Annalee taking joy in hurting her.

Annalee has never been the child Lane worries about. Life has been somehow easier for Annalee than for most. She's always had many friends, although now Lane wonders how many of them were real. And then there was that phone call from Kyle six months ago, angry with Lane for having told Annalee she should move to Europe with him when Lane never said such a thing. And twice, maybe three times, parents stopped Lane before they left Brooklyn to congratulate her on scholarships Annalee had been awarded—one to Columbia and one to Rutgers. Full rides, they said. Aren't you the lucky ones? Lane had said thank you, and when she asked Annalee about the scholarships that never existed, she said the parents were obviously mistaken.

Annalee always had an explanation. She was always confident

and strong-willed. Those were the words Lane tried to use when describing her daughter. Annalee's lies—or rather, embellishments, as Lane preferred to think of them—had been small, insignificant. Annalee's way of building confidence. Not the healthiest way, but harmless. And when the lies became larger and should have been concerning, the exhaustion of raising a child like Annalee made believing her explanations less complicated than attempting to tackle the real problem. Believing was the only option Lane could manage, though she knew it was wrong. Believing was easier, and it kept the peace. It kept the peace for Talley, kept the peace between Lane and Kyle. Annalee never worried, and so Lane never worried for her.

"I remember a few late nights," Mark says. "Or rather, early mornings." And for what seems like the first time since the rumors began about Lane and Rowland, Mark smiles at her. It's a small gesture, a nod toward their past. A first love might not be a lasting love, but some small part survives.

"I told you earlier that Annalee didn't stay mad about the breakup for very long." Lane pauses while Mark nods. "I think maybe she didn't stay mad because they didn't really break up." Another pause. "Do you think that could be true?"

"Could be," he says. "Either way, we're going to find her."

Lane shifts in her seat so she'll be able to see Mark's face. She wants to ask him a question, and she'll be able to tell if he's lying. "Do you think Annalee being gone has anything to do with Susannah Bauer disappearing?"

Rolling one hand over the other, Mark turns onto Palmetto Drive, and at the intersection of Palmetto and 3rd Street, he rolls to a stop and idles at the intersection. His smile is gone. Lane looks where he is looking.

To the left is downtown. It's the oldest part of the city and the hardest hit when people began losing jobs and tourists stopped spending money. Thomas Bruce is pushing a broom across the sidewalk in front of his store, and it reminds Lane she has dry cleaning to pick up. When she was still a reporter, people admitted to having these same thoughts. They told her they remembered the oddest things while praying their daughter would be found or their wife would finally call. They remembered the car needed an oil change or the credit card bill was due in three days. Why did they remember those things that didn't matter? they would ask her.

To the right, a half block down, the road ends at Rowland's Tavern, and beyond is the river. The bar won't open until eleven. Rowland is probably inside placing the food order for the weekend.

"What are you looking at?" Lane asks.

Mark nods in the direction of the bar. "Your car?"

Lane leans forward and scoots to the edge of her seat. The parking lot in front of Rowland's is empty except for her white Lexus, almost ten years old now. She'd have thought Rowland would be there, but his car isn't in the parking lot.

"Yes," she says. "That's my car."

"You worked last night." It's a statement because he already knows.

"I did."

"And I found you at home this morning."

"Yes."

"Just wondering how you ended up at home," Mark says, pausing and turning to look Lane straight on. "And how your car ended up here."

LANE SHOULD HAVE realized as soon as she found keys in her pocket this morning she didn't drive herself home. On those mornings when she woke and couldn't remember how she got home, she first looked for her keys. If they were in her front pocket, it meant Rowland drove her. Once he had her safely inside the house, he would tuck her keys in her front pocket so she'd be sure to find them the next day. Every other morning, finding her keys in her pocket would have made her renew her vow to drink less, be home more, stay clear of Rowland. But she'd been distracted this morning by the divorce and reporters in the bar and the picture of their house on the television. She'd forgotten to feel shame.

"Should be no surprise," she says. "I had a few drinks last night. Always park in the garage. Didn't even notice my car wasn't at the house."

Mark nods and puts the car back into drive.

"Good enough," he says. "And who drove you home?"

"Rowland, I suppose."

"You suppose?"

"Yes," Lane says. "I suppose."

Mark says nothing more. They continue through town, but when he should drive straight down the road that will take them on toward the river, he slows, pulls alongside the curb, and stops in the shade thrown by the water tower.

"I'm not asking for no reason other than I'm trying to track down your daughter," he says, staring straight ahead. "Who took you home?"

"Rowland. I think it must have been Rowland."

"You sound unsure."

Lane rests her head against the window and says nothing.

"So if you're unsure," Mark says, "why do you assume it was Rowland?"

"Because it's always Rowland."

"Okay," Mark says. "So we'll assume you're right. He go inside with you?"

"What?"

"When he takes you home, does he go inside with you?"

"Is that question necessary?" Lane says.

"Doesn't matter to me what you do," Mark says, still looking out the windshield and not at Lane. "Except it has to matter now. I need to know if that man was inside your house."

After Lane and Mark's one night together in their senior year of high school, she knew it would be their last. His hands and the way they quivered when he touched her were enough to drive her away. His touch would always remind her that he worried for her and felt sorry for her, and she knew he would never stop. So she went looking for a boy, a man, who wouldn't shake when he laid his hands on her.

She first gave a few of Mark's friends, including Rowland, a try. Some turned her away, as if whatever Lane had contracted all those years ago was catching. Others didn't know enough of her past to be afraid. They were distant, mechanical, tolerable. And then there had been Rowland, who at twenty-one was willing only because Lane wasn't Hettie. Already everyone knew he would marry Hettie, but he wasn't ready yet to succumb. Lane was something different for him, and her being different was more important to the younger Rowland than her being damaged.

They had grown up together—Lane, Mark, and Rowland. Rowland is older by a few years, and he was the same then as he is now. Like so many men from the South, he has a way of studying his surroundings as if no matter where he is or what he's seeing, he owns it all. Like so many men except Mark. He and Rowland are different in this way, and it's what so often put them at odds when they were younger. The silence between Lane and Mark now is as heavy as it was when Mark first learned all those years ago about what she'd done with Rowland and the others.

Mark had stood in her kitchen that day—a boy, almost a man, she'd known all her life—and asked her if it was true. His faded jeans set low on his hips, his white undershirt hung untucked, and his dark hair was mostly hidden by a baseball cap. She nodded, though she couldn't force herself to say yes. He stared at her across the kitchen table, waiting, it seemed, for her to say something more. When she didn't, he leaned forward, and grabbing on to the back of a kitchen chair, he lifted it, slammed it down, and asked again. Lane looked him in the eyes so he would believe her and said yes.

"'That man'?" Lane says. "You're calling Rowland 'that man' now?"

"Guess I am. Was Rowland Jansen in your house last night?"

"No," Lane says, but her voice is thin, as if she's out of breath. Mark will hear it straightaway. She can't be sure, because she can't remember leaving the bar or Rowland taking her keys, though he surely did. She can't remember the drive to her house, walking up the steps, Rowland unlocking the side door for her and tucking the keys in her pocket. She can't remember falling into her bed, and so she can't know if she was alone or not. She can't even remember seeing Annalee's truck in the drive.

"I don't know," she says. "I don't think he was."

"Did he ever come inside with you?"

Lane nods. "Months ago. One time. Never again. Never since."

Mark is looking straight ahead, has been since they parked. "But you can't really say that," he says. "Can you? You can't say, 'never again,' because you can't remember."

Again, Lane says nothing.

"Were you alone when you woke up?"

Lane nods.

"Were you dressed?"

"Mostly."

Things changed for Lane three months ago after that night with Rowland. She cut down on the drinking, kept her distance from Rowland, and made sure she was awake in the mornings to kiss Talley first thing, but none of that could change what she did to Annalee and to herself when she spent that one night with Rowland.

"He might have come in with me," she says. It's little more than a whisper. "It's possible he left before I woke up. And I don't remember seeing her truck last night. Annalee's truck. I just don't know. I could have brought that man into my house."

Like Mark, she stares straight ahead. Cars pass as if it's any other day. People start to shiver. This is another thing that happens. While interviewing a witness to a train derailment or maybe a liquor store robbery, Lane would make note of how her subjects began to knead their hands, hug themselves, shake out their fingers, anything to make the shivering stop.

"Do you think Rowland Jansen did something to my daughter?"

Mark puts the car in drive. "We're going to find her," he says, leaving Lane to think yes, Mark believes Rowland might have done something to Annalee.

ERMA

LEANING FORWARD IN her chair, Erma pulls a tissue from her apron, blots her chest and neck, and opens her eyes. That's her writing desk in the corner and her favorite afghan draped over the sofa. She's in her parlor where she likes to sit at the desk and write her prayers in her prayer book because maybe that'll be like having a whole congregation praying along with her.

Something woke her, maybe the heat. Or maybe some sound. It's hard for her to wake up sometimes. Yes, those are footsteps. Someone is coming. No mistaking it because the stairs leading up to the back porch have a way of creaking and whining when a person walks on them. That's another thing Susannah Bauer was going to see to fixing. Erma sure does wish she knew Susannah's parents. She'd pay them a visit, maybe take them a cobbler. She'd tell them what a sweet girl Susannah is and they should always have hope. Erma knows all about the frightening thoughts that fill a mother's head when her child is not where she's meant to be. Young girls come home, Erma would tell Susannah's parents, and she sure does hope she's right.

The footsteps are still coming. They're light, and they climb the stairs slowly. Erma closes her eyes again and inhales. It's that sweet, spicy smell. She coughs from the burn of it on the back of her throat. She smells it sometimes in the middle of the night and wonders if Bonnie Wiley is standing there at the end of the bed. Erma smells her so strong some nights, she weeps and begs Bonnie to leave her be. Pressing the tissue under her nose, Erma opens her eyes. That'll be Bonnie Wiley for sure outside on the porch.

Many times, since Bonnie moved in across the street, she has come here to the house, and she knows just how to poke at Erma's most tender spot. If Erma is, on one particular day, staring at her husband and wondering exactly how his hand got so crippled and stiff, Bonnie will come along and from the front porch yell out that Erma had best be careful. Aren't you afraid? Bonnie Wiley might holler. Aren't you afraid he'll use his knotted-up old hand on you or one of yours?

The footsteps reach the top stair, settle on the porch, and cross to the far end of the house. A tapping of some sort starts up. Sitting tall in her chair, Erma leans to get a look across the foyer into the dining room where the sound has started. It's odd, and she can't place it. There it is again. A tapping. No, not a tapping. It's a single tap. And then a few quiet moments, and farther along the porch, moving closer to Erma, another tap. And farther still and closer still, another. And another.

"Is that you, Bonnie Wiley?" Erma can't help that her voice cracks and that Bonnie will know she's afraid.

People say Bonnie was born here in Florida but grew up in Louisiana down near the Gulf, where people pray to who-knows-what sort of God. She does have the look about her, the look of something unholy or otherworldly or both. It's her hair, always popped out in a frizz, and those eyes edged in too much white.

Someone is still out there. Footsteps continue across the porch. Standing now in the middle of her parlor, Erma faces the windows that run along the side of the house. There is another tap. And more footsteps. And another tap. It's happening at each window. Erma walks into the foyer, closes her eyes, and listens. Now Bonnie has reached Neil's room.

"I told the sheriff what you're up to," Erma shouts, but maybe she didn't call the sheriff. Remembering is near to impossible sometimes, like lifting something far too heavy to be lifted. Try as she might, Erma can't get her memories to budge. "You better see to it Annalee comes home safe and sound."

It's never Neil who has to say the nasty things to Bonnie. It's always Erma saying them, screaming them, day in and day out, more so now that Lane and the girls are here. The curse circling the house is meant for Erma as much as it's meant for Neil. God forbid, that means it's closing in on Lane and her girls too.

IT STARTED ON a Saturday in April when Lane was thirteen years old. Erma and Lane had fought that day over something ordinary they'd fought about before. That's the most Erma could remember of it. Maybe Lane failed to finish her chores and so wasn't allowed to go to town. Or maybe she hadn't done her homework or had used foul language. No matter the cause of the fight, Lane shouted at Erma and ran from the house, slamming the door behind her.

After giving Lane a good hour to calm herself, Erma walked to the ruins where the slaves once lived, certain she would find Lane there. The remains of a dozen small houses were laid out in an arc near the back of the property. Now only the tabby slabs remained, most overtaken by brush and drifting earth, and the walls of five houses. All the doors, roofs, and windows had long ago rotted away. The empty sills and thresholds had crumbled over the years, and the tops of walls that no longer held a roof had been worn to rounded nubs. This was where Lane always went when upset. She'd sit in the shade of the tallest wall even though Erma warned her again and again the structure could topple at any moment.

When Erma first visited the Fielding house in the weeks before she and Neil were married, Neil led both Erma and her mother around the grounds and walked them past each of the tabby remains. See how smart the men of this family are? Erma's mother had said loud enough that Neil could hear and perhaps in hopes of convincing Erma the marriage was for the best. The Fielding men knew to keep their workers far enough away to be civil but close enough to be kept under watch. Then she squeezed Erma's hand because they'd made it all the way to this fine house and this fine land from their swampy, soggy home in south Florida.

While Lane had always found peace in these ruins where the slaves once lived, they were a painful reminder to Erma of what she really was to Neil. He'd never truly loved Erma, not in the way she had always dreamed of being loved. He was a man of a certain age when they met and was long overdue a wife. And Erma's mother believed she and Erma were long overdue a fine life with a grand home and a name people respected. Far enough away to be civil. Close enough to be watched over. That's how Neil kept Erma.

Walking slowly as she approached the worn patch of land and what remained of the small homes, Erma shouted out for Lane to come on in to lunch, but Lane wasn't sitting there in the shade where Erma had hoped to find her.

Continuing to shout out for Lane to come on home, Erma

walked to the road and back and checked along the river. She looked inside the house and twice walked around it. When she saw nothing of Lane, she grew angry. She drove into town, poked her head into the movie theater, and visited the houses of every one of Lane's friends. She drove up and down the dirt roads around their house but saw nothing of Lane. Later that afternoon, when she stopped being angry and started to worry, she called Neil at the school. Kids wander off, he said. She'll be home when she's hungry. When Erma called him a second time, again interrupting his workday, he sent two of his guards to help her look.

Neil arrived home at his usual time that night. He'd forgotten about Lane and the two men he'd sent to look for her until he saw the empty table in the dining room and no food on the stove. He stomped toward the stairs to check Lane's bedroom as if Erma hadn't already done that. Before he reached the first step, someone knocked at the doors off the back porch. He motioned for Erma to answer it and continued on to Lane's room.

Erma hurried to the doors, yanked them both open because maybe Lane was on the other side, and instead, one of the two guards Neil had sent over from the school stood on her porch.

"Yes?" she said.

"I see Mr. Fielding is home," the young man said, glancing at Neil's truck parked near the back porch. "May I speak to him, ma'am?"

"What is it?" Erma looked outside for who else might be with the guard. She had hoped to see Lane standing alongside him, a little dirty perhaps, hungry for certain, but safe. The porch was empty. Erma swallowed hard and her heart beat faster as she waited for what the man would tell her. "Have you found Lane?"

"Your husband, ma'am," the man said, removing his hat and tucking it under his arm. "Best I talk with him."

Erma left the doors open, and from the bottom of the stair-case, she hollered up at Neil to come on down. As she and the guard waited for Neil, Erma offered him iced tea. He told her no thank you, and because he wouldn't look Erma in the eyes and because he continually glanced over his shoulders as if something were sneaking up from behind, Erma began to worry Lane hadn't just run off and she wouldn't be home for supper.

"What is it, son?" Neil said when he reached the foyer. As he spoke to the man, Neil rolled up the sleeves on his button-down shirt. He smelled salty and sour from a long day at work, and his shirt had wilted. Neil's shoulders were still thick and broad in those days, and he led with his full stomach as he spoke to the man. "Out with it."

The man, boy really, looked from Erma to Neil and back again. He didn't want to say what he had to say in front of Erma, and this made Erma more certain. Something had happened to Lane, and this man knew what it was. It was a silly argument like every mother has with every daughter. Nothing more, and yet here Erma was, waiting to hear the worst.

"Son, either tell me or leave me," Neil said, brushing Erma away from the entryway.

"This." The man handed Neil a piece of paper no bigger than an envelope. "Found it over near the river."

Neil took the paper and pulled off his hat to get a better look.

"Anyone else seen this?" he said, yanking his hat back on and pulling it low on his forehead.

Erma leaned in to get a look. The paper was flimsy in Neil's hands and torn at its edges. Something was written on it, but Neil folded it over before Erma could read it.

"No, sir," the man said. "Ain't showed no one but you."

"And you ain't told that other fellow who come with you?"

Again, the man shook his head.

"Ain't my daughter who wrote this," Neil said. "You understand?"

But Erma didn't believe him. Neil saying that in the way he said it, looking the young guard straight on, dipping his chin, made Erma certain the note had something to do with Lane being gone.

"What is it, Neil?" Erma said, reaching for the paper but jerking her hand away when Neil looked at her. It was a look she knew well enough—narrow eyes staring down on her from under the brim of a hat.

"Tell me you understand," Neil said to the man, and ignored Erma's question. "My girl would never invite such a thing. Tell me you understand."

"Wasn't your daughter who wrote this," the man said, mimicking Neil's words. "No, sir, didn't find no note."

"Please," Erma said. "Do you know where she is?"

Again Neil ignored her question as he folded the paper over twice more and tucked it in his front shirt pocket.

Erma should have been accustomed to being treated as if she weren't standing right there alongside Neil, because that's how he so often treated her, as if she weren't quite as solid, not quite as human as other folks. Still, she should have been braver, should have risen just that once and snatched the note from Neil's hand before he tucked it away.

"I want you to hustle on back to the school and round up every available man," Neil said to the young guard. "Send them here to the house. And call the fellows who aren't on today and tell them to get over here too. Tell them bring flashlights, lanterns, whatever they got. I want every man here in thirty minutes. You tell them fellows they're to find Laney."

"Yes, sir," the man said.

"I'll be right behind you, and soon as I get to the school, I want to do a fresh head count. Last thing, you get someone started pulling together a list of every boy who's tried to run this past year."

That was the moment Erma knew something truly awful had happened to Lane.

"Neil," she said as the man jogged back his truck. "What is it? What's happened?"

Neil turned to her. "You call up the neighbors. Any who's home, ask them to check their barns and sheds and such. Tell them Laney's gone and we need some help finding her. Tell them if they find one of my boys with her, to hold on to him until I get there."

"Yes, Neil," Erma said, and followed him up the stairs. As she stood in their bedroom doorway, Neil changed into a fresh shirt. She clung to the doorframe, her heart pounding so loudly in her ears she could scarcely hear herself talking. "You're scaring me, Neil. What's happened? Was it one of the boys? Did one of them do something?"

"Never you mind," Neil said, pulling on fresh socks as well. "Just get on and do as I say."

Erma followed him back downstairs, grabbing at him along the way so he'd stop and talk to her. She was afraid now for the very worst. Neil swatted her away and left her standing on the porch as he crossed the drive to his truck.

"Do whatever you have to," Erma called after him. She didn't care what he did or who he did it to. "Just find our Laney."

ERMA TURNS IN a tight circle, following the sound of Bonnie as she makes her way around the house. Tap, tap, tap, she goes across the windows that run along the porch.

"You hear that, Neil?" Erma hollers from the foyer.

The entryway rises two stories high, empty space leaving Erma's voice to drift about as if lost. This foyer, being grand as it is, means you're somebody now, Erma's mother said on Erma's wedding day. As a child, Erma heard all the stories of the fine fertile land here in north Florida that had once belonged to her family, had originally belonged to her family. Old Southern money had pushed out Erma's people, stolen the land, and forced them deeper into Florida where the land was cheaper and near to worthless.

When Erma's daddy died, her mother packed what little they had and said they were going to find their way back to north Florida and the rich land that was rightfully theirs. People will sense it on us, Erma's mother had said. No matter how many years removed we are from the home that's due us, people will sense we're destined for something finer. Erma had dreamed of finding a man to love and maybe studying to become a teacher. She'd have babies and rock them on the porch. She wanted a small, sweet house surrounded by a magnolia hedge. That's what she wanted in north Florida. But Mother said no to all those things. We're due much more, she said. When Erma finally agreed to marry Neil, her mother was happy and said they were home at last. One year later she died, leaving Erma alone with a husband she barely knew and would never love.

"Look out them windows in your room," Erma calls out to Neil. "Look there and tell me. What do you see?"

Still watching over her shoulders, Erma walks into Neil's room, where he is staring at the television. A reporter, that same silver-haired reporter who stood in Erma's driveway this morning, is talking into a camera. He's just across the way at the school, all of those reporters are, and they're talking from in front of the small white building where those old men say they were beaten as boys.

If Erma would walk to the fence line and look through the trees, she'd almost be able to see them. The silver-haired man is talking about a picture of a boy, a sketch of his face. He uses words like "reconstruction" and "skull fragments" and "facial approximation," and as he talks, he disappears and the face of a boy takes his place. He was ten to twelve years old, the reporter says. Cause of death and identity are unknown.

Erma backs out of Neil's room. She backs all the way through the foyer, and when she bumps up against the credenza passed down from her grandfather's father, the one piece of her family's furniture Neil allowed in the house, she gathers the family Bible from the marble top and holds it to her chest. Its brown leather cover has split in places, and the binding is loose. All the names of all the family are written on the front pages. Dates of birth. Dates of death. She clutches it like it's all that will save her.

"Talley," Erma hollers, and when the girl doesn't answer, she calls out for Annalee. But Annalee is gone. Lane and Sheriff Ellenton are both off looking for her. And where is Talley?

"What is it you've done, Bonnie Wiley?" Erma says. She lifts her chin and cries out overhead: "What have you done with my girls?"

Erma slaps a hand over her mouth. She's done it now. She's said it right out loud, and whatever is out there has a way in. She grabs up the receiver from the telephone, presses it to her ear, but doesn't know what number to use. Her address book lies open on the marble tabletop. Erma starts to dial Lane's number, but the phone is dead. She shakes the receiver, reaches for the cord, and then remembers she pulled it from the wall.

Sliding her feet across the pine floors because she can't force herself to take a proper step, she makes her way to the tall, narrow window to the right of the large double doors that lead to the back porch. The heavy drapery, a single panel that requires no clothespin, hangs nearly ceiling to floor. Slipping one hand around its edge, Erma pulls it back and looks straight into the face of a boy. It's a drawing, crudely done. Pencil on white paper, and it looks much like the one they are showing on the television. This hand-drawn boy has the same round cheeks and large eyes. Erma drops the drape and stumbles back. On the other side of the double doors, she steps up to the next window.

Again, she pushes aside the drape, but this time, she stands as far away as her reach will allow. There is another boy, another drawing, much like the first. Black lead on white paper. Rounded cheeks and a small nose, two wide-set eyes. But this boy is not quite like the last. Another picture hangs in the next window. And another. Each one is a different sort of boy, and each one is staring in at her. Bonnie has summoned them, and now they hang in Erma's every window.

14

TALLEY

TALLEY STANDS ON the side of the road as two vans pass by. Across the street, the New Covenant Church where Daryl works is quiet. The front doors are closed, and not a single car is parked in the circle drive where the Little Sisters will soon be dropped off for their last meeting of the summer.

Once the vans have passed, Talley looks both ways and runs for the side of the church. For three weeks, since first meeting Daryl, Talley has been coming here every day to tend her garden, and it's never been this quiet. The door to the shed where Daryl keeps his tools is always propped open with a cement block, but today it's closed up tight.

Daryl's first job each day is to pick up the fronds that fall from the palms growing near the parking lot, but several lie on the ground, blown down by the winds last night. Like it is most days when Talley comes here, the spot where the reverend parks his long black car is empty because he goes to visit the old folks who can't make it to church anymore, but Miss Hettie is always here. Daryl says Miss Hettie is here at the church from sunup to sundown because she doesn't have anywhere else to be. He says her life is in shambles. He says Miss Hettie doesn't like Mama or Annalee, and for the first time this summer, the spot where Miss Hettie parks her small blue car is empty.

Not wanting to shout out Daryl's name because that is one of the things that makes him angry, Talley instead runs through the parking lot and around the other side of the church. When she reaches the front again and still has seen nothing of Daryl or anyone else, she squats on the curb, pulls her knees to her chest, wraps her arms around her shins, and waits.

Out on the road, more vans pass and some cars too, but none turn into the church's circle drive. None are Little Sisters. Not only is Susannah Bauer gone, but now Annalee is gone and Daryl and Miss Hettie and every Little Sister of the South. Talley jumps from the curb, runs toward Daryl's shed and down the mulched pathway to her garden.

When Talley and Daryl first planted her garden, he said it was too late in the season to be planting tomatoes, but they planted six of them anyway. Talley was going to have a garden of her own, and that meant she'd soon have friends of her own like she did in Brooklyn. No one in Brooklyn knew about Grandpa Neil or the boys who ran, and Talley had as many friends as anyone. But now only one of the tomato plants is alive, and Susannah and Daryl are gone and they were her only friends. Yanking the dead plants from the soggy ground, Talley tosses them off into the trees.

While the tomatoes mostly died, the peppers and butter beans are doing much better, but because of the rise and fall of the small patch of land and all the rain that fell, they stand in a few inches of stagnant water. Susannah taught Talley about stagnant water when Grandma left the hose running too long on her garden at home. Together Talley and Susannah used a hoe to dig troughs that drained away the water. Nothing worse for butter beans than too much water, Susannah said. Talley will do as Susannah taught her now. She'll dig a trough so her beans and peppers will live, but to dig a trough she'll need a hoe, and to find a hoe, she'll need to find a way inside Daryl's shed.

DARYL HAS NEVER allowed Talley inside his shed. There are sharp things in there and expensive tools, lots of things a girl Talley's age shouldn't get near. When he said that, Talley frowned because it was the first time he treated her like everyone else.

Standing on her tiptoes at one of the shed's back windows, she still must jump to get a look. Because the sun is throwing a glare, and because the glass is covered in thick smudges of something greasy, she has to squint to see inside.

One of the first times Talley came to water her garden, back when it was brand-new, Daryl locked himself out of the shed. He said curse words, and he slapped himself on the forehead as he walked back and forth along the side of the shed. When Talley said maybe she should go home, Daryl shouted no. He said no again, but quieter the second time, and then he stacked two cement blocks under the same window Talley is looking through now, slid it open, and jumped inside. He smiled when he opened the door, but his forehead was still red.

That was the day Daryl first told Talley about his brother. His name was Wayne, and he was at the school for boys a long time ago. Daryl said he was going to find his brother one day and then they'd be a family. He asked Talley if she thought that might happen. He asked Talley if she thought maybe her grandpa beat

Wayne. She told Daryl no but only because she was too scared to say otherwise, not only scared of Daryl but also scared that saying out loud Grandpa hurt someone might make it true.

The two cement blocks still stand under the window, but they aren't tall enough for Talley, so she grabs the rubber garbage can where Daryl dumps the palm fronds every morning. It's empty because he never gathered today's fronds. She pushes it upside down under the window and climbs on top. Standing on the outer edges of the can so it doesn't collapse under her, she slips her fingers under the window's bottom pane and pushes it open. She leans inside and scoots until her hip bones teeter on the windowsill. She is half inside and half out. A little bit more and her hands will reach the workbench that's just below her. Rocking side to side, she kicks with her feet, falls forward, and lands with her palms flat on the workbench. She pulls her feet in, and the rest of her follows.

Jumping down from the workbench, she brushes off the front of her clothes. Sometimes Grandma says Talley needs to start behaving like a young lady and stop coming home with cuts and bruises, but Mama says there's nothing wrong with a few bumps along the way if a young lady gets them of her own accord. Susannah Bauer always had bumps and bruises because she climbed on the roof and wiggled into the crawl space under the house, and Talley has always wanted to be just like Susannah Bauer.

It's warm and quiet inside Daryl's shed. The sun shining through the dirty windows is a milky yellow color, and flecks of dust glitter in the air. A few jars filled with nails and screws sit along the back of the workbench, a lawn mower is parked in the middle of the shed, and a blower and chainsaw sit together in one corner. Several long-handled tools—a couple of rakes, a shovel, and an ax—stand in another corner.

A few steps will take Talley to the corner where the hoe is

probably tucked back in among all the rakes and shovels, but before she can grab for any of them, something sparkles, catches the sunlight in a way other things in the shed do not, and she stops, can't make her legs move. It's small, round, and white. Actually it's blue. Blue-and-white fine porcelain china.

Grandma has a whole set of plates and bowls that look the same as this one, all stored where company can see them in the hutch made especially for china. Talley used them, plates exactly like this one, when she first started leaving food for the boys. She didn't know about the plates being special back then. They were easy to reach and to put back when Talley was done using them. Every day, when she'd go outside to check the fence post by the river, the plate would still be there and the food too. She'd take the plate back inside, wash it in the kitchen sink while Grandma was napping in the parlor, and return it to the hutch. But the first day the food disappeared, so did Grandma's plate.

That's the day, the first day her food was gone, Talley learned about fine porcelain china in classic blues and whites. Grandma noticed the missing plate right away when she set the table for supper. She fussed and blamed Grandpa. After that, Talley used only the white butter tubs Grandma didn't much like because they leaked.

Using both hands, Talley reaches for the plate sitting on the farthest corner of Daryl's workbench. It already has a chip in it that wasn't there before. She hugs it to her chest. She's not going to dig a trough for her tomatoes and beans. She wants to go home. She wants to see Mama and Annalee even though Annalee isn't always nice to Talley. She wants to tell Mama that Annalee plans to run away, and she wants Susannah Bauer to come back. But mostly, Talley wants to know why Daryl has Grandma's plate. At the sound of a key rattling in the lock, Talley swings around, squeezing the china plate with both arms, and the shed's door flies open.

DARYL

10 days before Susannah disappeared

IT'S A WEDNESDAY and still not time for Susannah Bauer to come to town again. But it is the day Annalee will be at the restaurant. I know this because Talley told me after she peeked in the church window to see the Little Sisters of the South. I know many things about Annalee I didn't know the first time I came to the bar. That was only a few days ago. I know which roads she drives each day. I know she has lived in Waddell for six months and recently graduated from high school. I know her grandfather once worked at the school and that he stores a gun in the room where he watches television. I know Talley leaves food for the boys who run. I know maybe Wayne was one of those boys, and one day I'll ask Talley if she thinks so too. I even know her family's secrets—the things they say her mother did with Miss Hettie's husband.

As Annalee did the first time I came to the Wharf, she works through supper, but she doesn't work like I thought she would. Dirty dishes cover empty tables while she talks with the man mixing drinks. She leans on the bar, resting her chin in her hands, and steps aside for the waitresses only when they ask. There is no game on the television, and no one buys a beer for the kid who mows the church lawn. At a quarter after ten, Annalee leaves, and I follow.

It's fully dark, the sun having long ago set, when Annalee turns into the drive leading to her house. I trail her, but not too closely, drive past her house, and park. It's late but not too late for a person to be out and about. The engine smelled funny, I will say if anyone comes along and sees me walking down the road, and I forgot my cell phone at home. I quietly shut the car door, though no one is around to hear, and begin to walk.

The house where Annalee lives is a good ways off the road. The long drive is wide and edged by oaks. I count twelve in all, six on either side. The porch lights from Annalee's house glow on the trunks and lower branches. My arms, if I were to wrap them around one of the trees, would not reach. At first, when people come upon this house, they must think these twelve trees are as grand a thing as they will ever see. It must occur to them that this house has been here since the beginning, that the South was in part born here in this very place.

Talley told me just yesterday she worries ghosts live here in these trees, most especially in the tree nearest the house. It's the biggest tree of them all, and people died under its branches. That's what Talley said, and she told me about one particular branch that stretches out thick and high and is scarred from the ropes. When the moonlight is just right and the breeze just so, she sees those people dripping like the moss from the branches. I've never seen a place where ghosts live, not up close like this where I can touch the bark and smell the dirt. Surely it's true. Ghosts are here and like Talley said, they drip from the moss, quiver in the broad, leathery leaves, and cling to the rough brown bark. I think they're holding on so no one will forget.

As I slip from one tree to the next, making my way ever closer, I watch the road for passersby. At the largest oak in all the county, I squat to the ground where no one will see me if they look outside. At the tallest point of the house, there is a single window. The attic window. Talley told me this and said she isn't allowed to go in the attic and never has. The windows up there used to be boarded over to keep the rats out, but now they're open, no glass even in them, and she's afraid of what's up there. She says the door to the attic is only half as tall as a door should be and something about that scares her too.

The mother comes home. She drives slowly past Annalee's truck and parks in the detached garage. Walking across the drive, she doesn't see me leaned up against the biggest tree. Once she is inside, the porch light goes out, and then another light, most surely the kitchen light, switches off. One by one, the slivers of light that trim the drawn curtains disappear and more rooms go dark. Bugs crawl through the grass and onto my ankles. They leak from the stringy gray moss. Mosquitos settle in around my face, and still I keep watch until the last sliver of light has disappeared. I'll have welts tomorrow on my ankles and behind my knees and on my forearms, but I won't scratch at them now. I wait thirty minutes more and then push myself off the ground.

WITH EACH STEP I take toward Annalee's truck, I stir up the scent of the night-blooming jasmine. I imagine it's the smell of Annalee's skin and hair. I inhale, close my eyes, even. The ground is rough under my feet, and I crush small rocks and bits of gravel. Something guides me to the truck. Knowing Annalee was just here quenches a thirst. When I am near enough, I let my fingers slide across the truck's smooth metal and open my eyes.

It's darker here than in town. No streetlights line the road, no overhead signs, no headlights or stoplights. I blink, waiting because I know my eyes will adjust, and once they have, I slide along the driver's-side door, drop one hand to the handle, and look in through the window.

I thought the truck would be clean inside. Instead, to-go cups Annalee must get at work, a half dozen at least, lie on the floorboards, and so do crumpled bags and the cardboard tubs that hold French fries. I bought whole wheat bread at the Food Lion because Annalee told me it was best and was all she ever ate, but now I think she was lying. I close my eyes again, hoping, letting out one slow, long breath, and I pull. The door clicks and opens. I shiver, excited, frightened. I hold the door there, where it's open just a crack, and look behind me because maybe I hear something. There will be all kinds of things out here that would make such a noise. I don't hear it again, so on the count of three, I throw open the door, reach inside, and fumble with the dome light until it switches off.

Keeping one foot on the ground, I lean into the truck and rest a knee on the front seat. I thought it would be wonderful inside Annalee's truck. Instead the truck smells of stale food and damp floor mats never allowed to dry through and through. Only the feel of the seat, warm and soft under my hands, is how I imagined. And I hear it again. Something behind me. A footstep? A door opening? I push off the seat, swing out of the way of the door, but I have no time to see to closing it. In three steps, I'm behind the truck where I squat and listen.

Something is crushing the bits of gravel again. Not my footsteps this time, but someone else's. I drop to the ground, lie flat, and from here, I look under the truck. The feet coming toward me are small. Those are white sneakers like the ones Annalee wears to work and with each step, she lifts onto her toes. She'll see the door has been left open, and she does. The feet stop at the driver's side. There is a long pause. She doesn't make a sound. I imagine her hand resting where mine had been a moment ago. I shiver again and wonder if the handle is still warm from my touch. She must be looking around, though her feet don't move.

Tiny rocks dent each palm as I push myself up. I don't stand tall yet and instead stay crouched. I brush my hands together and place them on the rear bumper. I lift higher and listen. Annalee must feel what's between us, the something in the air that makes it sizzle and pop. She must know I'm here. I could step forward, no more than a few steps, and I would be upon her. She would be warm and soft. Her glossy hair might tickle the side of my face, and her voice would be gentle, her words kind. Sometimes I ache for being so far away. Now I ache for being so close.

The truck's door opens wider. I drop my hands and fall backward when the truck rolls forward. I never heard the door shut, and the engine has not started. She's pushing it away from the house so no one hears. As the truck rolls down the drive, the door closes. I push myself up from the ground and stand. The engine starts. She rounds the side of the house, never seeing me in the rearview mirror.

I stand in the dark, not moving, until I no longer hear anything. She'll be gone and I'll never find her by the time I run back to my car and follow. From here in the driveway, I no longer smell the jasmine. I smell the river instead, though I don't hear it. It's low, everyone says. What with no rain, the river is so low it's barely more than a trickle.

Just yesterday, Talley told me she leaves food for the boys on the limestone fence post near the river. It's also in the path the boys took when they would run. Maybe that's why Wayne never came home. If he was one of the boys who ran and if he got away and came looking, he wouldn't have found Mother and me. Father was already dead when they took Wayne away, and Mother said if Wayne never came home, if he never found us, the bloodline would end.

It's vile, Mother said of our blood. As she spoke, she ran one fingertip along the blue veins on the inside of my wrists and said vile. Her dark hair, so dry the ends were nearly white, hung in her face, and she smelled of the ashtrays stacked in our sink. If another one of us is ever born, I'll never see it, she said, and it will never find me and the line will end. And then she held me by both hands because I was still small and begged me never to spread my vile seed. Promise me, she said, kneeling and looking up at me. Let the family die. But if the family died, I wondered as a child, who would care for me?

In the dark, it takes me some time, and when I do find the fence post, I nearly trip over it. I stumble, and the food Talley left falls. It hits the ground with a soft thud. I shuffle through the tall grass that has nearly covered the fence post. First, I find a small plate. Running my hands around its smooth edges, I feel a chip. I keep looking until I find two biscuits. One at a time, I throw them as hard as I can toward the river. It will make Talley happy to think the boys are taking her food, and if I ask, she'll go into the attic at night in hopes of seeing one of them take it again. Holding the plate tight to my chest, I run for my car.

LANE

WHEN LANE WAS in high school, they called it "the Tracks," the spot where the train tracks cross over the river. They would meet there as kids to drink the beer someone had managed to score. In the spring, they'd dare one another to steal honey from the hives farmers had hoisted onto platforms high among the tupelos that bloomed only a precious few weeks of the year. In the coldest months, they'd huddle together under the train tracks, using the thick concrete supports as shelter. And when the river was especially low, they would wade upstream to the limestone caves. It was cooler there at the river than any other place during the summer months. Lane was always the one to take the dare, whatever the dare, and that was enough to make some forget she'd once been the victim. The higher she climbed or the more she drank, the more they forgot. Except for Mark. He never forgot.

While Lane would have missed the narrow dirt road just past Breakers Auto Supply, Mark doesn't. He slows, flips on his blinker, but instead of taking the road that will lead them to the Tracks, he switches off the radio and pulls into the ditch again.

"What are you doing?" Lane asks, pointing off toward the dirt road. "It's right there, yes?"

Her cell phone vibrates in her front pocket. She yanks it out, hoping to see Annalee's name rolling across the screen.

"Don't have no business taking you down there." Mark lays his arm over the back of Lane's seat.

"Then don't," she says. Bonnie Wiley's name appears instead of Annalee's. "I'll take myself."

Bonnie calls nearly every day to tell Lane how glad she is Lane has finally come home, and every day Lane takes her calls. There is little Lane can do for people like Bonnie. Listening is one of the few, but not today. She stuffs the phone back in her pocket and reaches for the door handle.

The wail of a siren stops Lane from opening the door. By the time she turns to look, the flashing blue and red lights are upon them. That's why Mark switched off the radio. He heard code 3 or running hot or some other phrase Lane should have recognized, and he turned it off. The ambulance passes them, slows, and disappears down the dirt road.

"What is it?" Lane says, grabbing Mark's sleeve. If Lane had been awake all these months instead of drinking her nights away in a bar, she likely wouldn't be here wondering if the ambulance that passed is intended for her daughter.

"How about you stay here while I find out," Marks says. He shifts in his seat and looks Lane straight on. It's a trick to make her trust him, one she used often enough to get someone to agree to talk to her while reporting on a story.

"Take me down there," she says. "Take me or I'll go by myself."

The clearing is only a few hundred feet off the paved street, but the rain has made the dirt soft so Mark drives slowly, his tires slipping in and out of the grooves cut by someone who came before them. As they approach the bend the road takes before reaching the river, he pulls over and parks.

"We have to leave the car here and walk," he says, grabbing Lane by the wrist as she reaches to open the door. "You can't go running in there. You have to let me walk you in."

The clearing is smaller than she remembers. She was a few months from being eighteen the last time she was here. She had just met Kyle. He was the first person she knew who wasn't from Waddell, and he didn't plan to stay, not a moment longer than he had to. That went for the South as well. He was a writer, even then, and planned to move to New York. Lane was also a writer, having started when she was thirteen. She wrote after school and on the weekends and at night when she was in bed. It was something she could do alone, and being alone was what she had wanted most.

Kyle liked that she was a writer, though he never asked to read her work. He also liked that she studied and made good grades. She never told him she studied so she could one day get out of Waddell. She liked Kyle because he promised a different sort of future and because they shared no past.

Kyle didn't grow up hearing the sirens sound at the school for the boys, and he wasn't sitting in the classroom the day Lane finally returned to school and all the kids watched her slide into her desk like they were wondering if it hurt her to sit. He must have heard rumors when he moved to town, but either he didn't believe them, didn't care about them, or was intrigued by them. Lane often wondered about it over the years, and her question was finally answered when his third book told the story of a thirteen-year-old girl who was abducted from the front porch of the Southern mansion where she lived with her mother and father.

But no matter the reason, Kyle could hold Lane and press down on her with the full weight of his body. He wasn't careful about peeling off her clothes, not like Mark had been, and didn't stop or slow himself down to ask if she was okay or was he hurting her. He never worried or cared about what lasting damage he thought had been done to Lane by that boy.

The air is immediately cooler as Mark and Lane walk into the shade of the tupelos and Southern magnolias. She's chilled even when they walk through the patches of sunlight shining through the tops of the upland trees. Mark slips an arm around Lane's shoulders and cradles her elbow with his free hand. He must feel the weakness in her legs, the wobble in her ankles. She's slipping away again, into a place where she can't quite hear his voice, though he stands right next to her. As he leans into her to talk, his chest vibrates against her arm. The magnolias are in bloom somewhere nearby. The sweet scent comes and goes with the breeze. As Lane crosses her arms to warm herself and the arm that cradles her shoulders tightens, she can't rid herself of the feeling that Rowland Jansen has done something terrible and she let him do it.

BECAUSE THE RIVER is still up, the ambulance stopped just around the bend, and it took a wide turn so it's parked lengthwise. It'll be easier and faster for it to pull out when the time comes. Though the vehicle's lights still flash, the siren has gone silent. Walking on a slight downhill slope toward the river, Lane can see the top of a white truck, Annalee's truck, even though the ambulance stands between it and her.

As they near the river, Mark is a half pace ahead of Lane, and with one arm still wrapped around her, he is coaxing her along now. Her pace has slowed, each step shorter and slower than the last. In her front pocket, her phone vibrates again. And again, she pulls it out, hoping to see Annalee's name. Instead, for the second time, it's Bonnie Wiley. Lane shakes her head at Mark so he'll know it's no one.

"We don't have to go no farther," Mark says. "Can stop right here. In fact, it's better that we do."

Lane dips from under his arm and steps away, shoving him when he reaches for her. Taking slow, careful steps so as not to sink into the muck and silt, she walks beyond the ambulance. A man is sitting inside Annalee's truck, his muddy shoes hanging out the open door. Three patrol cars are parked nearby, one next to the other, each with its front end a safe distance from the water's edge. Men wearing boots are high-stepping it this way through the shallow black water. Here in this spot, when the water is still, it throws a perfect mirror image of the trees along the bank. It's dizzying to see, especially for kids drunk on one too many beers on a hot July afternoon.

Lane takes a few more steps toward the river. Another car is parked behind the farthest patrol car. It's a truck, maybe here to help out in case anyone gets stuck. There are more men in the water. Voices crackle over radios. Other voices grow louder, or they're not growing louder, but Lane is only slowly able to hear them. A group of men, four or five of them, walks together through the shallow water. Behind them, farther downriver, the tracks cross, the span of iron and concrete throwing a heavy shadow on the water below. The men in the water are cradling something. It's a tarp or a stretcher, bright blue. As Lane lunges, a set of hands grabs her from behind.

If she is saying anything, yelling anything, she can't hear herself. She swats at the hands holding her, pushes at them, twists and pulls away. They aren't Mark's hands but a stranger's. Mark has waded out into the water and is talking with the men high-stepping it this direction. They all pause to stare at her. She stops pushing, goes still. He's standing right next to her, almost within arm's reach. It's Rowland, standing at the water's edge. Rowland, who took her home last night. Rowland, who maybe came inside, who maybe she invited into her bed. Rowland, who was maybe walking through her house while her daughters slept right upstairs.

Like the men who are carrying the tarp, Rowland turns to stare at Lane. His face is unshaven. He's wearing the same clothes he wore the night before, and while he is staring in Lane's direction, his eyes don't settle on her. It's as if she isn't there.

"What have you done?" Lane says to him.

Now his eyes focus on her but only for a moment. Then he looks at the ground at her feet, at the river to her left, at the ambulance behind her. It's as if he doesn't know her and doesn't know this place.

"Answer me," she says, louder this time. Everything around her—the trees, the officers, the muddy banks of the river—begins to fade and then disappear. Everything but the men in the river. They must be carrying a body. They must be carrying Annalee. "What have you done here?"

She lunges for Rowland, wants to grab at his shirt, shake him awake until he tells her what he's done to Annalee, but her feet slip from beneath her. They're heavy with mud, and someone is dragging her backward. She falls to one knee. Both hands hit the ground in front of her and sink into the silt.

"God damn you, what did you do?"

"Lane, stop."

It's Mark's voice in her ear. He pulls her up and draws her into his body, wraps his arms around her, presses his mouth to her ear.

"It's not Annalee," he says. And again. "It's not Annalee."

TALLEY

WHEN THE DOOR to Daryl's shed swings open, the sun hits Talley full in the face. She squints, shifts Grandma's chipped plate to one hand, and holds up the other as a shield against the light.

"What are you doing in here?"

It's Annalee's boyfriend, and he's holding the extra key to Daryl's shed that the reverend keeps just in case. It hangs from half a paint stick Daryl got from the hardware store. When Jimmy came to take Annalee on their first date, Mama was happy because Jimmy had a part-time job and had already been accepted into college up in the Northeast. He was planning to play baseball like his dad. Jimmy was the right kind, that's what Mama said. And he was a heap-load better than the characters Annalee had known in Brooklyn.

But Jimmy doesn't look like the right kind now. His hair is

flat like he only just woke up, and his eyes are red where they're supposed to be white. He missed a button on his sleeveless flannel shirt, and his body and head and eyes look to be worn-out—right worn-out. That's what Grandma would say.

"What are you doing in Daryl's shed?" Jimmy says in a sharper voice when Talley doesn't answer him the first time, and he takes a step deeper inside. "You damn well shouldn't be in here."

Clutching the blue-and-white plate that belongs to Grandma, Talley backs away from him. She wants to go home. Annalee must be back at the house because Jimmy is here. Knowing Annalee is home makes Talley feel better, but Daryl isn't here like he's supposed to be and the Little Sisters never came and Susannah Bauer is still gone. Home is a safer place to be.

"Looking for a hoe," Talley says. "Why are *you* here?"

"Got my reasons." Jimmy crosses his arms and stares down on Talley. "Is Daryl around?"

Talley shakes her head. With Jimmy inside, Daryl's shed is much smaller. No matter if she goes left or right, there isn't enough room for her to slip past him, and her hands start to tingle like they do when she sleeps on them funny.

"You seen him today?" Jimmy asks.

Again, Talley shakes her head.

"Then how'd you get in here?"

Talley points at the window. "I needed a hoe."

"Pretty sure your grandpa has a hoe at his place. Besides, you shouldn't be taking things from the shed." He takes another step and blocks out most all the light. "That's stealing, you know?"

"I'm not stealing," Talley says. She doesn't like Jimmy, and she never thought he was the right kind. "Just borrowing."

"What about that?" Jimmy points at the plate Talley has wrapped up in both hands.

"Belongs to my grandma," Talley says, turning a shoulder on

Jimmy so he can't grab hold of the plate. She swallows and clears her throat and wishes he would go away so she could leave.

Talley finding Grandma's plate here in Daryl's shed must mean Daryl is the one who has been taking her food, and thinking about Daryl sneaking around her house in the dark and tricking her into thinking the boys had taken her food makes her stomach ache and her mouth turn dry.

"Well, you shouldn't be here," Jimmy says. "You need to stay clear of that Daryl, you hear me?"

Talley nods and takes a step to the right so she can squeeze between Jimmy and the door, but he slides right, blocking her path. She takes a step left and Jimmy steps left.

"What about my mom?" Jimmy says. He smiles like he was only kidding and backs away, giving her some space. He leans against the doorframe and glances at the parking lot where Miss Hettie's car should be parked.

"Haven't seen her."

Jimmy asks Talley if she's sure and then nods down at her shin. "You better clean that up," he says. "Then let me take you home. Your mama won't like you being here."

Talley looks down at her leg. Blood has dripped along the front where she skinned it crawling through the window. Stooping to reach under the workbench where Daryl keeps his rags, she pulls out a white undershirt covered in grease. She tosses it aside, and the next shirt she pulls out is wet, so wet it drips when Talley lifts it from the pile. She tosses it aside too. On her last try, she pulls another white undershirt from the box, and a blue-and-yellow kerchief falls out with it. Unlike all the other rags, the kerchief has been folded up until it's a perfect square that can almost fit in the palm of one hand. Talley tucks it in her front pocket and uses the white undershirt to wipe the blood from her leg.

"You sure you ain't seen my mom?" Jimmy asks, looking hard into Talley's eyes as if he's checking for signs she's lying.

Talley shakes her head, and still holding Grandma's plate, she slips past Jimmy. She doesn't even care if Mama and Sheriff Ellenton catch her running around where she shouldn't be running around. She doesn't care about her garden anymore or the Little Sisters of the South. She doesn't care anymore about silverware and napkins and boys who stand when she enters a room. She wants to go home and never come here again.

JIMMY'S MOTHER DOESN'T like Mama or Annalee, and that's why no one can know Annalee and Jimmy are still in love. When Miss Hettie called Mama to say her boy would never date the likes of Annalee again, she called the Fieldings butchers and whores. Talley heard Mama telling Grandma Erma all about it as they sat at the kitchen table. Talley didn't know what that meant—butchers and whores—but it definitely wasn't a good thing. Even though Talley and Annalee had a different last name, she was pretty sure Miss Hettie and most everybody else didn't see the difference.

"Hold on there," Jimmy says as Talley squeezes past him. He drapes an arm around her shoulders, trapping her. "Let me take you home. You shouldn't be walking around here by yourself."

Talley jerks away so she won't feel his damp underarm. He stinks too, smells worse than Grandpa ever does. Her chin is starting to quiver in that way it does right before she cries.

"Annalee's in trouble because of you," Talley says as soon as she's outside the shed.

"What do you mean?" Jimmy says, dropping the key to Daryl's shed and grabbing for Talley's arm. His eyes are wide now like something jumped out and scared him.

"She's in trouble for being out all night," Talley says, and walks away as fast as she can.

"What do you know about it?" Jimmy jogs a few steps ahead of Talley, then swings around so he can look her straight on.

"I saw her leave last night," Talley says, darting to the right.

Jimmy darts with her, blocking her path to the road. His eyes have changed. They've narrowed, and he stares down on Talley. The quivering in her chin has spread to her lips, another sure sign she's about to cry.

"Where did she go?"

"She went to be with you," Talley shouts.

Jimmy grabs her by the shoulder, and this time he gets a good hold on her. His fingers hurt where they dig into her arm. She jerks hard, stumbles backward, falls on her hind end, and Grandma's blue-and-white china plate flies into the air. It tumbles over the freshly mowed grass and cracks when it hits the edge of the sidewalk. Crawling on hands and knees, Talley grabs the two largest pieces. She tries to stand, but Jimmy leans over her, not letting her get to her feet. The quivering turns into crying, and holding one half of the plate in each hand, she lowers her head and tries not to make any sound.

"You telling me you seen her leave last night, and she still ain't home?"

"Well, she'll be home now," Talley says, wiping at her eyes before she looks up at Jimmy. Annalee isn't always nice to Talley, not like Susannah Bauer, but she's glad Annalee's home again. Mama and Grandma will be happy too, and they can all have a nice supper.

"Why do you think that?"

"Because you're home, you're here."

Jimmy reaches down with one hand. Still holding Grandma's plate tight against her body, Talley grabs hold of Jimmy. He gives a yank, and she pops onto her feet. She wants to run, but that'll make Jimmy grab for her again, and if he gets hold of her a second time, he might not let go.

"I didn't see Annalee last night," he says. "I swear. I told the police, the sheriff too. If she's gone, it don't have nothing to do with me. Hand to God, I ain't seen her."

"That's not true," Talley says, starting to cry again. She wants to pound her head like Daryl sometimes does because her thoughts are all jumbled up now and she can't straighten them out. "She was with you and now you're home and so she should be home too."

Jimmy shakes his head. "No, Talley. She wasn't with me. And she ain't home. Least not according to the police. I think something real bad has happened."

"I know something bad happened," Talley says. She takes a few backward steps. "Daryl told me all about you. He told me everything."

Jimmy grabs Talley by both shoulders this time. He pulls her close and lifts until only her toes touch the ground. He isn't only angry. He's scared. "Daryl told you what?"

"You lied to her," Talley says, twisting right and left, but Jimmy holds on tight, his fingers pinching her shoulders. She starts to feel dizzy. "You told Annalee you loved her and were going to run away with her and marry her, but that was never true, and your mom called us butchers and whores."

Jimmy lowers Talley until her feet are firm on the ground again.

"Daryl said you're a liar," Talley says, stumbling a few steps. "You won't marry Annalee, not ever. He told me and I told Annalee. Just last night, I told her you're leaving to go away to school without her and will never marry her. Daryl said he knows what you did."

Jimmy drops his hands from Talley's shoulders, and his arms hang at his sides. "What did he mean by that?" Jimmy says.

"Annalee isn't supposed to love you anymore," Talley says, sliding one foot off to the side.

When Jimmy doesn't grab for her, Talley slides the other foot over to meet the first. She blinks, her vision narrowing on her like she's looking through the cardboard tube that's inside the paper towels. Jimmy's eyes don't follow her. Instead he continues to stare at an empty spot in the grass.

"I'm going to tell Mama that Annalee's gone because of you." And she runs.

DARYL

7 days before Susannah disappeared

TODAY IS SATURDAY, the day Susannah is due to work one last time at the Fielding Mansion. As I wait all day for her to come borrow tools, I pace in front of my shed and my heart beats faster each time a car slows near the church entrance. Hour after hour passes, and I stop imagining how Susannah will look and smell and sound and start to pound one fist in the palm of my hand. Over and over I pound until I stop feeling it. When she never comes to borrow a rake or the wheelbarrow, I go to the Food Lion.

Listening and watching for her and rubbing my sore hand, I walk the aisles, forcing myself to take slow, steady steps so no one will take notice of me, but she never comes to the store either. Last time she stopped by the church, two Saturdays ago, she promised she'd come one more time to say good-bye. When I finally leave the store, I go home to my apartment and write down on my list of things about Susannah that she didn't come this Saturday like she was supposed to, and I write that I should watch for her again next Saturday. Then, as the sun begins to set, I put my lists away and leave my apartment because while I watch for Susannah only on the first and third Saturdays of the month, I have begun to watch for Annalee every night.

I could wait for Annalee where the dirt road meets the paved county road because this is the way she'll come when she sneaks out again, but instead I watch for the mother. I watch for her first because Annalee won't leave the house until the mother is home. I park on the side street within sight of the bar where the mother works and sit on a picnic table outside the bar's side entrance. For three nights in a row, this is where I have waited and watched for Annalee's mother.

A can of bug spray sits on the ground because there are always bugs. Day or night, no matter the season. This is one of the first things I learned about Florida when I moved back. Tonight, it's the no-see-ums. That's what Mother called them. They hover in the air, clouds of them. They swarm near my head and light unseen on my skin. I would cry from their sting when I was small and slap at my arms and ankles. Mother would look me over and see nothing. Stop that crying, she would say. See. Look there. Nothing. You ain't got nothing to cry about. Wayne, before he was sent away, would tell me to put on socks and not sit near the trees. Giving the can a good shake, because that's what I've seen others do, I spray my arms and feet, the back of my neck, and I wait.

Annalee's mother is the first to leave, has been all three nights. She wears her hair loose tonight. This is where Annalee's blond hair comes from, though the mother isn't as slender and slight as Annalee. She wouldn't be as soft to the touch. The other nights, she walked out alone and left in her car, never seeing me. But tonight, the man she works for follows her through the door. He is much taller than me, and his hair is much lighter. I know him because he is married to Miss Hettie at the church, and he's the reason she works sunup to sundown, he and Annalee's mother together are the reason.

Annalee's mother doesn't know Rowland Jansen is there until he slides up behind her, blocking the light that hangs over the side door and throwing a shadow on her. She swings around, startled by him.

"You need to go back inside, Rowland," the mother says.

"No one's here." He steps closer, leans down to look her straight on. "No one'll see."

Annalee's mother, her back to the car, pushes him away with one hand, not a real push, but more of a touch. "It's not going to happen."

"He never asks about you, you know."

"Who?"

"Mark," the man says. "When he comes in and you're not here, he never asks about you. Nothing."

She tries to turn away from him, but he stretches out his arms, traps her by placing both hands on the hood. She is wedged now between him and the car, and she can't move. I think I might practice this later in my apartment even though I hope to never get so close to one of the girls. Rowland Jansen tilts his head and dips his chin as he looks down on her.

"It will never happen again," she says. Her voice is different. It's hard, each word coming loud and quick. "Never."

She says that because it has happened at least once before.

And she's angry with him. What he's said has hurt her, telling her some man doesn't ask about her. He must be a man she cares for. Rowland Jansen is trying to hurt Annalee's mother. Annalee is kind and good, and this would make her angry, so it makes me angry too. The mother jabs a finger at Rowland Jansen to be sure he heard her and then she ducks under one of his outstretched arms and grabs hold of the car door's handle. She won't look him in the eyes. She is waiting, hoping he will go away.

When the man finally leaves to go back inside, he pulls open the door and a flash of light spills into the alley. If I were a different sort of man, I might follow him and warn him not to be unkind to Annalee's mother ever again. But I'm not, so instead I blink and hold up a hand to block the brightness that is gone the moment the door closes. The alley alongside the bar is dark again except for the small light over the door. It shines on Annalee's mother, throwing shadows on her cheeks and neck that make her face too long and too narrow. She looks toward the car's rear bumper and then toward the bar's side door. It's as if she thinks she's heard something unusual. She stands still, one hand on the car door. She doesn't see me sitting here on the picnic table. If she were to listen, she'd hear me inhaling and exhaling, and if she would bother, she'd smell the bug spray on my skin.

Sometimes a woman will pause at this moment. She'll think maybe a door has opened somewhere nearby, hear some sound, scratch at some tickle on the back of her neck. She'll pause, and because I listen, I know she holds her breath. I hold mine too, wondering what will happen if she sees me or hears me. And at last she'll exhale, usually laugh quietly to herself, and turn and walk away. I will exhale too and sometimes close my eyes so I'll remember the sight of her better. But the mother doesn't bother with me on this third night. She starts her car, backs up, and drives away.

After the mother is gone, I walk to my car, don't run, and follow her only as far as the intersection where the asphalt meets the dirt. Though she is well ahead of me, I know she has turned down the road leading to her house. I drive on past the intersection, do a tight U-turn, pull into the flat ditch, flip off my lights, and wait.

LANE

LANE SWATS AT Mark so he'll let go of her. The river has left behind inches of watery silt, and when her feet come to settle on the ground again, they sink up to her ankles. Mark's arms loosen from around her and fall away. Mud drips from her hands and down each leg. The sun has broken through the treetops. Here and there, men, police officers, hold up a hand to shield their eyes or pull a set of sunglasses from their front pockets.

"It's not Annalee," Mark says again.

The men carrying the tarp walk past, four of them. They step in tandem as they move slowly, steadily from the deeper water onto the spongy floor of the floodplain. Once they reach the spot where the cars are safely parked, more men slide up and take some of the weight. One of them presses a hand in the center of Rowland's chest when he tries to grab hold. Two men inside the ambulance reach for the tarp, and taking care to keep it level, they lift it inside.

"Who?" Lane whispers. And as quickly as she asks, she slaps a hand over her mouth. "Not Susannah," she says.

Mark shakes his head. "Hettie Jansen."

"She's . . ."

This time, he nods.

Lane squints into the sun filtering through the trees. The slivers of light reflect off the water, spread like glitter. Her neck begins to itch where sweat has gathered. The itch grows until she wants to claw at her skin. She leans forward, braces herself with her hands to her knees because Hettie is dead and the fear of what that means for Annalee is making Lane dizzy.

"Did you even know?" Lane asks. "Did you know Hettie was missing too?"

Two victims didn't necessarily indicate a pattern, but it was something to hang a story on, a hook. Lane had done it herself more than once. Two women missing, one of them now dead, is enough to solidify the unimaginable. What had only loomed, shapeless and distant just an hour ago, is now close enough to touch.

"Don't go assuming these things are connected," Mark says, resting a hand on Lane's back and telling her to take deep breaths.

"But they were both here. Obviously, they're connected."

"We need to get you out of here," Mark says, taking Lane by the arm as she straightens, and he signals to one of his deputies. The man wears a uniform like Mark's, but he's likely not yet shaving. "Olin here is going to drive you back to the house."

"What aren't you telling me?" Lane says, jerking away. "Why is Rowland here? Did you tell him to come? Does he know something?"

Mark tips his head at the deputy and ignores Lane's question. "Take Miss Fielding home, please."

"Answer me," Lane shouts. "What aren't you telling me?"

Mark walks away without saying anything and twice looks back to make sure she isn't following. This must be why Mark was asking all those questions about Rowland on the way over here. He was wondering if Rowland had been inside Lane's house, walking freely from room to room. He must think all of this is somehow Rowland's doing.

"Ma'am," the deputy says, taking hold of Lane's arm.

Rowland is leaning against one of the patrol cars and is bent at the waist, his hands resting on his knees. He wears a baseball cap backward, same as he always does. His hair hangs down his neck and is curling up with the humidity. A man has squatted next to him and is taking his pulse with two fingers to his wrist. Mark joins them, and the officers from the Waddell Police Department who carried the tarp head back into the river.

"Where is she, Rowland?" Lane shouts, her arm still hanging from the deputy's hand. "Where is Annalee?"

The night three months ago, when Lane and Rowland were together, comes back to her in flashes, often when she's waking first thing in the morning. She's told Rowland more than once, apologized, really, that she doesn't remember much of that night but knows it shouldn't have happened and is certain it never will again. But her lies do nothing to keep those moments from sneaking up on her. The feel of his hands, his lips. The weight of his body. The fullness of his shoulders under her hands. Next time one of those moments wakes her, she'll have to wonder if it's a memory from that night three months ago or if she brought him into her home again last night, a mistake that may have led her here today.

"Ask him, Mark," she yells, swatting at the deputy until he drops her arm. "Why is there blood in my daughter's truck?"

The young deputy steps in front of Lane so she can't see Rowland and again directs her to leave. Men who are nearby turn to look at her. A few exchange glances as if preparing to deal with her. Lane backs away. To her left, someone has closed the ambulance doors. The men wearing boots are walking downriver where the shallow water has spilled into lower ground, one within reach of another so they'll not miss anything. The banks there are clay, and they'll be taking care where they step. Upriver, limestone lines the riverbanks, rising steep on either side—large slabs worn round and smooth by years of the river washing over them. Still more men, and one woman too, stand in the clearing among the cars, some taking notes. Others walk among the upland trees, shoulder to shoulder.

"It's better you're at home, ma'am," the deputy says, waving off the others because he thinks he has Lane under control. "Annalee might call you there. Sheriff Ellenton will see to Mr. Jansen."

"I'm not leaving here until my daughter is found."

It's a crime scene now. She saw enough of them during her days reporting to recognize it. They'll force Lane to stand at a distance if they allow her to stay at all, so before Mark can come back and insist again she leave, she walks behind the ambulance where he won't see her. They'll be marking off a grid, picking through the brush and roots where they found Hettie. They'll be looking for clues as to what happened to her and for any further trace of Annalee.

"Has anyone called the Tallahassee department?" Lane asks the young deputy.

"Ma'am?"

"The Tallahassee Police Department? Did anyone call them?"

Someone would call Tallahassee if they suspected a connection between Susannah and Hettie Jansen and possibly Annalee.

"I believe so, ma'am."

"And what about Rowland Jansen?" Lane asks. "How did he end up here so quick?"

"I couldn't say, ma'am."

Keeping herself behind the ambulance where Mark won't see her and send her away, Lane watches the men who are searching downriver until the ambulance's engine starts up. The driver waves at her to step aside, and he pulls away without turning on the sirens or lights. She can see Rowland again, and Mark, who is still talking with him, and they can see her. In her front pocket, her phone vibrates. She turns her back on Mark and looks at the screen. It's Bonnie Wiley again.

"What is it, Bonnie?" Lane says. "I can't talk right now."

"Mama."

It isn't Bonnie Wiley on the other end of the phone.

"Talley? Is that you, Talley?"

The soft voice is what finally makes Lane cry, but not in a way she ever has before. Not like she did when she called her husband and heard another woman's voice instead. Not like she did when she offered to stay despite it all and Kyle said he would rather she not. She doesn't choke on her sobs or shake or bury her face in her hands. She only has energy enough for the tears.

"I need your help, Mama."

TALLEY

TALLEY STANDS IN Miss Bonnie's foyer, holds the telephone to her ear, and tries not to inhale through her nose because the house is filled with a heavy perfume. Miss Bonnie's telephone is not like any Talley has ever seen. It has a black twisted cord attached to the part she talks into so she can't walk into another room to get away from Miss Bonnie.

"What's wrong?" Mama says, almost yells. It's the same voice she uses when Talley calls her at work and it's after Talley's bedtime. It's an angry voice Mama says isn't meant to sound angry. Calls that come at an unexpected time scare Mama. She needs for Talley to say straightaway that she's safe. Mama is more alone now than she's ever been, and everything is on her and up to her and she doesn't mean to sound angry. Still, the sound of Mama's voice and Miss Bonnie standing so close and worrying Jimmy Jansen is going to find her make Talley cry all over again.

"Why are you calling from Bonnie's phone, Talley? What's happened?"

AS TALLEY RAN from the church, Jimmy called out after her. Over and over, he shouted he wasn't with Annalee last night. And the more he shouted, the faster Talley ran.

"You can't believe that Daryl," Jimmy yelled. "I wasn't with her. I promise."

But Talley didn't believe Jimmy. And she knew Annalee was a liar. She'd lie about things that didn't even matter, like saying a friend gave her the socks she was wearing as a gift when Talley knew Mama just bought the new socks. Annalee was a liar, and so was Jimmy. As hard and as fast as she could, Talley ran across the church lawn. Once she reached the other side of the street, she leaped over the curb and turned to look back. Jimmy was still shouting out to her as he pulled open the door to his car and jumped inside.

Talley ran as far as the county road, keeping to the backs of buildings and staying off the streets, before she slowed to a walk. She had been running and crying all at the same time, and she had to stop so she could take at least one full breath. Bending forward, she rested her elbows on her knees, and afraid to look out at the road, she stared at the ground instead. Once she got home, everything would be fine again. She just had to keep running.

When she reached the houses built to look like Grandma and Grandpa's, Talley was almost safe. These people were neighbors but weren't very neighborly. That's what Grandma was always saying, and Mama would say a person could hardly blame them. They were younger, new families who hadn't always lived in Waddell, not like the regular customers Mama served at the bar. These newer families, seeking a small town where they could raise a family, afford a home, escape the traffic, didn't like seeing their town mentioned alongside the school for boys and Neil Fielding.

Talley forced herself to look left and right to be sure no one was following her. There wasn't a single car anywhere as far as she could see, so she ran to the other side of the asphalt road. Once across, she started down into the ditch that would lead her into the backyard of the first house, being careful where she stepped because the grass was overgrown and still wet from last night's rain. Holding her side that had started to ache, she imagined she was one of the boys who ran. They must have hidden behind bushes just like Talley and peeked out from around houses and sheds to see who was chasing them. They must have been scared, but they did it anyway, and Talley could do it too. The hum of tires on asphalt made her stop and turn. A car, a small black car like Jimmy's, was turning off Highway 90 and headed her way.

Holding the two pieces of Grandma's plate tight to her chest, Talley ran down the ditch, slipping and stumbling at its lowest point, up the other side, through a hedge of pink oleanders, and into the first backyard. She squatted there among the tall plants, listened, but the hum of tires was gone. As fast as her legs would take her, she walked across the yard.

When she neared the edge of the lawn, Talley stopped and leaned forward to look around the side of the house. The small black car was there, rolling slowly down the road that would lead to Grandma and Grandpa's. She pulled back, but she'd have to look again, no matter how scared she was. The boys who ran were brave. They ran without knowing where they were running. They didn't have food or water and didn't know which way to go. They were brave, and she could be too. She counted to five, squeezed her hands into fists, and looked. The black car was gone, and the tightness in her stomach and jaw loosened. Running through the next yard and the next, she paused at each to look between the houses. By the fourth house, the last before she reached Grandma and Grandpa's, she heard Jimmy's voice.

"You can't believe him."

The voice wasn't loud because he was calling out from inside his car. He must have reached Grandma and Grandpa's house and turned around, because when Talley saw the car again, it was headed the other way.

"I didn't do nothing."

He was out on the road, shouting as he drove. Leaning against the fourth house, Talley hugged herself and pinched her eyes closed. She wasn't going to be afraid.

"Whatever he told you, it's a lie. I didn't do nothing."

His voice continued to fade, and once it was all the way gone, Talley ran across the last yard. When she saw the crumbling walls where the slaves once lived, she had made it home.

AS SHE WALKED past the tabby ruins that looked to be made of concrete but for the chunks of oyster shells trapped inside, Talley took care not to step on or even touch any part of them. Before the television began showing her picture and saying she was missing, Susannah Bauer had said the ruins deserved more attention. People should always remember this place, and she was going to see to that. What she really said was she was going to damn well see to that, and she had smiled and winked as she said it so Talley wouldn't tell anyone Susannah had cursed. That's what Talley liked best about Susannah and what she missed most. Susannah thought about other people more than she thought about herself. But ten days ago, Susannah disappeared, and now everyone Talley knew was slipping in after her.

Setting down the two halves of Grandma's plate, Talley reached in her front pocket and pulled out the kerchief she found in Daryl's shed. At some point between the church and home, she'd lost her other kerchief, so she gave this new one a good shake, folded it into a big triangle, pulled it across her forehead, and tied it off in back. It was exactly like the kerchiefs Susannah always wore—bright blue with golden stripes. Putting it on would for sure make Talley as smart and strong as Susannah, and she wasn't quite as scared anymore of what might happen next.

Before walking up the path toward the back of the house, Talley looked and listened for any sign Jimmy was still out there somewhere. She heard nothing and saw nothing, but that also meant Mama and Sheriff Ellenton hadn't come back yet. No cars were parked where they should have been parked. Grandma wasn't working in her garden or taking in the laundry. Annalee wasn't running out the door, late to work and in a hurry. The house was quiet, and just as it had scared her to see the church quiet and empty, it scared her to see her own home the same way. Talley was ready to tell Mama and Sheriff Ellenton every secret she had, and no matter what Jimmy had been yelling from his car, she was going to tell all about him too.

Halfway up the path that was slick and muddy like the ditches, the limestone fence post stood off to Talley's left. Grandma's laundry still hung on the line and would be dry by now. Talley leapt over a puddle and ran toward the river. While no one was around to see, she would grab the tub of food she'd left for the boys. No one would ever know what she'd done, and she'd never leave food for them again.

There were no boys anymore, hadn't been since the school closed. A long time ago, they had been real. They'd run through those very trees and along the river right over there. Mama had left food for them so they'd be safe, and probably Mama was alone like Talley. Probably Mama didn't have any friends back then either. But the boys are gone now, and Daryl had been taking the food all along. She didn't know why he would do that, and she should have been angry about him sneaking around in the dark and lying to her and pretending the boys were still out there running, but she wasn't. She was sad. She'd never go in the attic again in hopes of seeing one of those boys, something she dreamed of even though some part of her knew all along they were never out there.

Like it was when they first moved to Florida, Talley would have no friends because the boys were gone and Susannah was gone and Daryl too. The thought of being alone made Talley's head hurt and her stomach ache. As she neared the fence post, she slowed and then stopped. Instead of finding the tub where she'd left it, the fence post was empty.

Dropping to her knees, she parted the grass where she'd found the tub before. She crawled around the post twice, searching the tall grass, scrambling forward as fast as she could, but the white tub filled with food for the boys was gone. Talley stood, and as she backed slowly away, she looked out into the cypress trees and black gums that edged the river and at the blood grass, wild azalea, and wax myrtle that hid the chain link fence. Someone was out there and took her food right in the light of day. She wasn't sad anymore. She was afraid.

"Daryl?" she said in little more than a whisper. "You out there?" And then she thought about the man, whoever he was, people thought was taking the blond girls. "You out there, Daryl?"

She stood still, not letting any part of her body move, and listened. When Daryl didn't answer her, she backed all the way across the drive and didn't turn until she neared the house. Still carrying the two halves of Grandma's plate, Talley went to step onto the first concrete stair that led to the side door but stopped and pulled her foot back before it touched down. Bits of wood were scattered on the top step, and the door leading inside stood open a few inches.

When they first moved to Waddell, Mama said most kids didn't have to worry, not for real, about broken windows or doors or strangers walking right up to the house. But now that they were living with Grandpa Neil, they did have to worry about those things. Talley had to be older than her years and had to, simply had to, understand that.

"Grandma," Talley said, leaning toward the door but not taking a single step up the stairs. "Annalee?" She tried to yell, but she couldn't get enough air.

"You in there, Grandma?"

NOW, AS TALLEY stands in Miss Bonnie's foyer and holds a black phone to her ear and presses a forearm under her nose because the smell of Miss Bonnie's house is making her queasy, she wonders why Grandma never answered when Talley called out to her. And Talley thought Annalee would be home, but Annalee didn't answer either. Now she wonders if Jimmy Jansen driving by and that broken door have something to do with Annalee still not being home.

"Someone broke the kitchen door," Talley says to Mama. "You said never go inside if the door is left open." Talley's chest is shaking, and tears are running down her cheeks and into the creases alongside her nose. She can't be brave anymore, not even with Susannah's kerchief.

"Talley, please, I can't hear you. What is it?"

Talley can't get any more words out. Miss Bonnie's front door stands open, and all her curtains are open too, and twice a small black car rolls past the house, first going one way and then the other. Talley backs away from the open door as far as the phone's cord will allow. As if she's angry, Miss Bonnie snatches the phone from Talley's hand.

"Something is amiss over at your place," Miss Bonnie says in a loud voice Mama is sure to hear. "The child says it's the door there off the kitchen."

Miss Bonnie pauses. Reaching into the pocket of her long housedress, she pulls out a wadded-up tissue and hands it to Talley.

"It's been all broken up is what. She says somebody's been messing about with it, left it to stand open."

Another pause and Miss Bonnie motions for Talley to wipe her nose.

"Lord if I know," Miss Bonnie says as Talley unravels the tissue and blows her nose into it. "And Lord knows why this child come to my house."

Miss Bonnie stretches the cord as she walks across the foyer, opens a small drawer in a long, narrow table, and pulls out two fresh tissues.

"No, it's just the one here with me. The little one. Says she called out to Erma but didn't get no answer."

She hands Talley the tissues and waves a hand at her whole face so Talley will dry her eyes and cheeks. Talley does what Miss Bonnie tells her to and feels the littlest bit better with a clean face.

"Good Lord, no," Bonnie says. "You call the police yourself. I wouldn't dare get so involved. That mother of yours will blame me for sure."

Holding the phone with one hand, Miss Bonnie uses the other

to lift Talley's chin. She looks down on Talley's face, brushes her hair from her eyes, and tucks it back under the kerchief Talley is wearing and gives a nod.

"For heaven's sake," Miss Bonnie says, "leave the girl here for now. Just see to your house and then you come see to this child."

DARYL

7 days before Susannah disappeared

FOR THREE NIGHTS, I've sat on the picnic table outside the bar
where the mother works and then have followed her as far as the
intersection where the dirt road meets the asphalt. The other
nights, I've waited two hours, talked to Annalee from my car,
tried to coax her from her house, and when she never snuck out,
I eventually went home. Tonight, I hope to see something more
of her, to find out some new thing about her life so I can breathe
easy again, at least for a short while.

While I spent all day waiting for Susannah Bauer to come to
the church, I made myself think of Annalee. I drew maps of her
house and the roads to and from it. I wrote that the attic door in
Annalee's house is half as tall as a door should be and is never
locked. I learned this from Talley. She has started going to the

attic to watch for the boys who run because she thinks they are taking her food.

I have done the same thing for Susannah Bauer, for all the girls. I keep the maps and notes because they soothe me and so that when I must leave, I'll always remember them. For eight years, ever since Mother died, this is what I've done. I know I can never let the girls notice me, no matter the spark I feel in that moment when their eyes land on mine and they see me, really see me. Because if they do see me standing somewhere nearby in the shadows of an alley or pushing a cart in the grocery store, they tell a father or boyfriend about the strange man following them and I must take my notes and maps and go. Only Susannah is different, because she will be the one to leave. I don't have to be so careful with Susannah, but with all the others, I do. I hope I never have to move from Waddell, because I don't know where else my brother might be.

As I sit in my car at the intersection where the dirt meets the asphalt and wait for Annalee, I close my eyes and try to calm myself by thinking of the silence and warmth of her truck. At first it works, but as one hour turns into two, I begin to slap the steering wheel with my hands. I beat on it and shout out until the center of each palm aches. I slap my forehead, beat my fists on the dashboard, rock side to side, and knock my head against the glass. With the windows rolled up, the heat builds and will suffocate me if Annalee doesn't come soon. I fall back in my seat, and as I call out her name, two white spots appear out of the darkness.

Inhaling and exhaling heavy through my nose, I still my hands, use my shirtsleeve to wipe the sweat and spit from my mouth. The lights are tiny and dim, but they grow larger and brighter, and as they reach me and I think I'll have to duck, they swing away, off to the driver's right. I start my engine and follow the taillights of a white truck.

LANE

IN SEPTEMBER OF Lane's eighth-grade year, her class studied the historic sites of Milton County. Her teacher, Mr. Wolfson, was new that year and didn't realize his student, Lane Fielding, was the same Fielding who lived in the Fielding Mansion or that she was the daughter of Neil Fielding, the man who ran the school for boys.

Slavery here in Florida didn't end with the Civil War, Mr. Wolfson said. Not really. Convict leasing replaced it, and when a cry went up to exclude children from the horrors of this practice, the school for boys in Waddell was conceived. Children once sentenced to convict-leasing camps were instead sentenced to the school, and the land-owning men who could no longer survive on the economies of the changed world began to take their slaves a new way. Directly behind the school for boys, Mr. Wolfson said as he pointed to a map taped to the room's back wall, you will find the Fielding Mansion, where some of the school's earliest students, or rather inmates, were made to work.

Mr. Wolfson didn't know Lane lived in the house that had bullet holes splattered across its front, put there by Union soldiers, or that she was the Fielding girl who had been taken the year before and only returned after God knows what was done to her. But at the end of the two-week-long series of lectures, which included photos of Lane's house, Mr. Wolfson asked if Lane had anything to add. At some point, he had figured out she was one of those Fieldings. No relation, Lane said, though everyone, even Mr. Wolfson, knew she was lying.

"You wait here," Mark says, stopping his car at the side entrance to Lane's house. He's changed into dry shoes, but his pant legs are still damp from the river. "I'll have a look around, then we'll go get Talley."

On the road behind them, a sheriff's car slows and parks at the curb outside Bonnie Wiley's house, sent there by Mark as he and Lane left the river.

"Absolutely not," Lane says. "Talley will stay at Bonnie's for now."

Mark nods as if he understands that one death makes the possibility of another all the more real. Lane won't have Talley anywhere near it.

"Good enough," he says. "But you stay put."

Lane waits as Mark walks around the front of the car and up the three steps to the side door before she gets out and follows.

"You do this?" he says, shaking his head at her but not sending her back to the car. He nods down at the chipped doorframe and scattered bits of wood. "Break this lock?"

"Of course not."

There's a tightening in Lane's stomach like the one she feels when driving over the top of a hill too fast.

"Didn't even bother trying to hide the mess," Mark says.

"It was probably Annalee." Lane pushes past him, certain now she'll find Annalee inside. Annalee would be one to lose her keys, and she'd be one to break into the house with a crowbar or a hammer and leave the mess for someone else.

Once in the kitchen, Mark grabs Lane by the arm to stop her from running into the foyer and presses a finger to his lips so she won't call out to Annalee.

"Erma and Neil home?" he says.

"Should be," Lane says, matching Mark's quiet voice as she follows him into the foyer.

They hear Erma before they see her. She sits in one of the two straight-backed chairs on either side of the credenza. Her head is tipped back, her eyes are closed, and the family Bible rests on her chest. Each breath rattles as she exhales. Mark sets the Bible on the table, and, motioning for Lane to stay put, he disappears into Neil's room.

"Mother," Lane says, squatting next to Erma's chair. "It's me. You need to wake up."

Erma's eyelids flutter open. She looks past Lane as if expecting to see someone else in the foyer. "Laney? Is that Laney?"

"Yes, Erma, it's me and Mark."

At the mention of his name, Mark walks into the foyer and waves for Lane and Erma to follow him back into Neil's room. Again telling them all to stay put, he leaves to check the rest of the house.

"Did you find Annalee?" Erma says, letting Lane guide her.

"No, Mother," Lane says. "But someone broke through the kitchen door. I need you to listen to me. Who broke in through the door?"

Erma shakes her head and glances around the room as if it's unfamiliar to her.

"Think hard," Lane says, touching Erma's shoulder so she'll focus on Lane. "What do you remember?"

"She was outside," Erma says. "Didn't you see all them pictures?"

From his chair, Neil is fumbling with his glasses while at the same time reaching for the remote that has fallen to the floor. Lane grabs it and hands it to him.

"What do you mean?" she says. "What pictures? Was Annalee outside?"

Neil points the remote at the television, pokes at it, shakes it. "Goddamned worthless thing," he says.

Erma holds on to the back of the sofa as she makes her way toward one of the windows. When Lane was a child, Neil never allowed hands on the upholstery. Have some Goddamned respect, he would say. His tone now is the same as it was then, and it ignites the same fear Lane felt as a child, except now her fear is for her daughters.

"Erma, please," Lane says. "Was Annalee here?"

"No," Erma says. "That Bonnie Wiley was here."

"Bonnie was here inside the house?" Lane says.

"Not inside," Erma says, yanking open a set of drapes. Two clothespins pop off and fall to the floor. "Didn't you see?"

"Leave them draperies be," Neil says, scooting to the edge of his seat. "You've all but ruined them."

Lane rests a hand on Neil's shoulder so he'll not try to stand. "Bonnie is the one who called me," she says to Erma. "She and Talley together, they called me from Bonnie's house."

"I told her to stay upstairs," Erma says.

"You told who?" Lane is beginning to shake. It's impatience working its way out. And more of that childhood fear. "You told Annalee to stay upstairs?"

"No, Talley," Erma says. "I told her to keep herself upstairs because Bonnie was here, hollering and making a fuss. Where is Talley?"

"Erma, you need to tell me what happened here," Lane says.

"The pictures," Erma says. "Didn't you see them pictures?"

Waving Erma away from the windows, Lane stoops to pick up the clothespins. "What pictures?" she says, drawing the drapes shut. "What are you talking about?"

Erma yanks at one of the drapes, pulling it from Lane's hands. "They was right there," she says, jabbing a finger at the window. "One was hanging right there. And there was another in that window there. And every other window."

Lane stares down on the window.

"How are all them pictures gone?" Erma says, dropping onto the sofa.

"Did you open this?" Lane asks.

The window she and Erma have been looking out has been unlocked and the bottom pane pushed up a few inches.

IN HER PERSONAL life, Lane was never much good at knowing which details mattered. She overlooked Kyle's late nights, his cell phone that was always flipped over so she couldn't see who was calling him, his angry answers to her simple questions. But as a reporter, she always knew what details mattered most. The open windows matter.

"And what about this one?" she says, throwing open the drapes on the next window. Like the first, it has been unlocked and opened a few inches. "Did either of you open this one?"

Still sitting on the sofa, Erma shakes her head. "No," she says, crossing her arms as if Lane has frightened her.

"Damn sure wasn't me," Neil says, pushing himself up and out of his chair. "It was that Mark Ellenton. He done it."

Overhead, Mark's footsteps cross from one end of the hallway to the other. He's checking each room. As he continues, Lane checks the rest of the windows in Neil's room, and then the parlor, and lastly, the dining room and her bedroom. She's certain of it. Those open windows mean something. After five minutes have passed, Mark's footsteps hit the stairs, and he reappears in the doorway of Neil's room.

"What are you doing in my house, son?" Neil says, shuffling around his chair in his stocking feet until he's facing Mark. He's confused, has forgotten twenty years have passed since Mark was last in this house.

"I'm here looking for Annalee, sir," Mark says, and shakes his head at Lane, signaling he found nothing. "And I'm interested in who tore up the door off your kitchen. You know anything about that? Anybody giving you trouble these days?"

Neil's bottom lip pops out. He lifts his chin but says nothing.

"I don't think they saw anything," Lane says. "But look at this." She pushes aside the drape so Mark can see one of the open windows. "When you were in here before, did you open this?"

"Tell him about them pictures," Erma says.

Mark walks across the room and squats before the single pane of glass that's been pushed open a few inches. He leans in but doesn't touch it as Erma tells him about the dozen or more pictures Bonnie Wiley taped in every window.

"That one too," Lane says, pointing to the next window. "But none of the rest. They're all closed and locked."

Groaning as he stands, Mark shakes out his one bad knee. "I'm guessing Bonnie changed her mind about them pictures and gathered them up," he says to Erma. "We'll look into it." And then he rests a hand on the small of Lane's back. "Come join me in the kitchen, would you?"

"We never open our windows," Lane says, not moving from her spot. "Never. They are always locked. The doors too."

"Didn't think to open no windows," Neil says. "Air is on."

"It's them reporters make us pin our drapes closed," Erma says. "Make us lock everything up too."

"Yes, ma'am," Mark says. "I do understand. Lane? The kitchen?"

Once in the kitchen, Mark pulls out a chair, but Lane refuses to sit.

"Whatever it is, just tell me," she says. "I want to go pick up Talley."

Lane and Mark had been right to leave Talley with Bonnie Wiley and the deputies, but now Lane needs to see her and touch and hold her. The need is sudden because those windows mean something bad has come right here to the house. She wants to run from the kitchen, down the drive, and across the road, and Mark must see it in her because he grabs her by the wrist.

"Erma and Neil telling the truth?" Mark says, holding tight.

"I assume so," Lane says, tugging against him. "Don't imagine either one of them could open a window even if they wanted to."

"Talley? Annalee?" Mark loosens his fingers from around her wrist. "Window could have been open for a while."

"Annalee never goes in that room. And Talley knows better."

"Using the attic fan lately?" Mark asks. "Maybe Erma or Neil opened the windows for the draw."

"Even when we do run it," Lane says, turning toward the door, "we don't open the windows anymore."

Mark takes a few quick steps and grabs Lane's wrist again before she touches the doorknob. "You notice anything missing?"

Fingerprints. Mark will want to take fingerprints from the knob and doesn't want Lane ruining them. This is another thing she should have known, but she's on the other side of the story now.

"So much clutter," Lane says. "Not sure I'd notice if anything were gone, but I don't think so." She steps away from the door. The windows do mean something, and Mark isn't telling her what.

"It's likely nothing," Mark says, pulling out a chair for her again. "My guess is Neil opened the windows ages ago. And Bonnie was snooping around outside, so maybe Erma messed with them."

"But we do check," Lane says. Her fear begins to grow. He's going to tell her something. There's something about those windows. "Neil is scared. Almost all the time. He still has his pride, so he won't let on." She talks quickly, so Mark won't say it. Whatever it is. "He's the one who insisted on pinning the drapes. He's always having Erma and me check that things are locked up. Only way to keep him calm some days. Those windows were not open until today."

"All right. Then I'm guessing whoever came in through that door is likely the one who opened them. Picked Neil's room because it doesn't face the road. Easy access off the porch."

Lane drops into the chair and rests her hands on the table. "And they opened those windows because they're coming back," she says. "And that'll be their way in."

Mark nods. "Would be my guess. Didn't even bother taking your tip money. Lying right there in the middle of your bed. They weren't here to steal nothing, that's clear enough."

"So why leave the windows open? Why come back?"

Mark lets the silence between them settle. He's giving her time to think, knows she has the wherewithal to answer her own question. It also means he'd rather she be the one to say it.

"Talley wasn't here," Lane says, and stares up at him. "And Annalee's already gone."

It's a small gesture, the way Mark's lips form a hard line and the way he exhales as his head nods forward.

"Someone came and left those windows open," Lane says, "with the intention of coming back when Talley is here? That's what you think, isn't it? They're coming back because they want Talley too."

Mark inhales, and his lips form that same hard line. "We have to consider it."

LANE MADE A terrible mistake bringing her girls to this town and this house. Staring across her kitchen table at Mark, she knows she'd been a coward to marry Kyle. It had been an easy way out, and she'd taken it. She knows that now. In the beginning, Kyle had needed someone to prop him up until he was ready to stand on his own. Even then, she'd known that, but she went with him anyway, because she needed an escape. Neil did all those things the newspapers say he did. Even if no one has ever proven it and even if they never do, she knows because she lived with him for eighteen years, and now she's trapped again in a world all his making. If Lane had never married Kyle, she'd have found her own way out of this town and would have never been forced to return with no place else to go. Her being a coward led her back to this town, and now Annalee is gone. The guilt settles on her chest, makes it heavy so she can hardly breathe.

"What happened to Hettie Jansen?" she says.

"Not certain. Didn't look to be an accident."

"Was it Rowland?"

Mark sits next to Lane, reaches for her hand, but she pulls away, won't let him touch her.

"Tires on his truck didn't look to have been anywhere near the river before this morning, but we'll be making certain. Tough call with the weather being what it was."

"But he was there already. When I got there, before they brought Hettie's body in. Why?"

"Found Hettie's car there this morning, same as Annalee's."

"You didn't tell me that."

Mark shakes his head. "No, I didn't."

There were other cars parked along the dirt road where Mark stopped when he took Lane to the river. One of those cars must have been Hettie's, but Lane hadn't noticed and Mark hadn't told her. He had to consider that if something had happened to Hettie Jansen, Lane or maybe Annalee could have been to blame.

"It was only one time," Lane says, staring at the white kitchen cabinets beyond Mark's shoulder. "Rowland and me. I don't remember if he came inside last night. But I don't think he did. To be honest, I was too drunk to remember. But I do know nothing more happened." Lane closes her eyes and turns away from Mark.

"I'm going to have a deputy here in a few minutes, a good many of them, in fact. What with all the reporters in town, we'll keep an eye in case anyone is thinking to give Neil trouble."

Lane has seen the men a few times since she moved back to Waddell, men of a certain age she doesn't recognize from the bar or around town. They usually travel in small groups. Some smoke cigars and have thick middles. Others are silver-haired and wear pressed shirts and belted pants. Still others wear baseball caps and frayed button-downs. She assumes but never knows for certain that they're all men who have returned to Waddell to see the school they still visit in their nightmares all these years later. And surely they've come to see, maybe confront, the man they can't believe is still alive.

"This is payback," Lane says.

This isn't a repeat of what happened back in the seventies. No one is hunting girls with blond hair. And Rowland Jansen isn't to blame.

"You're talking about Neil?" Mark asks. "You think this is payback for something Neil did?"

Lane nods. She's trapped now, by all of Neil's misdeeds and by her own.

Before moving back to Waddell, Lane read about Neil and his troubles in newspapers, on blogs, and in reports issued by the Department of Justice. She watched news clips and depositions on YouTube, sometimes having to close her eyes at the sight of her father. In the years since she left home, he had become an old man. She heard about Neil's troubles too from Erma over the telephone. Erma would cry and say, I'm sorry I couldn't make it better for you, Laney. Lord knows I tried. I wish you'd come home. Your father, he really can do no more harm.

"Doesn't make sense that it's some kind of payback," Mark says. "Not if you believe one has anything to do with the other. Susannah Bauer disappearing. Hettie. They don't have nothing to do with Neil."

"So then they're not related," Lane says. "Doesn't make it any better. I've always known it would come back on us one way or another."

Not all the abuse happened under Neil's watch. Some happened long before he came along. Those who suffered or died during the school's early years are gone and no one will ever know their stories. But those men who are still living will see to having their stories heard.

"Neil beat those boys," Lane says. "All of those years he was working at the school, he did it. Now this has happened."

"We'll deal with Neil later," Mark says. He talks in a quiet voice and places a hand flat on the table in front of Lane but doesn't touch her. "You need to think about calling Kyle. There's a chance Annalee's contacted him. And he needs to know what we're dealing with here."

Lane nods. Now is not the time for blaming. Now is the time someone tells Annalee's father that his daughter is suddenly gone.

ERMA

IN NEIL'S DRAWING room, where Lane has told Erma and Neil to stay put, Erma pulls the drapes together. It means something that those windows are open, but she doesn't know what. With one hand, she pinches the drapes together, no matter how her fingers ache, and with the other, she squeezes until the clothespin opens enough that she can clip it on. She wants to protect her girls from every terrible thing out there.

"Be careful," Neil says. "My own grandmother hung them. You should be changing them out. Summer's here, ain't it?"

"Yes, Neil," Erma says, though she hasn't changed out the drapes for years.

It used to hurt Erma, this being told what to do and how to do it. When, as a young bride, she complained to her mother, she told Erma she was blessed to live in such a house and used a tone meant to warn Erma against squandering her good fortune.

Over the years, Erma found her way to fooling Neil into believing she was an obedient wife. Before he would go off to work in the mornings, she would set the table to his liking, serve his cream in the creamer and his sugar in cubes. But after he left for the day and before he came home again, she did as she liked. She cared more for crocheting and not for quilting as Neil's mother had, so she would piece a few squares together first thing each morning before sitting down to her yarn and hooks. She tended her garden, baked fresh bread, stitched loose buttons, and mended socks. As Lane grew older, Erma taught her how to do those things too. Most days, Erma fooled Neil into believing she did as she was told and only as she was told. Most days, but not all.

The hardest years began when Lane was thirteen. Erma did her best to soothe what was between Lane and Neil during those teenage years, but still Lane packed up and left Waddell with Kyle Wallace the moment she graduated high school. She wanted no more of the Fielding name. No more of the money, whatever money there was. Blood money, Lane called it. Erma begged her to stay, apologized that she hadn't done better, promised she had done her best.

Life finally eased for Erma three years ago when Neil stopped leaving the house and began to slip away. By then, he'd seen the men plant their tree at the school, been questioned by those attorneys, been advised the federal government had issued a report detailing all manner of horrific abuse that had taken place at the school. That's when Neil started fussing about intruders, and twice a day every day he would insist Erma check the locks on every door and window. She could tell him she had tested them all when really she hadn't, and he would believe her.

This brought a strange, likely sinful happiness into Erma's life.

With Lane gone and before Susannah Bauer came along, it was Erma's only happiness. She could warn Neil to stay in his room because people outside were trying to get in when really they weren't. His eyes would stretch wide to hear this, and he would pull back in his chair. It was fear. She should have felt guilty for the pleasure it brought her, but she didn't.

Even though Neil has been easier to fool in more recent years, the memories of what he did when he was a younger man are still enough to make Erma flinch. She worries some days, as Neil slips further away, if she isn't slipping too. She used to have a whole town to hold on to, friends she'd had for years, but now she's alone and slipping. Or maybe she's worked at fooling him for too long and now she's fooling herself.

THOSE ARE BOOTS walking through the foyer, boots that will leave prints and track mud. Erma has such a time keeping up with the house, and the older she gets, the larger it seems to get.

"Who's that I'm hearing?" Neil says, struggling to turn in his seat so he can see into the foyer.

"It's fellows from the sheriff's office," Erma says as a large man, wearing heavy black boots and a navy blue shirt and trousers, walks past the drawing room.

"Police in my house?" Neil tries to stand, rocks from side to side, and pulls at the armrests of his chair. "Why, by God, are there police in my house?"

"Sit yourself down," Erma says, keeping well beyond his reach as she walks past him. "Wait for Lane to help you."

Neil falls back in his chair. His skin has gone gray, and he exhales short puffs of air through his nose.

"I didn't do nothing to that boy," he hollers toward the foyer. "To none of them boys."

Erma takes careful steps these days. She holds railings, always steps one foot straight ahead of the other, and never rounds off the corners. That'll lead to a twisted ankle, or worst yet, a fall. With Lane home and her girls too, Erma has reason now to keep herself healthy.

She wasn't always so careful. The last time deputies walked through her foyer, wearing those same heavy boots, Erma didn't struggle with the thoughts in her head or the weight of her memories. She wasn't afraid of old age and fragile joints. She was afraid of Neil. And after that night, and up until the day she left Waddell, Lane was afraid of him too. Maybe she's afraid of him still, or rather she's afraid, like Erma, of the memory.

By ten o'clock that evening, on the day thirteen-year-old Lane went missing, Erma had been left with nothing to do as the others continued to search. Lane had been missing all day, and by suppertime, Neil had called in every one of his guards and staff not already on duty to help in the search. He called them because of that note. Something on it had worried him, scared him even, but he wouldn't tell Erma what it was.

Neighbors came too, because Erma called them. After checking their own barns and sheds and anyplace they figured a young girl might hide, they'd come to the house to help. The wives came too, bringing with them leftovers from supper or casseroles they'd had tucked away in their freezers.

As the men searched, their flashlights sparkled in the trees out back, but in the past hour, the search had moved beyond the house to neighboring fields and ditches. The ladies had all gone too. They meant well, but Erma sent them home to tend their own. We really should stay, they said, but all their efforts to comfort Erma—the reassurances Lane would be home any moment, the hands that rested on Erma's shoulders to steady her, the constant suggestions she sit and save her energy—only fed Erma's fears. She'd heard the ladies talking when they didn't think Erma was nearby. Do you suppose it's all happening again? they asked one another. Oh, I remember it well. Seems like just yesterday they were all searching for the poor young girl that fellow Ted made off with. Go, Erma pleaded, because it was all too frightening, and finally the last lady left.

While the others were searching, Erma was to answer the phone and be home in case Lane returned, that's what Neil ordered before leaving with the others, but it wasn't enough. Wanting to do something, anything more, Erma unlocked the attic door. She would go looking for Lane herself but needed a good flashlight first. Somewhere up in the attic, Erma would find the lantern Lane had used when she last went camping with the Little Sisters of the South. Before ducking under the low-hanging doorway, Erma reached for the switch in the hallway and turned off the attic fan that ran all winter and throughout the spring. It was a steady noise Erma hardly noticed until it was gone. Having only a small flashlight to guide her, she climbed the stairs slowly and stopped when she reached the top.

Straightaway, Erma knew what had happened. And straightaway, she knew to be afraid. Her breathing turned shallow as if to help her hear better. She closed her eyes, and as she took a step into the attic, the floorboards underfoot creaked. She knew the sound immediately, the quiet in and out of Lane's breath as she slept. She was right there in the attic, had been all along. Instead of sitting down among the ruins to sulk about her argument with Erma, Lane had come here to the attic to hide. Probably she was wanting to make Erma worry, punish her, even.

Dropping onto her knees next to Lane, Erma shook her arm to wake her. Like Erma, Lane seemed to know straightaway she'd made a terrible mistake. It must have been the way Erma's voice shook or how her eyes stretched wide or the tremble in her hands. Scrambling to her feet, Lane grabbed for Erma.

"Oh, Laney," Erma said. "Come with me. Come quick."

Erma called Neil first and only.

"Laney was hiding up there in the attic," she told him, whispering into the phone, though she wasn't sure why. "Locked herself in. She was asleep when I found her. It was my fault. She was hiding from me. It was our fight, our silly fight. All my fault."

After cleaning Lane's face with a cool washcloth and running a brush through her hair, Erma led her into the foyer and there they waited. When Neil's boots hit the first stair outside the back door, she grabbed Lane's hand.

"Don't say nothing," Erma said. "Don't even look him in the eye."

The door flew open. Neil had come alone.

First thing, he ordered Lane to dress in something modest. Not knowing what that meant, she looked to Erma. Your white blouse and black skirt, Erma whispered. Once Lane had changed, Neil sat her in one of the two straight-backed chairs in the foyer. He told Erma to keep the lights low, so she turned off every light except one of the two table lamps on the credenza. Having changed into the calico belted dress she normally wore to church, Erma stood next to Lane, every so often smoothing her blond hair and whispering that everything would be fine. Do as your father says. Say what your father says. Lane sat silently, her hands crossed in her lap, her head lowered. The glow of the single light fell on one side of her face and along one shoulder.

The deputies came next, only a handful of them. They gathered to see for themselves that Lane was safely home. Everyone else who had been searching for hours—neighbors, the school's guards and staff, other deputies—had received word Lane was safe and had gone home. Signaling it was time for the deputies to leave, Neil slapped the last few on their backs, shook their hands, and thanked them for their good work.

"We're grateful to them, aren't we, Erma?" Neil said.

The deputies wanted to ask questions, talk with Lane when she felt up to it, talk with Erma about what she'd seen, but Neil assured them he had tended the situation.

"One of my boys made off with her." That's what Neil called him—one of my boys. "Can't blame my girl for the likes of one of them. Wrong place. Wrong time. But that boy won't be causing no more trouble. I seen to that. Didn't get nothing he didn't deserve."

At hearing Neil say this, Erma squeezed Lane's shoulder, not to comfort Lane but to steady herself. Neil was telling lies to the deputies, but that wasn't what frightened Erma and made the floor begin to tip and sway under her feet. The fear Neil was also speaking the truth was the thing that made her dizzy. While he was lying to the deputies and making them believe someone had really taken Lane—a lie his ego surely commanded—maybe he was at the same time telling the truth about having seen to it a boy wouldn't cause no more trouble. He must have lined them up when he went back to the school after that guard found the slip of paper. He must have questioned them one at a time. Or maybe he picked out one particular boy he'd always had a disliking for. Maybe he asked the boy, that child, again and again what he'd done with Lane. And when the boy didn't answer, couldn't answer, what else did Neil do to get him to talk?

Erma had told Neil, begged him, to do whatever it took to find their daughter. She knew what he'd been doing to those boys over the years. No matter how she tried not to think about it, she knew. He'd whipped boys for things like smoking, walking on the grass, and getting a poor grade. So when Erma asked Neil, begged him, to do whatever it took to find Lane, she had known exactly what she was asking.

She wondered now, as she listened to Neil lie to the deputies, what he had done between the time he read whatever was on that slip of paper—which must have seemed to him like proof positive one of those boys took Lane—and the moment Erma called to tell him she'd found their daughter. Lane hadn't been the one in the wrong place at the wrong time; it had been, may have been, one of Neil's boys. What had Neil done because Erma begged him to?

"What about a doctor?" one of the deputies asked, glancing at Lane and then Erma. "Is your daughter in need, ma'am?"

Lane's face showed no bruises. She sat up straight, feet squarely on the floor, and stared at the pocket on Neil's shirt where he had tucked that slip of paper the guard handed him earlier in the evening. Nothing about Lane's posture suggested she was in pain, but the deputy was wondering about her virtue. Neil likely hadn't considered that particular side effect of his lie. Erma didn't have to look at Neil to know how to answer the deputy. Still clinging to Lane's shoulder, Erma shook her head.

Just as Neil had a way with the ladies on potluck Wednesdays, he had a way with the deputies, and the police in town, as well. Neil had his plate full at that school. Everyone knew it, the police officers most of all, and he'd done a damn fine job with it for a good many years.

"Don't need no doctor," Neil said. And he repeated himself, squeezing the deputy's shoulder and looking him straight on. "You understand? No doctor required."

But it was too late. Why else would a boy take a girl?

"DO YOU HEAR ME?" Neil says, slapping the side of his chair to get Erma's attention. "You tell that Sheriff Ellenton. Tell Lane. I didn't hurt that boy. Didn't hurt none of them."

"Yes, Neil," Erma says.

Neil's gray hair sticks out from his head in greasy clumps. "Fetch my gun," he says.

Erma swings around as quickly as her sore hip will allow. As she knew he would be, Neil is pointing at the chest pushed up against the wall.

"It's right in there. Fetch me my gun and I'll see to who is in my house. By God, I'll see to them boys."

Erma stares down on the chest where she keeps her finest blankets, the ones she crocheted in hopes Lane would pass them on to her children. In the days and weeks after deputies last gathered in Erma's foyer all those years ago, some of the ladies from the church asked, quietly and discreetly, if Lane would still be able to have children. Erma nodded, let them believe Lane had been tarnished. Neil figured Lane had it coming. If that's what folks believed, well, so be it. Erma could never tell them Lane had been hiding, that no one had ever taken her. Now Lane has children, two beautiful girls who will one day inherit the blankets stored in the chest. It's also where Neil keeps his gun.

Still hollering at Erma, Neil continues to push and scoot and try to make his way out of his chair, and he does it. He makes his way onto his feet. He's not straight, he's certainly not as tall as he once was, but he's as upright as he can be. His tan trousers buckle at the waist because every month he must draw his belt a notch tighter, and his white shirt hangs on his empty, sunken chest.

Just as Erma wishes for it, Lane and Mark appear in the doorway again.

"Laney," Neil says, as if surprised to see Lane. "There you are, girl. Come and see. They found the boy. The one who took you. He's there on the television."

"Stop that, Neil," Erma says, shaking her head at Mark as if such things don't often happen in her house.

"But he was right there," Neil says, pointing at the television where a commercial for cat food now plays. "The boy who took you. Erma, get to it." He waves at the chest again. "Fetch me my gun."

"You want your gun?" Lane says, taking a step into the room. "You say you want your gun?"

Lane is hollering.

"You haven't done enough?" she says. "These men, these officers, all of them are here because of you."

"They're here about the boy," Neil says. "The boy who took you. He's right there on the television."

Lane takes a quick look at the screen. "There is no boy there. Annalee is the one who's gone. Gone because of you," Lane says. "Talley's next, and you want your Goddamn gun?"

"I'll not have anyone take the Lord's name . . . ," Neil says, tries to say.

"Don't you dare," Lane says. "Don't you dare try to tell me one Goddamn thing."

"You're getting ahead of yourself there, Lane," Mark Ellenton says, and tries to quiet Lane by resting a hand on her shoulder, but she slaps him away.

"What is it, Lane? Mark?" Erma says, bracing herself against the back of the sofa. "What's happened? Is it Annalee? Susannah?"

"Hettie Jansen is dead," Lane says, but really she spits the words at Neil. "Someone beat her and drowned her. And Annalee was right there where it happened. Her truck, right there, and now we can't find her. Hate to think what it means for Susannah."

"We don't know none of that for sure," Mark says. "You're not thinking clear. We don't know—"

"We know enough." Lane shoves at Mark again. "This is all because of you, Neil."

Erma reaches for Lane to stop her from pushing Mark away.

He's been one of the only people to stay by Erma's side in the years since Lane left and the investigations into Neil began. But she drops her hand when Lane pushes her away too.

"Someone broke in here because of you," Lane says, taking another step toward Neil. "Annalee's gone because of you, and they're coming back for Talley."

Neil looks to the floor and then to Erma. A clump of his greasy gray hair falls over his forehead and into his eyes. She used to cut it for him every Sunday. Not anymore. Now it hangs in his face. He says nothing but instead begins to swat at his back pocket like he did when he still carried a wallet, and then he dips a hand in his front pocket like he did when he still carried keys. He's imagining he's a younger man who goes to work every day and reads the *Waddell Chronicle* and flirts with the ladies at the church socials. He's imagining he'll gather himself and leave because, by God, no one speaks to him like that in his own house.

"Where is your gun, Mr. Fielding?" Mark says, using one finger to flip the latch on the chest, opening it and looking inside.

Neil doesn't answer but instead continues slapping his pockets and again looks to Erma. He's wanting her to remind him where he is and what he's doing and who these people are. He needs her. She says nothing.

"Mr. Fielding? Mrs. Fielding? Lane?" Mark says. "Should there be a gun here?"

"I've never seen him with one," Lane says, shaking her head. She closes her eyes and turns away from Neil most surely because the shrunken, helpless person before her doesn't fit the man she wants to punish. Erma so often struggles with the same. After a long pause, Lane opens her eyes again. "I guess I'm really not sure. Erma?"

Erma stares at the chest. The lid stands open, and inside her best blankets are folded and wrapped in tissue paper.

"This is important, Mrs. Fielding," Mark says. "Does he usually keep a gun here?"

Erma knows Neil's confusion because she feels it herself, the painful moments that surprise her more every time. A person should grow accustomed to what has become of her. She doesn't, hasn't. She'll look at her hands, the thin skin that creases like rice paper and the long, fingers with thick, round knuckles, and wonder who they belong to. But she comes back from it quicker, easier than Neil, and especially since Lane came home because now Erma has hope. She is certain there used to be a gun in that chest. She knows because Neil threw open the latch more than once when he was a younger man and grabbed it up when the school's sirens woke him. He grabbed it a few times too and pointed it at Erma, usually late at night when his words slurred from too much drinking.

She knows a gun used to be there because when Neil began ordering Erma to pin the drapes shut and started to confuse Erma for his own mother, she took it away and stored it in the credenza in the drawer just below the family Bible. She covered it over with church bulletins she kept from the years when she could still go to services. The gun would be hers to protect herself from Neil. And when Lane called to say she and the girls would be moving back, Erma asked Susannah Bauer, sweet Susannah Bauer, who knew about so much, if she knew about things like shooting a gun and would she mind teaching Erma.

"I don't know about a gun," Erma finally says. "But I think no. There isn't supposed to be no gun there."

"Was there ever?" Mark asks.

Erma shakes her head and holds her eyes steady so they don't drift toward the foyer and betray the gun's new hiding place.

"No," she says.

She can't live here in this house without the gun, not even

now as Neil continues to sputter, unable to string together a single thought. Everyone else will look at Neil and see a weak man who can barely stand from his chair, but Erma remembers. She's lived in fear too long. It's exhausted her, and she can't do it any longer.

"Very well," Mark says. He then asks Erma and Neil to please not touch the chest until he tells them otherwise and directs Lane back toward the kitchen.

"Our dear Annalee may be gone," Erma says, once they've left the room. "I think most certainly she's gone."

Neil turns to her, and his eyes, small and tired as they are, widen. He's surprised by her, not by what she has said but by the simple presence of her. It's as if he forgot she was in the room, or maybe he's forgotten her altogether. Out in the kitchen, Lane is quiet. Mark is talking on his cell phone or maybe into that radio of his. Neil shuffles back to his chair, lowers himself. He's better once he's in his chair, and like he so often does, he wraps his left hand over his right and with his thumb rubs the crippled part of his hand.

IT BEGAN WITH Neil clenching his fingers and straightening them, clenching and straightening, over and over. Usually during supper at the end of a long day. And in the mornings too because his hand would stiffen up on him while he slept. Some evenings, when he got home from work, he would hold a towel to it and every so often peek underneath until he was certain the bleeding had stopped. He would dab at it with peroxide because it didn't sting so bad as alcohol. Eventually, it would scab over and that would cause itching and more tightness.

Every morning and every evening, clenching and straightening. And then a few days would pass, or maybe as much as a few weeks or months, and his knuckles and the back of his hand would bleed again and scab over again. Years and years of this caused the crippling. Years and years of clenching and straightening and tending to fresh wounds. Now that hand, that right hand, is frozen, half-open, half-closed. The fingers are forever stiff. Morning, noon, or night, he can scarcely move them even to press at the buttons on the television's remote control. The skin on that hand is dark and thick, callused over the doctor said, and damage has been done that can never be undone.

A reporter once noticed Neil rubbing that spot with the thumb of his good hand. It was on the first day Neil sat in the icy-cold room at the county courthouse, his sweater buttoned up under his chin, and answered the lawyers' questions. One question after another about how many spankings he gave and with what did he give them and when does a spanking become a whipping and how many boys did he kill? As they asked and Neil answered, he rubbed small circles on the back of that crippled hand with his one good thumb.

Around and around, Neil kneaded what had grown into a hard lump. The next day, the reporter who sat through the entire day's questioning wrote about allegations that Neil had swung his leather strap so high and so hard that his right hand would scrape against the low-hanging ceiling in the old white building. The reporter wrote about allegations of beatings that went on for fifty, sixty, seventy lashes, each time the strap lifted so high Neil wore away the back of his right hand.

To look at him now, the reporter wrote, it pains him still.

Outside the house, more cars pull up and grind to a stop, surely kicking up dust Erma will be scrubbing from the windows later today. The engines shut down, doors open and slam closed. More men wearing boots cross the gravel. More men wearing navy blue uniforms. They kick up their own dusty clouds and climb the stairs. No one knocks. More dust and grime for Erma to clean. But she won't mind if only Lane and her girls will stay when this is all over. Neil keeps his eyes on the television screen in front of him and continues to knead that callused lump.

Erma knows it now. In truth, didn't she know it all along? Didn't at least some part of her know, or does she only now see? All those times he sat at her table, Neil, as he nursed his wounded hand, never asked her to fetch the cloth and peroxide. He, a man who never fetched his own paper or poured his own coffee or laid out his own clothes, never asked her to tend that wound.

"You believe yourself, don't you?" Erma says to Neil as three large men wearing dark-blue trousers and long-sleeved shirts appear in the doorway. "All these years, and you really do believe you didn't do nothing wrong." One of the men stretches out a hand to Erma, says ma'am to her, wants her to follow him.

"Lane is right," Erma says. "You brought this on us all. This is your doing. Whatever has become of our poor Annalee is all your doing."

DARYL

7 days before Susannah disappeared

I'VE WAITED THREE nights for Annalee's headlights to appear out of the darkness, and now they have. My heart slows. The knotted tangles inside loosen, and I can breathe easy again. I'm no longer angry Susannah didn't come today. I have Annalee to think of now. Trailing her through town, I'm careful to stay at a distance. I'm sweaty from beating the steering wheel and from all the shouting, and the air rushing through the car dries me.

We are near the river where the train tracks cross over and old men come to fish. I hear them talk about it at the church. They have their favorite spots, the best place to land a good catch. You fish? they'll sometimes ask. I say yes because they don't think anything of a man who fishes. They'd think poorly of one who didn't.

Up ahead, Annalee takes a sharp turn onto the dirt road directly past the shop that sells me the parts I need for the mower. Turning off my lights, I drift toward the ditch, make a three-point turn so my front end is pointed in the opposite direction, and park long before the bend in the road that leads to the river. I shut off my engine and roll down my window. Annalee is somewhere not so far away.

I walk slowly, and I choose a path where the ground is hard and littered with leaves and pine needles so I leave no tracks. After a few minutes, I hear the music. It's only a couple of notes in the beginning, but the more I walk, the more those notes stack one on top of another and they become a song. I walk faster, and I round the bend in the road. Up ahead, Annalee's truck is parked such that its lights would shine on the river if they had been on. A car, an ordinary sedan type of car, blue, maybe black, is parked next to it. It's a car that I'm almost certain will end up belonging to a boy.

I could say the music led me to the river, but that would be a lie. Annalee drew me. She's pure like the others, kind and loving, a craving. Long before I see her, I see the glow of a light, a lantern, and I smell the same pine I sprayed on my skin as I waited outside the bar for Annalee's mother. I walk where it sometimes floods when the river runs high, but the ground is dry now, even crunches underfoot. Just beyond Annalee and the boy—I was right, she's come here to meet a boy—the yellow light from a lantern reflects in the black river that has spilled between the trees with swollen trunks. There's a breeze here, and it's why they've come. Among all these trees, it won't be enough to keep the bugs away, but they'll be able to bear the heat. I walk toward them until I'm just beyond the lantern's reach.

I know the boy straightaway. He is the one who was talking to Susannah Bauer in the grocery store the day I met Annalee.

He also comes to the church sometimes to talk to his mother. His name is Jimmy, and his mother is Hettie Jansen, the church secretary, the one who gives me $325 in cash at the end of every week. He took the lantern they are using from the large closet at the church. There are six of them on the shelves. They sit there, side by side, in case we lose electricity. They are large lanterns powered by large square batteries. Reverend put on my list that I'm to check the lanterns every Sunday morning so we're sure to have them if we need them come Sunday night. The building is old, and when the weather is hot and we run our air conditioners, we sometimes lose power.

Reverend does his most important work on Sunday nights, and the boy's mother, Miss Hettie, agrees. You should come, she sometimes says when she hands me a stack of limp bills at the end of the week. She tells me her life is in shambles too, and when I ask what are shambles, she smiles and touches my face. I jerked away from her the first time she did this, but she reached out again, right away, and I let her touch me. Her fingers were cool and dry. Shambles are what happen when bad things befall good people.

The boy who brought Annalee here brought the bug spray too. He holds a green can, shakes it, sprays it on one of Annalee's arms and runs his hands over her, smoothing it into her skin. Overhead, small, dark shadows dart through the edges of the light thrown by the lantern. Bats shooting through the sky. They roost in the limestone caves upriver.

The boy isn't so different from me. He's taller, I know, and his hair is light whereas mine is dark. But he isn't so different. It should be no harder for me. I could do the same for Annalee. I could spray each arm and each leg, and I could rub her skin, smooth it with my hands.

First crossing her arms, Annalee grabs the bottom of her

blouse and lifts it over her head. She's bare underneath. In the flickering light, her skin glows in some spots and is clouded by shadows in others. The boy sprays all of her, and with both hands, he smooths the fine mist into her skin. I could do the same.

TWICE I'VE HAD to replace batteries in the church lanterns. This makes Reverend angry because they cost too much money and burn out though we've yet to use them. Now I see this boy has been taking them. He must return one lantern, trade it for another when it begins to dim. This one sitting between him and Annalee burns strong. I take yet another step, standing so closely I can smell her skin, not only the pine but also the flowery lotion she must rub onto her hands and elbows, and I think to close my eyes so I'll better remember the sight of her. It's Annalee sitting tall, her bare skin glowing. Her yellow hair shimmers, falls over her shoulders. The boy's hands, his mouth, are on her. He's in a hurry, a frenzy.

Trying to slow the boy, Annalee strokes his hair with one hand and ducks her head to his. I imagine she presses her lips to his ear and whispers. I can almost see him trembling. I press my hand over my mouth so they won't hear me breathing because I'm that close, and I hear her voice. She is asking him do you love me? Will you even when you leave? I can't unless you promise me. And do you promise me we'll stay together? Will you love me forever?

If he answers, I can't hear him, but he nods over and over, and his hands and mouth continue to move across her skin. Annalee looks to the sky as she cradles his head. He slides a hand between her shoulders and lays her back, slowly, as he nods yes to each of her pleas.

I back away from them, moving closer to the bend that will lead me back to my car, and rest my head against a tree. Its rough bark digs into my skin. I lean there, eyes closed. I can't look again because I'll see Annalee and I'll tremble like the boy. I can't watch him cover her over with his body. Instead, with my head still pressed against the tree, I stomp one foot and listen. I want him to stop, to take his hands from her. She's mine, and this boy is taking her. The music is slow, the notes deep and muffled. I have to look, at least enough to see if they've heard.

The boy has tried to slow himself. He has rolled to the side of Annalee. He pushes the hair from her face, leans over her, and kisses her mouth without touching the rest of her. I grab a low-hanging branch, take hold with both hands, lift my feet off the ground because the branch is that thick, and bounce until it breaks and I drop back onto my feet. I stomp on one end so it's the length of a cane and look again.

They've heard this. The boy stands. I've made him stop. His pants hang open at the zipper, and like Annalee, he's bare-chested.

"Hey," the boy calls out.

Annalee sits tall, doesn't bother trying to cover herself. The boy looks down on her, motions for her to pick up her blouse, and takes a few steps into the darkness. Annalee squints into the trees, calling out to the boy to be careful. Her voice should be higher, strained. I should hear fear. The boy takes another step toward me. I tremble like he did. I want him to see me, if only a glimpse. I want him to see something among the trees. I want him to wonder if the something is real or if his fear has made him see it, and I want him to be afraid. I want him to stop touching Annalee.

"Who's there?" the boy yells.

I slip behind the thick trunk and take shallow breaths that

make my stomach swell instead of my chest because it's quieter. It makes me angry when a Saturday that Susannah Bauer is meant to come to town passes without my seeing her. I can't stand still or sit still on those days, and I don't know which wrench to use or which direction to turn a screw. Those are the days my knotted insides turn brittle and the sharp edges jab at me. I feel that now as I wrap both hands around the stick.

The boy will continue looking for me. He'll take a few more steps, and he'll pause and look back at Annalee. This is what I want her to taste in the air, the same fear the boy will taste. Their fear will stir the hairs on my arms. I want Annalee to feel something, and only I'll know it's because of me. I want her eyes to stretch wide. I want her to pant. I want her hands to shake and her legs to grow heavy so she'll fear she can't run. This will make us close, Annalee and me, and my insides will soften and quiet.

But Annalee isn't afraid. She stands now, still bare from the waist up. She pushes her hair off her face. Something about the curve of her cheeks and the way her head rolls slightly off to the side makes me think probably she's smiling. I think probably she's amused. She doesn't feel me here alongside her and isn't afraid. We're not so close as to touch. The ache inside turns to anger.

"Hey, there," the boy calls out again.

In the dark, he doesn't know how far away I am. He has no sense of depth or distance. He walks slowly, testing each step before he takes it because he wears no shoes. He'll be slow to chase me. I'll run through the trees, a quicker way around the bend, and back to my car. He won't be able to follow. Annalee is leaning forward, looking into the dark, calling out to the boy, telling him to keep going. Each time the boy looks back at her, she pushes him on.

"I seen you," the boy says. "Come on out, or I'll come in after you."

My eyelids flutter. I imagine saying nearly the same. Come on in, or I'll come out after you. One more step. I'll make sure Annalee knows someone was here, though she'll never know it was me. Pine needles rustle but don't snap under the boy's bare feet. I know his height because I see him at the church. He's taller than me, and he's broader through the chest and shoulders. His hair is light; mine is dark. But he's not so different from me. One more step.

When I swing the branch I've broken from the tree, I know where to catch him. Directly below the breastbone in the soft spot above his belly. Wayne taught me this before he was sent to the school. Stand with your feet just so, he would say. And hold your elbows high. Wayne was always teaching me stuff and telling me that one day he'd be old enough to take care of me himself and we'd leave Mother. It would be just him and me and things would be good. Real good. But that day never came.

When the stick hits the boy, it makes a loud crack. His head and shoulders drop, and he rolls forward at the waist, stumbles soundlessly to his knees. I run.

LANE

LANE'S GREAT-GREAT-GRANDFATHER ON Neil's side built the small house across the road from the Fielding Mansion for the children he had with his first wife. When she died giving birth to their third baby, the next wife insisted the dead wife's children live in a separate house. And so the great-great-grandfather built them a house with walls a full half foot thicker than those of the main house, and he shuttered each window on the inside for added protection. He did these things to keep the children and their caregiver safe, but he also hid his care from the new wife by making the house a single story tall. Now the house is home to Bonnie Wiley.

Two deputies already stand at Bonnie's door, and Talley stands between them. Seeing the deputies with her young daughter makes this day somehow real—a day that has, up until now, drifted in and out of focus. Exhaustion is what nearly cripples Lane as she starts up the concrete walkway that leads from the road to Bonnie's house. Lane must think about every step to make her feet move. She'll grab Talley, take her home, tuck her into a bed made up with clean, crisp sheets, and lie down next to her. When they wake, this'll be over and Annalee will be home. All Lane wants is to close her eyes.

One of the deputies is squatted next to Talley while the other talks to Bonnie Wiley. Standing next to Talley, Bonnie is not much taller. Her white housedress flutters as a fan blowing through the open door rolls from side to side. It ruffles her hair too, the fan, spraying the silvery-gray strands across her face.

Lane stops partway up the path that leads to Bonnie's house. Even this far from the front door, the air is heavy and clouded with the musky incense Bonnie burns every day. Lane turns her face, tries to take in fresh air. She has to find a way to tell Kyle she doesn't know where his daughter is. She has to tell him she was too drunk to remember if Annalee was gone when Lane got home and that their daughter's truck was found at the river and another woman is already dead.

Lane will have to tell about the break-in at the house and the reporters and how everything Neil did all those years ago— allegedly, because that's the word the newspapers are always careful to use—may have finally come back to punish them. She'll have to tell him someone might want to harm Talley too because that's how badly they want to punish the Fieldings. And eventually she'll have to tell him maybe none of that is to blame. What she did with Rowland may have come back to punish them, and maybe the police are even wondering if Lane had something to do with all of this because Rowland's wife is the dead one. Butchers and whores. It's one or the other.

As if Lane has called out to them, and maybe she did without realizing, both deputies and Talley turn to her at the same time. Talley looks up at one of the men, surely asking his permission first, and then runs down the porch and into Lane's arms. Lane holds her, presses her face into Talley's hair, clears her throat so she won't cry, and then lifts Talley and turns to go.

"I didn't have nothing to do with what's going on over there," Bonnie shouts from the porch. "Tried to help your girl, is all."

"Yes, Bonnie," Lane says, though she doesn't bother shouting it over her shoulder so Bonnie probably doesn't hear.

Lane holds Talley close despite the heat. They're both sweating, but Talley doesn't pull away and Lane doesn't loosen her grip. She doesn't know what to do now except to go back home. She'll take one step and then another. While she needs this fear to ignite her, it has instead drained her.

"And you tell that mother of yours I did hang them pictures," Bonnie calls out.

"Yes, Bonnie."

"And if someone took them down, I'll hang more. Do it every day if I have to."

Lane wasn't here when Bonnie Wiley first moved in across the road from Erma and Neil. Back then, two years ago, folks in town were angry about the people who came to study the graves at the school. They demanded bygones be left in the past, and when that didn't work, they demanded the boarded-up school be sold, and when that didn't work, they demanded the people from the university who arrived with radar equipment, picks, and shovels be arrested for disturbing the dead. But even more than they feared the reporters or the state or the people with their radar equipment, they feared Bonnie Wiley. She told them those boys buried so long ago were not going to stay buried, and they feared she was right.

STILL CARRYING TALLEY in her arms, Lane continues down the walkway toward the road. The concrete underfoot has split where roots have grown under it, giving way to feathery weeds. With her eyes closed, Lane breathes in the smell of Talley's hair. It's not freshly washed but instead smells of cut grass and the black mud where she finds the best worms when Neil sings them from the ground. She smells like Lane probably did when she was a girl. It makes Lane feel all the more helpless, as if she's a child again.

"They put a Q-tip in my mouth, did you know?" Bonnie shouts out to Lane. "They tested me so now they'll know which one of them boys they dig up is my brother."

Lane was no longer working as a reporter when she saw the pictures online of law enforcement swabbing the cheeks of men and women who believed a family member had died at the school. Theirs was the kind of story Lane would have written about had she still been writing, a story rooted in suffering and tragedy. The stories had exhausted her, and yet again and again, she sought them.

"Any day now," Bonnie shouts from the porch. "They're going to match my DNA to one of them boys. Today, they only got a picture to show, but soon enough, they'll start having names."

"Thank you for the call," Lane says to Bonnie, again not bothering to raise her voice or turn her head because she doesn't have the strength. She's understanding it now. Neil's crimes alone didn't lead them to this end. It was her lies and silence and Erma's too, and they can never make amends for them. Maybe if the world is somehow fair to those who suffered, that will mean Annalee never gets to come home.

"She does this every day," Bonnie says.

Still holding Talley in her arms, Lane stops walking and turns back toward Bonnie's house.

"Every day," Bonnie says. "She comes running up your drive first thing and heads off down the road toward town. Would have thought she was too young to be doing that."

Lane loosens her arms enough to pull back and look Talley in the face. Her eyes are cast down, and even when Lane whispers her name, she doesn't raise them.

"Every day, Talley?" Lane says.

Every day first thing here in Florida, Lane is still sleeping, though since her one drunken night with Rowland, she's tried to wake early enough to have breakfast with Talley. When she was living with Kyle up north, she never slept past six. She made breakfast back then every day, flipped laundry, signed homework, and packed lunches. She kept schedules on her computer and wrote lists on a pad that hung in the kitchen. She did all those things because Erma had done the same. When Lane left Waddell, she promised herself she would do better by her girls than Erma had done by her. She's failed.

"I've told these fellows this is nothing new," Bonnie says. She tips forward at the waist so her voice will carry farther. "Your girl wandering off is nothing new, and it ain't got nothing to do with me."

One of the two deputies sweeps an arm across the open door as if inviting Bonnie into her own house, but she shakes her head at him.

"She goes to the church over there on Walton Drive," Bonnie says when Lane begins to turn away. "Some Little Sisters of the South nonsense. Was raining and I drove her home one day. Lord knows I shouldn't have done that. Someone over there is helping her grow a garden. If I was you, that's what would be worrying me."

"And Annalee?" Lane says, talking over the top of Talley's head and using a louder voice so Bonnie will hear. "Have you seen anything of my oldest?"

One of the deputies shakes his head in answer. They've already asked this of Bonnie.

Bonnie steps back as if to close the door. "Your father is a despicable man. And if something bad has befallen that house, well, the all of you deserve it."

"I hope they find him," Lane says, pulling Talley close again and backing away. Bonnie has said the thing that frightens Lane most. They do deserve this. They should have been the ones, she and Erma, to know what Neil was doing and should have been the ones to stop him. But Lane wasn't strong enough, and she isn't strong enough for this either.

"Your brother," Lane says, her voice sticking in her throat because even as she says it, she knows she has no right. "I really hope they find him."

Lane turns away from the house, ignoring the deputy who calls out for her to wait and let him help. Like Mark, the deputy will be seeing the weakness in Lane's legs.

"You were at the church?" Lane says. She pulls back again so she can look into Talley's face. "Every day, you were at the church?"

"Jimmy was there," Talley says. Her chest begins to lift and lower, and her chin wrinkles as if she's about to cry. "He goes with Annalee at night. And it's his fault she's gone."

"Jimmy was where?" Lane says.

"At the church. It's his fault Annalee's gone. I should have told you before. I'm sorry. I shouldn't have kept secrets."

With one hand, Lane cradles Talley's head, inhales, and opens her eyes.

Talley started wearing the kerchiefs shortly after they moved back to Waddell, a fad Lane assumed Talley picked up at school. And then the students from Florida State came to the house for the second time after Lane and the girls moved back, and one of them was wearing a kerchief on her head. Talley hadn't picked up the fad at school but had been copying the girl from Florida State. This was the real reason Lane remembered Susannah Bauer when the police came to ask their questions.

It made Lane sad to see Talley admiring and imitating someone like another girl might admire and imitate her own sister. It felt like Lane's failure that Talley didn't love her sister like she loved a stranger. After that, Lane scolded Talley for wearing the kerchiefs. They'll tear your hair, she said, though they didn't. They'll make you overheat, she said, though they wouldn't. No kerchiefs in the house and no kerchiefs after baths. Talley should feel those things, that kinship, for her own sister.

Sliding her hand over Talley's head, Lane gently pulls off one of those kerchiefs. It's been tied loosely, and it comes off easily in her hand. This isn't one of the kerchiefs Lane bought for Talley, and it isn't one that usually hangs from a hook near Talley's bed.

The kerchief is bright blue with two golden stripes. It was the reason Lane first assumed Susannah was from Sweden. She always wore the same kerchief. Exactly like this one. It's the Swedish flag. Lane has wondered about Susannah's parents many times since their daughter disappeared. Did they have to fly in all the way from Sweden, or did they already live here in the States? Were they staying in a hotel in Tallahassee and joining in the searches? She's even felt guilty for being angry with Susannah because Talley liked her better than her own sister. Lane bends until Talley's feet touch the ground, slowly loosens her arms so Talley can pull away, and holds out the kerchief for her to see.

"Talley, it's very important you tell me the truth," Lane says. "No more keeping secrets. Where did you get this?"

26

DARYL

6 days before Susannah disappeared

IT'S SUNDAY. BUT not just any Sunday. It's the Sunday after the Saturday Susannah was supposed to come and say a last good-bye, but she didn't. I wonder now if maybe she won't ever come again. My fingers ache from breaking the branch off the tree and swinging it at the boy last night. My ankles and behind my knees are covered with red welts, and I'm tired. The wondering and hoping exhaust me most, always, with every girl.

As I'm stuffing palm fronds in the garbage, the boy's mother, Miss Hettie, comes to me with a bottle of pink lotion. She tips it over onto a cotton ball and dabs at my bug bites and raw patches. I close my eyes as she does this and wonder if Mother ever did the same for me. How on earth did you get so many? Miss Hettie asks, and then invites me to evening services.

She's done this before. When the Sunday-morning services have ended and the parking lot has cleared, she comes to the shed to find me. She wobbles on shoes with tall heels, wears belted dresses with pads in the shoulders, and her long hair hangs loose. Gray streaks cut through the brown waves, and the ends are frayed and uneven. It didn't always look like that. I've seen pictures in her office where her hair was smooth and brown and fell only to her shoulders. The pictures aren't so old, but she looked much younger than she does now.

On those Sunday mornings when she comes to find me, she tells me I work too hard, that I really shouldn't work at all on Sundays. I can't tell her that I work because my apartment is always empty and the loneliness makes my chest ache. I don't tell her that Sunday is the hardest and loneliest day of them all because it begins another week without Susannah. Instead I tell her I have nothing else to do and the work makes me happier. Miss Hettie says she understands. She doesn't work for money either. She works for the love of her church and of her Lord. The people in this town depend on her. They need a place to go where they come together and worship and lean on one another. And that's why she works.

The first time Miss Hettie came to me, she handed me a sweaty glass of watered-down lemonade made from too little powder. Sometimes she brings plain, icy water. Sometimes bitter tea. This Sunday, today, the tea is sweet, too sweet to drink. I pretend to sip from it while she dabs at my ankles and legs with the pink lotion. I close my eyes as she does it. Every touch makes my insides shiver, but I keep my body still so she won't know.

Every week, Miss Hettie tries to please me. She is watching what I will enjoy and what I'll hold but never drink from, the ice eventually melting. Her perfume is heavier today, or maybe it's the heat that makes her sweat and the perfume leach from her skin. She lays her cool, dry hand on mine and says that'll do it because my legs are covered over with pink splotches. And then she says, come tonight, and for the first time, because she treats me like I think a mother should, I tell her I will.

Once, soon after I started working at the church, Miss Hettie invited me into her office so we could look for my brother on her computer. I told her he was at the school for boys long ago and that when I found him, things would be good, real good, because that's what he said before they took him away in the back of that brown car.

Miss Hettie sat behind her computer that day, tapping at the keyboard while I sat next to her in a black chair that swiveled. I was sweaty from spreading mulch in the flowerbeds out front. An air conditioner rattled in her window, one of the air conditioners I tinker with, and the cold air blew in my face. It dried my eyes. I blinked and I shivered as my shirt slowly dried. She typed "Wayne Thompson" into her computer. She found several, but none were my brother. I knew she wouldn't find him because Thompson wasn't my real last name. It wasn't my brother's last name either. A shame, she said as she pushed back from her computer.

"You know," Miss Hettie said that day. "Neil Fielding beat those boys. He's a butcher, that's what they say. And that daughter of his, she's a whore. Butchers and whores, the whole lot of them."

MISS HETTIE IS already there, standing in the doorway when I pull into the church parking lot for Sunday-evening services. Because she told me to, I showered before I came, dressed in fresh clothes, and saw to my nails and hair. People hug Miss Hettie as they pass her by. Some stop and take hold of her hands and talk to her. They are comforting her. I've seen this before, though not from my car. I know they comfort her because her husband is the man

I saw at the bar with Annalee's mother. He's the man who trapped Lane Fielding against the car, leaned into her.

Miss Hettie will think I don't know about her husband and Lane Fielding. That's why she comes for me, because all the others know. On her tall heels, she wobbles from person to person, and I think she looks out into the parking lot and smiles to see my car.

When the line of people walking into the church has dwindled to two or three and music has started to drift from the back of the church, she steps away from the doorway and waves for me to come along and join her. I clear my throat. Come on out, or I'll come in after you. That's what the boy had shouted out to me last night at the river. I say it now, aloud, to myself in the car. Again, in a whisper. Come on out, or I'll come in after you.

She's happy with how I look. I know because as we walk down an empty hallway, she slips a hand around my arm and presses against me. Even though the air is cooler inside the church, her perfume is still too thick. It's musky and spicy, and I turn my head so I don't cough. I pat the hand she has wrapped around my arm. She'll like that, and I force my hand to stay there, touching hers so she'll think I'm not so different from her own boy.

At the end of the hallway, the double doors are closed, and the closer we get to them, the louder the piano. As we walk down the hallway, our steps fall in time to the drums, and lastly a guitar carries the melody. The music is fast. It's wild, frenzied like the boy at the river when he was touching Annalee. It races along, and when we are nearly close enough to open the doors, voices join in, many singing voices. And hands clapping and feet stomping. I think Miss Hettie presses her face to my shoulder, maybe inhales, and then she steps away, drops her hand from my arm, and pulls open the door. I want to brush away the feel of her, but I don't. She won't like that.

THE METAL FOLDING chairs I set up every week in fifteen even rows, ten chairs each, have been pushed off to the edges of the room. Some have been upended. Some have been folded and lean against the wall. This is how I find them on Monday mornings. Like the chairs, many of the people have been pushed to the edges. Some stomp and clap. Some sway with the music. Miss Hettie draws me through the outside ring of people until we are on the inside.

This is where the children are, mostly girls. All girls. Some I recognize as Little Sisters of the South. They wear simple dresses, flower prints or polka dots or colorful plaids. They have long hair like Miss Hettie, but theirs is shiny blond or rich, full brown. They are slow in walking toward Reverend, who stands near the drums and piano. Mothers stand behind the girls, guide them with hands to their backs. They whisper in their daughters' ears. One of the girls walks with her hands raised high overhead. She rocks from side to side, her arms swaying, her head hanging down. This mother fades away. She smiles, looks around to see that others see too. Another mother uses two hands on her daughter's shoulders to show her the way.

At the front of the room, Reverend bobs in time to the music. He lays his head back. His eyes are closed. He stretches out his hands, blindly. One lands on the girl whose mother is still guiding her. The girl lifts her hands high, stretches them tall. Reverend cups her head with his palm. The girl begins to pump her arms and jump and spin and the mother backs away. She is proud now too. The other girls see, and so they begin to jump and swing their arms and wave their hands overhead. The people sing and stomp and clap. I don't let Miss Hettie draw me any closer, but I clap like all the others.

When the night is done, Miss Hettie tells the men that I will see to the room, and then she turns and asks if I wouldn't mind putting away the chairs and sweeping up before I leave. She holds the door as the others walk from the room, all of them blotting their cheeks and necks with tissues or pushing their damp hair from their foreheads. The men tug on their belt buckles and shake hands. The mothers kiss their daughters' cheeks.

Miss Hettie holds the door until the last person has left and then follows everyone down the hall. I pick up the chairs, fold them, stack them on the cart I pull from the closet. My fresh shirt wilts and sticks to my back. The room still echoes with the clapping and stomping.

Outside, footsteps pass down the sidewalk. Voices drift by. Car engines fire up, fade, and fall silent. Miss Hettie appears in the doorway. She waves for me to come along and flips off the light before I have crossed the room. I walk the rest of the way in the dark.

"I still look for your brother, you know?" Miss Hettie says. Slowly the darkness lifts as my eyes get used to it. "Every once in a while, I try again."

She is quiet, but I say nothing because I know she won't find him.

"I think of him sometimes," she says. "Pray for him. Pray he wasn't hurt at the school and that you'll find him one day."

I tell her thank you but don't know what else to say. The dark room is hot and it crowds me, makes me want to run through the doors and into the parking lot.

"I know you watch her," Miss Hettie says. Her hand touches my arm. Her fingers are light and cool. "That girl. I know you watch that girl."

She must feel some change in me, or maybe because I don't answer, she drops her hand. I want to ask if she knows I watch

Susannah or does she know about Annalee. I blink, trying to bring Miss Hettie into focus, but see less of her than before as she steps out into the hallway. She becomes an outline, nothing more. She takes my hand again and draws me along with her. I stare at her fingers where they tangle with mine, and I shiver like the boy did alongside the river when he laid his hands on Annalee.

"It's okay that I know you watch her," Miss Hettie says as she leads me down the dark hallway. "I don't mind. She'd be better off with you." And then she stops, takes my other hand too, and turns me until I face her.

"Tell me," Miss Hettie says. "Why do you watch?"

I don't know how to answer her, but I know now she is asking about Annalee because she thinks Annalee would be better off with me than with her boy. I can't tell Miss Hettie I watch the girls because it's all I have. I live in an apartment where every room is mostly empty and I have no mother and Wayne is gone. The girls are the only thing to fill me up and ease the aches, even if for only a few moments. They feed the part of me that needs to be soothed. What else am I to do? I have no other plan. If I were really like the boy, like Miss Hettie's son, I'd have a plan.

"Am I so different than your boy?" I ask her.

She rubs the backs of my hands with her thumbs. Her touch is light, barely any touch at all. I want to ask if she was there in the woods last night. Did she see me strike her boy, and did it make her angry? Is that how she knows I watch Annalee? Or was it at Annalee's house? Maybe Miss Hettie saw me there or sitting in my car where the dirt road meets the asphalt. And I wonder, now that Miss Hettie knows I watch, what will she do?

LANE

UNABLE AGAIN TO move her feet, Lane stands at the end of the walkway leading to Bonnie Wiley's house. Holding Talley loosely by the shoulders, Lane stares down on the blue-and-yellow kerchief. The moment Talley said it belonged to Susannah Bauer, Lane dropped it on the ground. When one of the deputies finally notices her and comes to offer his help, asking does she need a hand, she tells him to call Mark Ellenton right away. The deputy doesn't move to make the call but instead reaches to pick up the kerchief. Lane slaps his hand away and screams at him. The kerchief is evidence, and she doesn't want him to touch it. Call Mark Ellenton right now, she says, as Talley begins to cry.

Lane's kitchen fills with deputies from the sheriff's office, men wearing uniforms, and women too, but Mark sends them away. A few go outside to study the door someone pried open. Two others sit in the drawing room with Erma and Neil, and every so often Neil's voice rises above the rest—Erma'll damn sure get me a cup of coffee if I want one—but Erma never comes into the kitchen. Still another few linger in the foyer, just beyond the threshold. Mark sits at the table across from Talley. Lane stands near the kitchen sink, her arms crossed, head lowered, coaching herself to inhale and exhale so she'll stay calm. It's what she always told people she was interviewing. Relax. Getting upset won't help anyone.

"First things first," Mark says to Talley. "I want you to know you're not in trouble for taking that"—he nods at a brown bag sitting between them, the blue-and-yellow kerchief inside—"but I also want you to know I won't be giving it back."

Talley puckers her lips and nods. "Yes, sir."

"Your mama says you wear a good many of them. That true?"

Again, Talley nods. "Only after school and not in the house."

"You had that one a long time?"

Lane's bottom lip begins to quiver. She tucks her chin to her chest so Talley won't see and waits for an answer. When she hears nothing, she looks up. Talley is shaking her head.

"So, this one here is new?" Mark says.

"I took it. I think I stole it."

"That's good, Talley," Mark says. "I mean, good that you're being honest." He leans back in his chair and glances toward the window over the sink. "Tomorrow'll likely be a good day for worms, huh? Once the rain drains off some." He turns back to Talley. "You think?"

"Grandpa says if the ground's too wet, the worms'll get drowned."

"Grandpa knows his worms." Mark takes a sip of his coffee. "So, you think maybe you stole the kerchief. Did you especially like it? That why you took it?"

Talley nods.

"And what makes it so special?"

"It's Susannah's."

Not wanting to distract Talley, Lane resists the urge to sniffle. She pulls a paper towel from the roll hanging under the cabinet, slowly so she'll make no noise, blots at each eye, and wipes her nose.

"You're talking about Susannah Bauer? It's her kerchief?"

"Yes, sir."

"And why do you think it belongs to Susannah?"

"It's Swedish," Talley says, using one finger to trace the lines in the marbled laminate tabletop. Lane did the same when she was a girl. "It's the flag from Sweden. She was born there but mostly lived here."

"Lane," Mark says, when Lane makes a move to comfort Talley. "I hear Neil fussing about a cup of coffee." He surely knows Lane's on the brink of something, crying maybe, shouting, collapsing. "Why don't you go on and take him one? No reason he shouldn't have himself a cup of coffee, is there, Talley?"

"Coffee's cold," Lane says, and smiles for Mark so he'll believe she's in control and let her stay. "I'll make more later."

"So then, Talley," Mark says, handing Talley a small packet of tissues he took from his front pocket. He keeps his eyes on Lane, a warning he'll send her away if he needs to. "Why don't you tell me where you found that kerchief?"

Still tracing lines in the marbled tabletop, Talley says nothing.

"Remember what I told you," Mark says. "You won't be in no trouble."

"I took it from Daryl's shed."

Lane covers her mouth with one hand and turns away, leaning over the counter and pressing her face toward the window as if she'll find fresh air there. If she could clear her head, she'd be able to sort through everything that's happened and figure what it means. But the window is closed up tight like every other window in the house.

She's been blaming Kyle for everything bad in her life since the day he said it was best she took her leave. What a ridiculous thing to say. Best she took her leave. But it's also made blaming him easier. Kyle had needed her in the beginning, never truly loved her. He needed someone alongside to weather everything that was new. New town. New apartment. New friends. And then he needed her to pick him up when the rejections came from literary magazines and publishers and agents. Lastly, he needed her to celebrate with him. They celebrated the first sale, the first great reviews, the first appearance on the *Times* bestseller list.

By the time Talley was born, he was done needing Lane. He'd found his footing and didn't need Lane to prop him up anymore. Love had never been between them. Only need. And so Lane has blamed him for her drinking, for the way she's struggled to wake every morning, for her sleeping with Rowland. She's blamed him for her not being the mother she should, for her having to work late every night, for them having to live in a house with Neil. But she can't do that anymore because she is the coward who married him, and she surely can't blame him for Annalee being gone.

"This Daryl," Mark says. "Who is he? How do you know him?"

"He works at the church," Talley says. "And I go there."

"The New Covenant Church? Is that where Daryl works?"

Talley says nothing, but because Mark continues, she must have nodded.

"And you found the kerchief when?"

"Today. This morning when I went there to check on my garden."

"And did you see Daryl today?"

"No, sir. He wasn't there. Only Jimmy."

With a hand still pressed to her mouth, Lane turns back around. Mark is pointing at two deputies standing near the entrance. Susannah Bauer is gone, has been for ten days, and this man had her kerchief. This man nobody seems to know except Talley. The deputies disappear, and the front door opens and closes. They'll go to the church, find this shed Talley has described, talk with the reverend there, and get an address for the man from his employee file. They'll do all of that, but they won't find him. It's never that easy.

SITTING AT THE kitchen table across from Mark, and every so often glancing back at Lane, Talley tells about the Tuesdays she went to the church so she could watch the Little Sisters of the South. She wanted to be one of them so she'd have friends, but they told her no because Grandpa beat boys with a strap. It's hard when no one likes you, Talley tells Lane and Mark. It's hard when you smile and say nice things and try to be the right kind of girl and still they don't want you. Lane closes her eyes to hear Talley say this. The Little Sisters hadn't wanted Lane when she was a girl either, at least not once she became the girl who was the victim. They looked at her differently after that April in 1990. They whispered when she walked by, turned their backs on her when she tried to join the group. They didn't invite her to their parties, didn't clap for her when she was the one to give a speech, didn't even want to be near her. Other than losing Mark, or rather giving him up, being cast aside was the hardest part of being the one who was taken.

It's all coming too quickly, the things Lane should have known, the things any other mother would have known. Lane wants Talley to stop, but she doesn't. She tells about the day Daryl asked a favor of her. Would she bring him his rake? He said they'd plant a garden and Miss Hettie Jansen would let Talley be a Little Sister if she had a garden of her own. Now she goes to the church every day to weed and water and sometimes Daryl asks questions. He knows about the big house she lives in and which bedroom is hers and that she has a big sister with a room of her own.

"I found those too," Talley says, pointing at the two halves of Erma's china.

One of the deputies brought the broken plate to the house and said Bonnie Wiley gave it to him. Talley had been carrying it when she knocked on Bonnie's door. For the past few weeks, Lane has listened to Erma fuss every day about being short a piece of china. She even got cross with Erma for caring so much about something so meaningless.

"Where did you find it?" Mark asks Talley, shaking his head when Lane reaches out to pick up the two pieces.

"In the shed. In Daryl's shed, but I knew it was Grandma's, so I took it."

"You think your grandma gave the plate to Daryl?"

"No, sir," Talley says. "I put food on it and left it outside for the boys who run. Same as Mama did when she was a girl. I thought one of the boys took it. But now I think Daryl did. He took the food and kept Grandma's plate."

"That's real good, Talley. Now, your mama told me you figured Jimmy might have done something bad and that you had kept some secrets," Mark says. "Want to tell me about those?"

"I told a lie." Talley's bottom lip quivers like Lane's.

"And what was that?" Mark says, signaling Lane to leave the room. Again, she shakes her head.

Even if she wanted to walk away, her legs have gone numb. She's remembering being Talley's age and leaving the food. Beginning at dusk, Lane would sit on the back porch and listen and watch for the boys, ready to wave at them and point them toward the river. When she was Talley's age, those boys were like hope to Lane. They were a way to break free of her life and escape all the way to Georgia. She clung to them when she had nothing else. Talley must have heard that in the stories Lane told, because she's been clinging to the boys in the same way.

"I saw Annalee leave."

"Seen her leave where, here? You seen her leave home?"

Talley nods.

"And when was that?"

"During the night," Talley says. "Annalee did it all the time. She did it last night after Mama got home. She goes to see Jimmy. She loves him. She said she was going to run away and be married. But I don't think she did."

"And why do you think that?" Mark asks.

"I found a bag in her room."

"Yes," he says, nodding as if he already knows about it.

"It's under her bed, and it's packed like she was really leaving but she didn't take it. Jimmy was going to marry Annalee. That's what she thought. But Daryl told me that will never happen because Jimmy is a liar. He's going away to college all by himself. He doesn't love Annalee, and he will never marry her."

"What exactly did Daryl say about Annalee and Jimmy?" Mark says.

"He said Fieldings are butchers and whores, and he made me promise to tell Annalee that Jimmy didn't love here and would never marry her. Daryl said no matter where she goes, Annalee will never be safe. Never, ever again."

LANE

IT ISN'T THAT Lane's knees buckle or that she falls to the kitchen floor. She doesn't scream or slap at the hands trying to calm her, at least not at first. Instead she walks to the other side of the kitchen table where Talley sits, not able to feel her feet beneath her. She speaks to Talley, though she doesn't hear the words coming out of her own mouth. She cups Talley's shoulders, kisses the top of her head, but she can't feel the warmth of Talley's skin. With so little sun, the room has gone cold, and Lane is suddenly chilled.

She tells Talley how wonderfully brave she's been and says maybe she should go on upstairs. Take a bath. Use your bubbles. Put on fresh clothes. It'll be lunchtime soon. Grandma Erma will make us something special. I bet she'll make some of her peach tarts too. You'll help her, won't you?

As Talley pushes back from the table, Lane holds her own hands at her sides, forces herself to smile, clenches her stomach to keep her body still. She does all these things until Talley's feet hit the staircase.

Mark is there to grab her. He wraps his arms around her, grunts as she twists and pulls away from him. She doesn't think it anymore. Or fear it. She knows it. Annalee is gone, and a man named Daryl has done something terrible to her. Lane is trapped now, all of them are, more than ever. By the closed windows and drawn drapes. By reporters and Erma hobbling down the drive and Neil shouting from his chair. For nearly twenty years, Lane has tried to be a good mother. She tried and hoped that would be enough, but she brought her girls here, and now Annalee is gone. Still holding Lane in his arms, Mark shakes his head because someone must be coming toward them to peel her away. His arms squeeze tighter until she can't slap or beat at him.

"He was at our home," Lane says, her mouth pressed to his chest so Talley won't hear. "The food. That man, that Daryl, came here. How many nights? He came to our house and he knows Talley. And that kerchief. It's definitely Susannah's. I saw her wearing it, every time she came here. How did he end up with Susannah's kerchief?"

And then she looks beyond Mark to the back door.

"The door," Lane says. "It was him. He was here today and broke into the house."

She wants to pull away and run into the foyer, the drawing room, the parlor. She wants to run through every room in the house, searching so she'll find him and be rid of him, but Mark already did the searching, and the man, Daryl, is gone. He came into the house, walked past Erma and Neil sleeping in their chairs, and he left the windows open so he could come back for Talley. So he could take Talley too.

Lane pushes away from Mark, shakes her head from side to side, but his arms don't let go. He presses her face into his chest, where he smells so much like home. Like mud and the river and the gray moss hanging in the oaks. He whispers in her ear in that voice of his, that deep, slow, meandering voice. It'll be all right, he whispers. Over and over, it'll be all right. Lane stops slapping and twisting.

"Jimmy," she says, pulling away enough to look up at Mark. "She was going to see Jimmy. He'll know something. He has to."

Mark's arms loosen. He inhales deeply, signaling for Lane to do the same, and when she doesn't beat at him again, his arms fall away. He pulls out a chair, guides her to sit, and squats next to her.

"Some officers have already been to talk to Jimmy," he says, his hands resting on Lane's knees. "Says he wasn't with her."

"Well, he's lying. They've been keeping it secret. I didn't know. Surely his parents didn't either. He's lying."

"And if that's so, we'll flush it out. A few officers found him at his house this morning. Showed one of them his cell phone. There was a call from Annalee last night. Just like Jimmy said happened. Rowland was there with him. Both say they were home all night. Rowland did drive you, told me that himself at the river. Said the same to the officers who went to his house. He dropped you and went home and says Jimmy was there all night."

"But Annalee didn't leave until late, until after I got home. He could have met her. Jimmy could have left the house without Rowland knowing it."

"Possible, yes."

"What about Hettie and Rowland?" Lane says. "Did they know the kids were still together?"

Mark shakes his head. "Not according to Rowland."

Lane sits back in her seat. Her shoulders drop and roll forward.

The air rushes out of her. She should have thought of it right away. She braces her hands against the table as if to stand, but Mark's hands close tighter around her knees.

"Hettie, she worked at the church, the same church as that Daryl." She leans back. "Oh, Mark. Susannah, she and some of the other kids from Florida State, they went to the New Covenant when they needed tools we didn't have. They're all tangled up with that man. And now Annalee too. Why is he suddenly everywhere?"

"We'll figure all this out, Lane," Mark says, leaning in and looking directly into her eyes so she'll believe him.

Lane stares at him. It's only been a day since she was standing in the bar alone. Rowland had gone out to move their cars from the side of the bar where they normally park to the lot out front, and she was listening to the rain on the roof when a man stumbled through the door, a strange man who slapped himself in the forehead. She called Mark because she'd made him a promise but hung up when the reporters arrived.

"What is it?" Mark asks.

"He came into the bar," Lane says.

"Who did?"

"That man. That Daryl. He was at the bar too. It had to have been him."

"What do you mean? When?"

"I started to call you about him last night. He came in before everyone else, before the party. He was strange. I thought he was probably here for whatever brought the reporters. And then he told me Annalee wasn't working. He was watching her and he wanted me to know."

"Did he say anything else?"

"Called us butchers and whores. Wasn't the first I heard that.

I texted Annalee right away. She was at home. Then the man left. I got busy and didn't think anything else of it."

"Okay, I need you to slow down and tell me everything he said to you. Everything you can remember about him."

"He's here because of Neil," Lane says.

"You don't know that," Mark says. "You can't know that."

"I do," she says. "Why else leave those windows open? It's personal, whatever brought him here." Mark takes her hands in his, rubs his thumbs across the backs of her fingers. This kindness of Mark's has made Lane ashamed over the years. She didn't know how special it was back when she first lived in this town, how special it made Mark. She thought it was ordinary, conventional. Men like her ex-husband survive on mistakes like that. Women like Lane suffocate on them.

"How did you know about Annalee and Jimmy?" Lane asks.

"Didn't know for sure," Mark says, still trailing his thumbs over her top knuckles. "Figured it was likely. Tell a teenage boy he can't have something, and he wants it all the more." He stares at Lane, his lids heavy. He isn't only talking about Jimmy Jansen. He's talking about himself too and about how much he's wanted Lane all these years.

The smell of fresh coffee fills the room. Lane must have set some to brew when Neil started hollering for a cup but she doesn't remember doing it. The air conditioner switches on, and cold air blows down from overhead, chilling her damp skin.

That's Bonnie Wiley's voice coming from outside. Someone is telling her it's best she go back home but she wants to know what has that Neil done now. She's shouting out that they drew a picture of a boy dug up from the graves. She wants to know if Neil remembers the child. She wants to know if Neil whipped that boy until he died.

Lane was fifteen when she walked to the end of the drive and turned left instead of right. When she reached the entrance to the school for boys, a guard greeted her. He was leaning against a black pickup truck and had a thick gray mustache and a large stomach.

"Your father ain't here," he said.

Tall, ragged pines stood on either side of the cracked asphalt road leading into the school. Thick patches of brown needles covered the ground beneath the trees. The needles splintered under the guard's heavy boots as he pushed off the truck and walked toward Lane.

"Working on a school project," she told him. "Mind helping me?"

He drove her through the school, the asphalt road sinking below ground in some spots and turning into a dirt road. They passed simple white buildings with black pitched roofs, one just like the next. Dirt footpaths cut between each. A few boys dressed in pale blue pants and shirts walked from one building to another, but when they saw the black pickup truck, they turned their eyes away or lowered them to the ground. Any one of them might have suffered because of Lane. Every one of them might have, and she felt like they looked. Empty inside, moving stiffly and without reason. She wanted to jump from the truck, run to each one and ask if he was the boy Neil hurt, did he know which boy it was. Was the boy dead or alive? She wanted to cling to them, beg them, though she wasn't sure what she wanted to hear. Would one particular boy matter to them? What about all the others? She wanted to tell them she was so very sorry.

The last building Lane and the man drove past before starting up a shallow hill was single story and white much like the rest but smaller and topped by a flat black roof. The kids at Lane's school said this building set off by itself was the one where the boys got their whippings. Some said boys also got shot in the back for running and that one boy was found, or rather his bones were found, under the front porch at the Harrisons' place. Some of those kids said things like that didn't happen no more. Others glanced at Lane and said maybe, maybe not. They had all heard the same as Lane—that on the day Lane disappeared when she was thirteen, Neil beat a boy until he told him where she was.

She couldn't remember when she first started leaving food for the boys. She would hear her father talking about them. Another one ran, he'd say at the supper table, or maybe he'd say that old Toby Timberland was hoping to earn himself an easy fifty dollars by tracking down another one. Lane would lie awake on those nights and imagine the boys creeping through the oaks, maybe pausing when they passed near a magnolia tree to take in the scent of it, before seeing the river just ahead. At some point, no telling how many years back, one boy told another and he told another— the river was the way out.

Lane would imagine them reaching the banks and following the river all the way to Georgia. As she grew older, she began to leave the food and notes so they would know she was here, thinking of them and that she wanted to be part of their dream to escape. She'd follow the river alongside one of those boys. It would be dark, and for once, the night would be cool. They'd run until their legs burned and they couldn't run anymore.

No one ever seemed to miss the boys who ran, no one ever seemed to care what became of them, and that would be true for Lane too if she ran away with one of them. She would escape heavy boots climbing the stairs that meant she was in some kind of trouble, slamming doors, breaking glass, cries in the middle of the night. She'd escape being careful all the time and scared all the time and she'd escape how tired the fear made her. Tired like she was an old woman already. But mostly she'd escape the way Mama's head hung most all the time.

At the top of the hill, the guard stopped in the shade of a few mulberry trees. He nodded for Lane to look out her window, and it was right there. The cemetery. Thirty or so white metal crosses had been driven into the ground. Brown rust stained each where its parts joined in the middle, and some had lost an arm or a top. Lane asked to see the newer graves.

"Only graves we got," the guard said. "Don't use this place no more."

The boy's grave, if it existed, would have been newer, only a few years old. Grass would have overtaken it like it had all the others, but still the newer grave would have looked different, somehow fresher. Lane opened her door, stepped lightly onto the ground, and walked toward the graves. The man joined her.

"Were you here that night?" she asked the man.

Dark patches of sweat stained the man's gray shirt at his underarms, and he rubbed his large stomach as if it ached. He started to ask what Lane meant but then nodded again because he understood.

"We all was," he said. "Damn near the whole town was out looking. Fellows from as far as Tallahassee, Greenwood, and Cottondale came looking."

"And do you remember anything about the boy?" Lane asked. "Do you remember what my father did to him?"

The guard said nothing but took Lane by the arm, guided her back to his truck, and helped her inside. When he settled in his own seat, he tugged at his buckle where it cut into his stomach, laid one arm over the seatback, and leaned toward Lane. He smelled salty and like cigarette smoke.

"Don't know what your daddy did or didn't do," he said, his

arm brushing the back of Lane's head. "But whatever it was, he done it for you. All them people who came here searching for you done it for love of your father. He's a damn good man, and folks know it. You should too." Then he pulled his arm away and shifted the truck into drive. At the entrance where Lane first walked into the school, he stopped and nodded for her to get out.

"Ain't going to tell your daddy you was here," he said before Lane closed her door. Like everyone else, this man believed someone had taken Lane. He believed a boy, one of Neil's boys, took her, and whatever that boy got, he had coming. "And you best hope no one else tells him you was here either."

"Lane." It's Mark, standing on the other side of her now. She rolls her head to the left. He bends his knees, lowers himself so he can look her straight on. "You still with me?"

There used to be a worn spot in the wooden floors leading into the kitchen. Susannah Bauer ordered the heart yellow pine from a shop up in Boston, and she and the others feathered the new wood into the old. It's perfect now, that patch where the wood was once worn. A person could never tell where the old ends and the new begins.

"They've found her, Lane," Mark says. "They've found Annalee."

DARYL

On Susannah's last day

SATURDAY IS HERE, and it must surely be the day I will see Susannah again. She was supposed to come last Saturday and didn't. As I wait for her, I scratch at the red welts on my ankles that I got watching Annalee and the boy down at the river. I scratch at them as I think of Susannah not coming to town when she was supposed to and I wonder if she'll ever come again. I scratch at them until they bleed, and now, even a week later, they've still not healed over. Miss Hettie says it's because I won't leave them alone. Stop that scratching, she hollers at me when she leaves in the evenings.

Talley never comes to water her garden on Saturdays, because her mother can't know she comes here. When lunchtime nears, I leave my shed and do the watering for her. After today, I won't water again. I know all I need to know from Talley.

I eat my sandwich at twelve noon, and when Susannah still has not come to borrow a tool by three o'clock, I begin to pace in my shed. I close the door so Reverend and Miss Hettie won't see me. Even with the windows open, the heat grows inside the shed. It's like a tin can in here, Reverend once said when he stuck his head in to check on me. As I walk three paces this way and three paces that way, I pound one fist into the palm of my other hand. There and back, I go. There and back. It's Saturday and Susannah should come. Last time, she said she'd see me again. No need yet for good-byes.

I stop waiting at five. Susannah never comes after five. I open the door to my shed, stumble out, and with my hands resting on my knees, I stand in the shade of the oaks. Susannah promised to say one last good-bye, but I'm afraid she'll never come again. From over near the church, Miss Hettie calls out to me.

"Are you okay there, darling?" she says. Stepping up onto the curb, slowly so as to not stumble in her high heels, she takes a few steps in my direction. "You don't look well."

I run both hands through my hair, pushing it off my forehead like the boy did down at the river, and force myself to stand straight. Miss Hettie talks to me the same as she did before I went to services with her. When I left her that night, she said Annalee would love me one day and I was a fine young man.

"Doing just real well, ma'am," I say, because that's what people here at this church, here in this town, say. "Have yourself a nice evenin'."

My shirt, my hair, and even my jeans are still damp when I reach the grocery store. A burst of cold air spills out as the double doors open. The shock of it makes me draw in a single, quick breath. The chill clears my thoughts, and I remember why I've come. It will stay light until well into the evening, so Susannah may come here for sandwiches and water and ice-cream bars she'll pack on ice. I've come for Susannah.

Pulling a cart from a long line of carts, I push it down the aisle where they keep the fruits and vegetables. The left wheel wobbles, and I push with my left hand and pull with my right. It's the same cart I pushed the day Annalee knocked the wind from my lungs, the day I first saw her. Susannah was in the store that day too. Someone was with her, talking to her. I heard him and recognized him as Miss Hettie's son, and so did Annalee.

Just as I think about the boy from the river, he appears. Carrying a bag of ice in both hands, he is walking toward the cashiers. Others walk with him, people his own age, but Annalee isn't among them. She'll be working at the Wharf because it's Saturday. At the beginning of the summer, she didn't start work until six, but she's been there a month, at least a month, and she's a waitress now and a closer. Someone asked if she was the closer the last time I was there. She said yes. Been here since five. Be here at least until ten.

Some of the others carry ice too. A few carry bags of hot dog and hamburger buns and still others carry chips and plates. I push my cart closer, slipping in between all of them, pushing with my left hand and pulling with my right. They stumble out of my way, frown that I've forced my way between them, but the boy smiles. Not at me. At someone else. Handing his bags of ice to one of the others, he walks away from the group. I push my cart off to the side and turn to watch the boy as he walks quickly, with long steps, toward the deli at the far end of the store.

"Susannah," the boy calls out. "Hey, wait up."

SOMETHING HAPPENS TO me each time I see Susannah. I want to be near her, not only so I might get close enough to touch her but also so she'll notice me. She knows me like none of the others have. This is what makes her more special than the rest. I have to hide from the others so they don't see me and tell a father or boyfriend. The others will never remember me. They'll never say my name or brush past me, letting our arms touch. Susannah will be the first to leave me, but she'll also be the first to remember me. Now, here in the grocery store, I want to hear her say my name one last time and for her to look in my eyes and know I'm here. I become something more when Susannah is near. The girls are what make me real, Susannah most of all. If Susannah sees me and remembers me and thinks of me in the years to come, that will surely mean Mother was wrong. Our family didn't die with her.

Susannah wears a kerchief on her head today like she does so many days. It's bright blue and yellow. She told me once it's the Swedish flag and reminds her of home, though really she didn't live there long. I almost told her about Wayne that day. I thought I might even tell her his real name and that when I find him, it will be just him and me. I won't even need the girls anymore, and we'll do real good.

Since Susannah was honest with me about missing home, I could tell her the truth about my brother too. I could tell her he taught me about salting watermelon and how to slide the tail from a honeysuckle bloom to get at its honey. Maybe she'd help me find Wayne. Like Miss Hettie, Susannah would know how to use the computer to type in his name, his real name, and find out if he'd been one of the boys who ran. Maybe she could find out if he got away and where he went and why he never found me. Or if he didn't get away, and if that's why I never saw him again, was he one of the boys Neil Fielding beat?

There are boys in the cemetery over there at the school who have no name, boys they've dug up from unmarked graves. Some of those boys died a long time ago, almost a hundred years ago, some of them. Others died not so long ago. Miss Hettie told me this. She said probably the poor kids and the ones with no mamas or daddies were the ones who got it worst. There was no one to look out for those kids, and she asked if Wayne was alone like that. I said yes, I think so, and she said I should let them stick a swab inside my mouth so they could tell me if my brother was one of those boys in a grave. Discarded, she said of the boys. And I wondered by who.

I didn't know about swabs and DNA, but I did know Susannah could help me find out what happened if I told her Wayne's real name. We'd find him and I'd have a brother again. But then, after talking about home and Sweden, Susannah said there was no sense living in the past, and so I didn't say anything.

I get one glimpse of the blue-and-yellow kerchief, and then Susannah disappears behind the shelves where they keep the aspirin and bandages I sometimes buy. The boy shouts out to his friends that he'll be right back and runs after her. I swing around and follow, pushing my cart behind the tall display that holds thick paperbacks.

"Was hoping I'd see you here," the boy from the river says to Susannah.

Walking around her cart, the boy draws her into a hug. Like me, he has come here at this time wanting to see her. Or maybe he's lying and says it only to make her happy. When they pull apart, the boy keeps his arms around Susannah as he looks down into her face. She lets him do this and rests her hands on his forearms. It should be as easy for me. The boy leans in and says something in her ear. She lays her head back and laughs. The kerchief slips off and falls at her feet.

"You should come," the boy says.

As he waits for Susannah to answer, he presses one of her

hands to his lips. His hair is nearly white, much lighter even than the last time I saw him. He holds Susannah's hand there. He must be smelling her skin, kissing her top knuckles. I know he's begging her, pleading her to do something because I've seen him beg and plead before. The boy is large next to her, larger than he is next to Annalee. I want to beat him with a stick again until he crumbles at my feet.

"But you'll have to come get me," Susannah finally says. "I won't be ready until eight or so."

"Perfect," he says. "The burgers will be gone, but there'll be plenty of beer. The Tracks. You know the place?"

Susannah nods. "You'll show me the caves?" she calls out as he begins to walk away. "I want to see the bats."

I'll add that to my list. Susannah loves houses and history and horses and the gray bats that live at the river. She wants to see them because they live no other place on earth. Only there in the limestone caves.

"Sure," the boy says. "We'll find you some bats." And when his friends call out for him to hurry up and get a move on, he turns and breaks into a jog, but before he disappears around the end of the aisle, he calls out to Susannah, "Can't believe you was going to leave without saying good-bye."

Once he is gone, Susannah swings her cart around as I push mine out from behind the display of books. She glances at me and then looks again. The second time, she smiles and lifts a hand. Her blue eyes are brighter under the overhead lights, and her cheeks and the tops of her shoulders are red where she's gotten too much sun.

"Hey there," she says.

"Hey there," I say.

I want to reach out and grab her by the arm so she'll look me in the eyes and say my name and I'll be real for a moment. I want to tell her Wayne's real name, and I want her to help me. If she doesn't, I might never find my brother and I'll always be alone. But she's in a hurry to get her ice-cream bars and pack her cooler. She gives me one quick wave and then pushes her cart through the vegetable bins and turns toward the freezers. She walks quickly. Two leather gloves are tucked in her back pocket and the fingers flap as she hurries away.

The boy is picking her up at eight, driving to Tallahassee just for her. He and his friends are having a party because they are all leaving for college soon. But those friends don't matter as much to him as Susannah. Today was her last trip to the Fielding Mansion. She'll never come again to Waddell. Can't believe you was going to leave without saying good-bye, the boy shouted as he walked away.

Once Susannah is gone and the boy and his friends are digging money from their pockets to hand to the cashier, I leave my cart, pick up the blue-and-yellow kerchief that dropped from Susannah's head, the first thing I've ever had to remind me of the girls except for my maps and lists, and I press it to my face.

30

LANE

LANE SITS ON a metal chair in the hallway outside Annalee's hospital room, and Talley sits next to her. No visitors allowed yet. Mark said he thought they should leave Talley at the house. Three deputies were there and would be staying. She'd be safe and there would be no chance of reporters swarming her or her hearing something she shouldn't. Lane needed only shake her head once. Talley would be staying with her.

They're parked outside the hospital, reporters who came here for a story about the school but who are staying for the story about a killer. They're parked too at the end of the road outside Lane's house, kept at bay only by the sawhorses and yellow tape the sheriff's office set up. The reporters must see this as their great fortune, a once-in-a-lifetime story that makes the family of Neil Fielding the near victims of a possible serial killer. They shouted at Lane as she hurried into the hospital, Talley cradled in her arms. Lane shook her head and said nothing as they asked questions highlighting her greatest fears. Do you think this is tied to your father? Do you think this is tied to you? Given your past, why would you bring your children back to Waddell?

Before disappearing into Annalee's room and leaving Lane to wait outside, the doctor tells Lane that Annalee is dehydrated and shows signs of exposure. They are working to bring up her body temperature and examining her for trauma, head injuries, and such. All that limestone really does a number on a person, the doctor says. Her feet, her legs, shins especially. She took a good knock to her left cheek, right there under her eye. No telling if it was inflicted or a result of making her way upriver. She was likely moving quickly, recklessly, as if running away from someone.

And bug bites, lots of bug bites, but that is the least of their concerns. The body temperature is the thing they need to address. It'll likely lead to some confusion on her part and fatigue. It's being stubborn, that body temperature of hers. And before pulling open Annalee's door, the doctor leans in close. No signs of sexual assault, he says. Lane inhales sharply as if someone has struck her in the stomach with a fist. Annalee will live with it now, the same thing Lane has lived with. She'll live with being a victim, walking past people who whisper, learning to smile at tilted heads that mean she is pitied.

Annalee has always been the more difficult of Lane's two daughters. From the beginning, she cried more. Not in the way other babies cried, but she cried all the time, every waking moment, it seemed. People sometimes asked, why the long spread between your girls? Was it all those book tours? Was Kyle on the road too much? Lane would nod as if yes, it was something like that. She could never manage the truth.

After Annalee, Lane was afraid to have another baby. Talley was an accident, unwanted even in the beginning. That was reason enough for guilt, but there would be more. Talley went on to be an easier child. She was a pleasure after all those struggles. And so Lane carried the burden of wanting one child more than the other. Sure, she loved them both, but she would smile to see Talley every morning. She would brace herself to see Annalee. What kind of mother must brace herself to see her child? But it will be different now. It has to be. She has to find a way to know Annalee for who she is.

"They found her upriver?" Lane asks Mark. She whispers because Talley sits on a chair between them. Headphones dangle from both ears, and an iPad that must be Mark's rests in her lap.

"None of that matters now," Mark says, motioning to two men standing near the hospital's entrance that he'll be right with them. "Have you called Kyle?"

Lane nods. "But I don't understand. How did she get there?"

The officers had been looking downriver at first because that's where they found Hettie. The water was especially high in the wake of the rain, the rapids running heavier and faster than normal. It would have carried a body, a dead body, downriver. They thought, assumed, Annalee was dead.

"All you need to know is that Annalee's here," Mark says, standing. "She'll be well again, soon enough. You sit tight; I'll be right back."

As Mark walks away, his footsteps echoing up and down the long hallway, Lane can still feel the doctor's warm breath on her neck, just below her ear, and those words linger as if he just whispered them. Sexual assault. Something makes her turn. A sound maybe, a shift in the air as if a door opened, a stream of light as if someone pulled up the blinds. At the far end of the hallway, a man rounds the corner.

225

He walks with a long stride and a loose spine that makes his torso sway with each step. It's familiar, and it's suddenly summertime again and they're in high school and Rowland Jansen is one of the older boys. His blond hair turns white every June. He plays baseball and dates Hettie Martin. Her family has sugarcane money, old sugarcane money, so everyone thinks Rowland will marry her one day. Lane's friends all like him, but Lane says he's too old. They think she says these things because one of the boys from the school took her and ruined her, but really she says them because she likes Mark Ellenton. But there he is, Rowland Jansen. That's him striding down the hall, hands shoved in his pockets, except it isn't him, and Lane isn't sixteen years old. That's Jimmy Jansen. That's Rowland's son, the boy who says he loves Annalee.

"I DON'T THINK you should be here, Jimmy," Lane says when Jimmy is close enough to hear her. She stands and steps in front of Talley to block her from Jimmy's sight.

"That her room?" he says. With his hands still dug down in his pockets, he keeps walking toward Lane. His eyes are red, his hair hasn't been washed in days, and he smells of sweat and clothes left to mold in the washer.

"We can't go in," Lane says. "No one can yet."

Jimmy stares at the door and nods, but his eyes don't focus like they should. It's as if he's looking just off center. "My mom is dead," he says.

Lane swings around to check on Talley. The headphones still hang from her ears so she probably didn't hear what Jimmy said, but she is staring up at him as if afraid.

"I'm terribly sorry," Lane says, speaking in a quieter voice and hoping Jimmy will do the same. "I don't think this is a good time for any of us. You should be home with your father. Please tell him we're all so very sorry. I'll be over to the house just as soon as I can, and I'll tell Annalee you were here. But I really think you should go."

She's thinking about police investigations and eyewitness accounts, and she doesn't want to risk any of that by telling Jimmy something she shouldn't or hearing him say something she shouldn't.

"I can't hardly believe it, you know?" Jimmy says. "That she's really gone."

"I can't either," Lane says, reaching out to stroke Jimmy's arm, but he pulls away. "She was so very proud of you. Bragged on you all the time."

"Is it true?" He crosses his arms as if to keep Lane from trying to comfort him again. "Do they think it's that Daryl from church? That he killed my mama?"

"Talley," Lane says, tugging one of the headphones from Talley's ear. She is still staring up at Jimmy. "Would you run down there and ask the nurse where I can find some coffee?"

"Was it him?" Jimmy asks again before Talley has set aside the iPad and started down the hall. His voice has grown louder despite Lane trying to quiet him. "Did he kill my mom?"

"I don't know, Jimmy," Lanc says, waiting until Talley walks away. "That's what Mark seems to think."

Lane hurries Talley along with the wave of a hand when she glances back, and the way she starts to walk faster and the way she looks back two more times again makes it seem she's afraid of Jimmy.

"And Annalee," Jimmy says. "Will she be all right?"

"The doctor says yes. She needs rest, mostly." Lane glances one last time at Talley. She should have asked Talley to send Mark back. "Did you happen by our house today, Jimmy? Maybe try to get in through the back door?"

"He tried to kill them both, didn't he?" Jimmy says, shaking his head but not answering Lane's question. "Why were they both at the river? Annalee and my mom?"

"I'm sorry, I can't talk about this," Lane says.

"He followed us one time," Jimmy says. "Daryl did. Down to the river. I'm sure it was him. Hit me in the gut. Doubled me over. I'm sure it was him."

"I'm so sorry about your mother and whatever else has happened, but there's really nothing I can tell you."

This is Rowland's boy, and Lane should want to comfort him, but instead she wants him to leave. There's something about the way he won't look her straight on and yet is standing too close that is making her feel she doesn't have enough air to breathe.

"Annalee called me and said don't come," Jimmy says. He stares at the ground now, as if talking more to himself than to Lane, as if he's trying to convince himself of something. "We were supposed to meet at the river. We did that sometimes. But she said not to come because of the rain." He pauses, covers his mouth over with one hand but can't muffle the sob. "She was angry, you know, because I was leaving for college."

"You should tell all of this to the police," Lane says. She thinks again she should do something to comfort Jimmy, but the way Talley looked at him stops her from placing a hand on his shoulder. "Whatever it is, you should be honest, is all."

"My mom made me do it," he says, drawing a hand across his nose and lifting his head. His face is red and damp.

"Made you do what?" Lane stares up at Jimmy. She has to force the words up and out. "What did you do, Jimmy?"

He is crying openly now, wiping away his tears with the backs of his hands. "Mama made me lie to Annalee, made me lie and say I'd marry her. And I think Annalee found out."

"I don't understand." The sudden queasiness in Lane's stomach is realization. Everything Jimmy is telling her is swirling overhead, growing closer and moving faster, and soon it will land at the moment Lane slept with Rowland Jansen. "Why would your mother want you to lie? Why make a promise like that to Annalee when you knew it wasn't true?"

"I did love her," Jimmy says, again not answering Lane's question. "I hope you'll believe me. Never wanted her hurt."

"Jimmy, did you do something to Annalee?"

"I really loved her," he says, shaking his head. "But we're young, you know. I never thought we should be getting married, and I felt real bad telling her I did. I lied to her, Miss Lane. I'm real sorry."

There's no reason Hettie would tell her son to lie except for hatefulness. Hurting one of her children was the surest way to hurt Lane.

"People are saying my mom was with him, with that Daryl." Jimmy glances around as if afraid someone might overhear. "Like taking iced tea to him and taking him to services too."

"I'm sorry, but I don't know anything about that."

"She was doing it because she was mad at my dad."

"You need to go, Jimmy," Lane says, trying to speak gently but needing him to leave.

It's closing in, Jimmy blaming her for what has happened to his mother, and maybe he's right. If Hettie got herself tangled up with Daryl as a way to punish Rowland, then she did so because he slept with Lane.

"And that Daryl," Jimmy says. "Do they think he killed Susannah too?"

"Susannah's not dead," Lane says. Again, she must remind herself Annalee is here and she's safe. "We don't know anything about her yet. Nothing for sure."

Halfway down the hall, one of the nurses is handing Talley a stack of napkins, and another is coming out from behind the reception desk with two bottles of water in hand.

"That ain't true," Jimmy says. "Susannah is dead. The news said so. Rising water stirred up her body. They found her right there with Annalee. Practically side by side."

"I don't want to talk anymore," Lane says. "Talley's coming back and she can't hear this."

The panic that had exhausted Lane before is making her fidget now. She crosses her arms, shuffles from one foot to the other. Even though Annalee is sleeping in the next room, safe, another death reminds Lane that the man who left those windows open so he could come back for Talley is still out there.

"But is that what they think? Did the sheriff say so, that Daryl killed them both?" Jimmy is leaning forward as if he wants to grab Lane and shake an answer out of her. "They must believe that, right? It's settled? My mother and Susannah too? That Daryl killed them both?"

"I don't know, Jimmy," Lane says, wanting to shove him away, but that would be cruel. "Mark, Sheriff Ellenton, will sort it all out. He'll be sure to sort out exactly what happened to your mother."

In the wake of a tragedy, people have to sometimes be reminded it's over. Lane has done this before, sat next to a witness or victim after she was done gathering facts and patted a hand, offered a bottle of water. It's the moment she was constantly seeking when taking all those stories—the moment she could say it's over. She would sort out the facts, uncover the truth, give people a sense of order. All is well. You're safe. Now she's the one in need of reassurance so she will recognize the world around her again, know which way to turn next, which step to take. This is what the people in her articles needed, how badly they needed it, and Lane gave it to them for her own good, not theirs. She knows that now because she's one of them. She sought to comfort the people in her stories because she couldn't comfort the ones Neil harmed during all his years at the school, or, to be more truthful, she comforted them because she couldn't comfort the one she harmed by hiding in the attic.

It was a hateful thing Lane did all those years she was working as a reporter, selfish, at the very least. And she'd been wrong too. All the people from her stories, the ones she interviewed and wrote about, they never believed Lane when she said the worst was over. They still startled at a slamming door or grabbed her hand when a car passed by too quickly. Lane doesn't believe it either. Annalee is here in the next room, but she isn't safe. It isn't over.

JIMMY IS GONE by the time Mark reaches Lane, and before he can speak, Lane holds up a hand to silence him and also so the nurse walking with Talley will stop, turn around, and take Talley back to the nurses' station.

"Is it true?" she says. "Susannah Bauer was found?"

"I didn't want to tell you until you'd seen Annalee." Mark guides Lane back to the chairs. "You needed to see your daughter first. See for yourself she's okay. And she is. She will be."

There's desperation in his voice. Maybe it's the way he talks too quickly or with a slightly higher pitch, or the way he tips forward at the waist, ever so slightly so Lane will be sure to hear him. He wants to convince her that what happened to Lane, what he believes happened to Lane, didn't happen to her daughter. He needs Lane to believe it, wants to assure her before the wrong idea takes hold.

Lane jerks her arm away from Mark and drops onto the metal chair. "But I don't know that. I don't even know what she's been through."

"You heard what the doctor said," Mark says, sitting next to her. "A little time is all she'll be needing. This isn't like when we were kids, like when you were a kid."

"Stop it," Lane says, because every bit of Mark's concern for her is a reminder of how much she has hidden from him. "Stop worrying about me. None of this is about me, and none of this is okay. I don't understand why Annalee was down there at the river, or why Hettie was there. And now Susannah? That man, that Daryl, he means to come back for Talley."

"I'm not going to let that happen," Mark says, leaning back in his chair and resting his head against the wall. "He was careful with Susannah, but he wasn't with Hettie. He'll know he was sloppy, and that'll make him run. He's a simple enough fellow. We'll track him down."

"Jimmy told me the news is saying Susannah's body was found with Annalee. Is it true? And what does it mean?"

Mark rests his forearms on his knees. Annalee worked hard to get as far upriver as she did. That's how he begins. She traveled a good distance, all the way to the span of river where the banks of limestone rise sharply on either side. Cavities are carved into the stone there, hollows, dens, shallow caves. Of course, Lane remembers those caves. Some are barely above water level, and they would have flooded with the rising river. Some are higher on the banks.

When they were teenagers, she and Mark and the others would climb to the caves, and once there, they'd drink beer and sometimes smoke pot. The brave few among them would jump from the mouth of the highest caves out into the center of the river. Lane was always one of them. Always, even when Mark said it was too windy or shallow, she would jump. He was so worried something else bad would happen to her, and some part of Lane was trying to turn that lie into truth by jumping in shallow water or sleeping with boys she didn't love or running away from what she couldn't face. When Kyle came along, he never said the weather was too windy or the water too shallow.

"And what about Susannah?" Lane asks.

"She'd been tucked back in the first hollowed-out spot you come to when you're making your way upriver. We could swim into it when the water was up. Remember? Right there level with the surface. Someone put her there, is my guess."

"And did someone put Annalee there too?"

"We'll have to hope she can tell us the answer to that."

"Jimmy said the water stirred up Susannah's body."

Mark nods. "Rising river and all that rain. Floated her up and over the ridge in the stone. That's when they spotted her, when she floated out."

The door to Annalee's room opens. "You may come in, Mrs. Fielding," a nurse says.

Not able to stand until Mark reaches down to help her, Lane stares into Annalee's room and wonders if she'll be strong enough to help her daughter. All these years, she's not been strong enough to help herself.

31

TALLEY

TALLEY PINCHES HER eyes to clear away her tears when she, Mama, and Sheriff Ellenton step into Annalee's hospital room. The doctor said Annalee needed her rest. It drains a person to go through what she has. She needs time to get her strength back, and when she does, she'll remember. But no one could rest with lights so bright as these shining down, and Talley is glad of it. Annalee shouldn't get to rest when Susannah has to be dead.

Talley holds Mama's hand as the door closes quietly behind them, and because Mama is well ahead of Talley and their arms have stretched out between them as far as they can go, Talley knows she's walking too slowly. Out in the hallway, Mama told Talley about Susannah Bauer being found dead because she didn't want Talley to hear it from the television. She told Talley they were all safe, Annalee included, and not to be afraid. No matter what they saw in that room, it was Annalee, their Annalee, and with time, she would heal. But Annalee being Annalee is the thing that is starting to scare Talley most.

Inside Annalee's room, the lights turn Mama's skin and Sheriff Ellenton's a pasty white color, and shadows drop from under their eyes, nose, and chin. Sheriff Ellenton takes Talley by the shoulders and guides her to the end of Annalee's bed, their feet making tapping noises on the tile floor. Once there, he hands Talley a tissue, stands behind her like he thinks she might run from the room or from her only sister.

Annalee's eyes open, and the corners of her mouth rise the littlest bit. A smile, except her eyes don't look like a smile. That's always the thing with Annalee. She'll smile with her mouth, but the rest of her face stays flat, almost like a mask. Her cheeks that should plump with a smile, the corners of her eyes that should wrinkle, her head that should tilt off to the side, just off center . . . none of that happens.

Like the lights, the sheets Annalee lies on are bright white. Her hair, still damp, maybe from the river or maybe because the nurses scrubbed it clean, looks more brown than blond against the white sheets. Her blue eyes are big and round, too big and round, as if the rest of her has shrunk around them. Clear tubes run from her arm to a metal stand, and a single red light blinks and beeps steadily on a green screen that looks like a computer. This room, like the hallway, smells of the bleach Grandma adds to the laundry when she washes Grandpa Neil's undershirts. All of it together makes Annalee look small. Talley should feel bad for Annalee, but all she can think about is Susannah Bauer. She's the first person Talley has ever known who will never come back. Ever since Jimmy left the hospital, Talley can't stop herself from crying. Mama thinks the tears are for Annalee.

Sliding into the chair that sits next to the bed, Mama lifts one of Annalee's hands, wraps it in both of hers, and presses it to her cheek. She holds it there, inhaling through her nose. Mama still gives Talley hugs, but Annalee's too old for them. That's why her body is stiff when Mama leans in and loosely wraps her arms around Annalee. Except Annalee has always been that way, and if Talley knows that, Mama should know that too.

"Am I hurting you?" Mama asks, probably thinking that's the reason Annalee is hard to the touch.

One of the first times Talley and Daryl sat together on a Tuesday to watch the Little Sisters arrive for their meeting, long before Daryl said Jimmy would never marry Annalee, Daryl talked to Talley a good long while. You can't ever tell a secret and must always keep a promise, Daryl said. That's what being loyal means, and if you want to be a Little Sister of the South, you can't ever tell. That was when Talley's only secret was sneaking off to the church to tend her garden and having Daryl as a friend. Now she has many, but she thinks she's told Mama and Sheriff Ellenton every secret she has, except for one. She's never told how much she's started to fear Annalee.

STILL RUBBING ANNALEE'S hand like she's trying to work the kinks out of her fingers, Mama says, "You're doing remarkably well. Isn't that true, Mark?"

"Yes, you're in fine shape," Sheriff Ellenton says, his hands still resting on Talley's shoulders. His hair is flat where his hat normally sits, and bristly dark whiskers cover his cheeks and jaw.

It had been cold out in the hallway. The gray floors and the tan walls and the air blowing down from overhead made Talley wish for a jacket. Now her skin is warm where Sheriff Ellenton holds on to her, and sweat drips down her back and causes her to shiver. She has to think about every breath she takes in or there might not be enough air.

"They keep asking what I remember," Annalee says.

"No need to worry about that now," Mama says. "You're here and you're safe. That's all that matters." Mama pats the blanket draped over Annalee. "Feel, Talley. It's warm. It's what's making Annalee nice and warm again."

Before they walked into Annalee's room, the doctor told Mama that Annalee had some scrapes and bumps on her knees and shins, but they're hidden under the white sheets and warm blanket. One of her cheeks has a big red spot on it and tiny black lines at the center. Those are stitches. The doctor told Mama about those too. He said they wouldn't leave but the tiniest scar. Her face, he said, it'll be fine. Won't ever know it happened. Now all Talley can think about is what Susannah Bauer must look like since she's dead, and thinking about that makes her cry all over again, and Sheriff Ellenton squeezes her shoulders tighter.

"We'll talk about everything later," Sheriff Ellenton says. He dips his head and wipes the side of his face on his sleeve. He does the same on the other side. Like Talley, he's sweating. "I'm going to leave you ladies for now. Do you need anything, Annalee? Should I ask the nurse to come back?"

Annalee stares at the ceiling, and after a long pause, so long it seems she forgot Sheriff Ellenton asked her a question, she shakes her head.

"No," she finally says. "I'm fine."

Sheriff Ellenton pats the foot of Annalee's bed and gives Talley's shoulders a squeeze, a reminder to stay put as if he knows Talley wants to run. Then he walks slowly from the room, heel to toe like Daddy would do when he thought Talley was sleeping and didn't want to wake her. The cold air from the hallway spills into the room when Sheriff Ellenton opens the door. Talley tries to take it in, one quick lungful of the cool air, but by the time the door closes, it's gone.

"I keep trying to remember," Annalee says. "I remember hearing voices. It was like they woke me. But what was I doing there in those rocks? How did I get there?"

Mama says nothing more but sits still, only her fingers moving as she rubs and kneads Annalee's hand.

"What about Jimmy?" Annalee says, and when she tries to sit forward, she twists up her face and squeezes her eyes closed like someone punched her in the stomach.

Mama jumps to her feet and starts for the door.

"No," Annalee says, opening her eyes as she reaches for Mama's hand to draw her back to the bed. "I'm okay. Just moved too fast."

Mama slides into her chair again, but instead of lifting Annalee's hand, she lightly rests her fingers on her forearm.

"Is Jimmy all right?" Annalee says, lying back. "Was he there? He was supposed to meet me at the river. Is he okay?"

"Jimmy is fine, honey," Mama says, and glances over her shoulder as if hoping the nurse or Sheriff Ellenton will come back. Her face has turned red and shiny from the heat. "In fact, he was just here. He was very worried about you. But he's fine, perfectly fine."

"He told me to meet him, so I went to the river," Annalee says, closing her eyes. "I remember sitting in the car, and it started to rain. That's when I told him don't come."

While Annalee's eyes are still closed, Mama motions for Talley to go fetch Sheriff Ellenton. Talley nods and takes a few steps toward the door, heel to toe like Sherriff Ellenton did.

"I'd rather Mark talk with you about those things," Mama says to Annalee.

Annalee's eyes pop open, but she keeps looking at the ceiling. "His mother was there. Was Mrs. Jansen there?"

Mama stands, and Talley stops walking. A few more steps and she'd reach the door and could get away from Annalee, but she can't go any farther. There's something about Annalee's voice that frightens Talley. It's flat like the rest of her face when she smiles.

"Why would his mother have been there?" Annalee asks. "Why would she come and not Jimmy?"

"You're tired, Annalee," Mama says. "Let's leave all this talk until another time."

Talley slides one more foot toward the door.

"Did she follow me out there?" Annalee asks. "Could she have done that?"

The machine next to Annalee's bed begins to beep faster. Little by little, Annalee is taking up more space in the room and forcing Talley out the door.

"Come here, Talley," Mama says, motioning for Talley to take her seat next to Annalee.

Talley shakes her head and takes another sideways step toward the door.

"Why would she have been there, Mama?" Annalee says, reaching for Mama's hand. "What happened to me?"

"You need to calm down," Mama says, holding Annalee's outstretched hand in both of hers. "None of that matters just now. We don't know why Mrs. Jansen was there, but it doesn't matter. You've got to stop upsetting yourself. Talley, come here and sit with Annalee. I'm going to get the nurse."

Talley stares at Annalee's hand, wrapped tightly between both of Mama's, but can't make her feet move. She's shaking her head slowly from side to side even though she knows she should never say no to Mama. The machine beeps louder, faster. Mama drops Annalee's hand, knocks her chair over as she steps away from the bed, but before she reaches the door, it swings open and a nurse, the same one who gave Talley two chocolate chip cookies and bottled water, walks inside using long, quick steps. Sheriff Ellenton follows her, and like he did before, he stands behind Talley and rests his hands on her shoulders.

"Are you all right, dear?" the nurse says, placing a hand on Annalee's forehead and studying the machine that was beeping. It has slowed again. The nurse flips a switch. It stops altogether and she presses her fingertips to the inside of Annalee's wrist. "A little too much excitement. Better now?" she asks Annalee.

"Better," Annalee says.

The nurse lets go of Annalee's arm and hits the same switch again. The screen lights up, and the machine beeps like it did before, slow and steady with a long pause between each one.

"How about we wrap up this visit in the next few minutes?" the nurse says. She looks at Talley as she asks the question, and Talley nods.

The room is too small because something inside Annalee is growing too large.

ONCE THE NURSE has left, Annalee punches a button on the side of her bed and it rises until she's sitting up instead of lying down. She looks at each one of them . . . at Mama, at Sheriff Ellenton, at Talley.

"We were planning to be married," Annalee says, and her eyes settle on Talley. "He loved me. We were going to meet and make our plans. But I think Jimmy never came."

Talley wishes she could back away from Annalee, but Sheriff Ellenton has his hands on her shoulders again. When Talley cried because she had to pack a bag and leave Brooklyn, Mama told Talley to inhale and exhale. Remember to breathe, Mama had said. Talley does that now because her being afraid of Annalee has made her forget to breathe. Talley is afraid because Annalee knows Jimmy didn't love her. She knows he wasn't going to marry her and that Miss Hettie would never let him. She knows all those things because Talley told her, but that isn't what Annalee is telling Mama and Sheriff Ellenton.

"That'll be enough for now," Sheriff Ellenton says. "We'll let you rest."

"She called us butchers and whores," Annalee says. "Did you know?"

Mama nods. "Jimmy said his mama made him lie to you about getting married." She glances at Sheriff Ellenton, and he gives her a nod. "Do you know why she'd want him to lie? Why she'd want to hurt you like that?"

"I think because of what you did, Mama," Annalee says, resting a hand on top of Mama's. Mama straightens in her seat, but her eyes keep looking at the ground. "Where is Hettie Jansen now?" Annalee asks.

"She's dead," Talley says, because Annalee said something mean to Mama and she wants to say something mean right back. Sheriff Ellenton's fingers squeeze her shoulders. He wants Talley to say nothing more, but even though Mama will be angry, Talley can't stop herself. "And they think Daryl killed her. And he killed Susannah Bauer too."

"Hush about that," Mama says, wiping at one eye with the tip of her finger. "I'm sorry, Annalee. We didn't mean for you to hear any of this."

"They found poor Susannah?" Annalee says.

Mama nods and glances back at Sheriff Ellenton.

Annalee stares at Talley with eyes too big for her face. She smiles as if she wants Talley not to feel bad for blurting out the wrong thing, but only her mouth smiles. The rest of her face is flat.

"Who's Daryl?" Annalee says.

"You don't know him?" Sheriff Ellenton asks. "Works over at the New Covenant. Or rather he used to work over there."

Annalee shakes her head. "No," she says. "I don't know anyone named Daryl. But there was a guy. He came to the restaurant a few times. I remember some of the older men talking about him. The kid who mows for the church. That's what they would say. Could that be him?"

"Most likely," Sheriff Ellenton says.

"And he's out there still?" Annalee says, her eyes jumping from Mama to Sheriff Ellenton and back again. "They haven't caught him?"

Sheriff Ellenton shakes his head. "But you're safe. I don't want you to worry about that."

Talley looks up at Mama, who has closed her eyes. Sheriff Ellenton is patting Annalee's foot under the blankets and telling her they'll leave her for now and talk again later. Talley knows, but Mama and Sheriff Ellenton don't. Annalee does know Daryl. Just last night, Talley told Annalee that Jimmy was never going to marry her or run away with her. And when Annalee asked how Talley knew these things, she said Daryl told her. Annalee was angry to hear Daryl's name or afraid or both. Mama and Sheriff Ellenton don't know, but Talley does. Annalee is lying.

ERMA

ERMA'S BEANS ARE fine this morning, real fine. They remind her of Susannah. Every time she visited the house, she'd look over Erma's garden and talk about the day she'd have one of her own. Stretched out over her beans, Erma lets herself have a good cry about Susannah. The poor girl was nothing but kind and giving. She always had time for Erma, and if she had such kindness for Erma, she surely had it for others. What a tragic thing that someone so horrible could stamp out someone so very kind. If not for the relief she's feeling to have Annalee coming home today, Erma would have struggled even to get out of bed this morning.

Usually Talley would help with gathering the beans, but she's at the hospital with Lane, where they're picking up Annalee to bring her home. Lane insisted the doctors let Annalee come home today because she says Annalee will heal up better and faster if she's here at home, eating Erma's good cooking. It thrills Erma to hear Lane say these things. Erma will make up a nice roast, some corn bread stuffing, and maybe even a banana pudding. She's already put fresh sheets on Annalee's bed, washed and put away every scrap of clothing the child owns, and tidied that room of hers top to bottom. Everything will be good now, at last. Lane and the girls are home and safe, and they'll stay that way. So many years, Erma has waited, and now Lane is really, truly home again.

Those deputies are staying on until they catch the fellow who took Annalee. They say maybe the same fellow killed Susannah and Hettie Jansen. Those deputies tell Erma not to worry and that they'll see to keeping the whole family safe. They do so love Erma's cooking too, and just this morning, after one of those deputies fixed Erma's telephone, he asked if she would make up some of her butter beans because she sure does make them smooth and creamy.

Once in the kitchen, Erma wipes her face with a cool cloth and hollers out to Neil that he'll have a fresh cup of coffee in a few minutes. Erma's thoughts are sharp today, none of them trailing away like a puff of smoke. And with no cloudy thoughts swirling in her head, she is surefooted too. She knows what she's already done and what still needs doing. She works her best knife through the roast a half dozen times over and has dredged it, salted and peppered it, seared it on both sides, and layered it in her pressure cooker when tires roll up the drive.

Talley is first through the side door. Lane is next and carries a small overnight bag. Behind her, Annalee appears on Mark Ellenton's arm.

"Food's not quite done," Erma says, hugging Annalee lightly. Even after only a day, she feels as if she's lost weight and even a few inches of height. "Go lie down a bit and I'll holler when it's ready."

As Lane helps Annalee from the kitchen and up to her room, Erma returns to the stove. She even has strength enough today to lock down her cooker. She waves at Mark to sit himself at the table. The poor man looks to have not shaved in a week. A good meal will help him bounce right back. Erma checks her beans and cracks the oven to get a look at her corn bread stuffing.

"I think Daryl came to our house again," Talley says, standing in the threshold. She chews on the inside of her lip in the same way Lane did when she was a girl, sometimes still does when she's reading the newspaper.

"Who on earth is Daryl?" Erma says, reaching for an empty coffee cup so she can pour Neil a cup.

Mark shushes Erma with a finger to his lips. "What do you mean, Talley?" he says. "When was Daryl here?"

"Yesterday, when the door was broken into."

Mark stands, holds up a hand to silence Lane, who has walked back into the kitchen, and squats next to Talley. "Why do you say that?"

"I have been leaving food for the boys like you did, Mama," Talley says.

Lane nods but says nothing. Erma rests a hand on her daughter's back to steady Lane and to steady herself. The two of them have never spoken about those things Lane did as a girl. Erma always reasoned that silence and time would help them all to heal and forget, but if she'd been right, Lane wouldn't have left for twenty years.

"Yes, Talley," Mark says. "You told us about the food. We understand."

"I left food for them, and it was still on the fence post when you first came here looking for Annalee. It was in one of Grandma's tubs. I thought you came because I was leaving food. I thought I was in trouble."

"And why does that make you think Daryl was here?" Mark says.

"I went to the church yesterday too," Talley says. "After you and Mama went to look for Annalee, I went to the church. Daryl wasn't there, and Daryl is always there. And when I came home, the food was gone."

"You're certain?" Mark says.

Talley nods. "Yes, sir."

"That's real good, Talley," Mark says, motioning at Erma to fill the coffee cup. "Why don't you go on now and take some coffee to your grandpa before it gets cold."

ERMA FLIPS ON the fan to chase out the stale air. Talley's been leaving out food like Lane did when she was a girl. But it isn't the same, not really. There aren't any boys living over there at the school anymore, and Neil is an old man now. Erma shouldn't be afraid to talk about it after all these years or to have others talk about it. Neil can't do harm like he once did.

"What do you think it means?" Lane asks Mark when Talley has left the room. "Her food disappearing?"

"Could be one of my deputies found it," Mark says. "I'll check the log. Just to be on the safe side, we'll give another look. If he was here, we'll find sign of him."

"See there," Erma says, trying to comfort herself as much as Lane and to stop all this talk. "Mark says they'll find him."

Despite the years that have passed and despite Neil being an old man, the talk of the boys who run and the food frightens Erma. Keeping busy has always been her way of soothing herself, and she needs that now. Hoping to find some green onions to dice up for her beans, she pulls open the refrigerator, but it's filled with covered dishes people have been delivering the last few days. She starts sorting through them, looking for her onions and hoping all this talk will stop.

It's all those fellows from down at the bar and their wives who are bringing all this food. Not a one of them has been to the house in recent years. Erma's rarely even seen them since she and Neil were shuffled away by the elders over there at the New Covenant. But now they're all back, saying they're sorry it's been so long. Lane says not to judge because they've been good to her since she came home, but Erma sure could have used a friendly face during these past years. Lane also said the New Covenant isn't the only church in town, and Lord knows that's true.

"No, Erma," Lane says. "I think Mark is telling us he has no idea where that man is. Am I right?"

Mark nods.

"You said you'd find him," Lane says. She pulls out a chair and sits. "That you'd have no problem."

"Yes, I did."

"Getting upset won't do anyone no good," Erma says, dicing the handful of green onions she found as finely as her fingers will allow. "At least Mark knows who he's looking for."

It's all those darn casseroles cluttering up her refrigerator that are making her take after these green onions with such a vigor. She shouldn't be harboring grudges, certainly not now. But she wants Lane and Mark to stop. She doesn't want to think of things that happened long ago or what's happening now outside her kitchen door.

"What have you done so far?" Lane asks Mark. "Where have you looked for him?"

"The church, his apartment over on Third. Assuming he left,

he took nothing with him. Abandoned what appears to be most everything he owned. We found maps he'd drawn of your place, Susannah Bauer's place. Found lists, schedules of when the girls worked, when they went to school. Gibberish mostly. Boxes and boxes of gibberish. Found a good amount of cash too."

"He drew maps of our house?"

"Susannah's too. Lots of others."

"What do you mean, 'assuming he left'?" Erma says.

Erma looks from one to the other, trying to follow what they're saying because they won't stop and it's all getting too confusing. This time Lane nods because she must want to know the same as Erma.

"Have to consider he might be dead," Mark says. "That he died that night. Can't even be sure he made it out of the river."

Now Erma wants to leave the room and not hear another word. They're talking about people being dead and that'll get her to thinking about Susannah again.

"Even if one of your deputies found Talley's food," Lane says, waving a hand off toward the back door and nearly knocking the salt and pepper from the table. "Someone still broke into our house."

"Yes," Mark says. "Someone did."

"Dead men don't break into houses," Lane says.

Erma wants Mark to say everything is okay. Today is supposed to be a happy day, the deputies even said so, because Annalee is home and safe, but now Lane is talking about dead men breaking into houses and food for the boys and it's all clouding Erma's head with unhappy thoughts.

"You need to speak to that Bonnie Wiley," Erma says. "She put them pictures in every window. I tell you, she's up to no good."

"Stop all this nonsense about Bonnie Wiley," Lane says. "You're lucky she was there for Talley. You certainly weren't."

Erma pulls back, feeling as if Lane struck her across the face. Behind her, the beans have begun to boil. "It's not nonsense," she says.

"Lane, there's no need," Mark says.

Leaning across the table, Lane speaks in a quieter voice but not a softer tone. "You said he was a simple enough fellow. Those were your exact words: simple enough. Said you'd track him down in no time."

"And we hoped we would."

The ripple always starts in Erma's chin, and that means tears are working their way up and out. She rubs her nose with the back of one hand to stifle them. After crying all those tears for Susannah, she'd have thought she didn't have any more to shed.

"He'll find the man, Laney," Erma says. "Stop badgering him."

"And are we just supposed to sit around and wait for him to come back?" Lane says, ignoring Erma again. "Climb back in through those windows he left open?"

Erma stares at Mark, wants him to take her by the hand and tell her not to worry. Susannah is gone and Hettie too, but that's the worst that will happen. Everything bad is behind them, has to be. Things will get better now, but plenty of the folks stopping by with their casseroles are talking about this fellow being a killer like that fellow all those years ago. They say, watch over the blond ones. This isn't ended yet.

"You mean some fellow is coming back here?" Erma says. All her years in this house, she's been plenty afraid of things inside but never of the things outside getting in. "He opened them windows so he could come back again?"

"Yes," Lane says. "That's exactly right. He left those windows open so he could come back whenever he wanted. Maybe even get Talley next time."

"Someone's going to get me?"

Talley stands in the doorway, her hands hanging at her sides, her long hair pulled back loosely from her face.

"No, Talley, no," Lane says, jumping from her seat and pulling Talley into her arms. "That won't happen." She holds Talley at arms' length and looks down into her face. "Sheriff Ellenton would never let that happen. No one will ever take you."

"Your mama's right," Mark says, resting a hand on Lane's shoulder. "She's extra scared, is all. But we have deputies at the road, two of them. Be there until we take care of all this."

"Are you extra scared," Talley says to Lane, "because one of the boys took you when you were a girl?"

Erma presses a hand over her mouth to silence herself. Lane's lips are parted. Her eyes are fixed on Talley. She nods but doesn't answer Talley's question.

"You know about what happened to your mama?" Mark asks.

"Yes, sir. Grandpa told me," Talley says. "Did it really happen, Mama? Is that why you stopped leaving food and notes for the boys?"

"We don't talk about that, sweetheart," Erma says. She started the day steady and clear, but now she's looking down on Talley and seeing Lane instead. But no, that isn't Lane. She's grown now. Erma is slipping, forgetting all the years that have passed, just as Neil does. "Let's you and me go upstairs and check on Annalee."

"What did Grandpa tell you?" Lane says, holding up a hand to keep Erma from reaching for Talley.

"That the boy on the television took you."

"What boy?" Lane says. Her skin has gone pale. Her mouth hangs open.

Erma doesn't need to see Neil or hear him to know he's just there across the foyer. Talley asking these questions about Lane's disappearance is making Neil young again, younger anyway, just as they're taking Erma back in time. Her questions are unearthing the fear Erma had of Neil. Her heart pumps faster as if he'll stomp across the foyer at any moment, knock a lamp from a table, slam a cabinet door in Erma's face.

"They showed the boy's picture on the television," Talley says. "Grandpa said his name was Garrett Wilson. They dug him up at the school and drew a picture of his face." Talley looks at Erma. "Is it true, Grandma? Is he the one who took Mama?"

AFTER THE DEPUTIES left the house that night when Lane was thirteen, each of them shaking Neil's hand and saying thank the good Lord your girl is home, Neil pulled out the slip of paper the young guard had handed him earlier in the evening. It was the same slip of paper Neil had read and tucked away before Erma could see it. Holding that note now, he pressed it flat and held it up for Lane. Erma leaned in, squinted at the faded print: MY NAME IS LANE. MR. FIELDING LIVES HERE AND HE HURTS BOYS AND BEATS BOYS. I KNOW YOU'RE RUNNING AWAY. I WANT TO RUN WITH YOU.

Lane didn't have to look, so she must have already known what it was and what it said. Her chest lifted as if she were preparing to say something, but before she spoke, Neil grabbed her by one arm, gave a good yank, and dragged her across the foyer and up the stairs. Lane stumbled to keep up, hollering when she slipped and cracked a shin on one of the runners. Her black skirt tore at a side seam. Erma followed behind, her arms spread wide to catch Lane if she fell.

"How many of them notes you leave?" Neil shouted as he

pulled at Lane's arm. When she didn't answer, he stopped at the top of the stairs, knelt on one knee, grabbed her by both wrists, and asked again. "You better speak."

Standing behind Lane, Erma leaned in and whispered, "Go on and tell the truth."

"Left them mostly every day," Lane said. Her long hair fell over her shoulders and hid the sides of her face. "But I always picked them up."

"You whoring around with them boys," Neil said, still looking her straight on. His dark hair hung in his eyes, and his voice, quiet like it was, gave Erma more of a chill than when he yelled.

"No, sir," Lane said. "I never saw them boys. Never talked to them. Never did nothing with them."

"Looks to me like you damn sure want to," Neil said. "Sounds like you want to do plenty with them. Sounds like you want to run off with them."

With her eyes squeezed shut, Erma stood silent and willed Lane to do the same. She willed Lane to keep her mouth shut, her eyes lowered, her body still. When Neil asked a second time, Lane shook her head but said nothing more. Neil knelt there, staring down at the ground. As the silence stretched out, Erma's fingers unclenched and her shoulders relaxed, rolled forward. She gathered a strand of Lane's hair, let it slide through her fingers. Slowly Neil stood and in one motion grabbed Lane by the arm and began yanking her toward her room again.

"That note don't mean nothing," Erma yelled, as she trailed after them. She grabbed at the back of Neil's shirt, but he shoved her with one hand and she stumbled backward. "Don't mean nothing against you," she said, righting herself with a hand pressed to the wall.

Neil threw Lane into her room, and after pulling the door

closed, he turned back to Erma, grabbed on to her, and drew her close.

"Did you know?" he said, his face pressed so near Erma shut her eyes. He smelled of a pipe and stale coffee. "Did you know about her being up in that attic and that she'd been leaving them notes?"

Erma shook her head. "I didn't. I didn't know nothing about her being up there. But you can tell folks the truth. They'll not fault you for it. She didn't mean to cause no trouble for anyone."

Even as Erma said the words, she knew Neil would never tell the truth. He was a man who kept boys in their place without even a fence to contain them. Neil kept a whole town safe, and it was indebted to him. He couldn't have folks thinking he wasn't able to keep his own daughter in place, but that's what he surely feared if folks knew Lane had been right there in the attic the whole time. Didn't matter that she was up there sulking like children do, not meaning for anyone to set off searching for her. Neil wouldn't have folks thinking he'd been outwitted by a thirteen-year-old girl. That was worse even than the fear people would find out Lane had been leaving those notes.

Neil wouldn't care if folks knew his own daughter thought he beat those boys. Folks had been thinking the same for a long time, even if none of them spoke about it, and no one had ever made a fuss. But he couldn't abide folks thinking his daughter got the better of him.

"Never another word about this," Neil said, pressing so close Erma inhaled what he exhaled. "Not a word about where you found her, and you better hope to God that young fellow don't say nothing about finding that note."

Neil wasn't a young man by that time, and Erma wasn't a young woman. She wasn't a rash one either, so when Neil left to go outside, she stood quietly, her back pressed against Lane's bedroom door. She waited and listened for sounds of him.

"It'll be all right," Erma whispered as she kept watch for Neil to return. "I'm sorry, Laney. Real sorry, but no more sneaking off like that, not ever, and no more notes."

Erma did not move from in front of Lane's room, not even when Neil returned with a sledgehammer. She stood motionless as he drew the hammer overhead, scraping the ceiling, and brought it down on the doorknob leading to the attic where Erma had found Lane. Twice over he struck the knob. Then he turned to Erma, his face red. Sweat dripped down one dark sideburn and trailed along his cheek.

"I'll never do it again," Lane cried out from the other side of her door. "I didn't do nothing with them boys."

In two long steps, Neil reached Lane's room. He shoved Erma aside, widened his stance, and brought the hammer down on Lane's doorknob. A scream rose up from inside the room at the same time the hammer's head struck the knob. Twice more, he struck the door, splintering the wood and knocking the knob clean off.

"There ain't no lock on Laney's door," Erma shouted. "Stop. There ain't no lock."

"It was one of them boys took you," Neil said into Lane's closed door, his chest pumping and the hammer hanging from one hand. "And your daddy saved you. That's all you say if you are to say anything at all. You ain't going to be no whore, and I ain't going to be made no fool."

Neil had told the deputies that night he'd seen to it the boy wouldn't cause no more trouble. He had found the culprit. No more need to worry. He said those things to make the deputies believe he'd saved his daughter and restored order, or better yet, that he'd always maintained order because that's how good he was at his job. But when he said those same things to Lane and Erma in the months and years that followed, he did it to taunt them and punish them.

It would begin with Neil getting angry about shoes Lane had left in the foyer or a sweaty glass she'd set on the hatstand, but always the argument, no matter where it began, would return to that night. Do you know what I did for you, girl? Neil would shout at Lane. This is when Erma would try to send Lane away. Go and fetch the laundry, or see about the weeds in the garden.

In the beginning, Lane would do as Erma asked, but as she grew older, she buckled her fists and pressed her shoulders back. Erma would try her best. She'd stand herself between Lane and Neil, talk sweetly to Neil about what a good man he was and what hard work he did. At this Neil would lean in and sometimes yell at Lane, sometimes whisper, what would you think of yourself if one of my boys got himself a good beating because of you? The whispers frightened Erma more than the yelling. You hiding like you did, leaving them notes like you did. Course it made us think one of them boys got you. What do you suppose a man is willing to do when he's worried for his daughter?

"I'll tell," Lane whispered back, but only once. "I'll tell I was right there in the attic and you didn't even know. I'll tell I left them notes, and I'll tell you hurt one of them boys."

"Go on and tell," Neil said the one time Lane dared such a threat. "And you'll see how many more of them boys get themselves a good whipping because of you."

Year after year, even though Lane never threatened him with the truth again, Neil dangled the possibility that maybe nothing happened to the boy. Or maybe something did. Because of Lane, maybe the very worst happened to one of them boys. While Neil hit Erma many times during their years together, he never struck Lane, never with a hand or a fist, but what he did was worse than any beating he could have given her.

Neil used their good natures against them and knew the uncertainty of what did or didn't happen to that boy would torture them as much as or more than the truth. He taunted them, punished them both with the mystery of what became of that child. Everyone knew Neil had beaten plenty of boys over the years, but he made Lane believe one of those beatings, maybe one of those deaths, was on her account. He must have not remembered what Erma said to him that night when she begged him to do whatever he had to, or he'd have punished her in the same way. But while he may not have remembered, Erma did.

"A man like your daddy'll do anything to keep from being shamed," Erma said to Lane the day she threatened Neil with the truth. Erma had seen enough of Neil's shame, felt enough of it every time he had to slice off a section of the family land and sign it away to satisfy bills he couldn't pay. "You can't never tell the truth. Not about any of it. Not about hiding like you did. Not about your daddy hurting that boy. And who would care even if you did? Your telling will do no good. Not for you, not for me, most especially not for them boys."

"Tell Daddy to build a fence," Lane said to Erma when she must have felt she could do nothing else. "Tell him to build a fence so the boys can never come this way again."

Eventually Neil did build that fence. It wrapped around the entire school, and he pried the two-by-fours and plywood from the attic windows and pulled out the glass panes. Lane may well have heard them calling for her, even with that attic fan running, if not for the boarded-up windows. Eventually Neil replaced both doorknobs he broke too. He used ordinary gold knobs with no locks. The cheap imitations stayed there until Susannah Bauer ordered new ones, or rather old ones salvaged from some other house. It was one of the first things Susannah did for Erma. The knobs, glass like the originals, were complete with oil-rubbed bronze back plates and were near perfect matches to the rest in the house. Ain't got locks on them, do they? Erma asked as Susannah pulled the first from its box. No locks, she said.

33

LANE

LETTING HER HANDS drop from Talley's shoulders, Lane stands. "Run up to your room, Talley," she says, forcing a smooth and even tone. "I'll be up in a few minutes."

"But I want Grandma to tell me," Talley says, stepping beyond Lane's reach. "Is that Garrett Wilson the boy who took Mama?"

"That boy lived a long time ago," Erma says. "I don't know if he's the one who took Laney, but if your grandfather said he was, then I guess he'd know."

"Now, Talley," Lane says. She can't help that she nearly shouts. "Please run upstairs. We'll talk about this later."

Talley backs out of the kitchen, her eyes jumping from Erma to Lane to Mark and back again. When the stairs begin to creak from her footsteps, Lane turns to Erma.

"What are you saying?" she says.

"She asked me," Erma says. "What am I supposed to tell her? I can't lie to her."

"But you did lie," Lane says.

"I'm not lying," Erma says, looking to Mark as if most concerned about him knowing the truth. "I don't know that boy, but if Neil says it was him . . ."

Lane grabs onto the back of a chair, needs it to steady herself. All those years of living up north protected Lane. She never had to tell her daughters what happened, what didn't happen. But now they're back among it, all of it because she brought them here, and if she doesn't tell the truth now, her girls will eventually hear the lies, and they'll believe them like everyone else. Eventually, they'll look at Lane like everyone else.

"It never happened," Lane says, no longer trying to control her voice. And louder still, she shouts, "You know that. You know it never happened."

Erma pulls back at Lane's words. It's the same motion, a flinch, Erma would make when Neil moved a hand too quickly or unexpectedly. Lane saw it as a child, Neil striking Erma in the face. It would double her over, knock the wind from her lungs, but still she'd lift a hand so Lane would know she was all right. Lane has brought out the same in Erma as Neil did all those years ago. That flinch is as familiar as the smell of Erma's corn bread baking in the oven. But it's all Lane's doing now, and though she should stop and say nothing more, if only out of compassion, she can't. Not even as it turns her into her father.

"You know it never happened," Lane says, leaning forward and spitting the words at Erma. "No one took me that day. No one hurt me."

Erma shakes her head and hugs herself. "Your father said . . ."

"No," Lane says, pulling back and dropping into a chair. "No more. You have to tell the truth, Erma. Did Neil kill that boy, that Garrett Wilson, because of me?"

Mark stretches out a hand to Erma and helps her to sit. Once she is settled, he stands at her side, making it the two of them against Lane, and tells Lane to take it easy.

"You owe me the truth," Lane says, ignoring Mark.

Neil is the one who deserves Lane's anger, but he's old now. No one would look at him, not even Lane, at his narrow shoulders and bony knees and skin that so easily bruises and believe the things he's done. When she looks at her father now, whatever anger she can muster is anger he's outlived his crimes and his guilt. Erma is the only one left for Lane to punish.

"I don't know," Erma says.

"You do know."

Erma shakes her head and grabs onto Mark's forearm, looks across the table at Lane. "You was gone so long that day, Laney. I looked everywhere. And all them people came. And then I found you right there in the attic. Your daddy was so angry. He told us how it had to be."

Erma presses a tissue to her mouth and stares out into the foyer. She hugs herself, makes herself as small as she can. Lane's seen it before, the way Erma watches every doorway. She'll be worrying Neil might hear them. Even now that he's old and can do no more harm, she can't tamp down her fear.

"It was never my lie," Lane says, speaking mostly to Mark. She reaches for him, wants to pull him to her side, but he doesn't move. Lane's lie didn't change only her life; it also changed his. He never married after she left town with Kyle. Surely there have been other women over the years, but he loved Lane, truly loved her, and she squandered it.

"Never." She's begging him now, begging him to believe her

now though she's lied for twenty years. "I never said I was taken. Mark, you know that."

It's been a secret for too long, and letting it go makes her weak. She leans forward in her chair, rests her forearms on the table and lets her head hang. All these years, she's been like everyone else who never told.

"You never said you was taken," Mark says. "But you never said you wasn't either."

"And what do you think I could have said?" She stares up at him. "I couldn't tell. He said he'd hurt more of them if I did. And what if I had told? Was anyone going to care? Even now, after everything we know about that school, what has anyone ever done?"

"I don't know, Lane," Mark says. "I guess I wish at least you'd told me."

"Told you what? Should I have told you I hid in the attic because of a childish argument with Erma I can't even remember? That I sat up there for hours, doing nothing? That I fell asleep while they were all looking? Should I have told you I left notes for the boys and my father called me a whore? Should I have told you someone might have died because of all that?"

Lane made one mistake. She ran off and hid. She wanted Erma to miss her, to worry, to be sorry. It's what children do. She should have been able to forgive herself, but if she hadn't hidden that day, there would have never been a search and Neil's guard from the school would have never found Lane's note to the boys who ran. But he did, and that's why Neil called in more guards and all the neighbors and that's why he was sure one of those boys somehow had something to do with Lane disappearing. But that hadn't been true. Lane had been under Neil Fielding's roof the entire time, and he'd be made a fool if anyone knew that.

Lane made it bad for those boys by hiding, but she made it worse by having left the notes.

"You could have told me," Mark says.

"You were the last person I could have told." It's mean, what Lane is saying, but she can't stop herself. "My God, the way you treated me after, so careful all the time. Always feeling so sorry for me. It got to where just the sight of you made me sick."

"Lane, please stop," Erma says, dabbing at her eyes. "There's no cause for this."

Mark pats Erma's hand, which still rests on his forearm. "No, Lane's right. I did treat her different after. But who wouldn't? Jesus, Lane, I thought the very worst, and you let me think that."

"It was better than telling you the truth."

All these years, Lane has searched for the boy, promised herself if she ever found him, she would reach out to his family, tell them what she'd done, apologize but expect no forgiveness. She took those actions, but could never really let herself think about the boy because she knew too well what it must have been like for him. But now every image of a younger Neil is fresh, and every image of what may have happened to that boy is forcing her to cling to the edge of the table.

"But you didn't do nothing," Erma says, stretching both hands across the table. "You was just a child, Laney. You didn't mean no harm leaving them notes. Thought you was doing a good thing. Much as it hurt you not telling the truth about that day, would have hurt others more if you had."

"I don't think that anymore," Lane says. "The only one who didn't end up getting hurt was Neil."

Erma will be listening for the sound of Neil's boots on the wooden floors. Lane knows because that's what she's doing. But Neil doesn't wear boots anymore. He's not coming for them.

"I'm sorry, Mark," Lane says, looking up at him. "I shouldn't have said that to you. You didn't make me sick. It was all my do-ing. I loved you so much, is all. How could I tell you?"

Twenty years wasted because of shame. That's what is here at the center of it all. She's always loved Mark, knew it as she lay with him in the back of his El Camino. She knew it as his hands shook when he touched her, knew it when they stood together in her kitchen and she told him yes, she'd been with all those other men. She knew it even as she packed up and moved away with Kyle. But she went rather than tell Mark or anyone else the truth.

"I was so careful," she says. "Always picked the notes up first thing every morning. I was only trying to warn the boys. It was like they were my friends somehow even though I never saw a single one of them."

Erma pushes herself out of her chair, steps up to Lane, touches her chin, and lifts it. Her fingers are cool against Lane's skin.

"I told your daddy to find you that night," Erma says. "I told him to do whatever it takes to find my Laney. If it was your fault, it was mine too. But it wasn't neither of us. Whatever was done that night, it was your father's doing."

"He beat that boy to death, didn't he?" Lane says, staring at Erma. She gathers both of Erma's hands, squeezes them, pulls them close, clings to them like she hasn't since she was a child. Clings to them like they'll save her from falling. "He killed Garrett Wilson. Neil found that note and picked out Garrett Wilson because God only knows why. Must have asked that child over and over where I was, and then he beat him when he couldn't answer."

"I don't know, Laney," Erma says. "I just don't know."

Mark steps around to the other side of Lane's chair and drops to a knee. "I'm sorry I couldn't help you back then," he says. He sees it as clearly as Lane, the shame that's been between the two of them, that's been between Lane and everyone she loves, though it takes him only a moment to face it down. It took Lane twenty years.

"Wish I'd been the one you told," he says. "But I couldn't hardly bear it, imagining the worst. All I can think to say is your father is a cruel man, and I'm sorry for it."

"You have to find out about him," Lane says, grabbing Mark's hands. "Garrett Wilson. You can do that. You can find out what happened to him."

"I can," he says. "I'll do my best, anyway. But we have other work to do. You all are going to see to taking care of Annalee, and I'm going to tackle finding Daryl."

Still holding Erma's hands, Lane glances overhead where Annalee will be sleeping by now and where Talley is probably sitting on her bed and wondering why Lane sent her away. She nods so Mark will know she heard him. Both girls are safe. That's what Lane must focus on now. She's told the truth. The rest will stay with her, the need to search for the boy, the regret for having done what she did, but for now, she's stepped away from the edge and can breathe. For now, she must think only of keeping her girls safe.

"He's coming back here, isn't he?" Lane asks. "That man, that Daryl, is coming back."

"Don't know. All we can do is find him, whether he's dead or alive, before he does."

34

DARYL

On Susannah's last night

WHEN I LEAVE the grocery store, Susannah's blue-and-yellow kerchief folded and tucked in my front pocket, I drive straight to my apartment. The entire time I'm driving across town, I feel the kerchief in my pocket, like it has a heartbeat, and I can smell Susannah. It's as if she's right here in the car with me, but it's also as if she's already gone.

It makes sense the boy and Susannah are friends. He works at the hardware store, and just as Susannah sometimes comes to the church to borrow tools, she sometimes goes to the hardware store to buy washers and bolts and duct tape. I've followed her there before, and the place where the boy works is circled on my maps. Tonight, the two of them will go to the river together so Susannah can see the gray bats. But also so she can say one last good-bye to the boy. It's the boy she wants, and he's the one she'll remember.

I wait and watch for the two of them from the auto parts store where I buy spark plugs for the church's mower. The store is closed, so this is where I park to watch the cars turn down the dirt road leading to the river. For the first hour or so, all the cars are coming and none are going. But at ten minutes to seven, a car leaves the party, the first one to go. It rolls to a stop and waits for traffic to clear before turning left. It's the boy, and he'll be driving to Tallahassee to pick up Susannah.

While the boy is gone, the sun sets. At first the sky turns orange and then gray, and then it's nearly black. I leave my car, dig my hands into my front pockets, and walk down the dirt road toward the bend that leads to the river. Before I can see the water, I step off the road and into the trees. I'm careful not to trip over fallen branches and that I don't step where a stump has rotted away, leaving a deep hole in the ground that could twist an ankle. I've been here before, the night I watched Annalee beg the boy to love only her, but now the boy is coming here with Susannah.

While the river is quiet, its rapids still, the trees are loud with the buzzing cicadas and the chirps and grunts of the frogs. I slap at my neck, swat the mosquitos from my eyes and ears, and scratch until my skin is red and raw. In between drinking from their red cups, the people standing near the river and on the lowlands where the water sometimes floods slap at their cheeks and necks like me. Their music is loud but not too loud so the police don't come here and see the fire they've started.

When I think of seeing Susannah here at the river, I don't feel like I have all the other times I've thought of her. Lowering myself to the ground, I lean against a giant tupelo. I pull my knees to my chest, dip my head, and cover it over with both hands, all of it to keep the humming from my ears, nose, and eyes. I've always wanted Susannah to notice me, but now I want to stay hidden. I want to blend into these trees and prickly branches and the buzzing and chirping and never be seen again. She doesn't think of me, not even to say one last good-bye. She won't remember me in the years to come. No one will. I think I'll stay here and never leave.

IT'S NEARLY TEN o'clock. Everyone has left the party, chased away by the bugs. I look up again because I've heard a car. It'll be the boy and Susannah. He parks up on the dirt road before the bend. He must think there are still people here and doesn't want to get stuck if the clearing is still filled with cars. Long before I see them, I hear them. Susannah doesn't wear a kerchief tonight, and I might not recognize her if I didn't know she was being picked up and brought here. I want to hate her now, but I can't.

Like the last time the boy came here, he's brought a lantern from the church. Susannah almost shimmers in its light, like she isn't all real. Like she's floating instead of walking. She doesn't wear her brown work boots and denim shorts cut off at the knees. Instead she wears a dress that brushes her thighs, floats just above her knees, and her hair glows where the light shines on her. Susannah will be unhappy to see no one else is here. It was supposed to be a party.

The boy hands her a red cup, and as she drinks from it, he spreads a blanket on the ground near the river. This is what the boy did with Annalee. It's the same blanket Annalee had lain on. It's the same lantern. It's the same music he plays on his phone. The boy shouldn't get them both. Susannah doesn't like what the boy is doing either. I know because she turns away from the blanket and walks toward the river, wandering right up to the edge of the black water.

The boy follows Susannah, and when they near the river, he reaches for one of her hands. Together, they stand at the edge of the lantern's light. Susannah lets the boy kiss her, lets his hand slide up her thigh and under her dress, and pushes him away only when his phone rings. Pressing the phone to his ear, he stares at Susannah for a moment, then turns away from her and toward me. If he would only look up in the dark tangle of tree branches, he'd see me.

I hear little of what the boy says into the phone. When he turns just right, lifts his chin as he speaks, I hear. He's telling someone don't bother. It's over. Party's over. See you tomorrow. It's nearly ten thirty. Annalee gets off work at around ten thirty. Sometimes closer to ten, and because the boy drifts away from Susannah as he talks into the phone, it's Annalee on the other end of the call.

Susannah tips her head toward the sky as the boy talks. I do the same, and I see them too. Bats darting overhead, shooting across the sky barely beyond our reach. Together, Susannah and I watch them. They come from farther upriver, skimming the water, swinging out over the banks, dipping and soaring into the sky. Susannah lays one hand on the swollen trunk of a cypress, steps over the roots that ride high because the river is down. In the glow of the church lantern, the cypress knees rise from the riverbed like stalagmites rise from a cave's floor. She stretches a hand out over the water, touches the tops of the woody formations.

Slipping in and out of the trees, Susannah wanders to the farthest edge of the lantern's light. Wrapping her arm around one cypress, she circles it and reaches for another. As she spins around the trees, she works her way downriver toward the clay banks and the spot where the tracks cross over.

I can hear her better than I can see her. She's flipped off her sandals and has stepped from dry land into the water. She kicks at the river, wading up to her ankles, splashing with her toes. Are there alligators? she calls out. I get only glimpses of her white arms and the tiny wakes her feet leave behind in the water. The moon is full and shines off the river, but I've nearly lost sight of her. And then the lantern begins to move in her direction.

I'll wait until they're settled on the blanket so they'll hear me when I make a noise. I can't watch the boy put his hands on Susannah like he did Annalee. Susannah might never see me or never remember me, but I can't let him do that. I'll do like I did the last time. I'll strike the boy. He'll double over and Susannah will be afraid and she'll be angry the boy brought her here when there's no party. She'll ask him to take her home. At least I'll have that.

Holding the lantern high, the boy trails after Susannah and calls out for her to come back. Don't go so far, he says. The bats are the other way. Upriver not down. But this is the way they're headed, she says of the bats. There will be more insects, more food for them downriver. This way, Susannah calls back. Downriver, the trees grow thicker, closer together. Downriver the overstory is heavier and so less moonlight breaks through. Downriver, the night is darker.

I'm close to the boy now, and if I stuck out one hand, my fingers would catch the light. He continues stepping through the mesh of roots, the ground surely getting softer with each step, and at last his footsteps splash when he hits the water. The two of them work their way downriver, and the divide between us grows. As I climb along the bank that lifts higher with every step, we are farther and farther apart.

When the light from the lantern finally settles on Susannah, she is sitting on a slab of limestone, running her fingers over its rough, jagged edges. The stone slab is wedged into the clay bank, high enough above the river that the water won't have worn down and rounded out its edges. She's climbed up there, leaving the boy down below in the river. She shakes her head and swats at the bugs swarming her face.

They talk, but I can't hear them. Susannah continues to swat and slap and shake her head. The boy steps up to her, presses her knees apart, and stands between them. Setting the lantern next to Susannah, the boy slides his hands up to her shoulders, presses her back so she lies instead of sits on the limestone slab. But Susannah pushes herself back up. She shakes her head. She doesn't like it here. Like I do, she slaps at her arms and legs.

Nudging the boy away to give her room, Susannah slides off the limestone and causes a small splash when she lands in a foot of water. She braces herself against the slab as she works her feet in and out of the tangled roots, cypress knees, and rotting stumps. I think she doesn't care about the bats anymore. It's not nice here like she thought it would be. I won't have to make a noise and draw the boy out because Susannah already wants to go home. I drop back against a tree, rest there, relieved. She knows better than to want the boy who doesn't love her. She will leave the boy now, and even if I never get to say good-bye to her, she'll remember me because she is the person I always dreamed she was.

I SEE ANNALEE before they do. She's followed them through the low-hanging branches and roots that knot at their feet. I know it's her because of the way she moves, tipping forward on her toes with each step. Like I do, she stands still, watching. She must have called the boy from just around the bend. She called to ask him if the party was still going on. No, he said. No party. I'm home already. I'll see you tomorrow. And she trapped him. His car was parked there on the dirt road and she knew he was lying and now she knows why. He had promised to love her and only her and he lied.

"Annalee," the boy says.

Holding on to a low-hanging branch she'll have to duck under, Susannah looks up. Water sloshes as she moves her feet, pulling one out of the spongy ground and setting it down again. The light from the lantern shines only on the lower part of her face, her neck, her chest, and down to her waist. She stumbles as if she's twisted an ankle in the soft mud or tripped on the supplejack that winds itself around the roots and branches and trunks, some of it thick as a man's arm. Surely she isn't thinking about the bats anymore or the boy who wanted one last good-bye. She'll be thinking of her home and of grad school and of how much she wants to get away from the bugs and heat and the silky ground she sinks into deeper with every step.

"There is nothing going on here," Susannah says.

I can barely hear over the buzzing and clicking and croaking that continues to rise from the trees. Susannah knows straightaway the boy has done something wrong. I know it too. I want to reach out and grab hold of Susannah, pull her from between the two of them.

"Truly . . . ," Susannah says. "Just asking him to take me home."

And then Annalee takes another step toward the boy, and the light catches her face.

"You're Talley's sister," Susannah says. "Is that right?" And she says other things. ". . . Susannah . . . Florida State . . . I know Talley."

I slip from one tree to another, working my way down the bank. We've had no rain, and the clay crunches under my feet. I need to get close enough to take Susannah by the wrist and yank her away, because the boy has done something bad. He's drawing her into his troubles. And something about the way Annalee is standing so still, not moving, not speaking, almost as if she's crouched and waiting to strike, tells me she is part of the trouble.

"I was telling the truth," the boy says. He talks loud as if he has nothing to hide. Just beyond where they stand, the tracks run overhead, and the span of iron and concrete lifts the boy's voice, makes it larger than it is, almost causes an echo. "No party. See, everyone's gone."

"Tell you what," Susannah says, smoothing her short dress and squinting at the ground so she'll know where to step.

I'm closer now and make out the curves of her cheeks and the tip of her nose. But the rest of her is a shadow. I want to make myself bigger and longer so I can reach out to her and protect her, but she's too far away and I'm not enough.

"I'll find my own way home," Susannah says, and as she lifts a foot to take a step, the boy reaches for her hand, a gesture to help her.

Annalee lunges at him and slaps him away. "Don't you dare touch her."

One slap turns into two and three. The boy drops the lantern to grab Annalee's hands. There is a thud, not a splash, and the light lands on the ground. They're both stumbling in the water now, Annalee and the boy. All three become shadows. There is more splashing, and I think the boy has wrestled Annalee's hands together. Their two shadows move forward and back, side to side, and there is grunting as they fall, stumbling through the shallow water, farther out into the river and back again.

Susannah cries out. Those are her arms, I think, flying into the air. I know every part of her. I know the color of her and the smell of her. I know she loves old buildings and horses and the bats that dart overhead. A sliver of light from the lantern catches her body as it falls backward. Only one shoulder and the top of one arm. A round slice of her cheek. I stretch out my hand, but she's so far away. She turns as if to break her fall with her arms. A bitter ache rises into my throat, fills it, but I can't scream. Can't make a single sound.

Susannah would have remembered me as the kid from the church, the one with tools to help with her work. I think her feet don't move. They're caught up in the roots or they've sunk too deep into the mud. Nobody catches her, and she falls. Her head flies backward. That cheek bounces in and out of the light, her head bouncing off the limestone's jagged edge, and the cry she had let out as her hands flew up goes suddenly and instantly silent.

The boy and Annalee are still.

"Jesus," the boy yells. "What happened? Susannah?"

He stumbles through the trees and grabs at the lantern. Once he has it in hand, he raises it high, the yellow light spilling across the dark ground, reflecting in the shallow waters, flashing in the branches.

"Where is she?" he says, running onto higher ground toward the limestone slab where she was sitting, where he thinks she was sitting.

The light bounces as the boy moves in and out of the trees and over fallen trunks, his feet sliding where the clay is smooth and crunching where it's dry. He climbs onto one slab, holds his lantern high, and looks out into the water. Seeing nothing, he moves to the next stone and the next. In the dark, he's confused, doesn't know where they were. I want to grab him and drag him to the right spot so his light will shine on Susannah, but I can't make any part of me move.

Down below, Annalee holds on to a tree with both hands as if afraid the water will rise up around her. The boy doesn't shine the light on her. She's a shadow, staring down at the ground where the water sometimes floods. She stares down as if she sees Susannah but won't tell where she is.

TALLEY

TALLEY SITS IN the front seat of Sheriff Ellenton's car, buckles her seat belt, and licks the tupelo honey Grandma served at breakfast from her fingers. Grandma opened the jar of honey special because Talley has been so sad about Susannah Bauer being gone. Missing Susannah makes Talley feel like part of her is missing too. She wanted to be just like Susannah, but she's gone and eventually Talley will forget what Susannah looked like and talked like just like she's starting to forget Daddy.

It's been three days since Talley last went to the church, since Annalee disappeared and was found, and it has yet to rain again. It's been hot, Goddamn hot as Grandpa says, and the plants in Talley's garden are probably all shriveled, but she doesn't care about her garden anymore because Miss Hettie and Susannah are dead and Annalee still isn't well.

Up near the car's front bumper, Sheriff Ellenton hugs Mama. He is wearing his blue uniform, and Mama is wearing a tan skirt that floats when she walks and her favorite blue blouse. When Sheriff Ellenton starts to let go, Mama holds on and Sheriff Ellenton buries his face in Mama's hair. Seeing that makes Talley's insides not hurt so bad. She looks away until Sheriff Ellenton pulls open his door and drops onto his seat.

"Mind Sheriff Ellenton," Mama calls out as they drive away.

At the end of the driveway, two deputies sit in a car because Daryl is still out there, maybe. Or maybe he's dead too. Sheriff Ellenton told Mama an abandoned car was discovered at the auto shop last night. They hardly noticed it back in there among all the other broken-down cars, but the reverend confirmed it was the same one Daryl drove to work every day. And they found a lantern at the river that belonged to the church. The reverend said it was Daryl's job to check the batteries every month, and those batteries had been dead way too many times of late.

Sheriff Ellenton doesn't think Daryl took Talley's food, but he does think they'll eventually find Daryl in the river like they found Miss Hettie and Susannah Bauer. Until they do, the deputies will stay put. Talley isn't sure if she should be sad or happy about Daryl maybe being dead. Mama says happy isn't the word for it. Relieved, maybe. Safe. A little less afraid.

At the church, the grass needs a good mowing because there's no one to mow it anymore. This does make Talley sad because the Daryl she knew here at the church doesn't feel like the same Daryl who might be lying at the bottom of the river. Near the back door where Miss Hettie would always come and go, bundles of flowers lie on the ground, and balloons that have lost their air hang from the doorknob, bouncing lightly in the breeze. Miss Hettie's funeral is tomorrow. Mama, Grandma, and Sheriff

Ellenton will go, but Mama says Talley is too young and Annalee isn't well enough yet.

No one will go to Susannah Bauer's funeral because her parents are flying her home to Sweden. Mama wouldn't have let Talley go anyway, so instead they planted rain lilies near the ruins where the slaves once lived. They'll bloom every year, and when they do, Talley will be able to sit among them and feel like Susannah is almost still alive. Mama said Talley will never stop missing Susannah, but the hurting will eventually stop. When Talley asked how long until eventually, Mama said no one quite knows.

"You sure you don't mind showing me around the shed?" Sheriff Ellenton asks as they walk across the church grounds.

"You've never seen it?"

"Oh, sure," the sheriff says. "Good many officers have."

"Need a key," Talley says, stopping at the shed's door. "Daryl always keeps it locked."

Sheriff Ellenton pulls out the same key Jimmy used the day he caught Talley sneaking into Daryl's shed. It's a single key attached to half a stir stick for a can of paint. He slips it in the lock and opens the door.

"You come in here often?" Sheriff Ellenton asks Talley, standing aside and letting her walk in first.

The shed looks exactly like it did the day Talley climbed through the window and scraped her shin. Jimmy scared her worse that day than Daryl ever did.

"No, sir," she says. "Just that once."

Talley already told Sheriff Ellenton about climbing in the window and cutting her shin and finding Grandma's plate and getting caught by Jimmy Jansen. It was the same day Mama found Susannah Bauer's kerchief on Talley's head.

"It was always open when I came here," Talley says. "But Daryl said I wasn't allowed inside." She points to the workbench where Daryl kept all his tools and wonders if anyone will ever use them again. "That's where I found Grandma's plate."

Sheriff Ellenton nods. His voice has a way of sinking in and taking root. That's what Mama says. It's like a song that gets stuck in your head. His words meander, take plenty of time making their way. Mama says Sheriff Ellenton's voice is like home to her, and now Talley thinks it'll be like home to her too. It stops her from feeling like something is gone and it'll never come back.

Ever since Annalee came home, Sheriff Ellenton has been at the house. He is sleeping in the extra bedroom upstairs, and at night, he and Mama have stayed up late, talking in the kitchen. Talley heard Mama crying a few times, and one of those times, she thought Sheriff Ellenton was crying too. Having Annalee in the bedroom next to Talley's isn't as scary with Sheriff Ellenton sleeping in the next room. Not only is Talley sad all the time about Susannah being gone, but since seeing Annalee in the hospital, Talley gets a bad feeling whenever her sister is near. Being close to Annalee makes Talley feel like she is falling from a tall building.

"Awful nice of you," Sheriff Ellenton says. "To leave food for them boys, I mean. Bet Susannah would have been proud of you."

"I know there's no boys, not anymore." Saying that out loud makes Talley's voice crack like it does when she's getting ready to cry. She swallows so the feeling will go away.

"Yes, that's true."

"Miss Bonnie says they're still real," Talley says, "but they're all grown up now."

"I would hear sirens sometimes when I was a kid," Sheriff Ellenton says. "When one of them boys ran. Not like your mama did, because I didn't live so close. You could have told your mama you were leaving food. She'd been proud of you too."

Talley kicks at the box of rags that's still under the workbench and shakes her head. "She would have been mad I was going into the attic. We weren't allowed up there, not ever. She said we'd catch a rusty nail."

Sheriff Ellenton smiles and bends down to look under the bench and along the back wall of the shed.

"You think Mama's okay at the house with Annalee?" Talley asks.

"Sure," Sheriff Ellenton says. He glances up at Talley. "Why do you ask that?"

"No reason."

When they were all together at the hospital, Sheriff and Mama didn't see the same things in Annalee that Talley saw.

"So how'd you manage it?" Sheriff Ellenton asks.

Talley squats next to Sheriff Ellenton and looks where he is looking. She likes how he talks to her, like she's smart enough to figure things out and maybe she'll be a police officer one day, or a sheriff like Sheriff Ellenton.

"What do you mean?" she asks.

"How'd you get ahold of the key to the attic? Talk your grandma into showing you where she hides it? When your mama was a girl, Erma hid it in the bathroom under the extra toilet paper rolls." He looks over at Talley. "Noticed it was still locked up tight when I was up there the other day."

Talley stands and looks down on Sheriff Ellenton. "That's not true," she says.

"What's not true?"

"That door's never locked. I never needed a key."

36

DARYL

On Susannah's last night

I STAND ON the clay bank. My legs are heavy and numb, like they're not really mine. Bugs fill the trees overhead. Some give off a steady hum. Others chirp in sets of three. In the distance, a bird cries. Down on the ground, one bunch of frogs grunts, another wails. The boy continues to scream for Susannah, my Susannah. He calls out her name again and again until his voice weakens and becomes hoarse, but the bugs and frogs and that bird keep on.

The boy scrambles from one limestone slab to the next. At each, he drops to his stomach, reaches out with the lantern, and hangs over the edge. When he sees nothing, he leaps to his feet and runs to the next, and then he runs back, stumbling in the slick underbrush where the sunlight never reaches. He looks upriver and down. Where was she standing? he shouts out to Annalee, but she never shouts back.

He's too far downriver now. I stare at the spot where Susannah fell, waiting for her to stand. My legs are hollowed out, my arms too. No more tangled brittle knots to fill my insides. I'm empty, a useless shell. Susannah's scream and the sudden way it ended, snapped off in the middle, lingers, but slowly, the grunting and chirping and buzzing fill in and drown out the silence.

The lantern the boy holds must be the same lantern he used the night he and Annalee lay on the blanket, because the light begins to flicker and then dims and finally goes dark. The boy throws it into the trees and calls out for Annalee to keep looking, but Annalee is gone too. He's crying now. Keep looking, he shouts. Jesus, we have to find her. Get back here, Annalee. Get back here and keep looking.

"We have to go," Annalee yells. She's far upriver, near the clearing.

The boy is only a voice now. And there's crackling and rustling as he climbs down the bank, sliding at times, and there's a splash when he finds the water again.

"We can't leave her," he calls back, his voice breaking because he's crying.

"We have to," Annalee shouts. "Please, come on. I promise I'll never tell what you did."

I continue to stare at the spot where Susannah disappeared, afraid to let my eyes drift because they might get lost in the darkness and never find that spot again. There's more splashing. Hoping to see Susannah's shadow lift out of the river, I lean forward. But it's the boy instead. He's scrambling again, but this time he's making his way toward Annalee. What she said has scared him, and I know because of the way she said it, loudly so the boy would be sure to hear—she meant to scare him. She'll never tell what he did. Her saying that has frightened the boy more than Susannah lying alone in the river.

"I didn't do this," the boy yells, and then he's closer to Annalee and his voice softens. I can't hear him anymore, and they've both become nothing more than shapes off in the distance. But I imagine the boy stops and turns. I imagine he's remembering someone was here watching him the last time he came. It was only a week ago when I hit him with a stick. His gut probably still aches from it. He'll be remembering and wondering if I'm here again.

"Don't you say that," the boy says, talking louder because now he's thinking of me though he doesn't know it. He's wondering who is here in the darkness, right alongside him, hearing everything he says.

He'll be telling Annalee he didn't do this. It isn't his fault. He'll probably even want to call someone. We should call the police, he'll be saying. But Annalee said she promised to never tell. You did this. This is your fault. She'll tell him again and again until he's too afraid to call for help. Now Annalee can make the boy do whatever she wants.

Our bloodline is vile. That's what Mother said before she died. She scratched at her arms as if she could tear open her veins and drain that vile blood. The family would end when she was gone, and she gathered both my hands, mine bigger and hers smaller, and told me it was hardest on her. She would be the last to go. She had suffered through every other death and so had suffered most. I wondered then, wondered for so many years, why my death wouldn't be the last. But now I know. Mother's death was last because no one will miss me or think of me when I die, and a person like that doesn't get counted.

I wait until the engines in their cars start up and fade. When they've gone, I make my way down the clay bank toward the limestone slab where I last saw Susannah. Like the boy, I stretch out flat, lean over the edge, and I touch the jagged corner where her head hit.

Sliding off the rock, I drop into a foot of water. As I move through the downed trees and thick bands of roots and long branches that form the underbelly of the river, I use both hands to skim the surface. Just as the boy did, I find myself drifting away from where I know she must be. I close my eyes. She's near, and I should be able to feel her.

I turn around and open my eyes so I can watch the river's flow and remember which direction will take me back to the clearing. There is no light to anchor me. Every slab of limestone cutting through the clay bank looks like the next. I call out Susannah's name, over and over as I wade toward the tracks, until my voice lifts and grows larger than it is. I drop low into the water, reach with both hands, use my feet to push myself forward. Maybe she isn't dead. Maybe she's afraid and being quiet, hiding, waiting until everyone leaves her. I'm shivering and spitting out water when at last her hair tangles in my fingers. I've found her.

Mother died last and so ended our vile bloodline. Annalee's blood is vile too. She isn't pure, not kind or loving like the other girls, like Susannah. I was wrong to think so. Annalee forced the boy to leave Susannah here, alone in the river. It's her fault Susannah is gone. I didn't know it before because Annalee's tiny chin would fit in my one hand and her hair glowed and shimmered in the light. But I was wrong. Annalee is cruel, and she is vile. Just like Mother, Annalee should be the last to die. And if that is to happen, the others must die first.

I'll begin by killing the grandfather. He should be the first. He beat those boys, filled a cemetery with them, and Wayne, I think, was one of them. The grandfather and the grandmother gave birth to the mother, and she gave birth to Talley and Annalee. Vile. All of them vile. The grandfather, the grandmother, Lane, and even Talley. All of them must die first so that when I kill Annalee, she'll die last and suffer most.

It takes some time to pry Susannah loose. Already she has become part of the river's underbelly. I bend her arm at the elbow, wiggle it out from under a thin root. I'm gentle with her because she's delicate and kind. My sweet Susannah. I twist an ankle slowly and slightly until it's untangled. I roll her body, first one way and then the other, working her loose. I fold one leg, jiggling the foot that is the last part of her trapped by the mesh. She is free.

The river is slow because we haven't had rain. This is what the old men at church say. No good fishing when the water is so low. It's too warm, too still. But it makes for easier walking. I move beyond the shallower wetlands into the river, and without looking down on her face because it doesn't look as it should anymore, because there's a dent and a hole where her eye should be, I walk with my Susannah cradled in my arms.

The bats remind me why she came here. As I walk, carrying her body, the small dark creatures shoot past me. My eyes jump to them but never are able to catch up. They dart from one side of me to the other, from high to low and low to high. Susannah didn't want the boy like Annalee wants him. She only wanted to see the bats. She wanted to know where they roosted during the day and where they darted to and from during the night.

I carry her until the clay gives way to steep, rocky banks of limestone. This is where I'll find the caves the old men at church sometimes talk about. My arms ache. I wish I could carry her with me forever. Susannah was the only one who talked to me. She let me show her the rakes I cleaned with steel brushes and is the one who told me to use more sunscreen.

If I were strong enough to carry Susannah forever, I'd never be alone. But I'm too weak, so I carry her only as far as the first cave I come to. It's just above the reach of the water, an oblong hole cut into the limestone that's the exact right size for her. She'll rest here where the bats will be nearby and where I can visit. I lift her over the limestone ledge, and she tumbles from my arms. It's deeper than I would have thought. I can hear but can't see that she rolls and then hits water. My Susannah has died first and so has suffered least. It's Annalee's fault Susannah is gone. She deserves to suffer like Mother suffered, deserves to suffer every other death. Annalee will die last.

LANE

LANE STANDS NEAR the side door that leads into the kitchen and waves as Mark and Talley drive off. When they're out of sight, she closes the door and drops the hook into the small eye one of the deputies mounted on the frame—a quick fix to make Erma feel safe until the door can be repaired.

Annalee is back in her own bed and finally sleeping through the night. She's been happy to have Lane sit with her, happy in a way she has never been to have Lane near. Again and again, Lane asks if Annalee is truly at home here in Waddell, but she can't bring herself to ask about the friends Annalee doesn't really have. Though Annalee has yet to tell them anything more of what happened that night, she has continued to remember odd meetings with a man they all think is Daryl. Him at the Food Lion. Him at the Wharf. Him at the Tracks where she and Jimmy had gone a few times. Either she escaped Daryl that night, or he left her for dead. Mark says they may never know.

In the kitchen, Erma is fishing the tea bags from the hot water. While it's still warm, she pours in the sugar and stirs it with her long-handled wooden spoon. And she already has supper on the stove—chicken, beans, and potatoes that will stew all morning. When it's done, she'll unlock the lid to the pressure cooker and cover the pot over with an upside-down plate, the signal it's ready. Cooking gives her something to do and has made her happier than Lane has seen her since moving back. In the front room, Neil is watching television. Mark brought earphones so now Neil can listen to the volume as loudly as he likes and no one will holler at him to turn it down.

"I need to run a quick errand," Lane says. "Keep an ear out for Annalee, would you?"

Erma glances from Lane to the kitchen door and back to Lane, obviously nervous at being left alone with Annalee, or maybe Neil is the one making her nervous. Erma was closest to Susannah, closer even than Talley, and her death has been hardest on Erma. She clings to Lane now more than before, tries harder to keep Lane talking, to keep her at the breakfast table a little longer. Lane isn't sure if it's fear or loneliness, nor does it matter.

"It'll be fine," Lane says, dragging a finger through the tea and sticking it in her mouth. "I won't be long and the fellows are still down there by the road."

It's one of Lane's earliest memories, sneaking a taste of Erma's sweet tea. Erma would swat at her with a dish towel and chase her off as if she'd been sneaking whiskey.

"Did you see?" Erma says, shooing Lane away with a wave of her wooden spoon because she remembers too, and then points at a cake sitting in the center of the table.

It's a Lane Cake, three tiered and coated with a fluffy white frosting. It was Lane's favorite as a child, and when she was still young, Erma would tell her the whole of the South named a cake just for Lane.

"Annalee asked for it," Erma says. "Ain't that nice she asked special?"

"It'll be just the thing," Lane says.

Even amid the tragedy of Hettie's and Susannah's deaths, life is somehow easier in the house now. Perhaps it's the shock. They're all looking to feel safe and protected, and that need has united them. They can name the evil now. They know where it lived and where it worked and Mark will eventually capture it. Even Annalee has a need for Lane now. And life is easier.

At the end of the drive, Lane slows her car, turns onto the dirt road, and says a good morning to the deputies out her open window. She tells them she'll be only a half hour or so and gives a wave instead of an answer when one of the deputies asks where she's off to. She'd rather Mark not find out where she's going and is hoping to be back before he and Talley return.

The reporters are still in town. Mark said the parking lot outside the diner was crowded this morning and there was a line for coffee at the gas station, but none of those reporters are parked on the road outside the house anymore. It was one of the reasons Mark said Lane shouldn't worry about sending Talley with him this morning. He and Talley would be able to come and go without the press noticing and giving them any trouble. He felt certain walking through Daryl's shed with Talley was important to the investigation. And he'd have her home in no time.

Lane hasn't seen the three reporters again who were in the bar the night of her party, but they're likely still here, along with all the others. Once they've filed this story away or grown tired of waiting for the police to find a man who might well be dead at the bottom of the river, they'll go home, but they'll come back.

Eventually, there will be DNA matches to report and more bodies unearthed over at the school. They'll come again, but Lane won't be serving the drinks next time.

Though it'll take an extra few minutes, Lane drives the back roads the out-of-towners never take. At every bend and turn, she gets a glimpse of the river that weaves its way through town and wonders if Daryl really is there, rotting away underwater, or if he's still alive, somewhere maybe thinking about Talley and those windows he left open in Neil's room. It's why Mark hasn't left them, not once, since this all began.

Every night, Lane stares out the windows and watches for Daryl until Mark pulls her away. She startles at every noise and won't allow Talley outside. Mark scolds her and says they all have to go about their normal business so Talley doesn't sense their worry. It's another reason Mark insisted Lane let him take Talley today. Besides, Mark had said, once Kyle gets to town, Mark won't want to cut into what little time Talley will have with him. They either went to the shed today or they likely never would.

Kyle will arrive tomorrow, his flight due in at noon. Once he understood Annalee was safe, he hadn't sounded surprised something like this had happened. Even through the phone, Lane could hear it in his voice. He hadn't wanted Lane to move the girls in with Neil, or "that man" as Kyle tended to call him. She'd been tempted to answer that she hadn't wanted him to sleep with "that woman" but took a deep breath instead. Kyle might never have loved Lane and instead have only needed her, but the same was true for Lane. She'd never loved him either. He was a way out and someone who cared nothing about her past or any pain she might have endured.

Kyle's novel, the one he wrote about a girl abducted from a Florida mansion, had been closer to the truth than he could have known. The girl in Kyle's story was never taken, and instead she hid from her parents for the joy of hiding. But the difference, the big difference that made Lane first realize Kyle had never loved her, was that in his story, the girl tortured her father with lies. She tortured him by saying terrible things happened to her. Why hadn't he saved her? Why hadn't he been man enough to save her? That's how wicked the girl was in Kyle's story.

No one ever questioned Kyle about the book's ties to Lane's history. Neil had made sure there was no record of that day when Lane was thirteen, and the folks in town who did know what happened to her believed they knew the truth. Kyle mined Lane's life for everything that had value to him, twisted it to serve him best, and when she had nothing left, he asked her to go. That's how it ended. But it began with Lane using Kyle as an escape. Maybe she owed him her story, no matter how badly he perverted it. Though Lane never intended harm with her lies, she caused plenty. If the last twenty years have been lost to Lane, it's her doing as much as Kyle's.

Once Lane reaches Rowland's Tavern, she slows and parks out front instead of along the side of the bar. She pulls out her cell phone to give Mark a quick call so she can check on Talley, but he'll say she's hovering and he might ask what she's up to. Not wanting to lie to him and not wanting him to know what she's up to, she puts away the phone.

TALLEY

STILL SQUATTED NEXT to Talley on the shed's floor, Sheriff Ellenton pokes through the box of rags under Daryl's workbench. The windows are closed up tight, so there's no cross breeze and the shed is already hot.

"No lock on the door, huh?" the sheriff says, taking his hat off long enough to drag a sleeve across his brow before putting it back on. "Used to be. When we were kids, no older than you, your mama took me up there to the attic a time or two. We'd sneak the key and then put it back without your grandma ever knowing."

This makes Talley laugh. It's hard to imagine Mama and Sheriff Ellenton were ever kids like her.

"Grandpa told me he broke the lock off because Mama hid up there," she says. "He thought one of the boys took her."

When Talley, Mama, and Annalee first moved in with Grandma

and Grandpa, Mama told them to never go in the attic. Never ever. She said because a rusty nail might get them, but Talley doesn't believe that's the reason anymore.

"So your grandpa broke off the lock?" Sheriff Ellenton says, still sifting through the rags with the paint stick.

"Used a sledgehammer. And the windows used to be boarded up to keep out the rats. He took off those boards too, and even took the glass out. Grandpa said that boy on the TV took Mama and that he got what was coming to him. But I don't think a boy ever took Mama."

Talley hasn't known what to do with all the things Grandpa's been telling her. They've been stacking up and getting heavier every day, but telling Sheriff Ellenton is like handing off her big load of troubles to him. Whatever needs figuring out, he'll figure out.

Sheriff Ellenton stands, shakes out his bad knee, but doesn't say anything.

"If no one took Mama," Talley says, tipping her head to look up at Sheriff Ellenton, "why did Garrett Wilson have something coming to him?"

"That's the question, ain't it?"

"I think Grandpa Neil whipped a boy and then lied about Mama getting taken. Made everyone lie." Talley rubs her hand over her shin that is still sore and scabbed over. That's the heaviest piece of what she's been carrying.

Sheriff Ellenton stares down on Talley as if he's thinking over what she told him. "Your grandpa tell you all this the day Annalee came home?"

"He told me things lots of times, but mostly that day. He wanted me to get his gun for him too because he thought a boy took Mama again. He thought that's why the police were coming in and out of the house. He liked to talk about his gun. Told me about it all the time."

"And what did you do with your grandpa's gun?"

"Nothing," Talley says. At first, Grandpa's gun scared Talley, but then she never saw it and she figured it was just another thing Grandpa was remembering from a long time ago.

"Wasn't any gun where he said it should have been," she says. "He got real mad about that too. Said you must have took it."

Sheriff Ellenton lowers himself again. He sits there quiet for a good long time, rubbing his forehead with one hand. "That where you caught yourself climbing in here?" he asks, nodding down at Talley's leg.

"Bled real bad." Talley points at Daryl's box of rags. "I cleaned it with one of those. That's where I found the kerchief too."

"You mentioned one of the rags you pulled out was wet."

"Yes, sir."

"Did you smell anything when you picked it up? Something that maybe smelled bad?"

Talley shakes her head. She can feel Sheriff Ellenton thinking, that's how hard he's working things over.

"So it was water, you think?"

"Yes, sir."

"And it was a rag like this, an undershirt or T-shirt?" Using the half a paint stick, he lifts an old T-shirt. "Or was it like this?" He drops the T-shirt and fishes out an old towel. It's torn, and that's why it's in the rag box.

Sheriff Ellenton is not moving, maybe not even breathing as he waits for Talley's answer, and that means whatever she tells him is going to be real important.

"It was a shirt, a blue shirt," Talley says. "Like a shirt Daryl used to wear."

"So the attic door." Sheriff Ellenton stares at the old towel hanging off the end of the stick. "You telling me there's no lock? None at all? Just open it whenever you want?"

Talley rests her chin on her knees. She's started to shake, and she doesn't know why. "Yep."

Staring first at the towel and then at the box of rags, Sheriff Ellenton slowly stands.

"Come on, Talley," he says, takes her by the hand and backs away. "Come right now."

Sheriff Ellenton doesn't wait for Talley to follow him. He scoops her up with one arm. In his free hand, he pokes at his phone, presses it to his ear, and runs toward the car. Talley bounces at his side, can hardly breathe because he has her wrapped up tight in one arm.

"Lane," he shouts into the phone and keeps running. "Don't talk. Just listen. Get out of the house. Get out now. Get everyone out of the house."

39

DARYL

I KNEW THIS window was here. I knew it long before my Susannah disappeared into the river. I knew it long before I climbed the attic stairs and saw it up close. I knew it was here because the girl, Talley, told me. It's the window in her house that she would look out when hoping to catch sight of one of those boys running for his life. That's what they were doing. Running for their lives. It's what Wayne must have done, but he didn't get away because if he did, he would have found me. I'm sure he would have found me, but he didn't and now he's gone and Susannah's gone and I'm alone.

I'm hollowed out again. There's nothing inside to make me whole. There are no tangles anymore, no sharp edges. Only emptiness. I imagine I was cracked open at the river like Susannah's head was cracked open, and as I carried her to the cave, everything inside me drained out and floated away in the dark black water.

Talley was doing a good thing by feeding those boys, even if they weren't real anymore. I told her that, and I took some of the food she left for them so she'd believe me when I said she was a good person. I think I'll close my eyes when Talley has to die. That'll be the only way. Talley will be the hardest.

It's morning, I'm certain. The sheriff came to the house earlier and drove away with Talley. Soon after, Talley's mother drove away in her own car. Only the grandfather and grandmother are still home to take care of Annalee. Two police at the end of the driveway won't come to the house to eat their lunch for a few hours. The others should be home before then. They won't stay away long now that Annalee is back. Yesterday, or maybe the day before, they brought Annalee home. This is what I've been waiting for since I climbed into the attic—the grandfather and the grandmother alone in the house with Annalee.

I wish I had my maps because I would trace the road Susannah used to take when she drove into town and I might feel solid again. But I don't have my maps. Instead I draw new ones, and I write my notes too on dusty box tops with the tip of my finger so it's almost like she's still alive. I drink from the bottles of water I took from the refrigerator while the grandmother slept in the entry, the family Bible resting on her chest, and I eat the food Talley stored away in the attic so she could leave it for the boys who run. Crackers and pretzels mostly, and I'm losing count of the days.

After I carried Susannah Bauer up the river, I went back every night to sit on the rock where she died. I stopped going to the Wharf to see Annalee, and I stopped following her home and making lists about her comings and goings, because I had come to hate her.

Talley still came to the church every day to see me, and we watered her garden because the ground was cracking all around it. She talked to me about the leaves on her plants that were curling in on themselves and the stems that had shriveled, asked if I felt sad to see the plants die. I told her yes, it was always sad to see something die.

"I have a secret," Talley said to me on one of those days after Susannah died. "I have a secret I promised not to tell but I think I should. I think I have to tell somebody."

She hugged the book I had given her only a few weeks earlier. It showed every badge a Little Sister of the South could earn. It also told how a Little Sister of the South should behave. Loyalty, I had once told her, is the most important of all the rules, but I didn't care about her secrets or her loyalty anymore because I no longer care for Annalee.

"Annalee says she's going to run away," Talley said, even though I didn't ask. "She loves Jimmy Jansen and sneaks out at night to be with him, and one day soon, they're going to sneak out and never come back. Annalee's going to marry Jimmy Jansen and live in another town somewhere far away."

I grabbed her by the shoulders, shook her. She tried to pull away but couldn't because I held tight. I grabbed her like it was her fault Susannah was dead. Almost as quick as I grabbed her, I let her go. She stumbled and nearly fell.

"I'm sorry I told," she said, and backed away from me. I had frightened her, and that day, we didn't water her garden.

After Talley told me her secret, I started to go again to the Wharf to see if Annalee was there working and not sneaking off to get married and move to a town far away. They thought they could run, Annalee and the boy, from what they had done to Susannah, but I couldn't let them. Annalee had to stay so she could be the one to suffer most.

On the nights I watched Annalee, I didn't sit at the bar or drink a beer with the old men. Instead I watched from my car until I saw her walk onto the back deck where the guitar player sometimes played his guitar. I made notes of the dates and times I saw her and drew lines from my shed at the church to the house where Annalee and the rest lived. I drew circles around her house, more and more circles until the paper ripped through. I didn't know what to do or how to do it. Every day that passed was another day Annalee might run away with the boy, and I would be too late. Then a week and a half after my Susannah died and I carried her up the river, Annalee and the boy came to where I work.

THE SAME AS I knew about this window in the attic, I knew where I would find the attic door. I knew it was half as tall as a door should be because the girl, Talley, told me. I knew it would be unlocked, because Talley told me. I knew the door opened in and not out. I knew the grandmother had a wooden doorstop at her kitchen door even though she could rarely open it. Too many reporters and lookie-loos, Talley told me. And I knew the grandfather maybe kept a gun in the chest in his room, but when I looked, reaching in among the blankets wrapped in white tissue, it wasn't there. No matter. I hadn't wanted it so I could shoot it. I didn't know how. I wanted it so no one could shoot me. I would use my stick instead.

I fashioned the stick in my shed before coming here. Wayne had showed me how when I was a boy. I'd been seven, I suppose, no older, maybe younger. You'll need to protect yourself one day, he said, and showed me how to cut a two-by-four to the length of a bat. He made me hold the saw's wooden handle and then put his bigger hand over mine and together we cut the wood.

Then he showed me how to drive a half-dozen nails into one end of the board so they all poked through the other side. Cluster them, he had said, and held up a single silver nail and tapped its pointed tip. Make sure they're at least four inches long.

I gathered it all—the doorstop, the water bottles from the refrigerator, the pictures of the boys I pulled from the windows, and my stick with a half-dozen nails driven through it. I cradled some of it in my shirt, tucked some under one arm, and opened the attic door. Once inside, I jammed it closed by hammering the doorstop into place with my stick.

It was morning when Annalee and the boy came to my work a week and a half after Susannah died. They weren't sneaking anymore, weren't trying to hide. They came in her white truck, the both of them. It was a cloudy day, and already Reverend had been out to tell me today was the day it would finally rain. God bless us, it's finally going to rain.

Annalee wore a blue dress and brown sandals that were a size too big for her feet. Her hair was pulled back and tied loosely. As she and the boy walked toward the church's back door, she reached for his hand. The boy wore a baseball hat, and before the two of them disappeared inside, Annalee glanced overhead at the sound of thunder and then motioned for the boy to tuck in his shirt. As he did, she took the hat from his head and smoothed his hair by running her fingers through it, lifted onto her toes, kissed the boy lightly on the cheek, and together they walked into the church.

As I waited for them outside the door, I walked four steps this way and four steps that, sometimes pounding my forehead with one palm. Annalee was vile. The grandfather too. All of them vile. Annalee and the boy were surely at the church to talk to Miss Hettie, admit their love, maybe even confess what they'd done to Susannah so Miss Hettie could help them run away and be married. The night Miss Hettie invited me to services, she told me she damn well knew how to get things done.

When the church's door opened again and Annalee and the boy walked back outside, Annalee's arm was wrapped around the boy. The edges of his eyes were red. His chest had caved, and his shoulders rolled forward. He had been crying. He carried Susannah's death with him as he walked. Annalee did not.

"I know what you did," I said as they pushed through the door and stepped outside. They looked straight at me, saw me clearly, but they hadn't heard me clearly.

"Pardon?" Annalee said. She didn't remember me from the grocery where she had rammed a cart into my gut. She looked at me like I was any other person she had never seen before. But the boy recognized me straightaway. He backed up and started shaking his head. Annalee grabbed him, held him at her side.

"You," I said, holding my hands tight together and slapping them against one thigh. "And you. I know what you did."

I needed them to know someone had seen them and someone knew what had become of Susannah. But as soon as I said it, I knew hearing it would only make them want to run more.

"No, you don't," Annalee said. "You don't know anything. He's lying, Jimmy. Don't listen to him." She petted the boy's arm and leaned into him. With her head pressed to his side, she looked to me. "You don't know anything."

Pulling the boy past me, Annalee opened the passenger-side door for him and pushed him inside. I watched them until she drove away, and when I turned to go back to my shed, the mother, Miss Hettie, was there waiting for me.

"They can't run away," I said. "Annalee can't run. I know what they did, and it's not fair they run away and be married."

Miss Hettie stepped up to me and rested a hand on my chest. She stood like that even when sprinkles of rain began to fall.

Even when lightning cracked, and everyone knew to go inside when lightning cracked a Florida sky.

"Did you love Susannah like you love Annalee?" she asked, and touched my face when I didn't answer. "That girl thinks she's going to marry my boy. She thinks they have a plan, thinks they're going to run away together. But she's wrong. I would never let him marry a Fielding. Never."

Miss Hettie lifted onto her toes, leaned in close, and told me the boy would be leaving this town just as soon as she could manage it.

"He's moving away, and Annalee will be left here for you," she said. "I would die before letting my boy marry that girl. So don't you worry. My boy will be gone soon enough."

Miss Hettie was making her boy lie to Annalee. Miss Hettie and her boy were both lying so Annalee would believe she and the boy were going to run away together and no one would ever know what they did to Susannah Bauer and they would be safe. But none of that was true. Miss Hettie was just keeping Annalee happy until she could get her boy out of town and far away from Waddell. She didn't care about keeping Annalee safe at all. Only her boy.

But Annalee wasn't the only one Miss Hettie didn't care about. There had been times when I thought Miss Hettie was almost like a mother should be. When she dabbed pink lotion on my legs and tapped at her computer while trying to find Wayne, I thought she was kind like a mother should be. She called me darling sometimes, but she wasn't like a mother. She was like *my* mother. And that day, when the rain finally started to fall, with her hand still resting on my chest, Miss Hettie said if I ever told what I knew about Annalee and the boy, she would say I killed Susannah. People would believe her because she lived in a nice house and was the church secretary. She came from money, sugar-cane money. Who was I? she asked. I was nobody.

For two days, maybe three, I have waited in the attic for a time like this to come. The mother and the sheriff are gone. Talley is gone too. The grandmother is still here, but she never leaves. It's the grandfather who matters most. I've always known he had to be first. He's the one who hurt Wayne and all the others and is the beginning of what turned into Annalee. My father was the beginning of what turned into Wayne and then me, and he died first. That's what Mother said.

When I came here, I knew they would eventually bring Annalee home and all come together, but before that happened, they would see the broken door. They would know someone had been inside, and so I walked past the grandfather sleeping in his chair, quietly so I didn't wake him. I could have killed him that day, the grandmother too, because I had my stick, but then Annalee would have suffered only those two deaths. Instead I opened the windows, because open windows would scare them. They'd think the windows meant I had come and gone and was coming back. No one would ever think they meant I was here all along.

40

LANE

THE SMELL OF warm beer hits Lane the moment she pushes open the door to Rowland's Tavern. From where he stands behind the bar, Rowland doesn't look up. Instead he pulls a baseball cap from his pocket and slips it on his head. He's wearing a short-sleeved T-shirt. It's pale blue today and wrinkled. That wrinkled shirt is another reminder Hettie's gone.

"Morning," Lane says, glancing at the clock that hangs over the register. "Wasn't sure you'd be open."

"Been busier than ever."

Lane slides onto a stool near the cooler where Rowland is loading in longnecks. He grabs the bottle of Woodford from the shelves behind him, holds it out to Lane, but she shakes her head. He pours himself a drink—two fingers, neat.

"Can I do anything for Hettie's service?" Lane asks.

Rowland shakes his head.

"People really loved her." Lane says it even though Rowland will know it isn't true. People feared Hettie more than loved her, but they'll praise her and leave flowers at her grave because she was a Martin. "I'm sure the whole town will be there."

This time, Rowland nods.

"Is there anything else I can do?" Lane says. "Erma would like to bring food to the house."

"Hettie's mother has it covered." Rowland tips his head back and finishes off the drink in one long swallow. "Annalee doing better?"

"Much," Lane says, straightening the stack of napkins that sits in front of her on the bar. It gives her something to do instead of having to consider that maybe she's about to hurt Rowland when he's already been hurt so much. "I owe you such an apology for everything I said down at the river."

Rowland pours another two fingers of Woodford, and again Lane shakes her head when he holds the bottle up to her.

"I worry that what we did started all of this," Lane says, pushing the napkins away and leaning on the bar with both elbows. She knows she'll hurt him because that night wasn't just one night to Rowland. He wanted it to lead to a future, but Lane never did. "That night between us, is that why they were both there, Annalee and Hettie, at the river?"

"Don't give yourself too much credit," Rowland says, starting to load in another case. As he works, he won't let himself look at Lane. "You were just the last straw. Plenty other straws came before you."

A corner of a white business card sticks out from under the register. With one finger, Lane slides it toward her, picks it up, flicks it with her thumb. It's the card the silver-haired reporter tucked under the tip jar the night Annalee disappeared.

"And I'll tell you right now," Rowland says, pointing the bottle of Woodford at Lane and finally looking her straight on. "If Hettie found out Jimmy was thinking of running off with your girl, she went to the river damn well intending to put a stop to it. She wasn't going to let that happen with any girl in this town, most definitely not a Fielding girl. Not her boy."

"He came to the hospital," Lane says, trying to change the topic. "Jimmy did. How is he doing?"

Rowland shakes his head. "Ain't doing well. I've asked him to check in on Annalee now that she's home, but he won't do it. Can't face her, I suppose. Think he'll do better once he gets off to school, gets himself away from this town."

"Make sure he understands it'll all still be here when he comes back someday."

"You quitting on me?" His tone is softer now, and his question isn't much of a question. It's more of a statement because he already knows. He and Lane's one night together won't lead to a future.

"I can't work here," Lane says. "Not after what happened to Hettie."

"Going back to writing?"

Lane shakes her head because she'll never go back to journalism, but she says nothing more. She could never explain to Rowland or anyone else why she'd never write again, nor could she admit how she used all those people by trying to pacify herself by comforting them. The only thing she knows for certain is that if she ever went back, she'd make the same mistake again.

"Should have sent you on your way a long time ago," Rowland says. The liquor is tilting his voice. He must have started long before Lane showed up.

"I should have quit as soon as it happened," she says.

This is the moment she could tell Rowland the truth, and

when she glances up at him, he's staring at her like he knows she has something to tell. Or maybe he's wanting Lane to say she loves him, but that wouldn't be true, and he doesn't really want it. As much as he might have hoped for a future with Lane, he'd have never left Hettie. Lane made him feel young again, and he mistook that for love. She knows because that's how she felt all those nights working here alongside him. She felt young and could forget, for a few hours anyway, the mistakes and lies and all the responsibilities. But mostly Rowland, like Lane, just didn't want to be alone.

That night three months ago when Lane and Rowland slept together, Lane wasn't as drunk as she likes to make him think she was. She remembers every moment. Just as he did the first time they were together as kids, Rowland kept asking if she was all right. Does this hurt you? Should I stop? He was afraid to touch her, and that's in part why she took him home that night three months ago. Without telling Rowland or anyone else the truth of what happened when she was thirteen years old, or rather the truth of what didn't happen, she was trying to prove she was nobody's victim.

If Neil hurt that boy, killed that boy, he did it before Lane even knew they were looking for her. No one ever said what the boy did or didn't do to Lane—not Neil or Erma and certainly not Lane—but people assumed. And ever since, they've felt shame on her behalf, relief it wasn't them or one of their own, and lastly, mostly, they've pitied her, the people of this town. Lane may well never know what happened to the boy Neil beat or if there ever was a boy, but she has to tell the truth, not just to the girls and Rowland and those nearest to her. But to everyone. It may be the closest she can ever get to making it right.

"I'll help you keep up with the books if you want," Lane says. "But that'll have to be it. I'm so sorry, Rowland."

She can do the accounting from the house. No one will ever see her car parked here again alongside Rowland's and wonder what might be going on between the two of them. When the phone tucked down in her pocket begins to vibrate, she excuses herself and spins around so her back is to Rowland.

"Hey, Mark," she says, already knowing she won't tell him she came here.

"Lane," he yells into the phone. His voice is strange and he's breathing heavily, almost like he's running. "Don't talk. Just listen. Get out of the house. Get out now. Get everyone out of the house."

She jumps from the stool.

"I'm not at home. I'm not at home, Mark."

There is a jostling on the other end. Lane screams into the phone, shouts for Mark to say something. She can hear his voice, but he's not talking into the phone. He's talking to someone else, directing them. It's the radio in his patrol car. He's talking to someone else on the radio.

"Mama." It's Talley's voice on the other end of the phone.

"Talley, what is it?" Lane says, running toward the door. "Tell me what's going on. Where are you?"

"Sheriff says Daryl is in the house," Talley says. "He's telling his deputies to get Grandma and Annalee and Grandpa out and to bust down the attic door. He says Daryl's up there, and maybe he has a gun. Maybe he has Grandpa's gun."

41

DARYL

AT THE TOP of the attic stairs, I hold the pictures of the boys who run in one hand and my stick as long as a bat in the other. I should have drawn a picture of Susannah to go along with the boys the old woman drew and taped in the windows because Susannah is dead like those boys. From where I stand, I try to hear the littlest bit of them, the grandmother and grandfather. A cabinet perhaps slamming shut as the grandmother works in the kitchen. A creak and a pop, the grandfather lowering his recliner. A chair scooting across the floor. I stand still, looking down the narrow stairwell that gets darker near the bottom, and give the grandparents time to fall asleep. When I imagine the house must be quiet, I walk slowly down the attic stairs.

AFTER ANNALEE AND the boy left the church and after Miss Hettie left me standing in the rain, I walked back to my shed to wait for Talley. She always came to water on the weekdays and I hoped the littlest bit of rain and the sound of thunder wouldn't keep her away. I was standing under the oaks, holding one hand with the other, when I saw her across the road. She waved and ran toward me. The sprinkles that had started to fall were making her happy, and she forgot to be scared of me.

She was red in the face by the time she reached the oak where I stood. Leaning forward, she braced her hands on her knees. Already the air had shifted. Even though the rain had barely begun to fall, a chill had settled in. She was smiling and her eyes were wide, but then she remembered I had grabbed her by the shoulders and yelled at her when she told me her secret about Annalee and the boy being in love, and her smile wilted.

"It's going to rain," she said, glancing overhead at the sound of thunder. The wind was blowing in from the south, and it ruffled her hair and clothes.

"Tell Annalee the boy will never marry her," I said, telling her exactly what Miss Hettie had told me. I crossed my arms and hugged myself to keep my hands close.

I didn't know anymore what I should say or shouldn't, knew only that I didn't want Annalee to run. Maybe if she learned the boy had been lying to her and would never marry her, she wouldn't try to leave. I didn't know the right thing to say and I was afraid of Miss Hettie, but I was certain saying what I did would hurt Annalee. I wanted her to suffer. I wanted her to suffer every other death.

"Hettie Jansen called you butchers and whores," I said. "She'll never let Jimmy Jansen marry Annalee. You go home and you tell her that. Tell her she'll never be safe. I know what she did, and she can't run from it."

Talley backed away, crossing her arms like me. I shouted at her that Little Sisters always keep their promises and she had to tell. Promise me you'll tell. She nodded, turned, and ran.

Later that day, I went to Annalee's work as I had done so many other days. It was raining hard by then and the wipers on my car didn't work. I squinted and leaned over the steering wheel, trying to see the road ahead. Annalee's truck was not parked where it usually was, and maybe I was too late. Maybe she was already gone.

I drove next to the bar where her mother worked. The rain had soaked my clothes and hair, and when I walked inside, I dripped on the floor and left wet footprints. It was dark inside the bar, and the mother and I were alone. I wanted to cover my ears over because the rain was loud on the tin roof. I tried but couldn't look at the mother straight on because she looked too much like Annalee and I hated Annalee by then.

The mother gave me a beer in a brown bottle. I told her Annalee wasn't at work and she should be at work. I wanted the mother to stop Annalee from running. Maybe Miss Hettie lied and Annalee and the boy were going to run away after all, or maybe Annalee would run away by herself. But the mother told me to leave her daughter out of it.

WITH TWO FINGERS, I work loose the doorstop that holds the attic door closed. It's jammed in there good. I wiggle it back and forth, scraping my knuckles on the landing, and when it pulls free, I set it on the bottom stair, don't drop it because someone might hear, turn the knob, and open the door. It pulls in toward me, so I step aside, squat until I'm the size of the door, and look into the hallway.

The lay of the pine floors leads me straight to Annalee's room. Even in my stocking feet, the boards creak. The first door isn't Annalee's. It's open, ajar really, and inside is the bathroom. There is no sun here like there was in the attic. All the curtains are closed. A few more steps and I'm standing at Annalee's doorway. Her door too stands partway open.

AFTER I LEFT the mother's bar, I drove to the river. As I did every other night, I parked among all the broken-down cars at the parts store and walked toward the bend in the road that led to the river, through the trees, down the clay bank to the ledge of limestone where Susannah Bauer died.

I had said the wrong thing. When I first told Annalee and the boy I had seen what they'd done, I knew I had made a mistake. If I knew what they'd done, then I could tell, and they'd be more afraid. They would run for certain. And then I made Talley promise to tell Annalee the boy didn't love her, not really, and would never run away with her. It was too hard. Knowing what to say and what not to say and how to make Annalee suffer the last death. Now Annalee's truck wasn't at work. She was gone, and she'd suffered nothing.

At the limestone ledge, I sat, pulled my knees to my chest, rested my head there, and let it roll off to the side so I could look upriver toward the caves where my Susannah lay. The rain continued, and as the hours passed, the gray sky turned slowly black. I thought I might never leave because this was where I could always be near Susannah. But then I saw something. I blinked and rubbed my eyes on my wet shirt sleeve, squinted to see through the heavy rain soaking my face. Those were headlights throwing a blurry yellow glow out onto the river.

I knew it was Annalee and Miss Hettie the moment I saw the simple dark outline of them walking along the river's edge. The boy wasn't with them because he wasn't quite like them. He was a coward, but he was also kinder. He had tried to find Susannah. He had cried for her, struggled for her. At least for a time, he tried, but then Annalee threatened to tell what he'd done. In the end, the boy saved himself instead of Susannah, but he was sorry to have done it.

Annalee appeared first, or rather the shape of her appeared. She was walking toward the ledge where I sat and was leading Miss Hettie to the spot where Susannah Bauer had died. They were making their way through the cypress trees with the swollen trucks and the roots that rose and tangled into knots. But Miss Hettie was slow and small, and she struggled more with the rain than Annalee. She hung back, falling farther and farther behind, not following Annalee into the shallow water seeping higher on the cypress trunks.

Miss Hettie carried the lantern, one she must have taken from the church closet, and her smaller shadow grabbed for every trunk she passed. Annalee, barely a shadow because the light couldn't reach her, urged Miss Hettie forward with her waving arms. From my spot, I pulled my knees closer, made myself as small as I could.

As the two of them continued toward me, the branches overhead whipped with the wind. The river ran faster. My heart beat faster too. The water was rising, running deeper into higher ground. Annalee, the shape of her, continued pointing this way and that, making Miss Hettie look in front and behind, making her dizzy. Making me dizzy. They were close, but not close enough.

Miss Hettie's feet didn't tangle like Susannah's had, because Miss Hettie didn't back into the twisted roots in quite the same way. Holding the lantern high over her head, Miss Hettie refused to wade out into the deeper water. So when Annalee pushed Miss Hettie, her feet weren't wedged between the roots or caught up in the vines. She was able to keep her balance. She grabbed for a tree. She stumbled, dropped the lantern, but righted herself. From wherever it landed, the lantern still glowed. It lit up the underside of both of them, lifted them, made them seem to float above the water. When Annalee pushed Miss Hettie again, she fell, but she wasn't as close to the limestone ledge as Susannah had been.

Miss Hettie cried out once and again. She didn't hit her head, splitting it on a jagged edge. They hadn't come far enough. In the dark and with the water rising all around them and the wind blowing the rain in her face, Annalee didn't get it quite right.

As Miss Hettie scrambled to her feet, a shadow of arms and legs, Annalee did the same thing I did the night I saw her with the boy at the edge of the river. Her first swing was at Miss Hettie's gut. A cry rose up, one muffled by a lack of air. The boy had collapsed when I hit him there, and Annalee had seen how easily he was hurt. Bare-chested and standing tall, she had watched the boy collapse so easily. She'd seen how easily Susannah died too and was surely hoping Miss Hettie would do the same.

Annalee hit Miss Hettie again, this time swinging from down to up. She knew Miss Hettie wasn't going to let her marry Jimmy. She knew Miss Hettie called her a butcher and a whore. Talley did as I asked, and she told Annalee all these things. Next Annalee caught the boy's mother under the chin, right where the light from the lantern still shined on her. Her head snapped backward. There was a splash. Miss Hettie was gone, but so was Annalee. I couldn't see either of them. Listening hard over the wind and rain and rapids rushing over the river's limestone bed, I didn't hear another scream. I hugged my knees closer and squinted. Only one shadow rose from the dark water. It was Annalee. I never saw Miss Hettie again.

It was easier for me to walk on high ground, though the clay had turned slick. Down below, Annalee stumbled through the trees, her feet surely sinking into the mud and the silt. We were both making our way toward the headlights still shining out onto the river. I was the first to reach the clearing where Annalee had parked her truck, and right away I knew she'd made a mistake.

North of the clearing, there is a spot where the river leaves behind rough, grainy sand and another spot closer, where it drops broken shells, pebbles, and stones. Here in this spot, where the water churns most, the river leaves behind silt. And this was Annalee's mistake. She parked where the glossy mud comes to rest. It's a low spot that floods first when the river swells. Miss Hettie had known better, had parked on higher, drier ground. That's what made me think Miss Hettie called on Annalee to come here, maybe so she could find out where Susannah's body was. Maybe she had wanted to move the body to protect her boy. It was too much to think about, and I tried not to slap my forehead. I couldn't know for sure if Miss Hettie had called Annalee to the river, or if Annalee had call Miss Hettie, but I did know Miss Hettie had parked on higher, drier ground and that meant she had planned to be the one to escape.

AT HER TRUCK, Annalee opened the door and struggled to get one foot up and inside and then the other. Under the glow of the dome light, she became real until she pulled the door closed and turned back into a shadow. The engine started, but the truck didn't move. Its tires would be spinning in the mud, spinning like tires on ice. She threw open the door, leaned out. The falling rain sparkled in the dome light, and where the headlights lit up the river, drops blew across the water.

She lifted something and held it near her face. Her cell phone. She poked at it, shook it, threw it out the door into the water. Then she began to beat her hands on the steering wheel, just as I have done before and just as I wanted to do now. I wanted to beat on something so my head wouldn't pound and so I wouldn't scream. When Annalee tired herself and her palms surely ached, she became still. The door hung open. The rain sprayed into the truck and across her face. After a few moments, Annalee pulled the door closed, the cab went dark, and the headlights disappeared.

The river continued to slide farther up the banks, higher up the trunks of the cypress trees. Rain dripped off my head and my clothes hung heavy. My shoes were like stones on my feet. My breathing slowed, and every part of me was exhausted. I slid down a tree and sank into the mud.

I thought someone would find Annalee here in the morning and discover what she'd done. Even if she left, waded through the rising waters, and made her way back home, her truck would still be here. The police would find Miss Hettie. They'd be able to tell, wouldn't they, someone had beaten her. They would see she hadn't hit her head on a limestone slab, something that could have been an accident. And they would find bruising. There had been those moments after Miss Hettie fell when I couldn't see Annalee because maybe she was holding Miss Hettie underwater. They'd be able to tell, wouldn't they, that someone had wrapped her hands around Miss Hettie's throat and drowned her.

If the police were to find Annalee sitting in her truck, trapped by the rising river, they would piece together that she loved Jimmy Jansen. They'd already know Miss Hettie had forbidden Annalee and Jimmy to be together because the Fieldings were butchers and whores. They might never know Annalee and the boy killed Susannah, but they would surely discover what Annalee did to Miss Hettie. Annalee might not suffer every other death, but she would suffer.

For an hour, maybe two or three, this is what I thought about as the rain dripped in my face and soaked into my clothes. I stayed because I wanted to watch them find her. The rain would wash away all signs I had been there, so I could stay and watch. I would wait all night if I had to, but then the truck's door opened. The sky was lighter. It was nearly dawn, but mostly the clouds had passed, giving way to a brighter sky. Annalee stepped out. The water was only shin-deep around her truck, but she was still trapped by the silt. She hoisted herself up into the truck's bed and climbed onto the roof. Once there, she looked out into the trees. Turning slowly, beginning with her back to me, she was looking for something. I crouched to the ground and pulled my arms into the sleeves of my dark shirt so my pale skin wouldn't give me away. I didn't know how much she'd see in the dim light, but I knew she was looking for me.

We were so alike, Annalee and I, both of us vile. She would know I'd been following her and watching her. She had realized, as she sat in her truck all night and reasoned things through, that I had been there when Susannah died. How many other times had I been there, following and watching? And she had wondered, was I there at that moment too, somewhere in the trees, watching her yet again? She had realized if I had been everywhere she had been, she could blame me.

I first saw him in the grocery store, she could tell the police. And he came often to the Wharf. He'd sit at the bar and watch me. Ask some of the regulars. They'll have seen him too. And there were a few nights, well, I hate to admit it, but I was down at the Tracks with a boy and the same strange man was watching me. He hit Jimmy Jansen in the gut with a tree branch. Just ask him. Just ask Jimmy Jansen. It had to be that Daryl. And I'm sure I saw him that night at the river, the night Miss Hettie was killed. Was it him, do you suppose? And did he mean to kill me too? This is what she would say.

"Are you here?" she called out into the trees. She stood silent, listening. "I do remember you. The grocery store, right? And you've been to my work."

She turned in two full circles and called out to me again and again. Her hair was still damp and more brown than blond. She stood straight, didn't cower or try to make herself as small as she could. We were so alike, yet she stood tall and I sank into the ground. I should have been strong enough to save Susannah, but I wasn't. Instead I only watched. All I ever did was watch. I'm everything Mother said I was. Vile. But so is Annalee.

"She was planning to blame you," she said. "Miss Hettie. That's what she told us. I couldn't let her do that, couldn't let her blame you. Rich people like her, they think they can blame people like us."

I tucked my head to my knees and closed my eyes, but I could still hear her. All the times I followed her and watched her, I had never heard this voice. From on top of her truck, she called out loudly, and her voice had the sweetness a mother's voice must have. She had a different voice with the boy, one that sounded like she was teasing him sometimes, scolding him others. And still another voice, lower in pitch and flat, for her customers at her work.

"How could I let her blame you?"

She wanted me to think she'd killed Miss Hettie for me so I would be on her side and not tell anyone all the bad things she had done. But I didn't believe that. Annalee knew Miss Hettie was only trying to keep her happy until the boy had gone. And

Annalee knew those things because Talley told her. And Talley knew because I told her. Whether she meant to or not, Annalee killed Miss Hettie to keep the boy and now she needed someone to blame. I buried my face and squeezed my eyes shut to stop Annalee from seeping inside. I sat that way, curled as tightly as I could, until the shouting stopped.

When I looked again, Annalee still stood on the roof of her truck. Her head was tipped back and she was staring up at the sky. She hadn't seen me, and she was surely wondering if she could still say I was to blame. She had wanted me to answer her because what if I wasn't there at the river but was somewhere else? What if she lied and said she saw me anyway and what if the police caught her in the lie?

Dropping into a seated position, Annalee slipped from the roof into the truck's bed and down onto the ground, where she made a small splash. I thought she would climb back in her truck, but instead, she stood there, her back to me. With both hands, she pushed the door closed, or rather not all the way closed, leaned forward, and yanked it open, hitting herself in the face with its edge. Her head snapped back and she stumbled. She closed the door again, almost, and this time, she fell when she yanked on it. She used the door handle to pull herself up, leaned into the truck, and rested there. When she was finally able to stand, she dumped something into the water and flung something else, and then she waded into the river and started to walk toward the caves.

No one would find Annalee sitting in her truck in the morning. They'd find her somewhere else. They'd find her beaten. She'd say she ran, ran for her life. The old men at church have been saying to keep an eye on the blond girls. Poor Annalee was a blonde. They'd think she narrowly escaped what Miss Hettie and Susannah Bauer had not. Or maybe they'd think Annalee narrowly escaped Miss Hettie.

———

THE DOOR TO Annalee's bedroom stands ajar, half open, half closed. I give it a push. It doesn't creak, but swings silently. For now, I want only to see her.

She lies in her bed, a white sheet pulled up under her chin. Baskets of folded clothes sit at the foot of the bed, and a red blanket is draped across her feet. Her head lies squarely on the pillow, her face tipped toward the ceiling, and her eyes are closed. I don't beat my head or wonder what is the right thing to do, because I know. I'll be back for Annalee after I'm done with all the others, but for now I squat slowly to the ground and set the pictures of the boys who ran just inside her door. Talley's mother told her and Talley told me—no one cared about those boys and they were discarded by the ones who were meant to protect them. I think Wayne was like them. I think I am too, and before Annalee dies, I want her to know someone remembers, because if no one is left to miss them, the missing will simply disappear.

I carry my stick with both hands as I walk down the stairs toward the grandfather's room. Near the bottom, I stop. Silverware rattles against a tabletop in the kitchen. It's the grandmother. She's not asleep like I thought she would be. I wonder if they knew, the two of them, what they would create one day when first their daughter was born. Or did they only realize when their daughter gave birth to Annalee?

The floors in the entry are smooth. I slide my stocking feet over them, let my two hands drop to the end of the stick. You know which end to use? Wayne had asked when he handed me the stick we made together. I nodded. And do you know which way the nails should face? Again, I nodded yes.

The television is on, but no sound comes from it. The grandfather wears large earphones over his ears. I step across the threshold into his room. The smell is different here than in other parts of the house. Something has spoiled, gone sour. The grandfather sits in his chair, his head sagging to one side. Something inside his chest rattles as he inhales and exhales. Swing it like a bat, Wayne told me. Coming at it sideways like that, you'll have a bigger target. Give yourself some room or someone will wrestle that stick out of your hands. I will do that now. I step into the room, four full steps, but not too close. I need to give myself room. In the kitchen, more silverware clatters, and that must be the grandmother humming. It grows louder. Yes, it's the grandmother humming a song I don't know.

ERMA

ERMA IS CLEAR in the head today, and this Sunday, she'll be going back to church. Not the New Covenant, but that nice new church over on Central. It probably isn't right to say damn you to any person who tries to block her way or any person who speaks unkindly to her because she isn't accompanied by a husband, but that's what she'll say. After all these years and all the pleasantries, that's exactly what she'll say.

She already has her salon appointment. Someone new is answering the phones over there at Belmont's, and the young girl didn't hesitate taking Erma's name and giving her a Friday-morning slot. It was too late to get an appointment this week, but next Friday, they'll be expecting her.

A few footsteps cross overhead. That'll be Annalee up and about, likely using the restroom, though she's supposed to holler to Erma for help getting around. Lane was right about Erma's home cooking being just the thing for Annalee. She's bouncing right back, well, almost right back. Today Erma made a Lane Cake, and she thinks Lane was happy to see it. She even dragged her finger through the sweet tea like she did when she was a little girl. She's getting all those years back, Erma is. Even though it's barely midmorning, Erma will slice off a piece of the cake and run it on up to Annalee with a glass of milk. That's how good Erma's feeling this morning.

The reporters are all gone from the school. Erma has walked out to the fence every morning for the past two days and strained to see if any more have come along. From the right spot, she can get a glimpse of the white building where those boys, now men, got whipped. That's where the reporters sometimes go with their cameras and microphones when the school's gates are unlocked and they're allowed inside. They take pictures of the narrow doorways, the slender windows set high on the walls, the small room where those boys were made to lie on a mattress while they got beat. Hold those railings, they say Neil told them. Don't you look back. Don't you cry out.

The reporters came this time because the scientists from Tampa drew up a picture of one of those boys. There's no telling if he's the one Neil thought took Lane. Even if Erma did know, she'd feel no relief. No disappointment either. Just sadness and regret for having not tried to stop Neil. And there will be no relief or disappointment if Mark one day discovers Neil didn't hurt anyone the day Lane hid in the attic. Even if Neil spared a boy that particular day, he beat so many others—others who might now be buried in a sloppy cemetery, no markers for their graves.

Erma's heard nothing of Neil this morning and probably won't for a few hours, not until it's near about dinnertime. It's the best part of her day now, phoning down to those deputies to tell them anytime they care to, they're welcome to come fetch a plate. After so many years alone, it's wonderful to have a full house.

A few more steps overhead—Annalee walking back to her room. Or maybe that's her headed down the stairs, for pity's sake. Erma will have to get after her for all that moving about. Using her best knife, Erma slices through the three-layer cake, the first slice, and uses her pie server to scoop it out because she wants it to be perfect. She can't remember when last she used her good silver, but from now on, she will. And not just on Sundays. So much is better now. After all these years, they've put things behind them. Atoned. That's what they've done.

Ever so slowly, Erma slides the sterling silver server under the cut slice, touches one finger to the top, and jiggles. As she pulls it toward her, she knocks a fork to the ground. There was a time she'd have worried about waking Neil with such a commotion, but not anymore. She gives the fork a kick, sending it under one of the chairs where no one will trip on it, and tips the perfect slice onto a plate. Then leaving that dirty fork on the floor to another time, she takes a fresh one from the top drawer.

There will be no other justice for Bonnie Wiley or any of the boys, now men, who were beaten or their families. Or for the ones who died. After the lawyers asked their questions of Neil some five years ago, asked them for hours upon hours, no charges were filed. Too much time had passed. Statute of limitations, they called it. Unless someone could prove a boy under Neil's care had been murdered, an unlikely event when working with bones so old, too much time had passed.

And yet for all the men who had found one another after so many years of silence and who still remembered the little white house, the passage of time changed nothing. They demanded something, to be heard perhaps, to be remembered. The state of

323

Florida instead posted a plaque to honor all those boys, now men, who survived, and the boys who never got to grow up. May this bring some measure of peace, the plaque read.

Plenty of folks did wrong at that school, some before Neil, some alongside or after him, and they died having never paid for their sins. Neil will do the same. Those folks from the university will continue to dig up bones, test for DNA, and the day will come when some of those bones, some of those boys, will be matched up to a family. They'll be reunited and will rest easy after all these years. It's the least and yet the most Erma can hope for.

Carrying her perfect slice with both hands, Erma's halfway through the foyer when the telephone rings. She wouldn't bother with it, but she's right here, so she lets go of the plate with one hand and picks up the phone. And dang it all, her thumb slips and she dents her perfect icing. She sets down the receiver, takes hold of the plate with her free hand, and pokes her thumb into her mouth. She sure did get a good make on the icing. She steps toward the stairs again but stops when something moves in Neil's room.

She drops the plate. A man is already looking at her. He's thick and tall and has dark hair. He steps backward, topples the tray set off to the side of Neil's chair, stumbles. Erma's hands, too heavy to move, hang at her sides. Neil rolls his head forward, looks to the man standing near the television. Rocking side to side, Neil tries to scoot forward in his chair. He yanks the earphones from his head.

If Neil is saying anything, Erma can't hear him. She lunges toward the family Bible resting in the middle of the foyer's credenza. She swipes at the handle on the small drawer just there beneath the Bible, slaps at it, her hands still heavy and stiff. She yanks open the drawer, yanks it clean out of the credenza. It falls to the floor. Folded and stapled pamphlets, old church bulletins announcing weddings, births, and deaths, scatter. She drops to her knees, shuffles through them, and grabs the gun that's meant to be in the chest in Neil's room.

"Stop that there." It's Neil's voice. "You get on."

Dropping the gun because she needs both hands to make her way, Erma crawls toward the threshold leading into Neil's room. Every few feet, she swats at the gun, sending it sliding across the pine floors ahead of her. As she scrambles forward, crawling and swatting, her hemline catches under her knees. At the seam between Neil's room and the foyer, she grabs at the gun again. There's a safety. That's what Susannah said and showed Erma how to flip it on and off. Erma rubs her fingers over the gun until she feels it. It'll be set when you grab for the gun, Susannah said. You have to remember that. You have to remember.

Something else falls, or Neil has thrown something, his remote maybe, with his good hand. Erma yanks at her skirt, tries to lift onto her knees. She wraps her hands around the gun. Hold on tight and use both thumbs to pull back the hammer. The first shot will be the easiest. You won't get off a second. The man is ducking because Neil has thrown something else. A book, perhaps.

Erma often imagined the day she might have to use this gun, but it had always been Neil on the other end. She practiced controlled breathing, knew if she were ever using it, it would likely be her girls and herself she was protecting. She could do it. She could pull the trigger.

The man shuffles his feet like he's holding a bat and readying himself to swing. Erma and Lane once went to watch Mark Ellenton play ball when he was a boy, a young man. Stepping up to home plate, he did the same. The man holds the piece of wood out at arm's length, appears to study the end of it, and pulls it back over one shoulder as Erma pulls the trigger. Keep your eyes open. You'll only get one good shot. The man drops.

Erma asked Susannah Bauer if she knew about guns because she was a girl who knew how to care for herself and would know about such things. They practiced one day while Neil was sleeping, but Erma wouldn't let Susannah fire a loaded gun. Neil would hear. Shoot to kill, Susannah said that day, and showed Erma how to grip with both hands, hold her arms firm, keep her chin level. Shoot to kill, Susannah said.

Erma has done just as Susannah taught her, and now still holding firm with a level chin, she lets the gun slide a few feet to the left. Neil has leaned forward in his chair and is staring down at the man bleeding on the rug. Neil looks up and turns toward Erma. She always thought it would be Neil on the other end, and now it is.

Somewhere in the house, a door bangs open. It will have scarred her wall. Footsteps cross the kitchen. It's the deputies from down near the road. A hand rests on Erma's shoulder, and one of those deputies drops to Erma's side. He lifts his hand from her shoulder and places it on her forearm, gently presses down. The second deputy stands at the other side of her. She looks up at him. He uses two hands on his gun like Erma did. His arms are stretched out, and his gun is pointed into the room, but he doesn't fire. The man is already dead.

"Let's have you lower that gun, ma'am," someone says in Erma's ear. She'll likely not be making services this Sunday. "There you go. Let loose of it now."

There is a smudge of white icing on the heel of the deputy's boot. He has stepped in Erma's lovely slice of cake.

43

TALLEY

IT WAS THE last morning Talley and Grandpa Neil would sing worms from the ground. School was to begin the next day, and Talley wouldn't be allowed to attend classes smelling of river water and black mud.

Grandma Erma had already gone off to church. After many years of not attending, she was going every week again. But instead of the New Covenant, she'd been attending a new church over on Central. When she came home from her first Sunday back, she said she had hardly recognized a soul. Bonnie Wiley, wearing a God-awful hat, was the only one to tip her head good morning. Grandma waited all through the sermon for someone to toss her out, but they never did. Mostly, folks hadn't known who she was.

On that morning, Talley's last day of worm hunting, Grandma

left for church with a batch of peach tarts. She planned to stay for social hour, at least for a cup of coffee and long enough to see how her tarts went over. Bonnie Wiley was going to give her a ride home so Mama was sleeping in.

"This'll do," Grandpa said, settling on the same spot he always chose.

Instead of sitting on a tree trunk like he once did, Grandpa Neil lowered himself onto the folding chair Sheriff Ellenton brought down from the attic a few weeks ago. Sheriff Ellenton had found the spot where Daryl lived for those days he hid in the attic and had cleaned things for Mama after the deputies were done up there. He also apologized to Mama and Talley and Annalee, Grandma and Grandpa too. He should have realized the wet rag Talley found in the shed was the shirt Daryl was wearing the night Miss Hettie was killed. It rained that night, and Daryl had gone back to the shed to change into dry clothes and to make that weapon of his. And maybe Daryl took Talley's food that morning too. Maybe he didn't.

But the sheriff's biggest mistake, the mistake he made for certain, was assuming the attic door was locked when he couldn't open it. After they took Daryl away, Sheriff Ellenton found the doorstop Daryl used to jam the door closed and knew right away what had happened. He'd been too close, Sheriff Ellenton had said. Too damn close.

Daryl wasn't his real name. It was Terrance Michael Lannister. Talley found it on the computer, even though Mama insisted she not go looking. People called him Terry when he was a boy growing up in Bangor, where his mother moved them after leaving central Florida some years earlier. Mostly they remembered a sad boy and a mother who didn't seem fit to care for him. Terrance was survived only by a brother named Wayne, who lived in Austin. The brother hadn't seen or heard from Terrance since they were kids. Yes, Wayne was sent to that school in Waddell. Didn't even steal that damn lawn mower like they said he did. Eighteen months he spent there. Yeah, he seen plenty, but he'd just as soon not remember. Hell on earth, he said.

KNEELING BEFORE GRANDPA, Talley used the same flat rock she used every morning and pounded his stob into the ground. More and more, Grandpa didn't have the strength to sing for the worms, and Talley ran around some mornings pretending to pluck worms and cover them over with dirt because there weren't any real worms to gather.

"Do you remember the boy, Grandpa?" Talley asked as Grandpa took the rooping iron from her hand. She'd been asking him the same question every day since they first saw the boy's picture. "The boy who was on the TV? You said his name was Garrett Wilson."

Grandpa glanced overhead at the one stream of sunlight cutting through the branches of the cypress trees and black gums. The breeze caught his thinning hair, left to grow too long because Grandma didn't see to it much anymore.

"Don't remember no Garrett Wilson." He said the same every time Talley asked.

Sheriff Ellenton eventually uncovered the truth about Garrett Wilson. He had been sentenced to the school for boys on September 27, 1957, for skipping school long before Mama was even born. Thirty-eight days later, he was dead of influenza. That's what was scribbled in a record book alongside his name. Sheriff Ellenton also found a letter Garrett Wilson's mother had written to the school saying her boy had always been a healthy sort. Were they sure it was her boy who died? she wrote. Didn't make no sense a healthy boy should die like that. Many boys who died at the school, healthy boys, strong boys, were said to have died of influenza.

By the time they found Garrett Wilson in the record books, Mama had told everyone the truth of what happened when she was thirteen. She called a reporter she had met when she was still working at Rowland's Tavern and told him the whole story. She told about her childish tantrum and hiding in the attic and about the notes she left for the boys who ran. Only the boy matters, Mama told the reporter. If he was hurt, if he was killed, it's my doing and I'm sorry for it.

That reporter worked just like Sheriff Ellenton worked to find out if a boy was hurt or killed on that April 7. Neither one of them ever found a name. Every month and every year, more boys taken from that cemetery were matched up with their families, but none dated back to April 7, 1990. Sheriff Ellenton figured Grandpa Neil had been lying about it the whole time. He might well have hurt a good many boys at that school, maybe even killed some, maybe even Garrett Wilson. They'd probably never know, but Grandpa Neil didn't kill a boy the day Lane disappeared. He'd been torturing Mama all those years, and there was nothing much the sheriff could do about a mean-spirited lie. Grandpa Neil had been just that cruel.

Picking up her pail, Talley gave Grandpa a nod so he'd know she was ready. She backed away from him, glad this would be her last day to gather worms, and started to walk among the trees.

Years later, long after Grandma and Grandpa had passed and Mama and Talley had moved away, Mama signed the papers to turn the house over to the state. A group of volunteers built a small visitors center, gave tours of the tabby ruins, cordoned off each room in the house with thick red rope so people were forced to peer in at the fine furnishings from the thresholds, and cut down the giant oak that dripped with such a lot of moss. It was dead or dying, they said of the grandest tree in all of Milton County, and they couldn't risk it infecting all the other trees.

When Mama signed the last paper, she asked only that, along with the history of the house and the people who once lived there or were enslaved there, the history of the school for boys be told as well. She insisted the tabby ruins where the slaves once lived be always preserved and that visitors be told of the school's one-hundred-year existence, about the boys who ran and about all the children who had been buried with no headstone and with no measure of peace.

Mama never went back to journalism. She said she couldn't trust herself to do it for the right reasons. She never returned to work at the bar either, though she did continue doing the book-keeping for Rowland Jansen. By the time Annalee left for school in the fall, which she did even though Mama thought it was too soon, Mama had four more clients.

Jimmy Jansen went off to school that same year, and for as long as Talley lived in Waddell, and she lives there still, he never returned. Annalee has yet to come back to Waddell either. That was partly why, mostly why, Talley stayed. She hoped home was the one place to which Annalee would never return. Though Talley couldn't have fully explained her fear, it began the day in the hospital when Annalee lied. Who's Daryl? she had said. As many times as Talley thought about it, she could come up with only one reason why Annalee would tell that lie. And this fear of Talley's, it grew the day Grandma opened the family Bible.

IN THE DAYS after Daryl died, Grandma Erma called everyone into the dining room. She sat at the head of the table and with two hands, because that's how thick and heavy the book was, placed the family Bible directly in front of her.

"I've made a decision," she said, resting a hand on the tattered brown leather cover. "I'll be adding Miss Susannah Bauer's name to these pages."

She paused as if waiting for someone to challenge her. Everyone else sitting around the table—Mama, Sheriff Ellenton, Talley, and Annalee—nodded but said nothing.

"I know she technically ain't family," Grandma said, flipping open the Bible. "But wouldn't be no family if not for Susannah."

The Bible's binding was loose, and the cover fell freely. Grandma scooted forward in her chair, but instead of touching her pen to the page where all the names were written, she stared down on the thick book as if frightened by something she was seeing and slowly pushed it away.

Sheriff Ellenton was the first to stand. He walked to Grandma's side, touched the open book, and read what was written there.

"I'm sorry, Erma," he said.

Grandma lifted both her hands and pressed them to her chest, held them there, and closed her eyes. "He took it right off my chest," she said. "He took it from me and then he put it back."

"I seen the same sort of thing in what we took out of his apartment," Sheriff Ellenton said. "He'd written all kinds of lists and notes, ramblings, mainly."

"What is it?" Mama said.

Sheriff Ellenton turned the Bible and slid it toward Mama. Talley leaned over too, and she saw what was written there before Mama could shoo her away.

It was a list of names, crooked print written with a shaky hand. Written as if by a child, as if by Daryl. The list began with Grandpa Neil. The grandpa, the grandma, the mother, Talley, and the final line read, "Annalee was last."

Those notes meant Daryl wanted to kill them all, even Talley. She should have felt relief Daryl was dead. She should have felt safer, but seeing Annalee's name last on that list and being the one person who knew Annalee lied in the hospital made Talley cross her arms, drop low in her chair, and scoot in her seat until she was as far away from Annalee as she could get.

"Found similar scrawled out across box tops in the attic too," Sheriff Ellenton said. "Looked to have used his finger. Scribbled it out in the dust up there."

"This was his plan?" Mama asked, pushing the book away. "To kill all of us? What does that mean? Annalee was last. Last at what?"

Almost as quickly as she said it, Mama apologized to Annalee. Sheriff glanced at her too. She was sitting quietly at the far end of the table and was staring at the open book.

"It's okay," she said, and brushing a strand of hair from her eyes, she turned to Talley.

It was the slightest gesture, one no one else would have seen. But Talley was certain. It was a smile on Annalee's face. It was a real smile. Her eyes were bright, her cheeks plumped up, her teeth shined. Annalee had won, and it made her happy. She was alive, and Daryl was dead.

"Go ahead," she said to Sheriff Ellenton.

"He meant to kill Annalee last so she would suffer most. Wrote it over and over in those notes of his, just never wrote nothing about why."

Annalee lied about not knowing Daryl, and she lied about her and Jimmy running away to get married. She lied so everyone would believe Daryl had killed Susannah and Miss Hettie and that he tried to kill her too. The only reason for her to tell those lies was if she had been the one who did the killing. Talley would never know exactly why or how, but she'd live her life knowing it was true. And the only reason Daryl would single out Annalee to suffer most was because he knew the same.

"Anything about Hettie and Susannah?" Mama asked, giving Annalee's hand a quick squeeze.

"Scribblings, mostly. Last we could decipher, he seen Susannah talk to a boy the day she died. No name for him, just the boy. And next to nothing about Hettie. Miss Hettie called to me. That's all he wrote about her. Don't know why he picked you for last," Sheriff Ellenton said to Annalee. "Some sort of obsession, I suppose. I'm real sorry, Annalee."

Grandma eventually wrote Susannah's name in the Bible that day. At first, she had wanted to tear the page out even though other names of other people from long ago were also written on it, but Mama said no. It was part of their family, everything on that page, and it shouldn't be torn out and thrown away. She'd never hide from the truth again, never hide from her own past either, nor would she or her girls or Erma be branded by what Neil had done. They knew the truth of his life, all of them now, even Talley, and knowing came with responsibility. The truth will eventually rear up, sometimes in the ugliest of ways, but it will always rise. They could never be afraid of it again because fearing it wouldn't change it. You fear the truth, Mama said, and one day it'll be bigger than you. One day, it'll come for you.

WAITING FOR GRANDPA to start his singing, Talley drifted closer to the river where the dirt was cool and damp. The water was bright green that morning, no runoff to muck it up, no rain to stir the silt. On such a day, the river didn't make a sound. From overhead came a steady buzz, some insect up among the trees' highest branches.

"Go ahead," Talley called out to Grandpa. "I'm ready."

There had been times Grandpa fell asleep on Talley when they were outside singing for worms. He'd be strumming his rooping iron across his stob and she'd be hunting and then the song would stop. She'd pick her last worm and know Grandpa had drifted off. Sometimes, if the shade was nice and the breeze was just so, she'd dump her pail and go inside, leaving him to some fresh air. Mama, not Grandma, would eventually go fetch him. Grandma had done her share by then, that's what Mama said, and it was time Mama took her turn. She'd left it to Grandma for far too long. Caring for Grandpa Neil was the decent thing, Mama said, and decent isn't always easy.

Maybe it was the stillness of the river that day or the way for once the birds in the trees weren't quarreling, but Talley knew, even standing down by the river and looking back at him through the trees, Grandpa was gone.

The ambulance was parked in the driveway by the time Miss Bonnie drove Grandma home. Mama had already called Grandma and she knew. Miss Bonnie knew too. They parked near the giant oak and walked over together to look at Grandpa sitting in the chair. Just like that, he got to be gone. Miss Bonnie was crying. Grandma was not. Instead she rested a hand on Miss Bonnie's shoulder, and they stood there together until the men put Grandpa on a stretcher and drove him away. Six months later, Miss Bonnie's brother was the third boy identified from his DNA. She took him home to Louisiana and never came back.

Just like that, Grandpa was gone.

TALLEY MARRIED AT twenty-nine, right here in Waddell. Her own daddy walked her down the aisle, because to have it otherwise would have been cruel. Sheriff Ellenton and Mama were married by then, and though he didn't walk her down the aisle, Sheriff

Ellenton and Talley danced one of the first dances together. Everything that made Talley feel safe in the days after Daryl died was right there in the richness of Sheriff Ellenton's voice.

Mama continued to miss Annalee and wonder why she'd drifted so far. She called home a couple of times during her first semester, but a few months into the term, her roommate notified the dorm's RA that Annalee had packed up all her belongings and was gone. Together, Mama and Sheriff Ellenton continued to look for Annalee, never understanding why she left.

Talley looked too. Even as she had a child of her own, she would sit at the computer, searching. Annalee Fielding. Annalee Wallace. Annalee Jansen. Every time she hit the search button, she braced herself to see a picture of her sister. What would she look like now? Would her eyes still be too large for her face? Would she still smile in that same strange way of hers?

ON WHAT WOULD have been Annalee's fortieth birthday, Talley sits at her computer and types in just one name: Annalee. The screen fills with pictures, mostly of a young girl with dark hair, much too young to be Annalee. Talley pages down once and then again, ready to feel the same relief she has felt every time no familiar face appears on her screen. She always feels safer finding nothing because if she ever were to find something, it would mean Annalee is still out there and might one day come home. After paging down three times, Talley stops and pushes away from the computer.

It's a wide shot. A woman stands in the center of the photo, waving a hand overhead. A river runs in the background, so clear it reflects the tupelos and cypress trees growing along its banks. The picture has caught the woman mid-stride as she walks toward the camera. Ever so slightly, the woman has lifted onto her toes.

The tupelos bloom only a few weeks a year. It's always in the papers around Waddell, and just last week, maybe only a few days ago, the *Waddell Chronicle* led with a photo of a farmer hoisting a hive onto a platform up among the tupelo branches. He would haul it down again the moment the bloom was over. This is the only way to ensure true tupelo honey, the article said.

Talley leans close to the screen, clicks the photo, and enlarges it. The woman has blond hair, not so blond as Talley's once was, but as blond as it is now. Talley's hair has grown darker as she has aged. So has Annalee's. And there in the right side of the photo, at the very edge, are the branches of a tupelo and a hive set on the platform. A hive set just a few days ago. Talley leans in close, enlarges the picture as much as she can without making it grainy. Something over the woman's head throws a shadow, maybe reflects in the water. Train tracks. It's the spot where the tracks cross over the river.

Now Talley will have to tell them, Mama and Mark, about Annalee's lies. She'll have to make them understand what all those lies mean so Mark Ellenton will see to it justice is finally done. She'll have to make them believe. She'll tell them how she's searched for Annalee all these years, not in hopes of finding her but in hopes of never finding her. That's how afraid Talley has always been. Mama once said the truth always rises, sometimes in the ugliest of ways. And if you fear it, it will come for you. Mama was right. Annalee has come home.

ACKNOWLEDGMENTS

MY THANKS TO Maya Ziv of Dutton for her guidance, patience, and commitment to this novel. My thanks also to Christine Ball for her ongoing support of my work and for her professionalism and expertise. Thank you to Emily Brock, Madeline Newquist, and all the fine folks at Dutton for taking such great care of this novel. I also owe tremendous thanks to Jenny Bent and Denise Roy for the many years of friendship and for their insight, guidance, and continued support of my work.

THANK YOU TO Dr. Barb Stein, MD, for sharing her knowledge of forensic psychology, and to Teresa Guarcello for sharing her knowledge of growing up in the South. To Michael Koryta, thank you for sharing some kind words at a time when I really needed to hear them. And to Stacy, Kim, and Karina, thanks for the talks over coffee (and Skype) all these many years.

AND LASTLY, THANK you to William, my first reader, and to Andrew and Savanna, who have yet to read any of my work—a fact that is always good for a laugh.

ABOUT THE AUTHOR

LORI ROY IS the author of *Bent Road*, winner of the Edgar Award for Best First Novel; *Until She Comes Home*, finalist for the Edgar Award for Best Novel; and *Let Me Die in His Footsteps*, winner of the Edgar Award for Best Novel. She lives in St. Petersburg, Florida, with her family.